ALL QUIET IN PEKING

BEHIND CLOSED DOORS

LIU HEPING

Translated by
Teng Jimeng

SINOIST

ACA Publishing Ltd
University House
11-13 Lower Grosvenor Place,
London SW1W 0EX, UK
Tel: +44 20 3289 3885
E-mail: info@alaincharlesasia.com
www.alaincharlesasia.com
www.sinoistbooks.com

Beijing Office
Tel: +86(0)10 8472 1250

Author: Liu Heping
Translator: Teng Jimeng

Published by Sinoist Books (an imprint of ACA Publishing Ltd) in arrangement with Guangdong Flower City Publishing House Co., Ltd.

Original Chinese Text © 北平无战事 *(Bei Ping Wu Zhan Shi)* 2019, Guangdong Flower City Publishing House Co., Ltd, Guangdong, China

English Translation text © 2022 ACA Publishing Ltd, London, UK

ALL RIGHTS RESERVED. NO PART OF THIS PUBLICATION MAY BE REPRODUCED IN MATERIAL FORM, BY ANY MEANS, WHETHER GRAPHIC, ELECTRONIC, MECHANICAL OR OTHER, INCLUDING PHOTOCOPYING OR INFORMATION STORAGE, IN WHOLE OR IN PART, AND MAY NOT BE USED TO PREPARE OTHER PUBLICATIONS WITHOUT WRITTEN PERMISSION FROM THE PUBLISHER.

This novel is entirely a work of fiction. The names, characters and incidents portrayed in it are the work of the author's imagination. Any resemblance to actual persons, living or dead, events or localities is entirely coincidental.

Paperback ISBN: 978-1-83890-545-3
eBook ISBN: 978-1-83890-544-6

A catalogue record for *All Quiet in Peking (Book Two): Behind Closed Doors* is available from the National Bibliographic Service of the British Library.

BEHIND CLOSED DOORS
THE ALL QUIET IN PEKING SERIES
BOOK 2

LIU HEPING

Translated by
TENG JIMENG

SINOIST BOOKS

LIST OF CHARACTERS

Fang Buting - governor of the Central Bank's Peking branch
Xie Peidong - brother-in-law of, and assistant to, Fang Buting. CPC underground agent
Fang Meng'ao - colonel in the National Revolutionary Army Air Force, instructor at Jianqiao Aviation Academy and captain of the Peking Economic Inspection Brigade. Son of Fang Buting and brother of Fang Mengwei
Cui Zhongshi - deputy treasury director at the Central Bank's Peking branch, CPC underground agent
Fang Mengwei - Fang Buting's youngest son, deputy commissioner of the Peking Police Bureau and deputy director of the Investigation Department of the Peking Garrison headquarters
He Qicang - vice-chancellor of Yenching University and economic adviser to the Kuomintang government
He Xiaoyu - Yenching University student and Vice-Chancellor He Qicang's daughter
Xie Mulan - Yenching University student, daughter of Xie Peidong and cousin of Fang Mengwei and Fang Meng'ao
Chiang Ching-kuo - eldest son of Chiang Kai-shek, also known as Comrade Jianfeng
Zeng Keda - inspector-general of the Ministry of Defence's Bureau of Reserved Cadres

Hou Juntang - deputy director of the Air Force Operations Department
Lin Dawei - former staff member of the Air Force Operations Department, CPC underground agent
Fu Zuoyi - commander-in-chief of the North China Headquarters for the Suppression of Communist Insurgency
Xu Tieying - director of the Liaison Office of the Communications Bureau of the Kuomintang Central Membership Committee, chief superintendent of Peking Municipal Police Bureau
Du Wancheng - general auditor of the Ministry of Finance, head of the Five-Member Working Group
Ma Linshen - deputy director of the Kuomintang's Central Commission on Citizens' Food Distribution
Wang Benquan - secretary of the Central Bank
Ma Hanshan - deputy director of the Peking Citizens' Food Distribution Committee, and director of the Civil Affairs Bureau of Peking Municipality
Gu Weijun - Chinese ambassador to the US
Yan Chunming - professor, and head of the Communist Party's Student Committee at Yenching University
Cheng Xiaoyun - second wife of Fang Buting
Wang Yunwu - minister of the Ministry of Finance
Liang Jinglun - Yenching University professor, assistant to He Qicang and leading member of the Iron and Blood Congress of Nation Saving
Shao Yuangang - member of the Youth Aviation Brigade

CHAPTER 1

"Evidence?" asked Zeng Keda, as he and Fang Buting stood beneath swaying bamboo in the Fang family courtyard. He had seen calm people, but he had never seen Fang Buting so calm. "Governor Fang, do you really want me to produce evidence that Cui Zhongshi is a Communist?"

"We have a constitutional government now. That means separation of powers. So without evidence, even if you were to take Cui away, no court would convict anyone from the Central Bank."

Zeng Keda bowed his head in silence before saying: "So you think it would it be OK for us to bring evidence that Cui Zhongshi is a Communist to a public hearing in Nanking?"

Fang Buting didn't answer at first, and just stared at him.

Zeng Keda carried on. "If you insist, it might take me ten days, it might take me three, but I will get it. And it will show that a CPC agent worked side by side with you, sir, for three years, gaining as much financial information as he could get his hands on. How does that work for you? For three years, a Communist agent has exploited his connections to you and to your Air Force son. How does that look for him too, sir?"

Zeng's kind eyes flashed in Fang's direction as he waited for a response. But when the director finally spoke, he said the one thing Zeng was afraid of. "In this case, let me get some clothes to change into before you take me in." With that said, Fang left the bamboo grove and walked slowly back to the house.

Zeng hesitated, "Governor Fang…"

Fang had more to say on his way back. "As for Meng'ao, he might be my son, but we're not in touch. When you catch him, be sure not to imprison us together."

Zeng froze for a moment before coming to his senses and striding forward in an effort to catch up with Fang, but the man had already left the bamboo grove.

The new moon was about to set over the hills east of Shichahai, Zhonghai and Nanhai. From afar, you could see lights on at Commander General Fu Zuoyi's headquarters, and they shone especially bright at this late hour.

The security contingent which Zheng had brought was divided into two groups and kept away from the scene, probably because Fang Meng'ao had lost his temper again. They were watching from two hundred metres away as Fang Meng'ao and Cui Zhongshi, trousers wet and torsos bare, sat on the shore of Houhai with their backs to them.

Zheng looked on in bemusement at the pair, one with tendons like iron, the other with bones jutting from his skinny body.

"Was it you who distrusted me, or your boss?" Fang Meng'ao asked.

Cui Zhongshi replied: "There is no boss. Meng'ao, I've told you, I'm not a Communist."

"You're a bad liar. I can tell that by how you jumped in the water."

"And you are too honest. I dared to jump in, knowing how you're a fish in water."

"It's so dark that no matter how good I am, I wouldn't be able to find you."

"So I'm screwed then."

Every sentence tugged at the heart like spring rain dripping on burning charcoal, smoking still. Without warning, Fang Meng'ao turned to stare at Cui Zhongshi.

For three years, he had seen him as a confidante, someone close to him. But this bony man in front of him appeared far from the well-dressed Cui Zhongshi he knew. He did not know what to say. This man had become a stranger. He decided not to ask any further: "I have told you the truth every step of the way for the past three years. I've told you things that no one, not even my own dead mother, knows about me. So if there's one person in the world who knows this, it's you. I despise cheats most of all. Get dressed and I'll take you back." He picked up his coat and stood up, quickly putting on his uniform and cap.

Cui Zhongshi was short-sighted. He had left his glasses on top of his clothes when he dived in, and now he rummaged around for a few minutes in search of them. "Do me a favour and help me find them, will you?"

Fang Meng'ao slowly turned around and saw Cui Zhongshi, with a helpless look in his eyes and a scrawny torso, and sadness involuntarily crept up on him. He bent to pick up the man's glasses, fake collar and gown, and passed them to him.

"Thank you," Cui Zhongshi murmured.

"The National Government cannot work without the Central Bank for one day, just as the Central Bank cannot work without the Peking branch for one day. As for the Peking branch, it needs Fang Buting." Zeng spoke solemnly as he and Fang stood in the living room on the ground floor of the Fang Mansion. Fang had heard these words on many occasions, but this was the first time they had come from Zeng, who had mustered as much conviction in his tone of voice as he could.

Fang Buting paused on his way up the stairs. Zeng Keda added: "Governor Fang, I must tell you, these words are not from me."

Fang Buting turned round and looked at Zeng Keda. "It's not the Qing Dynasty any more, and I'm no Zuo Zongtang. It's now. These words of Pan Zuyin and Guo Songtao moved Emperor Xianfeng, and saved Zuo Zongtang. We now have constitutional government, a republic for heaven's sake. If I, Fang Buting, really did something to harm the country, laws would kick in. Right now, no one can protect me. It matters not a bit what words are used."

"It's both different and the same. At that time, the Qing court protected Zuo Zongtang and he did nothing to endanger his protectors. Similarly, the Nanking government will understand that you, governor, never intended to endanger the Republic of China before entrusting me to convey these words. As with the Qing court and Zuo Zongtang, Nanking is not protecting you as governor or your son as brigade captain, but China as a place in peril. It is our country that is in crisis. In the Northeast, battle with the Communists is about to break out in earnest. We need the Peking branch to ensure military supplies get through and cities such as Tianjin remain stable. In this role, no one can replace you, governor. Regardless of what you think of what I've just said, we need the one who brought you the tea set to evaluate you and give you confidence."

Fang Buting's eyes fixed on the tea set on the table. The characters were a bit fuzzy from a distance, but nevertheless the words jumped out: "Given by Mr Chiang Ching-kuo."

Closing his eyes without thinking, Fang felt the night wind blowing on the bamboo grove in his garden. In his head, it sounded like the tide.

What Zeng Keda said next floated above the tide in his head. "You saw it just now. Why does this tea set only have three cups and a pot? I see it like this: The pot as the Peking branch and the three cups as your honourable self and two sons. Perhaps the governor can appreciate the symbolism."

Fang heard this as the waves in his head got rougher and the boat he was drifting on slammed into his chest. They looked at each other, eyes flickering in the candle light. No, the set should have had four cups, but one was lost. All he could do was compare it to father and sons. Why would Chiang devise something so deep and yet so simple?

Fang Buting came down the stairs to inspect the tea set some more.

Zeng Keda followed him quietly as he walked over to the table.

"I accepted this gift," said Fang Buting. "Please convey thanks on my behalf, General Zeng."

Zeng Keda held up the tea set in both hands and ceremoniously offered it to Fang Buting but did not let go, as Fang took it.

"I'll call the Nanking side tonight, but Nanking needs to hear that Governor Fang will do something about the CPC lurking about. The Peking branch is the financial heart of the party-state in the north, and information about our economy can no longer leak to the CPC. More importantly, we must prevent this person from laundering money for the CPC through secret channels. Furthermore, he must be prevented from leading your son and his flying brigade astray. For nation and for family, Governor Fang, this person must vanish. And Nanking hopes he does so in secret."

En route from Deshengmen to Dongzhong Hutong, the medium-sized jeep behind Fang Meng'ao's small jeep was being forced to drive on to clear the way. The roads of Peking were quiet under martial law this late at night, but the driver chose to drive slowly for fear of losing track of Fang Meng'ao's jeep.

Behind him, a clearly impatient Fang Meng'ao was hitting the horn constantly, causing the guard driving the car ahead to seek support from Zheng sitting beside him, to which Zheng helplessly said: "What can I do?"

"Speed up!" The jeep sped up.

Fang Meng'ao's foot hit the throttle and he squinted as he looked at Cui beside him.

The breeze hit his face, but Cui Zhongshi's countenance remained calm.

The road ahead was long and straight, Fang Meng'ao loosened his grip on the steering wheel and drove straight ahead. He took off the Omega watch from his left wrist, switched hands on the wheel and put the watch in front of Cui's face without looking at him.

"Take it," Fang Meng'ao's right hand stayed where it was. "But not for you."

Cui Zhongshi only now looked at the watch, and said: "Then for whom?"

"Give it to Vice-Chairman Zhou for me."

Cui Zhongshi was shocked. "Which Vice-Chairman Zhou?"

"The Vice-Chairman Zhou you met. Don't fool around with me, Cui Zhongshi."

Cui still did not take the watch, sighing: "I have never seen any vice-chairmen, so it's impossible to do as you ask. I can't help you."

Fang Meng'ao's face sank. "Not the Vice-Chairman Zhou I mentioned but the Vice-Chairman Zhou you referred to. You must give him this watch, no matter if you ask a Communist or a Nationalist to help. One day I will find out if it has been delivered to Zhou Enlai."

"I'll do what I can," replied Cui Zhongshi, extending his hand slowly.

Fang Meng'ao looked to his side, heart trembling, to find Cui Zhongshi's eyes clear and sharp.

Fang felt something ominous as he went to put the watch in the palm of Cui Zhongshi's hand. Grabbing his wrist, he felt it lie unresisting and unresponsive, and the omen grew louder in his heart. The strange feeling was accentuated by the ticking of the two hands of the watch, until "beep!"

In front, the jeep sounded its horn, and the ticking in Fang Meng'ao's head stopped. The jeep in front was slowing down, and lights were shining ahead. They were close to Dongzhong Hutong. Police officers had been summoned by the deputy police chief Shan and plainclothes agents affiliated with many other unknown departments. They had reached Cui's home.

Fang Meng'ao had to release Cui's hand as he slowed the jeep.

Back in his bedroom, Governor Fang was lying in bed as if he had become an entirely different person. His face was pale and he was sweating profusely.

His wife Cheng Xiaoyun was beside him, carefully piercing the needle tip of the infusion bottle into a vein in the back of his hand. "Does it hurt?"

Fang Buting closed his eyes and said nothing.

Cheng Xiaoyun put a plaster on it, took a towel out of the basin, wrung out the hot water and wiped his brow.

"Go and call Uncle Peidong to come back at once."

"Where is he?"

"Always at the same shareholders' homes, why don't you ask there?" Fang Buting said impatiently.

Cheng Xiaoyun let out a silent sigh. "Don't worry," she said, "I'll make a call."

Just then, the clock in the ground floor living room chimed. It was ten at night.

At the Mirror Spring Garden Lodge to the north of Weiming Lake, Yenching University, He Xiaoyu walked into the house to find Comrade Liu standing just inside, smiling. "So, the get-together will be great fun in the army barracks, won't it?"

He Xiaoyu offered a faint smile: "Male classmates were still checking the accounts and female classmates were still busy with the pilots' laundry."

With one hand, Old Liu began opening the door, still standing in front of He Xiaoyu, looking at her as if intentionally stopping her from rushing in. "Coming back early didn't raise any suspicions?"

"Everyone knows my father is not well," He Xiaoyu replied. "My classmates all know." Old Liu nodded, still standing in her way.

"Comrade Xiaoyu, we summoned you back so urgently to introduce you to a leading comrade. You must be prepared."

This explained Old Liu's strange behaviour today. Nodding, she tried to calm down. "I will leave you two to talk alone." Old Liu called out, opened the door and told her to go in, so he could close the door from the outside.

He Xiaoyu slowly looked inside, eyes widening in astonishment. Although Comrade Liu had prepared her, He Xiaoyu still did not believe who was at the table. The leading comrade was, of all people, Xie Mulan's father, Xie Peidong!

Xie Peidong got up slowly, without the usual formality such as reaching out for a handshake or other encouraging greetings. Standing there was the same old Uncle Xie she saw all the time, with his hand clutching the hem of his gown, looking at her kindly.

"I get it now." Cheng Xiaoyun sat down next to Fang Buting's bed and replaced the hot towel on his forehead. "Peidong is with Mr Xu to discuss a share transfer."

"At the Xu residence downtown or in his Yenching house?" asked Fang Buting.

"At his house on the western outskirts," Cheng Xiaoyun replied.

"How can he get back into the city this late?" asked Fang Buting. "Call Mengwei and ask him to pick him up."

"All right," replied Cheng Xiaoyun.

"Mulan is still with Meng'ao, right?" Xie Peidong put down a glass of water on the table next to He Xiaoyu, and asked regular questions as if this was an ordinary meeting.

This time, they made her unusually emotional. Tears began to flow down her face. He stood there in silence, knowing that her mood would be complicated and excited at this moment. It seemed wise just to let her cry it out.

"I'm sorry, Uncle Xie." Xie Peidong's silence calmed her down somewhat. She saw he was still standing so she stood up herself to dry her tears on a fresh handkerchief. "Sit down, please."

"We should both sit down. Have some water." Xie sat on the edge of his chair as he would in the Fang household, reminding Xiaoyu again that he was the same old Uncle Xie.

He Xiaoyu also sat politely, staring into the middle distance beyond her cup. She thought – Uncle Xie was a leading comrade in the party. I could not have imagined.

"I scared you coming here tonight, didn't I? said Xie Peidong, warmly.

"No," He Xiaoyu replied, gripping the cup more tightly with both hands. She asked softly, "But I have to ask, how could you have worked side by side with Uncle Fang for so many years?"

"And I know you are curious about how, since I've hidden it so well, I've decided to break my cover in such a sudden way today?" said Xie Peidong. "And why I decided to come and see you? Am I right?"

He Xiaoyu nodded as Xie's tone changed. "The organisation has a serious issue. It's not your problem. But it involves the safety and security of an important comrade, fighting on behalf of an important person. The organisation has given it a lot of thought, a lot of research, and has come to the conclusion we should take on this task together. Only we can guarantee the security of these two people."

Xie Peidong's sincerity and firmness at his sudden revelation caused her shyness to dissipate. She had a dignified look in her eyes as she considered his words. Xie Peidong said it was someone important in the party, but who was the comrade? She did not know right now. But she immediately guessed who the important person to be fought for was. Fang Meng'ao's image flashed in front of her.

At this point, Xiaoyu stood up. "Uncle Xie... can I still call you Uncle Xie from now on?"

"It's not about still, you must always call me Uncle Xie. We will have more time to meet from now on. We should treat each other just as we did before. If I can do it, so can you, right?"

He Xiaoyu insisted on looking at him, letting out a sigh as she bowed her head and answered: "Uncle Xie, I'm afraid I can't do it."

He was silent for a while, then smiled with understanding. "I won't force you."

"It may be that we can't meet again exactly as before. It's normal for things to be somewhat unnatural for a while. Because everyone knows I'm your uncle."

He Xiaoyu raised her head awkwardly. "Uncle Xie, what do you mean?"

"Meng'ao calls me uncle. You should know what it means."

"I'm afraid this is something I can't do. The organisation will have to reconsider."

Xie Peidong's face dropped. "Why?"

"Because I don't love him, I can't call you uncle in that way, the way that Fang Meng'ao does."

Xie Peidong fell silent.

"I can't even persuade myself, let alone foolish Uncle Fang. And I certainly won't be able to hide that fact from the Nationalists behind him."

Xie Peidong had expected He Xiaoyu to be embarrassed and shy in accepting this task, but was surprised she had rejected Fang Meng'ao himself. This was a critical part of the conversation. He stood up and paced the room before coming back to stand in front of He Xiaoyu, saying: "The organisation was not expecting this. Maybe we can change our perspective, Xiao Yu. We can say, for example, that Meng'ao is an orphan."

"I don't understand."

"He has no mother, and is without the love of a father."

He Xiaoyu appeared as if struck by lightning, and a trace of love and compassion flashed across her eyes.

"In his heart he has a mother," said Xie Peidong, "but this mother can never see him again. The only people who can give him access to his mother are now at risk and cannot come close. Would you not be more willing to get together with Meng'ao if you saw it this way?"

He Xiaoyu held back but was moved. "I would still find it hard."

"If it weren't so hard, the organisation wouldn't go out of its way to entrust you. We are not the same generation, you and I. I cannot fully understand how you feel. You just said you don't love Meng'ao, but add one character before love to make it compassion, and I think you have that in you, am I right?"

He Xiaoyu nodded wholeheartedly.

Xie Peidong didn't sit down again. Mengwei was going to pick him up in about twenty minutes. "You shouldn't stay out late either. It's best to get home early. By the way, isn't Comrade Liang Jinglun of the Ministry of Education staying at your house?"

He Xiaoyu was again tense and anxious. "It seems he has some business with Nanking's Ministry of Finance. My father is writing a note regarding the currency reforms. Professor Liang has been helping him with some research. So yes, he sometimes stays in my house. Is there a problem with that?"

"The organisation knows all this," Xie Peidong replied immediately. "The issue is Fang Meng'ao. He may visit you at some point, and you should be prepared."

He Xiaoyu's eyes widened. The organisation makes this kind of arrangement?

"The organisation won't be involved. I've just told you, Meng'ao is now deemed an 'orphan'. With his current situation and character, he will definitely come to consult you."

He Xiaoyu was stunned again. "What identity should I use to contact him?"

Xie Peidong said: "According to Comrade Liang Jinglun's request to you from the CPC Peking Student Committee, you should contact him in your role as a student. When you meet, tell him that the Urban Works Department has arranged for you to take over from Cui Zhongshi. Set up a one-to-one conversation with him."

He Xiaoyu couldn't help but ask: "Uncle Xie, the CPC Peking Student Committee is also a party organisation led by the Urban Works Department. Why can't Professor Liang know my true identity?"

"You and Fang Meng'ao will work as a single channel of communication," said Xie Peidong. "This is a top-secret task that only me and old Comrade Liu will be privy to. Comrades Liang Jinglun and Yan Chunming can't know the identity of the party members in the Urban Works Department. As for your personal relationship, the organisation trusts you will act appropriately."

At this point, He Xiaoyu was silent, as was Xie Peidong.

The lights were off and the road was dark as a small military jeep was driving at full speed.

Not far to the left, the lights of the Youth Aviation Service Barracks appeared. Breaking suddenly, the small jeep came to an abrupt halt at the intersection. The medium-sized jeep behind the small one had its lights off too and was caught out, causing the soldier driving to hit the brakes as well but the medium-sized jeep clipped the tail of the small jeep in front.

Those sitting in the jeep behind were startled and hit the roof.

The man in the front passenger seat received the biggest jolt. His head hit the windscreen and his military cap flew off and flipped onto the seat behind him. It was Lieutenant Colonel Zheng.

He steadied himself and slapped the guard driving with the back of his hand before leaping out of the car. Lieutenant Colonel Zheng's bare head was throbbing, but he still saluted the jeep in front. "Excuse me, did we hit you, sir?" he asked, leaning over to take a look.

Fang Meng'ao in the little jeep lit a cigarette and drew on it heavily. "Are the brothers injured?"

When Lieutenant Colonel Zheng saw Fang Meng'ao, he breathed a sigh of relief, straightening up again. "Sir, no one is injured. Our comrades are fine."

"As we're all OK and have reached the barracks now, you don't need to stay," said Fang.

Zheng glanced at the bright lights not far from the intersection and said firmly: "Reporting. Our orders from above are to provide round-the-clock protection."

Fang Meng'ao looked at him in the shadows outside the car. He was silent for a while and illuminated the car with his cigarette. Zheng bowed again.

Fang Meng'ao whispered in his ear. "There is information that someone is going to make a move against General Zeng tonight. You must rush back and strengthen your defence."

"No way," Chief Zheng replied suspiciously. "Who would dare attack General Zeng at the ambassador's residence?"

"Why did your leader ask you to protect me? Why did the Group of Five not stay longer this morning? All of them left Peking, didn't they? General Zeng is in the most danger now, not me. Understand?" Zheng was slightly more convinced, but he still hesitated.

"Would you prefer me to bring everyone in the flying team to Ambassador Gu's residence so we can protect General Zeng together?"

"Sir, please return to your barracks. We'll head back to the ambassador's mansion." With that, Zheng returned to the medium-sized jeep, calling for everyone to get back in.

All the guards scrambled back to the jeep, with their lieutenant colonel waiting until the last one was in. He found his cap and jumped into the front passenger seat. "Reverse! To the ambassador's mansion!"

The jeep turned its lights on and made a U-turn in one fluid movement.

Fang Meng'ao leaned on the seat of the car, looked towards the nearby barracks, and threw his cigarette out of the car, exclaiming: "Shit! Can nothing get done without telling lies!"

It was pitch black, the road was bumpy, and Fang Meng'ao jumped the lights ahead.

He parked quietly outside the barrack gates, unseen in the dark.

In the courtyard, red lamps shone as bright as day. The students sat at the long tables helping to clear the accounts. The girls were helping the pilots wash their clothes next to the running-water tanks. Someone was singing.

Together with a group of more than a dozen pilots, Guo Jinyang was distributing all their cake, sugar, fruit and coffee.

Chen Changwu led Xie Mulan quietly out of the iron gates towards the jeep stationed by the roadside.

On walking up to the vehicle, Xie Mulan saw Fang Meng'ao standing there. "Big Brother? Why don't you get in?"

Fang Meng'ao glanced at Chen Changwu, then turned to Xie Mulan. "What about He Xiaoyu?"

Xie Mulan smiled and replied: "You're waiting here for Xiaoyu?"

Fang Meng'ao looked serious, and turned to Chen Changwu. "She left an hour ago. I heard her father is not well. She had to return to look after him."

Fang Meng'ao thought about it and said to the two of them: "Let's both get in the car."

"Where are we going?"

"To He Xiaoyu's house. Changwu, take my cousin's lead. You drive."

Chen Changwu immediately opened the door and sat in the

driver's seat. Xie Mulan didn't move. "Brother, it's a bit late to visit Xiaoyu like this. What will Uncle He say?"

Fang Meng'ao opened the passenger door for her. "I will meet Vice-President He, what's not to be happy about? Get in the car."

Stunned by this, Xie Mulan asked herself why he would be rushing to see Uncle He at this hour?

But Fang Meng'ao had already closed the car door and got in the back, telling Chen Changwu to keep the car lights off, and not to wait for him when they arrived at the He residence. "After taking my cousin home, you will immediately return to barracks."

"Yes," replied Chen Changwu, getting ready to drive off.

"Wait!" Xie Mulan opened her door. "Brother, if you don't tell me what's going on, I will neither lead you there nor go home."

"I'm going to ask him about the 'four lines, two games, one bank and one session.' What more do you need to know?" Fang Meng'ao countered with an enigmatic comment, reaching from behind to lock Xie's car door, so that Chen Changwu could get on the road. The blazing lights of the barracks flashed in the reflectors, soon dimming too.

———

In the accounts room next to the living room in the north of Cui Zhongshi's residence, a single bulb hanging from a wire gave out at most fifteen watts of light. The densely packed words in the books on the table appeared dim and hard to read.

Cui's glasses had been put aside as he pressed his face close to the ledger in order to deal with the accounts. Even though it was late at night, the door was closed tightly, the curtains were drawn and his naked torso was covered in sweat.

Unlike all the other rooms in the house, Cui Zhongshi's accounts room was locked from the inside.

As soon as it was pulled closed, it was locked, and needed a key to open it from the outside. Just then, the handle of the inner door turned slowly and the door was pushed open from the outside.

Cui Zhongshi immediately closed the accounts book, put on his glasses and turned his head to look. It was Ye Biyu standing at the door holding a tray.

"What are you doing? How come you have the key?" Cui Zhongshi had never spoken to his wife in such a harsh tone.

"What do you mean? I got a new one cut, did I do anything illegal?" Ye Biyu kept the same tone, but this time a little guilt had crept into it.

Cui Zhongshi stood up with a start and walked to the door. "What on earth did you have a new key cut for? Have you looked at my accounts?"

Ye Biyu had never seen her husband look like this, yet despite knowing that she was in the wrong, a Shanghai woman never succumbed to this kind of pressure. "I had the key cut when I was out today. So no, I've never stepped inside, let alone looked at your accounts! Throughout the past few days, you've had all the doors and windows shut, so I wanted to bring you something to eat. And tonight, you are so off with me!"

Cui Zhongshi stared at Ye Biyu standing outside the door. "Who asked you to bring me snacks? Did you have so much money left over you didn't know how to spend it? Give me the key!"

Confused, Ye Biyu subconsciously felt her right hand being lifted up as Cui Zhongshi grabbed the key and closed the door.

She almost dropped the tray she was carrying. "Cui Zhongshi, I will take the children back to Shanghai tomorrow. I hope you drop dead in Peking!"

The door opened slowly from the inside again, and Cui Zhongshi looked regretful this time, his gaze downcast.

"I will go to Governor Fang and Deputy Xie tomorrow, and ask them to make arrangements. You may take the children back to Shanghai." After saying this, he closed the door again, this time without a bang.

The stunned woman was full of regrets about her rash outburst.

The bedroom door was also pulled shut by Cheng Xiaoyun from the outside. Half the bottle was left, with the top off. Fang Buting leaned on the head of the bed and looked profoundly at Xie, who had just hurried back to work in front of the window.

On the table in front of the window was a large wooden tray of bamboo cups of various sizes that had clearly been used many times. There was a bottle of Chinese *shochu* liquor next to them. Xie Peidong was skilfully rubbing a piece of yellow straw paper into a root by the wooden plate.

"Did you take a shower?" asked Xie Peidong. She put the wooden tray on the bedside table and set fire to the paper roll. "You most certainly can't tomorrow."

Fang Buting started to take off his pyjamas: "Xiaoyu scrubbed me just now."

Xie Peidong lit the paper in the open flame again. "Lie down and let's talk while we work."

Fang Buting laid his head down towards the end of the bed.

Xie Peidong took a big sip of *shochu*, and sprayed more on Fang's back.

The liquor was like a puffy rain mist, evenly sprayed on Fang Buting's neck, shoulders and back, all the way down to the waist.

Fang Buting's eyes were still downcast and now they were closed.

Xie Peidong rolled the paper in his left hand, stretched the open flame into the fire pot on his right, and took it. He shook his left hand to extinguish the flame and held the cup on Fang Buting's back with his right hand. Xie started rubbing his boss's back from top to bottom.

Soon, purple stripes appeared on Fang Buting's back.

"Do you know what Zeng Keda said tonight?" For Fang Buting, it seemed that this was the only way to start a conversation with Xie Peidong.

Xie Peidong once again lit the paper and heated the cup he was holding, scrubbing the right side of his back.

"What did he say?" asked Xie Peidong.

"That he'd borrow a knife to kill someone!" replied Fang Buting.

"Who?" Xie Peidong's hand tremble stopped.

"You know."

"Deputy Director Cui?" Xie Peidong's hand stopped. "Is this too hard?"

"Carry on," urged Fang Buting.

Xie Peidong had to repeat the scraping movement, this time along the spine. "There's a saying – 'Borrow a knife from the

Central Bank to kill someone from the Central Bank,'" said Fang Buting between gritted teeth, not just because of the pain in his back.

Xie Peidong was silent, and the blaze was out now. He heated a hot cup and sucked on it abruptly, lit another cup, sucked it, and attached it to Fang Buting's left shoulder.

"What do you think?" asked Fang Buting.

Xie Peidong stuck another cup near his right shoulder blade. "It depends on the back."

Fang Buting, with his eyes open at this time, asked: "What did you say?"

Xie Peidong continued to attach cups. "They could use our knife to kill Cui Zhongshi, then they could use it to destroy us. This has nothing to do with the Communist Party."

"So what is it connected to?"

"The same old thing, money!"

"Oh, and when do you think Cui Zhongshi's account will be handed over?"

Xie Peidong kept kneading the cupping jars. "It's such a complicated process. We're working on it day and night. At the very least it will take three more days."

"That's simply not OK." Fang Buting moved a bit, and the cup Xie Peidong was fixing did not hold. "I need you to have that account in our hands tomorrow."

"Impossible," Xie Peidong replied crisply. "I asked in detail. Not only does the account involve transactions between the Songs, Kongs and the US, but also plenty of merchants connected with Fu Zuoyi's Northwestern Army. And now Xu Tieying has entered on behalf of the Central Committee, eager to convert Hou Juntang's Air Force shares into party and private property. Without levelling the account, there's no way we'll pass muster with the Iron and Blood Congress of Nation Saving."

Fang Buting's eyes, which had been wide open, were closed again. "You can say it time and time again, but this is my strategic undoing. Peidong, could Cui Zhongshi have transferred money to the Communist Party?"

Xie Peidong placed a cup on his back without answering.

"I'll ask again."

Xie Peidong sighed softly, before replying: "If the governor has an answer in mind, why is he so determined for me to address it?"

"But you believe Cui Zhongshi is not a Communist?"

"Let's say he is a Communist Party member then. As such, would he have helped the elites launder so much precious money from all over the place? Surely the Song and Kong families would have no wiggle room at this point. What's more, his transactions also involve the Northwestern Army, the Central Army, the Military Bureau of Investigation, the Central Bureau of Investigation and even the Central Party Committee. Governor, if you want to call him a Communist, you may find this case can only be tried by the president himself."

"So you mean we cannot recognise Cui Zhongshi as a Communist?"

"You don't need me to deny it. Zeng Keda and his people also have no wish to out him as a Communist. Since they are the ones who keep charging Cui Zhongshi as a Communist, they should come and get him themselves. The thing is, they don't dare, so they use the governor to do their dirty work. This was exactly Zeng's plan in arriving tonight."

"About this I am clear. But I asked you and you haven't answered me yet. Could Cui Zhongshi have transferred Central Bank money to the Communist Party?"

"The governor has forgotten that Cui Zhongshi never managed money from the Central Bank's Peking branch."

Xie Peidong finished putting the last cup on Fang Buting's back and covered him with a thin towel. "All eyes are on the money running through his hands now. No one will let even a single cent out of their sight."

"You still don't understand the Communist Party," Fang Buting replied, countering Xie Peidong's analysis at once. "The Communist Party will definitely find ways to divert these kinds of people's money. For them it's all about injustice, not being rich and famous. It is for this reason that we must take over Cui Zhongshi's account tomorrow. No amount of money can be transferred to the Communist Party."

Xie Peidong dismissed Governor Fang's decision out of hand. "I forgot to tell you, Xu Tieying sent police to guard Cui Zhongshi's house. He can't take even a step outside now. So stop worrying about him sending money to the Communists."

Fang Buting thought for a while. "You must bring the account on board within three days."

"I'll do my level best," Xie Peidong replied. "Once we have it, how does the governor plan to deal with Cui Zhongshi?"

"It won't be me dealing with Cui." Fang Buting became agitated as he repeated what he had already said. "Zeng Keda gave me an ultimatum on behalf of the Iron and Blood Congress saying he has to disappear!"

Xie Peidong said nothing.

Fang Buting tried to calm down. "Peidong, I know what you're thinking. If it wasn't related to the Communists, I would do everything to protect Cui Zhongshi. He has done so much for me over the years. I just don't understand how such a talented person could be in the Communist Party... and he implicated Meng'ao too." He let out a long sigh.

"Governor, allow me to speak, as you have done."

"That's exactly what I want."

"If Cui Zhongshi were not a Communist, you'd protect him. If he were a Communist, you'd be smart not to kill him."

"Give me your reasons."

"You need to give yourself a way out."

Fang Buting opened his eyes and pondered sharply, then shook his head. "I simply can't see a way out of this."

"Think of something. We have to find a way out, and we do need an escape route."

"What are you thinking?" Fang Buting moved to lift his back, and in doing so knocked many of the cups off his back.

"Don't move." Xie Peidong set him straight, and as it was almost time, unwrapped the towel and began pulling the cups off his boss's back.

Fang Buting lay still again. "Carry on."

"Didn't Zeng Keda want Cui Zhongshi to disappear from your side? Then let him go. That's what you should do."

"Give me more details."

"The Kong family's Yangtze Construction Company has said countless times that they'd like Cui to help them in Shanghai. If the governor agrees, I'll get in touch with the Kongs. They will take him on, and then if anyone wants to kill him, it's simply not our problem any more. More importantly, the governor will no longer need to worry about Cui's links with Meng'ao."

Governor Fang sat cross-legged on the bed wearing a towel Xie Peidong had thrown him. Thinking, he turned to Xie Peidong and asked: "Is the police department guarding Cui Zhongshi day and night?"

"Twenty-four hours a day."

"That's good. Didn't Xu Tieying want that twenty per cent stake? Peidong, talking to the Kongs should be left up to Xu. For this twenty per cent stake, he should be willing to cooperate with the Kong family. He will have Cui Zhongshi sent to Shanghai. We should make them do the work on this.

"Governor, won't it make things more complicated?" interjected Xie Peidong, startled.

"That's not the issue," noted Fang Buting. "You shouldn't get involved, and you shouldn't tell Mengwei either. You are absolutely right about having an escape plan. And you know what the most important escape plan is right now? To get Meng'ao to the US."

Although Xie Peidong mentioned that Fang Meng'ao would come to find her, He Xiaoyu did not expect that he would come to her house so quickly or so late.

Late that night, the second hand of the wall clock could be clearly heard, and twelve midnight was five minutes away.

He Xiaoyu poured boiling water into a cup filled with a spoonful of milk powder and slowly stirred it with a spoon. With the milk and two pieces of fried *mantou* steamed bun, she closed her eyes.

In her imagination, Liang Jinglun was sitting behind her, reading a book as she took notes. But turning around, it was Fang Meng'ao wearing his Air Force uniform who was sitting at the dining table.

He Xiaoyu smiled and put the milk and steamed bread pieces in front of Fang Meng'ao. "In the afternoon, you gave up your dinner for our classmates, so you must be starving."

"Thank you!" said Fang Meng'ao in English, as he stood up.

He Xiaoyu frowned. Even though she was learning English at the best English teaching institution, Yenching, hearing Meng'ao's standard American English was somehow jarring.

She smiled back quickly. "Let's not speak English, OK?"

Fang Meng'ao thanked her in Chinese, but asked the same thing again: "Do you have a knife and fork?"

He Xiaoyu hid her annoyance: "It's not Western food. What do you need them for?"

"Sorry, I have been used to the Yankees for a long time being with the Flying Tigers." He sat down, picked up the buns, bit one in half and ate the other half in one go, then picked up the glass of milk and drank it in one gulp. He Xiaoyu had to think of what Xie Peidong had said: this was a lonely child!

"Let me see if there is anything else to eat." He Xiaoyu looked at him tenderly.

"No need. Even if you look, you won't find anything."

"How do you know our family hasn't got anything else to eat?"

"If there were, you wouldn't just fry two buns. So many professors are facing hunger. Your dad could get more food, but he won't."

When He Xiaoyu looked at Fang Meng'ao again, her gaze took on a completely different aspect. People who are very difficult to get along with have such a delicate mindset and to understand other people is such a challenge!

Fang Meng'ao was sensitive enough to realise why he had been sent there that night.

Now that he could see it, he didn't hide it, looking closely into He Xiaoyu's eyes.

He Xiaoyu was panicked and looked self-consciously at the clock on the wall.

Both long and short hands were pointing at twelve o'clock! Fang Meng'ao's eyes were still watching her, without even a glimpse at the clock.

"Why doesn't it chime?" he asked.

"My father can't bear the clock and wakes up if he hears it," replied He Xiaoyu, surprised. "Odd, you can't see the clock, how do you know it's twelve?"

Fang Meng'ao smiled slyly. "If I had only one pair of eyes, how could I see a surprise attack from behind when I'm in my plane?"

He Xiaoyu knew now why the organisation valued Fang Meng'ao so much.

These eyes seemed to be able to see the stars beyond the boundless sky. But this made Xiaoyu look at him, and become even more flustered. There was a way for him to see her directly through her clothes. Physical, inner panic!

"My dad won't get up until five o'clock tomorrow morning." He Xiaoyu subconsciously held her arms in front of her, pretending to look up to the first floor, and avoiding Fang Meng'ao's gaze. Can you come back tomorrow morning?"

Fang Meng'ao seemed hurt, but kept his pride. "Tomorrow morning I will go to the Citizens' Food Distribution Committee." He had already walked to the door and took his military cap from the hook on the wall. "Thank you for the milk and steamed bread. Next time I will gift you a bag of flour."

"Don't," exclaimed He Xiaoyu as she walked timidly to see him off. "My father wouldn't want it."

Fang Meng'ao said softly: "I said it would be a gift. Goodbye!" The most handsome of all soldiers saluted her, before turning, opening the door and walking out into the night.

Just at that moment Fang Meng'ao looked over his shoulder, and He Xiaoyu could still make out some of that loneliness.

He Xiaoyu stood at the door, looking in Fang Meng'ao's direction as he disappeared behind the courtyard gates. Should I catch up with him and see him off properly? she wondered.

Just after receiving a news report from the Ministry of Defence that the Communist Army would attack Taiyuan within a week, Zeng Keda peered at the military map above the big desk, his face dignified.

The man in sunglasses wearing the military uniform of the Youth Army was still sitting tight on the sofa. Zeng raised his head and looked at him. "No one else is here. There was no need to wear the sunglasses. Put the military cap down. Cool off a bit."

The man slowly took off his sunglasses. It turned out to be Liang Jinglun! He neither stood up, nor took off his cap. His temperament matched the standard military uniform. With his straight body, he could have been anyone from the army or officialdom.

When he didn't move, Zeng Keda noted something odd about him. "Comrade Jinglun, have you got a problem with that?"

"No problem at all," Liang Jinglun replied. "I just wanted to ask Comrade Keda if the organisation has reassigned me."

"Why? What reassignment?" Zeng Keda's face changed colour. "Comrade Jianfeng personally arranged for your work. To which department are you going to be reassigned?"

Liang Jinglun stood up. "Comrade Jianfeng arranged my first job to establish links with the Communist Party in northern China. To earn the trust of the party and keep abreast of the CPC-led Peking student protest movements, Comrade Keda asked me to put on military uniform for a briefing at a place closely watched by CPC agents. Does that mean I don't have to go back to Yenching University after reading the report?"

Zeng Keda's tone grew stronger. "I brought you here because of an emergency. Naturally, you are also well protected. Comrade Liang Jinglun, you are taking your personal safety too seriously, aren't you!"

"Comrade Keda, I beg to differ with you. Ever since I accepted instructions from the organisation to join the CPC underground, I have experienced only danger, never security. Comrade Keda, you must take back that statement. Otherwise, you leave me with no choice but to report to the organisation that I will be unable to complete my tasks, especially with the upcoming currency reform."

Zeng Keda did not expect Liang Jinglun to be so tough today, putting reform of the currency system to the forefront. Was it possible that Comrade Jianfeng had given him something else to do from another line? Thinking of this, the sound of Comrade Jianfeng's voice on the phone that evening rang in his ears: "Regarding Comrade Liang Jinglun, I will answer you clearly now. What he can do within the Communist Party system is a role unique to himself.

Especially in the upcoming reform of the currency system, this role cannot be played by other comrades. You cannot replace him, either."

"Comrade." Liang Jinglun called out softly and brought Zeng Keda's gaze back to him.

"If my attitude just violated the fourth discipline of the organisation, I would like to apologise for it."

"Don't do it." Zeng Keda's attitude was improving. "According to the fourth discipline of the organisation, subordinate violation of the instructions of the superior must be reviewed, and the person reviewing it should be me. Maybe I didn't properly understand the spirit of Comrade Jianfeng's instructions. The tasks assigned to you in the past did not take the overall situation into consideration. But there is one thing I have to tell you – it was Comrade Jianfeng who called for you to come in tonight. He gave me the instructions long ago, asking you to look at the latest report from the Ministry of Defence with me. This was specifically part of his instruction."

"Yes." Liang Jinglun touched his legs together, his expression more solemn now, as he carried on with the report.

The pencil in Zeng Keda's hand pointed to Taiyuan on the map. "As of yesterday, most of Shanxi region has been occupied by Communist forces. Now Xu Xianqian personally commands the First Corps of the North China Field Army and three independent brigades from the Seventh Column of the Jin-Sui Military Command and Shanxi Military Command, a total of more than eighty thousand soldiers, are pressing on towards the city of Taiyuan and are prepared to lay siege to it."

"A siege of Taiyuan! Comrade Liang Jinglun, analysed from your perspective, what is the fundamental purpose of such a military operation?"

Liang Jinglun's gaze moved from Taiyuan to Peking on the map.

Zeng Keda immediately passed the pencil to him, in search of his opinion.

Liang Jinglun took the pencil and used the blue end to draw a circle around Taiyuan, then picked up the red pen to draw even larger circles around Peking, Tianjin and Shanxi. "Our economy will be in much bigger trouble!"

"Go on," prompted Zeng Keda.

"Taiyuan is the economic centre of Shanxi," noted Liang Jinglun. "To put it bluntly, it is the main source of military supplies for the Northwestern Army. If the Communists cut off the supplies for hundreds of thousands of Northwestern Army troops, it would force Fu Zuoyi's troops in northern China to rely on the central government for everything, which further threatens our existence in Peking!"

"Brilliant!" said Zeng Keda, promptly praising his analysis.

"Comrade Keda, I completely understand why Comrade Jianfeng has had me briefed on the battle report. To fight the Communists, we must first fight corruption. Our first priority is to get to the bottom of the corruption in the Citizens' Food Distribution Committee. We are also thoroughly investigating corrupt accounts in the Central Bank's Peking branch, and squeezing out every last cent to give back to the people. More importantly, the old *fabi* legal tender must be abolished immediately and a new currency issued. Finance can no longer be manipulated by corrupt groups. The government must take control!"

Zeng Keda saw something of Comrade Jianfeng in him as he looked at Liang Jinglun again. "Specific plans, specific steps?"

"No matter how arduous the task may be, you still need people to carry it out. Today I met Fang Meng'ao, and I understood what Comrade Jianfeng saw in him. In the fight against corruption in Peking, Fang Meng'ao and his team are truly a sword. The question is who is holding the sword."

"Of course, this sword mustn't be in the hands of the Communist Party."

"What if he only recognises the Communist Party in his heart?"

Zeng Keda felt Liang Jinglun was getting closer and closer to his viewpoint. "You see now why I asked you to arrange for He Xiaoyu to contact Fang Meng'ao?"

Liang Jinglun was silent.

"Any ideas?" asked Zeng Keda.

"No." Liang Jinglun's tone was heavier this time. "The Communist Party has already agreed with me that He Xiaoyu should make contact with Fang via underground channels."

"Any problem?"

Anxiety crept into Liang Jinglun's eyes. "It's just that I feel the Peking Urban Works Department shouldn't take my suggestions so literally."

Zeng Keda was startled, and then waved his hand. "Caution is right, but you don't have to be too sensitive."

"If we take Fang Meng'ao so seriously, the Communist Party has to let He Xiaoyu make the contact. This is why they accepted your suggestion."

"But today Yan Chunming made a clear request that I shouldn't go to He Qicang's house any more. I'm in touch with her too often. Comrade Keda, I feel the Urban Works Department already has tabs on me." A cold suspicion was revealed in his eyes.

Zeng Keda was concerned now. After thinking about it, he said flatly: "From tomorrow on, if anything happens, you come and find me. I will no longer take the initiative to contact you. I will tell any comrades who are in regular contact with you to stop too. They won't be in touch either. From now on, do whatever the Communists want of you. Is that clear?"

"Thank you for your understanding. Please tell Comrade Jianfeng about what I'm going to complete next."

"Go ahead," said Zeng Keda.

"First, I will be sure to push He Qicang to come up with a currency reform plan and let him go and convince Ambassador Stuart to fight for US reserve assistance," said Liang Jinglun. "Second, I will try my best to carry out the request of the Urban Works Department that I become Fang Meng'ao's direct contact."

"Very good!" replied Zeng Keda, excitedly. "I will report to Comrade Jianfeng tonight. What else do you need logistically?"

"There is only one other thing, completely cutting off the other links between the Communist Party and Fang Meng'ao."

"Rest assured," said Zeng Keda, placing his hands on the table. "Everything has been arranged; the only other person with a one-way connection with Fang Meng'ao will soon disappear."

"Comrade, can I leave now?" asked Liang Jinglun.

Zeng Keda immediately walked to the sofa, picked up the pair of sunglasses and handed them to Liang Jinglun. Liang Jinglun took the glasses. Zeng Keda helped him pick the cap up off the coffee table.

As Liang Jinglun reached out to pick them up, Zeng Keda said: "Allow me." Putting the military cap on with both hands, Liang Jinglun went to shake hands, when the phone rang suddenly.

"Hang on." Zeng Keda walked over and picked up the receiver, only hearing a few words and glancing at Liang Jinglun.

Liang Jinglun also immediately felt something related to him, and looked at Zeng Keda quietly, who whispered into the receiver: "Got it. You will separate now. No one should contact Professor Liang any more."

Putting down the telephone, Zeng Keda turned to Liang Jinglun. "Fang Meng'ao went to He Xiaoyu's house tonight."

Liang Jinglun's eyes flashed with a trace of shock, and a hint of unspoken sourness. Zeng Keda went on: "It was Xie Mulan who took him there. And she's still waiting for you in the bookstore. Will you meet her there?"

Liang Jinglun extended his hand to shake Zeng Keda's, and Zeng Keda reached back.

"I'm off!" said Liang Jinglun, gripping Zeng Keda's hand tightly.

CHAPTER 2

In the afternoon, the sun was blazing down on the courtyard of Cui Zhongshi's house in Dongzhong Hutong and the heat was unbearable, even in the shade of the locust tree.

Under the tree were the calf-skin suitcase Cui Zhongshi often carried around, two large leather cases that were part of Biyu's dowry, and a large wooden case. These were all the belongings that the family of four could take with them.

Boqin, the elder son, and Pingyang, the younger daughter, were dressed in fresh, smart clothes. They were busy playing a clapping game in the shade, despite the sweat on their foreheads, while singing a nursery rhyme in the Shanghai dialect their mother had taught them:

> An errand man pulls his rickshaw to Lujiazui;
> He picks up a packet of melon seeds and stir-fries them;
> He feasts on melon seeds but their shells fall down his trousers;
> He unbuttons his trousers by the Huangpu River...

Cui Zhongshi wore the business suit again, and Fang Mengwei a short-sleeved police uniform. Both seemed intent on not noticing each other's sweaty faces, focusing on the children instead.

Obviously in a hurry, Cui Zhongshi took a look at his watch.

A light flashed in Fang Mengwei's eyes, and he recognised the Omega watch and couldn't help looking at Cui Zhongshi.

But Cui looked towards the room in the north of the house.

"Mr Fang is waiting! What are you searching for? Whatever it is, you won't be able to take it now," shouted Cui Zhongshi.

"I know, but we have nothing back in Shanghai. What will we live on?" answered Ye Biyu from inside.

"The train leaves at half past five," said Fang Mengwei, "so there's still time."

He was reluctant to leave.

Cui Zhongshi no longer pressed Ye Biyu, but turned to face Fang Mengwei.

They could do nothing but stare at each other while Ye Biyu packed everything in a sweat. A cloth-wrapper was spread out on the table, and on it were a table clock, a porcelain teapot and cups, and some household articles of various sizes.

Besides the table and chairs, nothing else was left in the room. Ye Biyu was still checking for items to take. Her eyes lit up when she spotted the half-consumed calendar on the wall, and the date: 21 July 1948. It was the thirty-seventh year of the Republic of China. Today was deemed suitable for travel and relocation, and highly auspicious in the southeast!

Ye Biyu's eyes twinkled with joy. She immediately took down the calendar, blew the dust off it, turned around, put it on the cloth-wrapper and started packing. Boqin and Pingyang were still playing clap.

"He was seen by the Indian patrol police and dragged to the police station to be fined."

"Was it Commissioner Xu or Governor Fang who told you to see me off?" asked Cui Zhongshi in a low voice.

"I promised you that as long as you left my brother alone, I would give my life to keep your family safe," replied Fang Mengwei.

"I'm leaving. Believe it or not, I have to tell you that I'm not a Communist and neither is your elder brother. I don't need anyone to protect me," sighed Cui Zhongshi.

Fang Mengwei looked deep into Cui Zhongshi's eyes, indicating neither agreement nor disagreement.

"It's done. Let's go," said Ye Biyu, walking through with the laden cloth-wrapper. Fang Mengwei smiled at her and strode over to take it from her.

"I can handle it," she said.

Fang Mengwei insisted and quietly put a pile of US dollars into her hand. "It's money from the case. Don't tell Cui," said Fang Mengwei in a low voice.

Ye Biyu held onto it tightly. Before she could react, he turned away with the cloth-wrapper.

"Carry the luggage for Mr Cui!" shouted Fang Mengwei to the gate. Several policemen came up at once.

"Here we go! Here we go!" cheered the two kids.

Ma Hanshan walked into the meeting room outside Xu Tieying's office at the Peking Police Bureau sweating and with an air of puzzlement on his face. He was carrying a scroll holder in his hand.

Secretary Sun waited for him outside Xu Tieying's office. Ma Hanshan hurried over and forced a smile.

"What's wrong? Why was he so angry on the phone?" asked Ma Hanshan in a low voice.

Without his usual smile, Secretary Sun looked directly at the scroll holder in Ma Hanshan's hand. "Mr Ma, please show me what's in it."

"A painting. I've promised to invite Commissioner Xu to view it," said Ma Hanshan, with an involuntary smile, as Secretary Sun unscrewed the holder and brought out the scroll.

Then he pinched it half way to make sure there was nothing else before putting it back and closing the lid. Instead of returning it to Ma Hanshan, he laid it out on the conference table.

"I'm sorry, Mr Ma, but please raise your hands," said Secretary Sun.

"Why?" Ma Hanshan was stunned.

"If you have a gun, please leave it here," said Secretary Sun.

"Gun? What would I be doing here with a gun?" Ma Hanshan suddenly understood. "Are you going to frisk me?"

"I'm acting under orders. Please don't put me on the spot," explained Secretary Sun.

"He is the chief of police and I'm the chief of the civil affairs department. Who made the rule that I have to be frisked before I see him?" Ma Hanshan was furious.

"Mr Ma, you've got it wrong. My chief is interrogating those involved in the Citizens' Food Distribution Committee on behalf of the Defence Ministry's Investigation Group. Please cooperate with us," said Secretary Sun.

"OK! I will." Ma Hanshan unbuttoned his coat and threw it onto the table, revealing a white shirt under the belt. Patting his belt with his hand, he turned around and stared at Secretary Sun. "Damn it, do you want me to take off my trousers too?"

"OK, you can go in." Secretary Sun blocked coldly. "By the way, I want to remind you that we work in the Party Headquarters and Director Ye and Minister Chen have never spoken rudely to us. Please mind your manners in the future."

"All right, I will bring out my humblest side with you. Is that OK?" Ma Hanshan contained his anger, and picked up his coat with one hand and the scroll holder with the other. Secretary Sun moved away and let him enter Xu Tieying's office.

Furious, Ma Hanshan stepped inside, stopping as he walked past the screen.

Xu Tieying was talking on the phone with his back to him. "OK, OK, I will investigate the account in Hong Kong as soon as possible... Please rest assured. I'm taking action..."

Apparently, the person on the other end of the line hung up. Xu Tieying put down the receiver and turned slowly.

"Brother Tieying." Seeing Xu Tieying's uncertain face, Ma Hanshan began to doubt. "Did Zeng Keda notice something and put pressure on you?"

"Zeng Keda represents the Ministry of Defence and I represent the Party Headquarters." Xu Tieying wore the party crown on his shoulders.

"He can investigate cases, and so can I. Why should I consult him?" Ma Hanshan glanced at the phone on Xu Tieying's desk and realised that the call was not from Zeng Keda, but from Party Headquarters. He wondered if he had somehow offended Xu Tieying and the party.

"What's going on? Tell me," Ma Hanshan said uncertainly.

Xu examined his elusive face firmly and wondered what he knew. "Do you want me to tell you what you are doing without me?"

Xu Tieying softened his tone.

"Who do you mean?" said Ma Hanshan, looking directly at Xu Tieying. "What did we do without you? Come on, just give me a name."

"Sure. I can give you a name. Hou Juntang!" said Xu Tieying.

"He was shot long ago!" blurted out Ma Hanshan as the realisation suddenly hit him. "You mean the Air Force Hou Juntang's twenty per cent share?"

Xu Tieying didn't answer but instead just looked at him.

"The twenty per cent share was transferred to the Hong Kong account yesterday, wasn't it?" said Ma Hanshan.

"Which account?" asked Xu Tieying.

"Your… your account for the transfer."

"My account, is that right?" Xu Tieying took out a note from his pocket and put it on the table. "Look carefully. Is this your company account in Hong Kong?"

Ma Hanshan hurriedly picked up the note, scrutinised the account number and thought carefully. "This company account in Hong Kong isn't ours!" Ma Hanshan said firmly.

"What does 'ours' mean in this case? Cui Zhongshi or the Yangtze Construction Company?" asked Xu Tieying.

"Bastards!" said Ma Hanshan as the reality seemed to dawn on him. "It's a trick. This must be the new account they gave Cui Zhongshi. I'll call and ask."

Xu Tieying was cooperative this time and immediately pushed the telephone in front of him.

Ma Hanshan picked up the receiver before asking: "Should I call the Peking branch or Yangtze Construction Company?"

"Was Fang Buting involved in the transfer?" asked Xu Tieying.

"If he had been, Cui Zhongshi wouldn't have done it…" replied Ma Hanshan.

"Why are you still asking me?" said Xu Tieying.

"OK, I'll call Kong."

The telephone had a handle and there was no need for Ma Hanshan to crank it so fast.

The sound of the record player in the kitchen on the ground floor of the Fang mansion meant that the hostess was cooking today. Zhou Xuan's song *Blooming Flowers, Full Moon* was playing:

> The floating, scattered clouds.
> The bright moon shines on the reunited people.

There were two fans, one of which was blowing on Cheng Xiaoyun who was busy making bread in her oven, and the other blowing on He Xiaoyu and Xie Mulan sitting on the couch side by side.

"Mulan," said Cheng Xiaoyun to Mulan, looking back at the two of them with a smile, "turn up the sound."

Xie Mulan knew what Cheng Xiaoyun meant, but glanced at He Xiaoyu in all innocence and said: "It's so loud. Why do you want to turn it up?"

Cheng Xiaoyun was very careful and didn't want to embarrass He Xiaoyu, so she stopped smiling and turned her head. "Be smart. Just turn it up."

"I know. It's for eldest brother."

Xie Mulan rose, turned up the volume and set the fan to high speed.

Her skirt fluttered up, and she enjoyed the wind blowing through her thighs.

He Xiaoyu hurriedly grabbed at her skirt as it blew all over the place. "Why such a wind?"

Xie Mulan sat down beside her, yanking her hand away. "Don't worry. He won't come in now!"

He Xiaoyu's skirt revealed her slender legs.

Xie Mulan's eyes twinkled wickedly, but He Xiaoyu could see through them to her simple heart. She wanted her to be with Fang

Meng'ao so much, but even if that were the case, Liang Jinglun would not have accepted her.

"Enough. Get your hands off me," she said.

"Afraid of him coming in?" said Xie Mulan, staring at her.

"Why would I be afraid of him coming in?" asked He Xiaoyu.

Xie Mulan slowly removed her hand, looked at her with suspicion, and went over to the fan, setting it at medium speed. When she returned and sat next to He Xiaoyu, she was in a trance.

The breeze blew at the two girls' skirts like thick leaves in Mr Zhu Ziqing's *Moonlight Over the Lotus Pond*.

―――

There was no wind in the bamboo grove in the back garden of Fang's mansion, but the song floated from the mansion through the bamboo grove.

> Green lotus leaves holding red lotus flowers; twin lotus flowers are blooming, creating a scene of sweet love...

―――

Fang Meng'ao heard the song, as did Fang Buting.

Standing in the bamboo forest himself, Fang Buting was nervous and subconsciously felt Fang Meng'ao standing somewhere in his peripheral vision. Fang Meng'ao's back was straighter than the bamboo itself which was as motionless as he was.

Fang Buting felt a sense of loss and his tone was flat as he reported: "Cui Zhongshi has been transferred. You can check the accounts of the Peking branch on behalf of the Defence Ministry's Investigation Team."

Fang Meng'ao stood still as Fang Buting turned sideways to look at him. Fang Meng'ao knew what people thought even with their back to him. "I know how to fly planes, but I don't know much about economics. I don't understand the accounts of your four banks, two bureaus, one warehouse and one committee."

"Well, why did they send someone who doesn't understand economics to investigate the Peking branch?" Fang Buting looked up at the bamboo. "I'm the bank governor but the money is not mine, nor is it Cui Zhongshi's. He was working for me and I can't let him be blamed for what has happened. I told him to pass on the account books to your uncle, and he'll tell you how to check it."

On the floor of Fang Buting's office on the first floor of the Fang mansion were cardboard boxes stacked full of account books, some opened and some sealed. On the big desk many account books were spread out, which meant the ceiling fan couldn't be used. Xie Peidong flicked through the accounts with trepidation.

"That's why you transferred it to Deputy Director Cui?" Fang Meng'ao finally asked his father directly. "Maybe he could find some answers to the doubts Cui Zhongshi left him with for so many days".

"Yes and no," replied Fang Buting, retaining his reserved manner of speaking towards his son. But he soon found that he shouldn't have said that.

"Could you please talk with them?" The reaction of Fang Meng'ao confirmed Fang Buting's feelings.

"About what?" asked Fang Buting.

"Tell them not to play the song again," said Fang Meng'ao.

Fang Buting listened carefully. The song *Blooming Flowers, Full Moon* was playing on repeat in the kitchen of the mansion.

> *Today is the happiest reunion,*
> *Clean and shallow ponds,*
> *Mandarin ducks playing on the water*

Fang Buting had never been so embarrassed, even in front of Mr Song or Mr Kong, as far as he could recall. His legs felt like they were nailed to the stone path and he was not sure if he could move an inch.

In the kitchen on the ground floor of the Fang mansion, the record player was spinning and *Blooming Flowers, Full Moon* was coming to an end:

> *This soft wind blows upon the beautiful flowers,*
> *Blowing on the good flowers,*
> *Full of warmth and affection between the people*

"Mulan…" said Cheng Xiaoyun.

"I know. I'll play it again," Xie Mulan stood up and walked over to the record player. "Aren't you afraid of annoying him?"

Cheng Xiaoyun turned her head.

"I guess it's fine," said He Xiaoyu.

"Just play it again," said Cheng Xiaoyun thinking it over.

"Enough!" A voice came from outside the window. Cheng Xiaoyun looked back at once and saw its owner, Fang Buting, standing a few steps away from the window with a rare look on his face.

"Turn off what?" asked Cheng Xiaoyun, a little flustered.

"Turn off the record player," barked Fang Buting, and then he left.

Cheng Xiaoyun hurriedly turned, as Xie Mulan stopped the music, looking at He Xiaoyu.

Fang Buting stopped as he was walking back to the bamboo forest.

Fang Meng'ao, standing there, no longer showed his back.

His eyes, ten years estranged, were looking at him.

These were the eyes of an ace pilot who had flown over the Hump numerous times and had experienced countless air battles.

On closer inspection, the eyes were so familiar because they were just like those of his dead wife, revealing a thoughtfulness, tenderness and forgiveness he missed seeing.

Fang Meng'ao came towards him as he looked downwards in an attempt to relieve his tension.

"Sorry, I was supposed to talk with them."

Fang Meng'ao stood before his father. "Please sit down."

Next to Fang Buting was a stone bench. He sat, as he had never done so submissively before. Silence reigned as the son stood like a father, and the father sat like an obedient child.

"I'd like to ask you some questions, which you may not answer if you don't want to." Fang Meng'ao stood by his side.

"Is this on behalf of the Defence Ministry's Investigation Group?" asked Fang Buting.

"This is for me alone," replied his son.

"Go ahead," the old man gave in.

"Three years ago, Deputy Director Cui visited me in Hangzhou. Was it your idea?"

"The family planned it."

"I doubt it. You always have the last word in this house. Who but you would give him the go-ahead to visit?"

"Then you could say I planned it."

"How?" asked Fang Meng'ao.

Fang Buting was stunned. "What did Cui Zhongshi say?"

"You didn't answer my question," said Fang Meng'ao.

"I don't know exactly what you are asking."

"How did Cui know my mother liked that song so much?"

"Mengwei must have told him about it," replied Fang Buting.

"Two weeks ago, Cui saved me in Nanjing. Mengwei doesn't have that ability, right?" said Fang Meng'ao.

"He certainly doesn't have that ability," said Fang Buting.

"So you planned it?" asked Fang Meng'ao.

"Shouldn't I have?" doubted Fang Buting.

"Aren't you afraid that I'm a Communist?"

Fang Buting was afraid of this, but he recognised his fear. He hadn't expected his eldest son to ask him outright. Searching for the right tone, he replied: "You can't be a Communist."

"The Ministry of Defence charged me with colluding with the Communist Party. How can you be so sure?"

"I asked Party Headquarters to look into it," said Fang Buting.

"If they find out I am one, would you ask Cui to save me?"

"Yes," replied Fang Buting through gritted teeth.

"Why?"

"You are my son. I owe you."

"What if I weren't your son?"

"I don't know what you mean."

"If Cui were arrested, would you try to save him?" asked Fang Meng'ao by way of example.

Fang Buting reached for an answer but failed to find one.

In Fang Buting's office on the first floor of the Fang mansion, it was Xie Peidong who was surprised this time. One account in the book before him was growing larger and thicker, and from it a line of words appeared – Hong Kong Great Wall Trading Company Ltd. Xie Peidong stood up and thought hard. He walked towards the window at the back of the room and peered out at the bamboo forest. There was Fang Buting sitting on a stone bench, and beside him was Fang Meng'ao. Xie Peidong walked to the door of the office, left it ajar and checked if anyone was around. There was no one on the ground floor or in the living room on the first floor.

Xie Peidong closed the door quietly and turned the key in the lock before hurrying back to the desk. Sitting down, he rotated the chair to face the wall, revealing a radio transmitter hidden inside! With a gentle pull of the baseboard, the transmitter was released. He put on the earphones, switched channels and typed quickly.

In the twenty-square-metre office of the North China Bureau Urban Works Department in Fuping, Hebei, the keys of several radio transmitters rose and fell. All was quiet, except for the click-clack of the transmitters.

Occasional visitors to the room were wearing the uniform of the People's Liberation Army, as were the operators behind the transmitters.

On one of the transmitters, a telegram was being deciphered in Chinese. The receiver solemnly wrote "top secret" across the top right corner of the paper, and rose to look at an officer on duty pacing up and down.

When the officer came over, the telegram receiver reported

under his breath: "An urgent message from Peking, addressed directly to Minister Liu."

The officer took the message and passed through a curtained door in the room.

The inner room was modestly decorated, and Minister Liu took up position behind a square desk. It was easy to recognise this figure reading documents with his head lowered, though in uniform – it was Liu Yun, who had arranged a job for Yan Chunming in the Yenching University library.

"Comrade Liu Yun, an urgent message from Comrade Peking Number Three," said the officer, stepping lightly up to the desk. Liu Yun raised his head quickly. The surprise in his eyes showed the importance of the message. He took it. The telegram read: "Cui has transferred the secret funds to the Great Wall. Change rescue plan."

"What a pity!" sighed Liu Yun, approaching the map by the wall. He located the Peking-Shanghai Railway with his fingers, sliding them to point at "Cangzhou" after pausing at "Tianjin".

"When will the Peking-Shanghai train leaving at nine pm tonight arrive at Cangzhou?"

The officer on duty stepped forward to reply: "It should be between one and one-thirty in the morning."

"Make arrangements immediately," snapped Liu Yun, turning around.

"Could our comrades in the Enemy Works Department in Cangzhou help get an important person and three dependents off the train, and send them to the liberated area at night?"

Thinking for a while, the officer replied: "There should be no problem getting them off the train, but we don't have enough hands to escort them across enemy territory to the liberated area."

"Request support from the North China Field Army," said Liu Yun, thinking for a moment, before stepping quickly to the telephone and dialling the telephone exchange. "This is the North China Bureau Urban Works Department. Please transfer me to the North China Field Army Command. I have something important to report to the commander directly."

While waiting for the transfer, Liu Yun turned to the officer and said: "Send Peking Number Three's telegram immediately."

The officer went to grab a pen and paper. "Only a short

message," said Liu Yun, waving to stop him. "Protect yourself. Don't contact us via telegram again."

"Yes sir." The officer lifted the curtain and hurried out.

In Fang Buting's office on the first floor of the Fang Mansion, Xie Peidong still had his earpiece in, listening to the click-clack of a transmitter, audible only to himself, and writing down a series of numbers with a pencil in his right hand.

Without translation, he could read the combinations of numbers: "Protect yourself. Don't contact us via telegram again."

With a sigh, Xie Peidong turned off the radio, took off the earphones, pushed the transmitter into the wall and closed the hidden drawer. When he turned the chair around, his forehead was covered with sweat. Staring at the account book, he was lost in thought.

"The thing is," Liu Yun reported to the commander over the phone, excitedly, "this comrade risked arrest by sending the Central Bureau's bribes to Hong Kong, for the benefit of democratic advocates... It's a worthy deed. We must buy time to rescue this comrade and his family at Cangzhou station tonight and escort them to the liberated area, before he is discovered by the Central Bureau of Investigation and Statistics and the police. Besides, we need to know more about the currency reform to be carried out by the Nationalists, and this comrade will be very important. Commander, we request that the troops stationed nearest to Cangzhou come to our assistance. Thank you for your support, Commander!"

Putting down the phone, Liu Yun turned to the officer, who had been waiting for further instructions.

Xie Peidong piled up the books on the desk and carried them to the open box. Then he put a seal on the box, picked up another unopened box next to it and placed it on top of the other box. He took out a pile of account books from an unopened box, walked back to the desk and started checking the books.

In the bamboo grove in the back garden of the Fang Mansion, Fang Buting, now a gentle old man in his sixties, said: "I can tell you I changed the names of Cui Zhongshi's son and daughter."

Fang Meng'ao listened to him quietly.

"Li Bai's son was named Boqin and his daughter Pingyang," noted Fang Buting. "At that time, Li Bai's wife had died and he was adrift. His children were all in foster care with relatives in Shandong. He thought of his children all the time, so he wrote a poem and sent it to them thousands of miles away. The poem was called 'A Message to My Children in East Shandong'…" He glanced timidly at his eldest son and finally plucked up the courage to continue.

"When you and Mengwei were little, I taught you the poem. Would you like to hear me recite it?" Fang Meng'ao stood there silently, not daring to look at his father,.

Fang Buting recited with a Wuxi accent:

> *Pingyang is the name of my little girl,*
> *Who stands by a peach, holding flowers.*
> *She cannot find her father*
> *And her eyes are bursting with tears.*
> *Boqin is the name of my little boy,*
> *As tall as his sister's shoulders.*
> *They walk under the peach tree;*
> *Will someone help them, please?*
> *When I picture this scene, it is heart-wrenching.*

His voice was no longer calm.

Fang Meng'ao turned back with tears in his eyes. Fang Buting collected himself. "I hope Zhongshi will be safely reunited with his family," he said, forcing a smile.

"Uncle!" Xie Mulan called out, having showed up along the path. She had no intention of barging into their conversation. "Mama called me to ask you about dinner, so she can bake bread."

Fang Buting got up from the stone bench but did not immediately reply. He cast a glance at Fang Meng'ao.

"Tell your Aunt Cheng to wait for Mengwei," replied Fang Meng'ao. "Dinner will be at six."

"Got it!" Xie Mulan was not expecting such a quick answer, and she left light-heartedly.

But Fang Buting looked at his oldest son warily. "I have sent Mengwei to see Vice-Director Cui and his family off."

Fang Meng'ao said, "I don't know why he has been assigned so far away in such a hurry, and you won't tell me the truth. But I'm glad to hear you say that."

"Say what?"

"That you hope Zhongshi will be safely reunited with his family!" replied Fang Meng'ao.

"This is what you came for today?"

"Yes. I need you to guarantee the safety of Uncle Cui's family."

Fang Buting froze again, then shook his head. "I can't guarantee it, but I will try my best."

"So be it."

"May I ask why you are so concerned about Cui Zhongshi?"

"He saved my life", said Fang Meng'ao, "so I will save his."

The clock on the platform at Peking railway station said four-forty.

Peking was the starting station and the train was already on the track alongside platform one. In ten minutes, the passengers would be allowed to board. Fang Mengwei stopped his car and looked through the windscreen. A Peking police bureau jeep was parked on the platform. Beside it stood Deputy Police Chief Shan and several policemen.

Cui Zhongshi sat beside Fang Mengwei. His eyes flickered for a second, but soon he calmed down. Fang Mengwei was confused. He looked at Cui Zhongshi. "Let them get off. Bring your wife and children. I will walk you to the train."

Boqin and Pingyang jumped off the jeep behind.

"Don't wander off!" shouted Ye Biyu at the children, following them out of the vehicle. She screamed at the policemen handling their luggage: "Please be careful. Do not scratch them!"

"Don't worry, madam," said the two policemen as they handed over the suitcases. "We'll be careful."

Fang Mengwei and Cui Zhongshi got out of their car, as Deputy Chief Shan began walking towards them, smiling. "What brings you here, Chief Shan?" asked Fang Mengwei, looking at the deputy police chief.

"The leadership is concerned about Director Cui's safety, given the turbulent situation. The commissioner has ordered Deputy Director Fang to escort him to the train station, and me and others to Tianjin. When they arrive in Tianjin, the Central Bureau of Investigation and Statistics will arrange their trip to Shanghai. They will be safe all the way."

After that, Deputy Director Shan turned to Cui Zhongshi. "Director Cui, please tell Mrs Cui and your children to board the train before it becomes too crowded." He shouted to his men: "Help Director Cui with the luggage, and escort Mrs Cui and the children onto the train!"

Fang Mengwei was concerned about their safety before getting on the train. Now that Xu Tieying had made such comprehensive arrangements, he felt it better not to prolong his stay in front of Shan Fuming. His eyes reddened when he looked at Cui Zhongshi. "So I have to drop you here."

He walked over to Ye Biyu and the children. Ye Biyu was busy instructing several policemen handling the luggage when she heard Fang Mengwei from behind. "Mrs Cui, I've got to go."

"OK. See you later," she replied casually before realising it was Fang Mengwei, at which point she turned around rapidly. "Director Fang, there is still half an hour. You're leaving so soon?" she asked.

"Commissioner Xu has designated escorts for you, so I won't be your companion on the journey. Call me when you get to Shanghai."

Ye Biyu always found Fang Mengwei agreeable in Peking, and now she felt really sad. "Of course," she said. "Over the past three years, you have always treated me with such respect, even though you and Zhongshi are as close as blood brothers... By the way, a word in your ear."

Fang Mengwei leant over. Ye Biyu whispered: "There are

rumours about war every day. Try to leave Peking as soon as possible and go to Shanghai or Nanking."

Fang Mengwei smiled bitterly. "All right, I will try. Get on the train. I'm leaving."

Boqin and Pingyang came to their side. Fang Mengwei patted them on the head. Ye Biyu asked them to say goodbye to Uncle Fang, and the two did as they were told.

"Be good to your mother! Bye-bye!"

With no more time to delay, Fang Mengwei went straight to his car. Ye Biyu remembered their luggage. Seeing that all the suitcases had been carried onto the train, she held the children's hands and hurried to the train door.

Cui Zhongshi was watching Fang Mengwei bid farewell to his wife and children. As he opened the door of his car, Cui Zhongshi called out: "Mengwei!" Fang Mengwei stopped and turned around. Cui Zhongshi had something to say, but all that came out was: "Take care of the governor."

"I will!" Reluctant to show emotion in front of Shan Fuming, he got into his car. Cui Zhongshi's jeep turned around on the platform and went back the way it had come. Ye Biyu reached the carriage door with her two children and shouted happily to her husband: "Here we go!"

"After you."

Unexpectedly, it was Deputy Director Shan who replied to her, adding: "I'll have a few words with Director Cui."

"Come on!" Ye Biyu jumped onto the carriage with the children, not noticing that anything was wrong. Only then did Shan Fuming whisper to Cui Zhongshi: "Director Cui, you have to come with me to the stationmaster's office."

Cui Zhongshi knew what was going on and asked: "Anyone waiting to see me?"

There was a twinkle in Shan Fuming's eyes. "No, but I believe you must wait for a phone call."

"Should you ask my family to get off the train?"

"I can't tell you," replied Shan Fuming. "Wait until Mr Xu calls, please." Cui Zhongshi stopped talking and followed Shan Fuming unhurriedly. Passengers were already starting to check in at the station entrance. In front of them were the two young agents who had followed Cui Zhongshi from Nanking to Peking. They looked at Cui Zhongshi and Shan Fuming, walking to the stationmaster's office, and exchanged glances.

In the living room and dining room areas on the ground floor of the Fang mansion, the usual round table for Chinese dishes had been replaced by a long table for Western food. At the seat of honour was a single chair and set of cutlery; on the left were three chairs, placed side by side, and three sets of cutlery, and the same on the right side of the table.

At ten minutes past five, Fang Mengwei hurried in and his eyes lit up – his father was on the sofa in the middle, while his eldest brother was in the armchair beside him. They both looked at him enquiringly.

Fang Mengwei immediately took off his hat.

"Father. Brother!"

Neither of them replied, instead just looking at him. Fang Mengwei didn't know what the glance implied. It was his brother who had arranged for him to see Cui Zhongshi off and to keep it a secret from their father. Now he couldn't report his activities in the presence of their father. But he could talk about something else. Looking from the table to the kitchen, he exclaimed: "It smells great! We are lucky to enjoy Western food tonight for my brother's sake. I'm hungry. Let's have dinner!"

"Mengwei, you're back! We can start serving dinner!"

Xie Mulan breezed in from the kitchen. "Xiaoyu, take out the bread."

Fang Buting had something to add. "That's impudent. She is our guest. Do it yourself."

"Leave it to me," said Fang Mengwei, still saying nothing about his escorting of Cui Zhongshi, as he made his way to the kitchen.

Fang Meng'ao looked at Fang Buting rather than at his brother. "Have Director Cui and his family got on the train?" asked Fang Buting, standing, looking at Fang Mengwei's back.

Fang Mengwei was surprised to hear that from his father. Turning around, he glanced at his father and then at his brother.

"Don't worry, they're all on board. They'll give us a call when they arrive in Shanghai."

"You're sweating. Go and wash your face," said Fang Meng'ao finally.

"OK. Will do."

Fang Mengwei gave his eldest brother a meaningful look, heading for the kitchen. Fang Buting said to Xie Mulan: "Ask your father to come down for dinner."

"No, I won't do that. He gets irritable so easily."

While she talked, she went over to Fang Meng'ao and took his arm. "But be my guest, Meng'ao. I'm arranging the seating tonight. Please."

Looking at his younger cousin, Fang Meng'ao stood as steady as a mountain. She couldn't make him move, and realised why in a moment.

She exclaimed, "Uncle, have a seat, please."

Fang Buting was about to sit at the table when his office phone rang on the first floor. After a short pause, he reached the table. The phone stopped ringing. Xie Peidong must have picked it up.

Pale-faced, Xie replied in a tough tone: "Commissioner Xu, I don't think this is appropriate. If there is anything funny with the account, we can help check it. Director Cui ha been assigned to Shanghai under an official order by the Central Bank. You have no authority to keep him... The director is in no position to answer the phone right now. He's with Meng'ao. We shouldn't interrupt a reunion dinner between father and son after ten years. We can work out the matter in private, and do not disclose it to Meng'ao or the people with the Defence Ministry's Bureau of Reserve Cadres. Must the director answer the phone?"

"Uncle, dinner is ready!" Cheng Xiaoyun called out.

Xie Peidong closed his eyes in despair and spoke into the phone, "Commissioner Xu, if you take the money so seriously, I will ask the governor to speak to you directly."

Normally so calm, when he put the phone back on the table, his right hand was shaking. He had to complete the action with the help of his left hand.

Fang Buting was downstairs in the seat of honour. "I will sit next to my brother," said Fang Mengwei, laying a basket of bread on the table and going to the opposite side.

"Brother Mengwei, here." Xie Mulan, standing by the last chair on the left, pushed Fang Mengwei to the chair beside her.

Sitting in the first chair on the left was Cheng Xiaoyun.

Fang Mengwei was in the second chair. The third chair was left for Xie Mulan. On the other side, the first chair was empty, apparently for Xie Peidong. In front of the second chair stood Fang Meng'ao. The third chair beside Fang Meng'ao was surely for He Xiaoyu. Intentionally or unintentionally, everyone looked at He Xiaoyu, who hadn't been seated yet.

On Fang Meng'ao's face, there was a faint smile for the first time today. He stood behind the chair left for He Xiaoyu and gently moved it back.

"Thank you." He Xiaoyu walked over without any affectation. Now everyone was waiting for Xie Peidong. The door of the office on the first floor opened and Xie Peidong came out. With a strange laugh, he said: "Governor, there is an important phone call for you."

"I'm not answering any phone calls now. Tell them to call again in an hour." Fang Buting sensed it did not bode well but didn't move a muscle.

Xie Peidong was still at the door. "It's the Central Bank in Nanking."

Very reluctantly, Fang Buting rose. "It seems I'm going to have to resign as governor."

In his office on the first floor, Fang Buting, looking livid, spoke calmly into the phone.

"Are you afraid of me running away when you've kept them?"

Xu Tieying's voice was nearly deafening. "Why haven't you come over? This is serious."

"Serious?" replied Fang Buting. "This dinner is more serious to me! Before I finish the dinner with my son and come, Commissioner Xu, please, first take care of his family, and tell them there is a change in his assignment. And, second, do not make it known to Zeng Keda and others at the Defence Ministry, because Hou Juntang just died for the money!"

At that, he hung up the phone. He didn't look well, signalling another attack. "Governor!" Xie Peidong rushed to support him, grabbing a bottle of Tongrentang's *Huoxiang Zhengqi* liquid, prepared in advance, from the desk, and handing it over.

Fang Buting swallowed the liquid, opened his eyes and looked at Xie Peidong. "Is the account correct?"

"No," replied Xie Peidong. "There're too many accounts. I'll check it now."

"Stop." Fang Buting caught his breath. "Have dinner first."

Because of the great loss, Xu Tieying was anxious and sat blankly at his desk.

"Xu," Ma Hanshan said excitedly, pacing back and forth in the room. He changed the way he addressed Xu Tieying: "If you can't fix it, I'll call my men in the Bureau of Investigation and Statistics of the Military Council to do that. You can just pay their transportation fees after getting the money back!"

Xu Tieying was so anxious that he sent Ma Hanshan in, but unexpectedly Ma Hanshan had nothing to do with this matter. Instead, he told Ma the inside story. The way Ma Hanshan gloated made Xu Tieying laugh until he was angry. Soon, Xu Tieying calmed down and got his cup from the table, only to find that there was no tea in it. Ma Hanshan was staring at him.

"No tea to drink on such a hot day?" said Xu Tieying. "Are you sorry about that?"

"Secretary Sun!" said Ma Hanshan, as if he were the master, shouting towards the door.

Secretary Sun came in quickly.

Ma Hanshan was searching for Sun, and now he wanted to make up for that. He said calmly: "Why not serve your director a cup of tea on such a hot day? One for me, too."

Sun looked at Xu Tieying, who nodded. Sun, still looking serious, poured out a cup of tea and handed it to Ma Hanshan with both hands.

"Just put it on the table," said Ma Hanshan.

"OK." Sun put the cup on the table, picked up the thermos flask and refilled Xu Tieying's cup. Then he looked at Xu Tieying, who added: "Go ahead. Deputy Director Ma is one of us."

Sun continued: "Deputy Chief Shan has brought Cui Zhongshi back."

Ma Hanshan, who was drinking tea with his head down, immediately added: "Why not bring him here?"

A look of disgust betrayed Secretary Sun's feelings on the matter. Xu Tieying winked at him. "I see. Ask Shan to accompany him."

"Yes sir," acknowledged Sun, who then turned and backed away.

Holding a cup, Ma Hanshan watched Sun go out and turned to Xu Tieying, who smiled at him. "I wanted you to stay for dinner but I have to handle an urgent issue concerning the party's assets."

He paused at the words "party's assets".

Ma Hanshan looked crestfallen, waiting for him to go ahead and explain the urgent issue.

Xu Tieying continued: "You should know that it concerns the Central Party Committee. You'd better not say a word when you are out of this door."

Bastard, Ma Hanshan scolded him inwardly, and smiled portentously when he rose. "Yes, it's all for the sake of the party-state, and not easy for anyone."

"Let me show you out." Xu Tieying stood up slowly.

"You needn't bother. You have bigger things to attend to." Ma Hanshan stressed the words "bigger things".

He carried the Zhongshan suit over to the sofa in one hand, walked across to Xu Tieying's desk and picked up the scroll holder. "The painting was recognised by Zhang Boju as an original by Tang Bohu, but some laymen think it is a fake. I intended to ask you to help me authenticate it, but unfortunately you don't appear to have time."

Xu Tieying glanced at the holder and then turned and looked pointedly at Ma Hanshan.

"Goodbye." Ma Hanshan went straight to the office door with the painting originally intended for Xu Tieying.

"Secretary Sun!" Xu Tieying had never spoken in such a tone.

Sun entered at once, looked at Xu Tieying, grim-faced, and asked with concern: "Sir, are you feeling unwell?"

"I'm not going to die," continued Xu Tieying in a more relaxed fashion. "Throw away the cup Ma Hanshan used."

"Yes sir." Sun picked up the cup.

"You don't need to bother with the rat."

"Where is Cui Zhongshi being kept?" asked Xu Tieying, bringing up the next issue.

"With the felons," answered Sun.

"Tell Shan and the others to leave," added Xu Tieying. "Make the arrangement yourself. I'll see him in ten minutes."

On the dining table, there was a basket of seven loaves, a large plate of vegetable salad and trays of borscht for everyone.

This was Western fast food for all present. In front of Fang Meng'ao, it was inappropriate for the Fangs to prepare an authentic Western-style meal, given the situation.

At a simple dinner, no one touched the bread or vegetable salad. Cheng Xiaoyun, Fang Mengwei and Xie Mulan on the left, and Xie Peidong, Fang Meng'ao and He Xiaoyu on the right did not even pick up their spoons.

Aside from Fang Meng'ao, the other five were silently looking at Fang Buting.

But the man himself was behaving in a strange way today. He was eating his soup slowly with a spoon, head buried, not noticing anyone else in the room, nor the fact that they were looking at him.

Cui Zhongshi had been arrested without warning, and Fang Buting had to brace himself for a rare reunion dinner. Xie Peidong knew everything and worried more than anyone else. He made eye contact with Cheng Xiaoyun opposite.

Sitting on Fang Buting's right, Cheng Xiaoyun kicked him under the table. Fang Buting raised his head and noticed that no one had made any headway with the bread or vegetables, and that the others had not even had the soup in front of them. Today's hurdle was just too high. He forced himself to smile, miserably. "Why don't you eat?"

"Sir, after you," said Xie Peidong.

"Well…" Fang Buting used a fork to put some salad onto his plate.

"Please." Everyone looked at Fang Meng'ao at this moment.

He was the only one who didn't look at Fang Buting, but now he suddenly did so. "Father."

Everyone else was stunned.

Fang Buting's eyes widened. He looked at his son, who hadn't called him 'Father' for ten years. Fang Buting would rather Meng'ao did not do so.

The air froze.

Fang Meng'ao looked at him. "You want to eat with me, don't you?"

To everyone's surprise, he ate his soup. He picked up a loaf of bread, broke it in half and swallowed a few mouthfuls, ate a spoonful of vegetables and wiped his mouth with his napkin. "You'd better go."

The others had not yet realised what had happened when Fang Buting rose with the support of the table. He nodded heavily at his eldest son several times and turned to Xie Peidong, who was also looking at him in the same way.

"Peidong, get the car ready," said Fang Buting. "We should go."

Fang Mengwei was the first to realise the situation, and left his seat to help his father. "Dad, I'll walk you to the car."

Fang Buting declined. "No! Just stay at home with your brother and Xiaoyu to finish the meal."

He wiped his mouth with his napkin, and walked to the door with Xie Peidong.

The others rose to see them off.

Xie Peidong followed Fang Buting and glanced at He Xiaoyu as he passed by.

He Xiaoyu felt the shock and sensed a coming storm.

She was right. Fang Meng'ao had left his seat and said: "I beg your pardon. I'm seeing them off."

The others were surprised. Fang Meng'ao held his father's arm and walked to the door.

Xie Mulan, who had always been the simplest-minded, reacted to the scene. "Brother Meng'ao, will you come back for dinner?"

"I'll be right back." Fang Meng'ao and Fang Buting went out of the living room.

Xie Peidong had never been so uneasy, following them and thinking fast.

Fang Meng'ao turned around. "Uncle, please ask the driver to go."

"OK." Xie Peidong hurried past them. "Driver, move on!"

Fang Buting, supported by his son, who was as strong as a mountain, waited to be asked something that he didn't know if he could answer. "I believe in you today."

"You believe in me, for what...?"

They walked slowly. "The thing with Uncle Cui. You can deal with it if any one threatens you."

Fang Buting stopped. "You suspect that phone call..."

Fang Meng'ao refused to let him stop, but held him as he continued towards the gate. "I don't suspect anything. Fighting the Japanese in the sky, I would have been shot down if I had suspected too much."

Fang Buting felt his heart miss a beat but he had already reached the gate.

"I'll just say one thing," added Fang Meng'ao. "It's something you taught me yourself – 'a father and son united can win any war'!"

CHAPTER 3

The ten-square-metre cell for solitary confinement of serious offenders at Peking Police Station was windowless. A one-kilowatt spotlight cast an intense light on the interrogation chair. In such a hot summer, any man, strong or otherwise, would collapse in a few short hours. Cui Zhongshi sat handcuffed, eyes closed, sweating. So this is how they treat Communists, he thought!

He was fully aware that the moment of his darkest imaginings had come, but also that success awaited him if he survived. He envisioned the light as a halo in the shape of a red flag.

"Cui, some friend you are!" The voice of Xu Tieying pierced Cui's ears, dispersing the image of the red flag in his mind.

"You know as well as I do that we're not friends," replied Cui, testily.

Xu Tieying was struck by the unexpected retort, so much so that he felt on fire, despite being outside the circle of light. He tried to be as patient as possible. "That's just not something you would say. It's not you at all."

"It is exactly me," said Cui, as sweat dripped into his mouth. "Director Xu, you may have treated me as a friend, but I know that was the money talking."

"I like straightforward people. So let's talk about the money then," said Xu. "Where did you transfer that twenty per cent dividend?"

"Why do you need to ask? You have the account now."

"Who opened the account?"

"I did, of course."

Xu Tieying was sweating too. He couldn't wait to to be done with Cui once and for all, but he wasn't there yet. "Since you opened it, you can surely transfer the money back again, right?"

"What about the money I gave you earlier? Could I have transferred that back?" asked Cui.

"Cui Zhongshi!" The name burst from Xu Tieying's clenched jaw. "You are one of a kind. Let's put the money aside, and talk about what we are made of right now, just out of curiosity. A theoretical question. You won't say no, will you?"

Cui Zhongshi knew what he wanted to say. Covered in sweat, he smiled faintly.

"Fang Buting is such a clever man. How did you convince him to trust you?" said Xu.

"You are clever too. Why did you trust me?" asked Cui.

"Touché," replied Xu Tieying. "But I did read your files and found no trace of Communist training. Where did you get your wits and muscles from?"

"You think I'm clever and strong?" replied Cui Zhongshi.

"You have your tentacles all over the Central Bank, the Ministry of Finance and even Nationalist Party Headquarters," said Xu Tieying. "I doubt many Communists can match you for scope. And then you get yourself exposed for such a small sum of money? Is it worth it?

He was trying to draw Cui away from the party. "Keep talking," said Cui.

Xu Tieying felt as if a stone was dangling over his chest, but he had no choice but to carry on. "Onlookers see things the clearest, Mr Cui. I know the sort of ideals that fill the heads of people like you. Just try to set these things aside and think about what kind of a person you are. Let me tell you this. You'd be called a spy in the West, but for a Buddhist, you're grappling with an inferno. No one who gets into an inferno ever escapes death and their soul is cast away forever. They might not see it. They might wander around amid the living and the dead. But in fact, neither ghosts nor the living will want to get anywhere near you. That's why they ditched you today. Don't even think about trying to get away with it."

"Are you done, Commissioner Xu?" asked Cui.

"Tell me what you think," said Xu.

"It's too hot. I didn't hear a word you said," answered Cui.

"I'll tell you something you'll be willing to hear!" Xu Tieying got irritated at last. "You think you are sacrificing yourself for the Communist Party. But do your wife and kids have to die with you?"

"Sir," said Secretary Sun, showing up at precisely the wrong moment. "Governor Fang is here. He's waiting for you in the office."

"OK."

"Sir." Secretary Sun left at once.

Xu Tieying clenched his teeth and got up close to Cui's ear. "Don't even think that someone's going to save you and your family. Caught up in Communist affairs, unless you cooperate, no one can save you."

Seeing Xu Tieying leave the cell with sweat dripping from his face, Secretary Sun picked up a basin of cold water he'd prepared a long time ago and held it out to Xu as he came down the corridor. Xu Tieying took out a towel and wiped the sweat from his face and neck. Secretary Sun squeezed out the towel and took out a comb.

"Sir, you don't have to suffer." Secretary Sun took the used towel and passed Xu the comb. "Just move him to another place for interrogation."

"Some hardships are necessary," Xu said, combing his hair before walking through the iron door.

When Xu returned to his office, his clothes were still wet. Fang Buting was sitting on the sofa behind the screen. Although hot, he was not sweating. He remained seated as he caught sight of Xu, who slumped down beside him.

"Please tell me exactly how many shares in total, and how many dividends over the half year?" Fang Buting wasted no time on small talk as he spoke, head bowed and eyes turned away from Xu's.

Xu Tieying turned around and stared at Fang. "Have you checked Cui Zhongshi's account?"

"No. I didn't check that account and I never will," replied Fang.

"Such trust in your people. Aren't you concerned about getting into trouble because of them?" asked Xu.

"If so, would I be sitting in the Peking Police Bureau now? Please give me a number. How much?" asked Fang Buting.

"It's not much – about four hundred and seventy-five thousand US dollars in profit over the past six months," said Xu Tieying.

"I've brought Mr Xie here, too. You can talk to him. Just show him the account, and he'll write you a cheque," said Fang Buting. At that moment, he pushed himself up by the arms of the sofa. "There's a train heading to Shanghai tonight. I hope Cui Zhongshi catches it."

"You mean I should release Cui as soon as you transfer me the money?" said Xu, sitting still on the sofa.

Fang Buting turned to him slowly. "What do you mean, Director Xu? You want the money and his life?"

Xu Tieying, still sitting on the sofa, lifted his head and looked right back at Fang. "Why don't you ask Cui Zhongshi where he put the money that belonged to the company of the Party Headquarters?"

Even though he was prepared for the worst, Fang Buting was still hoping Xu Tieying was only after the money and wasn't aware of Cui's connection to the Communist Party. But seeing how Xu reacted, he realised Cui really had transferred the money to the Communist Party at the worst possible time. Without showing it, he cursed Cui in his mind – you will bear the consequences of your stupidity!

Realising he had hit Fang Buting hard, Xu Tieying stood up, walked to the office table and took out a telegram with the account and company name. "Would you care to examine this account?"

Fang Buting didn't take it, but instead just stared at the telegram in Xu's hand. Below a long row of numbers was written "Hong Kong Great Wall Economy & Trading Co. Ltd."

He turned to Xu. "I said I don't care about your accounts at all. No matter what account he transferred the money to, I'll just pay it back for him."

"What if he transferred it to a Communist Party account?" said Xu Tieying, playing his ace. "Can you just pay for him and that will be it?"

Governor Fang feigned astonishment. "Does it really belong to the Communists?"

"It's been confirmed," answered Xu. "The company was founded by the so-called democratic parties banned by the government, but is actually a front for the Communist Party in Hong Kong to raise funds for anti-government agitators. The China Democratic League, the Revolutionary Committee of the Nationalist Party and others like them."

Fang Buting shut his eyes before throwing out a barbed comment. "That's why I didn't want to come here and answer your questions. You always complicate things."

"We?" Xu Tieying couldn't stand him any more, and was getting increasingly upset. "Cui Zhongshi did it in secret, and he is one of your people at the Peking branch, Governor Fang. You were not involved, but Cui Zhongshi was sent to Nanking to save your son, right? A deputy director of the Peking branch vault, if he isn't working on your behalf, can't take even a single step into the Communications Bureau of the Nationalist Central Committee members. To save your son, friends at the Central Party Headquarters have spared no effort, to the point of trading him with a Nationalist lieutenant general. How dare you blame us now? That's right. I, Xu Tieying, owed you a favour before, but the people at the Central Party Headquarters and the Communications Bureau have no respect left to give you. If you give them no benefit, they'll chop your head off, never mind that one of your men is a Communist."

Fang Buting felt something burning inside, but he couldn't just confess it was his younger son's plan to send Cui Zhongshi to Nanking to save his son. So, he opened his eyes. "It's human nature for a father to save his son. You've read all the documents and files? Why didn't you tell me there was a Communist among us?"

"We have found out now!" Xu Tieying's face turned pale. "You want me to release Cui Zhongshi, right?"

Fang Buting paused before answering. "Of course not. If Cui Zhongshi is a Communist, I must be held responsible for it. You can contact Zeng Keda from the Ministry of Defence for a meeting at once. It would be better to force Cui to spill the beans, and leave him to be dealt with by the Nanking Special Criminal Court."

Xu Tieying's face changed colour, and his voice grew cold. "You want us to die together, like jade and stone burning together? I have to tell you, Governor Fang, you may be doomed, but I'm not. The twenty per cent share is not in my name. It's an asset of the party-owned company. According to the Company Law of the Republic of China, it's completely legal for party-owned companies to apportion equity."

Fang Buting clearly showed his revulsion. "Thanks for the reminder. You forget I've spent three years earning a doctoral degree in economics from Harvard, and another three years earning a doctoral degree in finance from Yale? When this government was establishing its financial law, I was fully involved. I'm well aware of the company law you just mentioned. There isn't a single article in the company law that says you can have shares without paying for the equity capital. How did you come about that twenty per cent share? You purchased the capital?"

Fang Buting was feared by people like Xu Tieying. He was one of those who had studied in America and came back grasping the economic artery of the Republic of China in their hands. And they had the Song and Kong families backing them up. He needed Fang to get rich, but was well aware that these shares were snatched from Hou Juntang's air force.

Xu Tieying closed his eyes briefly. "We have been friends for years. I didn't invite you here so we can hurt each other. The point is you and I have been set up by the Communist Party. Zeng Keda and his men cannot know this. I have two thoughts on the matter. First, as you said just now, we need to transfer that money to an account of our party-owned company as soon as possible. Second, we have to execute Cui Zhongshi tonight and no one must know."

"I can't agree to the second point," said Fang Buting. Xu was surprised and confused.

"To be frank, sending him to work in the Central Bank in

Shanghai was arranged by the Bureau of Reserve Cadres of the Ministry of Defence," said Fang Buting.

It turned out that Fang Buting had already prepared everything with Zeng Keda by keeping him in the dark. Xu Tieying pondered why through clenched teeth.

It was past seven o'clock now. Twilight tinged the edges of the sky. The lamps along the lane to the back garden of Gu Weijun's mansion had been turned on.

The back garden was large and Zeng Keda, wearing a white waistcoat, basketball shorts and running shoes, was running down the lane covered in sweat. At the entrance of Zeng Keda's residence, his adjutant and one of the agents of the Youth Army following Cui Zhongshi to the station were standing there, waiting. The agent was a little anxious and spoke quietly: "Adjutant Wang, we have only one man on monitoring duty there. If we don't take action now, we may lose sight of Cui."

"I'm thinking!" the adjutant growled quietly to the agent. "Pay attention. It's not something you should say."

Zeng Keda kept running along the path as it got darker and darker. His face was fading into the darkness, but his eyes were still shining. The adjutant and agent stood up straight. Zeng Keda finished his "pensive" run and entered the residence. He called for his adjutant and agent to follow him inside.

Xu Tieying finally realised that he had been set up by this canny fox. He looked at Fang Buting, feeling depressed. "Governor Fang, if I understand you correctly, if I hadn't tried to find out whether that four hundred thousand dollars had been transferred to the account of the party-owned company, I wouldn't have known that Cui Zhongshi had transferred the money to a Communist organisation in Hong Kong, and there's no way I could have discovered that he was actually a Communist. But the Iron and Blood Congress realised his true identity, and even arranged a secret arrest operation in Shanghai. Zeng Keda has supposedly discussed all this with you already. But you, in order to save yourself, worked hard at keeping us in the dark."

Fang Buting was actually more depressed than him. "Good theory. Anything else?"

"Governor Fang," said Xu Tieying, "don't think that the Iron and

Blood Congress won't be able to track you down because you didn't get involved in the deal that Cui Zhongshi and the Yangtze Construction Company struck with us and the Citizens' Food Distribution Committee. You put a Communist in an important position for years, and transferred a lot of money to the Communists during the period of counter-insurgency and nation saving. For this reason alone, you will definitely end up in a far worse situation than us if the Iron and Blood Congress gets Cui Zhongshi. What do you think of my theory this time?"

"I totally agree," answered Fang Buting. "Cui is now in your custody. So, Zeng Keda may come to find you in no time. You can just report your theory to the Defence Ministry's investigation team for it to be put on record."

After he had finished talking, he walked right towards the screen.

"Governor Fang." Even though Xu Tieying was highly experienced, he could not handle the composure of Fang Buting.

"So you are leaving just like that?"

Fang Buting stopped again. "I told you on the phone that my older son, the one so highly valued by the Defence Ministry's Investigation Group, is waiting for me at home. Maybe he is a Communist too. But he isn't, since you guys have investigated him plenty of times, right? I have no choice but to accept his investigation on behalf of the Peking Branch. Commissioner Xu, may I leave now?"

After returning to the residence, Zeng Keda did not issue any orders. Instead, he took a shower.

The adjutant and the agent were waiting in the living room, trying to keep calm and cool. After a while, Zeng Keda was seen wearing a white Hawaiian short-sleeved shirt, summer trousers and black cloth shoes.

"Tell the comrade monitoring the police bureau gate to come back too," said Zeng Keda, taking a glass of water from the table, and drinking it.

The agent was still awaiting details. Zeng Keda put down the glass, and stared at him.

"Sir, yes sir." The agent rushed out with determination and confusion written all over his face.

"Is Fang Meng'ao still at his father's house?" Zeng Keda asked his adjutant.

"Yes," answered Adjutant Wang. "Lieutenant Colonel Zheng called us twice. Fang Buting went to the Peking Police Bureau and has yet to return. Chief Fang has been waiting at home."

"Go and tell those who are monitoring the house of Cui Zhongshi to abort the mission," said Zeng Keda.

It was Adjutant Wang's responsibility to raise dissenting opinions at any time, so he asked: "Sir, with permission, may I ask why?"

"Xu Tieying will kill Cui Zhongshi. Let's not get involved. Fang Meng'ao should blame it all on them," answered Zeng Keda. "Tomorrow, we need to run a full investigation on the Citizens' Food Distribution Committee and the Peking branch."

"Smart decision, Sir," said Adjutant Wang sincerely, turning around and walking out too.

Zeng Keda picked up the phone on the table and quickly dialled. "Commissioner Xu? This is Zeng Keda. I heard you've captured Cui Zhongshi. Any word on the Yangtze Construction Company and the Citizens' Food Distribution Committee case?"

Fang Buting sat down, gawking at the ceiling and averting his eyes from Xu Tieying who was answering the phone call.

"Not really." When dealing with Zeng Keda, Xu Tieying gave full play to his composure as an experienced member of the Central Bureau of Investigation, "I'll inform you the moment we've got any new clues... It was Governor Fang. He told me that he had new plans to send Cui Zhongshi to the Central Bank in Nanking. As police, we needed to escort him, right? Of course, we took him to the police bureau on the way back. Governor Fang is with me now. Do you need to hear from him directly?"

Fang Buting jumped to his feet and strode back to pick up the phone.

He kept listening, before answering: "New plans are all from Nanking and they insisted on transferring Cui Zhongshi. Allow me to tell you, General Zeng, that over 1.7 million people in Peking need rations to survive and hundreds of thousands of General Fu Zuoyi's soldiers rely on the central government for military supplies. And all of these come from the US. I think we should send Cui Zhongshi to America to seek more supplies for the Peking branch. As for whether he can leave Peking safely, it depends on the Investigation Group of the Ministry of Defence as well as Commissioner Xu." He closed his eyes again.

Xu Tieying stood several steps away from Fang Buting, pondering Fang's words. But now he knew Zeng Keda was about to give his final decision. So he hesitated no longer and walked up to the telephone.

As if Zeng Keda was deliberately speaking quietly, Xu Tieying could only hear him faintly. "I totally understand your predicament, Mr Fang. I agree to change the arrangement of sending Cui Zhongshi to Shanghai.

However," Zeng Keda said in a raised voice, "we can't just let Director Xu interfere like that. Please tell him we'll let him handle this for your sake, Governor Fang. I hope he understands your predicament too and gets the job done tonight. He'd better not delay it until tomorrow. I don't think it would be a wise decision to force me or Chief Fang to take over."

Zeng Keda hung up the phone without any hesitation.

"Bastard!" Xu Tieying cursed like Ma Hanshan.

Fang Buting put down the telephone slowly. "I wanted to shoulder the whole responsibility myself. You shouldn't just barge in... Let's talk about what happens afterwards."

"What happens afterwards? How can we discuss it?" said Xu Tieying.

"I have to go back. Otherwise, my older son may come here," said Fang Buting, "I'll leave Mr Xie, my assistant manager, to represent me. You can talk it over with him. I wish we could come to an understanding. You get the money and I get this whole thing over with."

Fang Buting walked away with his stick. Xu Tieying wasn't inclined to see him off but did so anyway.

The Peking Police Bureau had been built as the Ministry of Personnel, the first of six ministries in operation during the Qing

Dynasty. It covered an area of about twenty-seven square metres, located east of Tiananmen Square. During the Republic of China, it was taken over by the police department but the gate and high walls remained virtually unchanged in order to demonstrate stateliness.

The eastern garden was where the minister of personnel went for a stroll after work. Now, it had become the commissioner's back garden, open only to certain staff. A tranquil spot, shaded by old cypresses, surrounded by walls in three directions, the crickets chirped in all corners and the lawn grew undisturbed.

In the middle of the garden stood a round, white jade table and four matching stools supposed to have been made for the Qing Ministry of Personnel. Xie Peidong sat alone at the table, facing the gate.

Outside, where the lamps shone, Secretary Sun took Cui Zhongshi into the garden.

Xie Peidong stood up slowly.

When Fang Buting drove his Austin sedan into the block where the residence was located, he noticed the jeeps of the Youth Army and Fang Meng'ao parked by the roadside. A squad of Youth Army guards saluted him on the way in.

Fang Buting had his car parked near the gate. The gatekeeper came over to the sedan, opened the rear door and put one hand on the car roof.

"Shut it," said Fang Buting. The gatekeeper paused with the door open.

"Shut it!" Fang Buting snapped quietly.

"Sir." The gatekeeper hurriedly yet gently shut the door.

Fang Buting sat in the sedan with his eyes shut.

The driver stayed where he was, hands on the wheel, breathing as unobtrusively as he could while taking glimpses at Fang in the rearview mirror.

The bank governor opened his eyes and looked towards his residence. He had never been more afraid of coming home.

Xu Tieying had promised to keep everyone away from the

garden. It was largely empty, with only Xie Peidong and Cui Zhongshi sitting at the table.

"They say you're a Communist," remarked Xie as they faced each other across the table.

He sounded upset. "I don't believe it and neither does the governor. But explain why you transferred money to that account! The governor has asked me to ask you. What is that account? Do you have your shares in it? If you tell me the truth, maybe we'll be able to save you. Is that clear?"

"Thank you, Mr Xie. And please convey my thanks to the governor. I kept you both in the dark about the transfer and I won't tell you the reason now. I won't tell any one." The faint lamp light shone on them. A wry smile touched the corner of Cui Zhongshi's mouth.

But his smile worried Xie Peidong. "It's a large number – four hundred and seventy thousand US dollars. If you don't make it out, what's the point? You won't get a cent."

Xie Peidong gave Cui Zhongshi a look that suggested he, as the superior, appreciated Cui's action. He continued: "Cui, did you ever give any thought to your wife and kids before making that payment?"

Cui Zhongshi's smile disappeared. He deliberated before opening his month, speaking in a low voice. "I had to do it, even though it was unfair to my wife and kids."

"You kept us and your families in the dark, and did just what you wanted. And you want to get away with it by just saying you are sorry?"

Xie Peidong nodded towards a chair. "Take a seat."

"It was my decision, right or wrong." Cui Zhongshi sat down, facing him, completely composed. "After I worked at the Central Bank and later as deputy director of the Peking branch vault, each sum of money I checked was sufficient to ensure that no one died of hunger in the whole of Peking. But I can't even use the money to help them. I've had to launder money for people, and transfer it to their accounts, and even give it to them myself. Recently, I've been checking these accounts at home every day. The moment I opened the accounts, it reminded me of what Lu Xun wrote in *A Madman's Diary*: every line is concluded with the two words – 'Eat people'.

Please tell the governor. No matter why he sent me to Shanghai, I'm not going to let Xu Tieying have that sum of dollars before I go."

"Is this why you sent it to Hong Kong?" asked Xie Peidong, interrupting him. "They've checked. The account is linked to the Democratic Party. It has nothing to do with the public, has it?"

"They represent the people," said Cui Zhongshi, smiling again at Xie Peidong. "Xu Tieying interrogated me just now. Poor guy, the look on his face was totally worth it. Please don't ask any more questions. My answer won't change."

Xie Peidong remained silent, and he looked back at the gate.

Secretary Sun had shown up under the lamp light, and coughed as if in cahoots with someone.

Xie Peidong had something more to say. "I'll ask no more questions. But there's something else. Did they force you to do it?"

"They asked whether I was willing to cooperate," answered Cui Zhongshi.

"You had to, no matter whether you were willing or not. They wanted you to write your family a letter. And, if you did so, the letter might keep your family safe."

The smile on Cui's face faded away. He stood up and walked towards an open area. "Please come here."

He had no wish to be recorded. Xie Peidong walked over, feigning reluctance.

Cui Zhongshi leant towards his ear. "You know, my marriage to Biyu was arranged by my family," he revealed.

Xie Peidong urged him. "Carry on. I'm listening."

"Getting married to her was to make my job in the Central Bank easier and more stable. I don't love her, but I had to marry her and we have two kids. Everything is resting on her now," continued Cui.

"It's the family's responsibility. The family must take care of her and your kids," said Xie Peidong.

Cui was lost in thought again. This time he spoke slightly more courageously. "There's someone else to whom I feel deep regret. If you happen to see them, please relay these words to them."

Xie Peidong thought he was going to mention Fang Meng'ao, so he said: "You shouldn't feel sorry for him. You'll always be an important person to him. I'll talk to him when the time is right."

"I've failed so many," acknowledged Cui Zhongshi with a bitter smile. "But it's actually someone else. You know, my original name was Cui Liming. And that person was orginally called Wang Xiaohui. If I hadn't come to work for the Central Bank, she would have been my wife. It's been ten years. I ran away when we broke up. I heard she went to Yan'an and has been trying to reach me."

Xie Peidong felt moved when he heard this. "What do you want to say to her? I'll make sure she gets the message," said Xie.

"Just tell her that my wife and kids love me very much, so she shouldn't go to my house when she comes to the city. I can't let Biyu and the kids know about my past," said Cui Zhongshi.

Xie Peidong agreed in silence, his eyes closed.

Cui Zhongshi looked relieved. He smiled and lowered his voice as much as possible. "And finally, please tell Meng'ao when you reach Deshengmen."

Xie Peidong had to open his eyes slowly again.

"Tell him, I'm proud to have nurtured him," said Cui Zhongshi

With this, Cui spoke at a normal pitch again. "There's no more. I'll write!"

Secretary Sun showed up outside the gate. Xie Peidong struggled to get up, pushing his hands against the jade table.

Somehow, Fang Buting had sneaked in, stopping in the lane where his older son had escorted him out in the evening. The sound of a piano being tuned drifted from the living room on the first floor of the Fang mansion.

Xie Mulan was surprised and excited. Unexpectedly, Fang Meng'ao could tune a piano, and with such professionalism and concentration.

He Xiaoyu hadn't expected it either, but just kept watching him silently.

Only Fang Mengwei showed no sign of surprise. He just

watched his brother tightening the strings and striking the keys in a rather complicated procedure.

Fang Meng'ao leant to one side, tried a few keys and stood up straight. "Almost done. How long has this piano been idle?"

"Only father plays it," replied Fang Mengwei, handing him a wet towel from the basin. "Since we moved here, he hasn't played it once."

"Students of Yenching University, any one of you want to give it a try?" Fang Meng'ao turned to Xie Mulan and He Xiaoyu. "In here, you can play anything, including revolutionary songs banned by the government."

"Uncle never taught me. I don't know any tunes," professed Xie Mulan, turning to He Xiaoyu. "I remember you could play a song called..."

She paused for a while, then lowered her voice. "*Yellow River Cantata*. How about that?"

"When did I learn how to play it?" asked He Xiaoyu with a mischievous look. She tried to relax a bit and forced a smile.

"Usually, when we sing together, you are responsible for the piano part, right?" said Xie Mulan.

"Shut up. That's an organ, not a piano. Just listen to your brother play," said He Xiaoyu.

———

Fang Meng'ao smiled slightly, so different from his expression as an ace pilot, and said: "I'm not tuning it for myself." He turned to the door of the living room. "The one who's going to play the piano is back already. Mengwei, fetch him please."

Fang Mengwei was a little shocked. He knew long ago that the two men he admired the most were going through something today. Sending their father out at dinner was only the beginning. Now, at the sound of his brother's words, he realised his father was in the front garden, and things were about to go down. Not knowing what to do, he simply stood there.

From the look Xie Peidong gave her when he left, He Xiaoyu understood she was going to be involved in a mission tonight. But she had no idea what was going to happen. She stood there trying her best to be calm.

Xie Mulan felt the same. Usually, she'd be the first to jump up in welcome. But today, right now, she only gave her brothers a nod, and stood there timidly.

"Why is it so quiet in here?" said Fang Buting when he showed up outside the living room.

"Father," greeted Fang Mengwei.

"Father."

"Uncle Fang."

Fang Buting, smiling, turned to the piano. "How did you move that heavy thing down?"

The questions brought Xie Mulan into the conversation. "I couldn't move it. The brothers did."

Now, Fang Buting had to look straight at his older son. "It has been years, and it's out of tune. It was a ropey old thing even before you moved it downstairs."

"Older brother has tuned it," said Xie Mulan, cheering up all of a sudden. "He tuned it for you to play."

"You'll lag behind if you forget to practise for even three days. And I haven't practised the piano for three years," said Fang Buting while walking slowly to the stool and sitting down. His shiny forehead was visible to all.

"It's too hot today," said Fang Mengwei, bringing him a towel. "Father, use this first." He handed him the towel.

Fang Buting took it and started wiping his face slowly, asking: "What shall I play?"

Fang Mengwei and Xie Mulan turned to Fang Meng'ao, as did He Xiaoyu.

"How about *Ave Maria* by Bach and Gounod?" asked Fang Meng'ao.

At that moment, Fang Buting was handing the towel back to Fang Mengwei. Their hands stopped in mid air.

Xie Mulan and He Xiaoyu secretively looked at each other.

Fang Meng'ao turned to them. "*Ave Maria* is the Latin name for it, isn't it?"

They nodded their heads in agreement.

"Can it be rephrased as *Bon Voyage, Maria*?" asked Fang Meng'ao.

The four of them were shocked. It reminded Fang Mengwei of Cui Zhongshi, adding a hint of begging when looking at his father.

Fang Buting seemed to be looking back at his younger son as well, but his eyes were blank. Fang Meng'ao waited for Xie Mulan and He Xiaoyu to give the go-ahead.

Xie Mulan said haltingly: "The literal translation should be *Wishing You Happiness and Luck, Maria*, but I think *Bon Voyage, Maria* is better."

This was the first time He Xiaoyu had agreed with Fang Meng'ao, and she did so with tears in her eyes.

All was quiet; everyone was waiting for Fang Buting's next move.

Without a sound check, Fang Buting raised his wrists and pressed the first key. He let the melody of Bach's *Prelude in C Major* flow through his fingers like a stream.

The beautiful melody had the power to torment performer and audience alike.

Cui Zhongshi's handwriting was exquisite, like music. Xu Tieying's office desk appeared just like this piano.

The letter was simply addressed: "To my wife, Biyu."

The content, though obscure from Xu's angle, was simple.

"The Central Bank Headquarters has ordered me to fly to Nanking to help prepare a delegation to America. The mission is confidential, so I'm afraid I can't say goodbye to you face to face. We may not be able to speak on the phone, either. You must wait for me in Peking with the children. If you need anything, Governor Fang and Mr Xie will help you."

The parchment cover was even simpler. It just said: "In Cui Zhongshi's hand."

Xu Tieying stood by the table and checked the contents, sighing at the handwriting. He took up the finished letter and inspected it carefully. "I think it's OK. Just address the envelope."

Cui Zhongshi wrote calmly: "I request Assistant Manager Xie to deliver this to my wife Ye Biyu."

Xu Tieying took the letter and walked over to Xie Peidong who was sitting on the sofa with his eyes shut. "Please take a look. You can leave if there's nothing else to modify."

Xie Peidong opened his eyes, took the letter, scanned it several times and raised his head after a while. "I can't leave now."

Xu Tieying stared at him. "You don't have to escort Deputy Director Cui, do you?"

"Governor Fang ordered me to leave after he called me, and requested that you escort Deputy Director Cui out after that," said Xie Peidong.

"What time is it? We've made a deal. Why are we waiting for some phone call?" Xu Tieying was upset, calling out: "Secretary Sun!"

Secretary Sun showed up like a shadow, as he always did.

"Commissioner Xu," he said. Xie Peidong was still sitting on the sofa. "My governor told me to wait for his telephone call. I have to answer his call so I can write you a cheque, right?"

Choked by his words, Xu Tieying thought for a moment before turning to Secretary Sun. "Escort Deputy Director Cui to the car and then wait for ten minutes."

"Sir," answered Secretary Sun.

Cui Zhongshi walked past the office table towards the folding screen without giving Xie Peidong a glance, before disappearing. Secretary Sun followed him at once.

"Mr Xie, please make the phone call to your governor," said Xu.

Xie Peidong did not move a muscle. "My governor told me to wait for his call."

Ave Maria, arranged by the French composer Charles Gounod over a hundred and fifty years ago, combined the innocence of Bach with the piety of Gounod. The song was immensely popular and stretched across time in a manner of cooperation, a classical ode to the Virgin Mary.

He Xiaoyu and Xie Mulan were students at Yenching University, founded by Americans from the church in China. They knew the song well but had no idea Fang Buting would be so well versed in it and able to play the accompaniment so convincingly.

Xie Mulan felt compelled to join in but knew she couldn't reach the high notes. She nudged He Xiaoyu several times. But all He Xiaoyu had eyes for was the piano. She saw the elder Fang and Meng'ao standing behind, and held her breath, not daring to interfere between father and son.

Her eyes widened as Fang Mengwei and Xie Mulan, aware of the older brother's singing talent, held their breath as Fang Meng'ao sang:

> *You suffer for us. You wear shackles for us.*
> *You relieve our pain. We all kneel before your altar.*
> *Virgin Mary, Virgin Mary, use your gentle hands*
> *to wipe away our tears, in our darkest hours.*

Fang Buting stopped playing, as if knowing his son wouldn't sing the final line – *lord we beseech you to save us.*

For the performance's sake, it was a bad moment to stop, as they all knew. Silence was restored, no one could muster a word.

Fang Buting rose to his feet and turned to He Xiaoyu with a complicated smile. "That's the best rendition of *Ave Maria* I've ever heard. What do you think, Xiaoyu?"

"Well..." He Xiaoyu seemed worried. "It's definitely the best version I've heard."

"It's definitely the best version I've heard, too." murmured Fang Buting again, before resolutely changing the topic of conversation. "I've got to make a call upstairs. You keep the brothers company down here."

Fang Buting turned around and caught his older son's expression of expectation. He walked away with the same *andante* pace as *Ave Maria* and went upstairs.

The phone on Xu Tieying's desk rang loudly. He was sitting within reach but hesitated to pick it up. Instead, he stared at Xie Peidong who was sitting on the sofa with his eyes on the phone. It continued ringing and Xu finally answered it.

In his first-floor office, Fang Buting spoke in a low yet calm voice: "Did Assistant Manager Xie write you a cheque, Commissioner Xu?"

"Yes, as I said. My condition is to hear Cui Zhongshi's voice once every ten days."

———

Meanwhile in the Commissioner's Office at the Peking Police Bureau, Xie Peidong saw Xu Tieying's face had changed. Xu spoke into the receiver: "What if you don't hear his voice again?"

"Please put Assistant Manager Xie on the phone. He'll answer you later," said Fang Buting, on the other end of the phone.

Xie Peidong took the receiver, the colour draining from his face. "I've got it. I'm telling him now." He held the receiver to his ear, and turned to Xu Tieying. "Our governor told me if you don't accept his terms, I can't write you the cheque."

Xu Tieying laughed. "OK, ask your governor if he can say that to my face," said Xie Peidong, handing over the receiver.

Xu Tieying took it, still smiling. "Fine, whatever you say, Governor Fang. You can transfer the money to the Communist Party instead of to a company owned by the Nationalist Party. You can just tell me if you want to do that. Why bother your assistant?"

The elder Fang was calm, "Then I'll say it to you directly, Mr Xu. First, I hope you report the case of Cui Zhongshi transferring money to the Communist Party to Nanking, according to the *Decree on Suppression of Insurgency and National Salvation*. I'm waiting for a summons to a Special Criminal Court trial. Second, if you don't report the case but execute Cui Zhongshi in secret, I will report it tonight, and you will have to wait for a summons to a Special Criminal Court trial. Third, why is there suddenly a twenty per cent share owned by you in the Peking civil and military food supply company? If Cui Zhongshi is dead, I'll report to the headquarters of the Central Bank as director of the Peking branch after I've got to the bottom of it. If possible, I reserve the right to submit the entire report to the legislature and direct enquiry of the Communications Bureau of the Kuomintang Central Committee members. Am I making myself clear and direct enough?"

Xu Tieying's smile froze. He gritted his teeth and turned to Xie Peidong, still holding the receiver. "Mr Xie, can you give us some privacy?"

Xie Peidong walked out.

"Governor Fang, are you still there?" asked Xu.

Hearing Xu Tieying on the phone, Fang Buting spoke calmly but with a hint of cruelty. "Commissioner Xu, it's the second time you've said we'll 'die together'. I don't want to hear you say that again. Now, there's only one way for me, which is that Cui Zhongshi can neither be released nor killed. But there are two options for you. You can kill him or hold him in custody. I don't think it would be hard for you to figure out how to secretly imprison someone. But if you're determined to kill him, you leave me with one option – putting the second and third terms I just outlined into practice right away. There are no other reasons why we must strike a deal. It's not related to the Nationalists or to the Communists. You have a wife and your three kids have been moved to Taipei for safe keeping. I've got two sons who will have to renounce me because of this. That is my reason. You say they are colluding with the Communist Party, right? Fine. Fang Meng'ao and Fang Mengwei are downstairs at this very moment. I can ask them to confess to you. What do you think?"

Known as a man of vigour, Xu Tieying looked exhausted. He rested the receiver away from his ear, as he simply had no idea what to do next.

He was quiet, knowing that Fang Buting was also collecting his thoughts on the other end. But he couldn't just give up and back off.

Knowing what they had to overcome, Xu Tieying took a sip of water and spoke into the phone in a rather dull and hoarse tone. "I accept your suggestion. I'll keep Cui Zhongshi alive today. But tomorrow, the day after tomorrow, or in one or two weeks' time, once the threat of his existence to the Nationalists has been proven, there will be other people who want him dead even if I don't kill him... I can do that. I'll inform you before making the decision... I agree with you, Governor Fang. Let's just work together to endure in hard times... Let's hope it won't take long."

"Secretary Sun," Xu Tieying called out, weakly. Secretary Sun showed up promptly.

"Where's Mr Xie?" asked Xu Tieying.

"Waiting in Deputy Commissioner Shan's office," answered Secretary Sun.

"Isn't there anywhere else for him?" Xu Tieying seemed unusually serious.

"Remember, you must trust no one in Peking!"

―――

Fang Buting was still on the phone. He heard Xu being angry with Secretary Sun too. He felt tired as well. Repulsed by the conversation, he put the receiver on the table. It would be several minutes before Xie Peidong spoke again.

―――

"Understood," Xie Peidong answered, "I'll go away as you command. Yes, I'll go to Cui Zhongshi's house first and get back as soon as I have pacified everyone."

After putting down the receiver, Xie Peidong took out a cheque book and pen, and sat at Xu's table.

Xu Tieying looked on begrudgingly. He sat on the sofa, refusing to look at Xie Peidong.

"Commissioner Xu," said Xie Peidong, rising to his feet.

Xu Tieying stood up slowly and walked over.

Xie handed him three cheques in total.

Xu Tieying was still suspicious of him. He focused on the cheques.

On the first cheque were written, in both upper and lower case, the words one hundred and fifty thousand dollars.

The second cheque was the same. His face turned sullen. He examined the third one – both upper and lower case words, and the number one hundred and seventy five thousand dollars, becoming more agitated by the second.

Turning to Xie, Xu said: "Why is only the first one signed?"

"Our governor told me to explain," replied Xie Peidong. "We will sign the second one ten days later, and the third one after another ten days."

Anger spread across Xu Tieying's pale face. He tossed the cheques on the table. "I'm not taking them. Return them to your governor and tell him maybe I'll be transferred back to Nanking tomorrow. Leave the money for my successor to handle."

Xie Peidong just stared at him earnestly. "Oh, I forgot. Our governor told me to tell you something else too, Commissioner Xu. There is a company registered in Taipei and they operate on a much larger scale than we do. There are not many shareholders but one of them is your wife. This is the registration form of the shareholders. Care to take a look?"

Xu Tieying was genuinely surprised. "Your governor cares about his friends too much... It almost makes people feel unworthy."

"As a friend," said Xie Peidong, "Governor Xu deserves our utmost attention and help."

Xu Tieying finally turned his eyes to Xie Peidong in an appreciative manner. "Had Governor Fang asked you to contact me earlier, we wouldn't be in such an awkward position now. Let me escort you."

"No, thanks," snapped Xie Peidong. He made a bow with hands folded in front, and picked up his briefcase. "If you need to talk with our governor, let me know first, Commissioner Xu."

"OK, OK," said Xu Tieying, stretching out to take Xie's hand so firmly that Xie Peidong felt the pinch.

The door to Fang Buting's office opened. Fang Buting walked out slowly, standing there in amazement.

There was only one person, Cheng Xiaoyun, in the living room downstairs. She walked across to him.

"Where are they?" asked Fang Buting behind the first-floor stairs.

Cheng Xiaoyun stopped at the bottom of the stairs and answered: "Meng'ao has returned to camp and Mengwei is escorting Xiaoyu and Mulan home."

Fang Buting stood there despondently. Cheng Xiaoyun smiled. "Meng'ao told me to arrange a room here for him. He may come back and stay here every now and then." This brought a weak smile back to Fang Buting's face.

Xu Tieying locked the three cheques and the registration form in a safe against the wall beside the office desk in the commissioner's office of the Peking Police Bureau.

He shut the heavy door, turned the privacy dial again, and called out: "Secretary Sun!" The latter appeared instantly.

"I'm counting on you," said Xu Tieying. "Don't let Deputy Commissioner Shan and Deputy Commissioner Fang know about it. Send Cui Zhongshi to the Communications Bureau prison in Peking tonight, as a Class One prisoner."

Secretary Sun said nothing, but kept his eyes on Xu Tieying. "What?"

"Don't ask questions you're not supposed to," barked Xu Tieying. He wasn't so satisfied with Secretary Sun today. He walked inside as soon as he'd finished speaking.

Sir!" said Secretary Sun, in a rather bizarre voice.

Xu Tieying stopped, turned around, and saw something peculiar in Secretary Sun's expression.

"Sir," he said, "Ma Hanshan and his troops came for Cui Zhongshi, and they're escorting him secretly to the Western Hills for execution."

Xu Tieying froze, wide-eyed.

CHAPTER 4

Secretary Sun was still in his Zhongshan suit in the commissioner's office of the Peking Police Bureau and Xu Tieying could imagine him in the uniform of the Youth Army as a member of the Iron and Blood Congress. All of a sudden, he remembered the words Zeng Keda had used on the phone: "The police chief's sudden intervention is very unusual. He is expected to make it tonight but had better not put it off until tomorrow. It is unwise to push me, as Chief Fang will step in."

Devoted to the Nationalist Party his entire life, Xu Tieying was a respected leader of its Communication Agency, formerly known as the Zhongtong, the Central Bureau of Investigation and Statistics. From the Communist Party of China to the internal affairs of the Nationalist Party, he had controlled and killed people in the name of the president and on behalf of the Nationalist Party Headquarters. Now, he found himself under the control of a young man with blood ties to the president! All his hard work for the party system over the decades had culminated in this. At such a critical moment for the Nationalist Party, he meant little more than sand and had nothing on actual blood relations with the leadership. It was a bitter realisation, but it also aroused his interest and ambition when competing with the young men around him.

Xu Tieying managed a smile, looking at him kindly. "We both

work for the party-state. I just wonder, when did you join the Iron and Blood Congress?"

Bemused by such a question, Secretary Sun kept silent and just stared at him.

Xu carried on. "If you find it hard to answer, forget it. Well, you know the discipline we keep. Anyone, no matter what department, who treads on party affairs will be severely punished. So tell me, who sent you?"

"Yes sir," Secretary Sun replied calmly.

Xu Tieying slowly lifted his teacup off the table, took a sip and splashed the remaining water and leaves in Secretary Sun's face. Sun stood still, silently wiping the tea leaves from his face.

"Chief..."

"Compose yourself and then answer!" growled Xu Tieying. "I could punish you right now, in the name of the Party Headquarters, and there's nothing you can do about it!"

"Yes, Chief," said Secretary Sun.

"Then, go ahead," snapped Xu Tieying, putting down the cup.

"You told me to send Cui Zhongshi to the car first and wait ten minutes," said Secretary Sun. "I waited ten minutes."

His reply froze Xu Tieying for a moment. He allowed a sneer to escape his inner thoughts as he waited for his next words to emerge.

"The Party Headquarters has iron discipline. I have to execute my superior's command right the way down the line," said Secretary Sun.

"Ha ha!" Xu Tieying's sneer became audible as he took his eyes off Sun and stared at the ceiling above him. "Was Ma Hanshan told to execute the orders of the Central Bureau of Investigation and Statistics?"

"I found you were seized by the Iron and Blood Congress and the Peking branch," said Sun. "You are a representative of the Party Headquarters in Peking. If you're controlled, the Party Headquarters would be controlled!-And as the Iron and Blood Congress has murdered others in the name of the Investigation Group of the Ministry of Defence, so the Bureau of Investigation and Statistics under the Secret Bureau of the Ministry of Defence had to perform the task. Don't let yourself be hijacked. The party's reputation will be stained. If I'm wrong, I'd rather be punished than let the party be dragged through the mud because you've been led astray."

Xu Tieying slowly dragged his eyes away from the ceiling.

Sun's face came into clear view again. As Xu Tieying looked at the tea stain and leaves on Sun's face, his doubts about Sun faded away.

"Foolish loyalty!" Doubts dispelled, he was somewhat soothed but his anxiety rose again immediately. He neither appreciated nor hated such foolish loyalty. More importantly, several critical minutes had been wasted on his doubts.

"Great loyalty! And a good cadre!" These words came through clenched teeth. "How long ago did they leave? Where's the execution site?" asked Xu Tieying quickly.

"Twenty minutes ago," replied Secretary Sun. "The site is the secret jail of the Bureau of Investigation and Statistics in the Western Hills."

Xu Tieying had finished with his questions. He picked up the phone on the table but hesitated before dialling. How could a phone call stop Ma Hanshan and save Cui Zhongshi?

Cheng Xiaoyun ran Fang Buting a bath, laid out fresh summer pyjamas for him and returned to his bedroom. She didn't turn on the electric fan, instead fanning him from behind with a cattail leaf fan. "I'm going to ask you some questions," Cheng Xiaoyun whispered in his ear.

"What?" said Fang Buting, lying back to enjoy the moment with his eyes closed.

"You play the piano well but you said you hadn't played in over three years," said Cheng Xiaoyun. "Where do you practice? Tell me the truth."

Fang Buting revealed a rare smile. "I practise at the home of my second concubine on Monday, Wednesday and Friday, and at the home of my third concubine on Tuesday, Thursday and Saturday."

Cheng Xiaoyun smiled with a certain amount of charm. "It must be Sunday. Where are you playing today?"

"I'm playing for the Virgin Mary in church. But I'm staying here with you."

Cheng Xiaoyun stopped smiling and fanning. "Don't comfort me... She is your Virgin Mary... You know how well you played today? And Meng'ao sang so well. I couldn't hold back my tears when I heard you. Your minds are in sync. I could tell you missed your wife and he missed his mother..."

Fang Buting opened his eyes slowly and looked up at her.

Cheng Xiaoyun looked back, murmuring with tears in her eyes. "*'Ten years parted, one living, one dead; Not thinking, yet never forgetting.*' I know how you feel."

Fang Buting stood up, took the fan from her hand, let her sit down and gently fanned her. He said softly: "*'Those who knew me said I was sad at heart. Those who did not know me said I was seeking something.*' In these turbulent days, I lost her but I met you. It's been a blessing from heaven. Xiaoyun, I don't know whether I can make peace with Meng'ao this time. The nation is in peril. I just want to protect my family, but I don't know if I can..."

At that moment, the office telephone rang. Fang Buting's heart missed a beat and he stopped fanning Xiaoyun for a second. Then he fanned her a moment longer, leaving the phone to ring.

"You must answer it," urged Cheng Xiaoyun. She stood up, took the fan away from him and pushed him gently. "Go."

"There's no time to explain," said Xu Tieying. "You'll be hard pressed to believe it even if I do. Governor Fang, Mengwei is at Yenching University, close to the Western Hills. At this moment, he has the best chance to stop Ma Hanshan. Of course, he can leave after I get there."

"Mengwei," said He Qicang, sitting on the sofa, looking up at him in the living room on the ground floor of He Qicang's residence in Yannan Gardens.

Fang Mengwei was standing in the living room in an ordinary shirt, holding a bag of flour, staring blankly.

He Xiaoyu and Xie Mulan stood by, embarrassed, and looked on with sympathy.

"Your father and I have reached a gentleman's agreement," said He Qicang. "Our students and teachers are starving. I will not receive any donation from him. If you respect me, you need to take it back."

Fang Mengwei respected He Qicang as he did his father. He said what should have been said earlier. "Uncle He, it's not from my father, but from my brother."

He Qicang looked surprised and he glanced back toward He Xiaoyu.

He Xiaoyu recalled that Fang Meng'ao had promised to give her a bag of flour that night when he left but she hadn't expected that it would be delivered by his brother.

It was not merely a bag of flour. Her father's questioning eyes made her feel awkward.

Just then the phone rang. He Qicang stood near the phone and as he took his eyes off his daughter he picked it up. "Still here. I will pass the phone to him. It's nine o'clock. I'm going to bed."

He Qicang held the phone, while Xiaoyu helped him to his feet.

He Qicang looked at Fang Mengwei. "It's your father."

In fact, Fang Mengwei knew it as well as He Xiaoyu and Xie Mulan.

Fang Mengwei put down the flour and took the phone with both hands. He stood aside, making way for He Qicang to pass, supported by He Xiaoyu, before answering.

His face immediately clouded over.

Xie Mulan noticed and asked with grave concern: "Cousin..."

Fang Mengwei stretched out his hand to stop her from saying any more. He whispered into the phone: "Father, don't worry. I'll go there right now and save him. I see. No conflict. Take care. Go and take a rest. Dad, I need to hang up."

Usually, his father hung up first, but this time he did so, gently. Then he rushed out.

"Cousin," called Xie Mulan behind him.

Fang Mengwei neither stopped nor turned round. "Nothing special. Get some rest," he said as he went through the door.

She was alone in a flash. Xie Mulan felt her heart beat arrhythmically. She knew where she would go, but not what awaited her.

The sound of her brother's jeep came from the courtyard and she followed him quickly out of the living room.

So much had happened and disappeared just as fast today.

He Xiaoyu walked out of the gate alone. The shadows of the trees, near and far, were caught in the dim light of the street lamps.

The campus had never been this quiet before and the night seemed endless. She had no idea what to do next. She thought of Xie Peidong's meaningful glance that day but it vanished in the mysterious night sky. She imagined the smile of Comrade Liu before it too disappeared in the darkness. The depth of Liang Jinglun's stare faded as she closed her eyes. Finally, Liang Jinglun's eyes also disappeared.

Coming down to earth, she was bewildered by her thoughts.

Slowly she turned around and walked back towards the gate absent-mindedly. She was aware of a faint sound in the distance. She stopped and closed her eyes, and tried her best to calm down. But she was haunted by the sound of a song sung to the accompaniment of a piano: "You suffer for us, you wear shackles for us..."

It was Fang Meng'ao's singing.

He Xiaoyu opened her eyes and found herself in quiet surroundings. The singing had stopped.

In the secret jail in the courtyard of the Military Council's Bureau of Investigation and Statistics in the Western Hills, a shout rang out: "A plague on Xu Tieying's forefathers!"

Ma Hanshan, with the muzzle of Mengwei's gun pressed against his lower jaw, raised his head high and shouted abuse. "He was trapped by the Communist Party but ripped me off. Cui Zhongshi is dead. There was nothing I could do."

The gun shook against his chin. "Don't lie... Give him to me, right now..." hissed Fang Mengwei, shaking with rage.

"Calm down," said the leader of the Military Bureau of Investigation execution squad. "Deputy Chief, please calm down. We were all witnesses. It was Chief Xu who gave the order to shoot Cui. It's a special period of time for suppressing the Communist insurgency and saving the party-state. We were simply obeying his order."

More than ten Bureau members stood there indifferently.

"... Take me there," muttered Fang Mengwei, heartbroken.

"Of course. Put the gun down first, OK?" Ma Hanshan kept one eye on the muzzle and the other on Fang Mengwei.

"It's loaded and it's likely to discharge accidentally if your hand shakes. You're in your twenties, but I'm in my fifties. Don't risk your life for me."

Fang Mengwei put the gun down slowly. His hand had never felt weaker. Following Ma Hanshan and heading inside, every step he took seemed to be on soft ground.

"Take it easy. It's OK. Please sit down," urged Liang Jinglun, standing by the table on the first floor of the Foreign Language Bookstore at the East Entrance of Yenching University. He spoke gently and reassuringly to Xie Mulan, who looked very nervous.

Xie Mulan was still standing at the door. "I came alone. No one knows, not even Xiaoyu..." Her lips and mouth seemed to be dry.

Liang Jinglun lifted the hot water bottle to pour water for her, but the bottle was empty. Hesitantly, he handed Xie Mulan his cup of water, saying: "I'm sorry, I've drunk from it. Do you mind?"

"Not at all," replied Xie Mulan, taking the cup. She could hear her heartbeat while lifting the cup to her mouth. Liang Jinglun's voice appeared close by: "No one will know that you have been here."

"Don't worry. Just take a seat and talk."

"You won't tell Xiaoyu?" After drinking the water Liang Jinglun handed her, Xie Mulan held his cup tightly with both hands and looked at him courageously.

Liang Jinglun nodded profoundly. Then he asked in a soft voice: "Shall I close the door?"

Hearing this, Xie Mulan's heart beat faster as she nervously nodded. When Liang Jinglun passed by, Xie Mulan closed her eyes tightly and felt that the breeze blowing past his gown could lift her up!

The heavy iron gate in the mortuary of the Bureau's secret jail in the Western Hills slowly opened from the outside.

Since the weather was so hot, the ice cubes melted and the light of the ceiling lamp seemed dimmer. A dozen beds were situated here, because this was a place where Communists and progressives were killed in secret. After being executed, their identity still needed to be verified by the higher-ups. Today all the beds were empty, except for one in the middle where a man lay with his face covered and a blood stain seeped through his chest to his jacket.

There was no disguising the fact that it was Cui Zhongshi. Fang Mengwei stood startled by the door. Ma Hanshan and the people of the Bureau stood behind him.

The mortuary was as quiet as a grave. Fang Mengwei walked slowly towards the bed where Cui Zhongshi was lying.

The execution team leader of the Bureau whispered to Ma Hanshan: "Director Ma, would you care to step outside for a while?"

Ma Hanshan said loudly: "I'm just killing a Communist, what's for me to avoid? I'm waiting here for Xu Tieying, the bastard!"

Walking over to Cui Zhongshi, Fang Mengwei reached out to the white cloth covering his face. But the moment he touched the white cloth, he stopped.

He gently uncovered his face little by little with closed eyes, imagining some other person's face beneath it. Ma Hanshan's, for example, or Xu Tieying's. Just as he took the white cloth in his hand, he heard a voice calling him. "Mengwei!"

It was Cui Zhongshi's voice calling him at the railway station that day.

Immediately, the look on Cui Zhongshi's face came to his mind.

Fang Mengwei regretted he hadn't recognised it as one of farewell.

Fang knew now that those eyes would be closed forever and the simple and honest face was no more!

He tried hard to restrain his grief but tears escaped anyway.

Xie Mulan was sobbing at the desk on the first floor of the Foreign Language Bookstore at the East Entrance of Yenching University.

Liang Jinglun sat quietly opposite her. It was his job to stir up pure and passionate youth in the name of revolution. But somehow his mind was in a whirl today. He was a lonely soul but he'd never felt as lonely as he did today.

Liang Jinglun's silence made Xie Mulan panic. Her tears dried up and, afraid to meet his eyes, she said in a choked voice: "I know, the things they did are unfair to the people and to the revolution but I don't think they are bad in themselves." She cast a timid glance at Liang Jinglun. "Mr Liang, am I not firm about the revolution..."

"How about you listen to me?" asked Liang Jinglun in a voice as warm as a spring breeze.

"Yes, of course."

"Then look at me," said Liang Jinglun.

After Xie Mulan had taken out a handkerchief to wipe her tears, she raised her head but still dared not look Liang in the eye.

"You told me what happened today," Liang Jinglun said, "and by doing so, you've proven your worth. You're an outstanding progressive youth."

On hearing these words, Xie Mulan had the courage to look into Liang Jinglun's eyes and said: "Mr Liang, I'd like to go further."

"Well, how do you plan to do that?" asked Liang with a smile of encouragement.

"I plan to leave my family," said Xie Mulan boldly, "and cut all ties with them."

"And then?"

Xie Mulan answered without a trace of hesitation: "I want to work with you."

At this, Liang fell silent.

Xie Mulan panicked again. "I know I'm not qualified but..."

Liang Jinglun walked over to the window. As Xie Mulan composed herself, he turned around and said two words to Xie Mulan: "Come here."

She hardly knew how she managed to walk towards him. All she knew was that the sun in her heart warmed her as if it was just a few feet away.

He held her hand forcefully but gently and said in a dreamy voice: "You're already working with me. But you have to go back home. There are things you must do now that are irreplaceable, arduous and glorious."

Xie Mulan was afraid to open her eyes. "Can I see you often? Just as we are meeting now?"

She put her head on his shoulder with her heart pounding fiercely, in tune with Liang's. He had held back for so long his deep connection with the beautiful, youthful and passionate girls around him. But now, it felt as though he'd been waiting for exactly this girl to lean on his shoulder

He felt so different with Xie Mulan than with He Xiaoyu. As he drew her close, he waited for her to face him, she who had ignored him for so long.

Xie Mulan telepathically raised her head and looked into his eyes. She wished she could wade in their fiery depths.

"I will read you a line from a poem," said Liang Jinglun. "You can read the line before if you like."

Since her face was so close to his, Xie Mulan held her breath and just blinked her long eyelashes slightly.

Liang Jinglun closed his eyes and said softly: "'Why need they stay together night and day...'"

In silence, Xie Mulan replied: "'If love between both sides can last for aye.'" Liang Jinglun kissed her and her body shuddered with delight.

Slap! Slap! In the mortuary of the secret jail of the Central Bureau of Investigation and Statistics in the Western Hills, Secretary Sun was still standing upright despite the beating.

"Why did you order Cui Zhongshi to be shot?" demanded Xu Tieying.

"Chief," said Secretary Sun calmly, "may I ask Deputy Director Ma?"

Xu Tieying glanced at Fang Mengwei as he dragged his eyes towards Ma Hanshan.

Fang Mengwei's face had turned from pale to blue, looking in front of him with a phlegmatic expression.

Ma Hanshan, heedless of Xu Tieying's gaze, said angrily: "Stop pretending. I will lie for you."

"At about seven o'clock on the twenty-first of July 1948, Ma

Hanshan, Deputy Director of the Peking Citizens' Food Distribution Committee, leading more than ten people from the Peking branch of the Secrecy Bureau, rushed to Peking Police Bureau to take Cui Zhongshi away by force. Cui's criminal identity as a Communist or a non-Communist had yet to be confirmed as they drove in three vehicles to the Western Hills to carry out the execution. He couldn't escape from the crime. The judge will ask, 'Ma Hanshan, how dare you! You forcibly took him and three vehicles away from Peking Police Bureau. How did you get the keys of the three vehicles?' No. I can't make up such a story for you! Chief Xu and Secretary Sun, you can continue!"

The reason why the Central Bureau of Investigation and Statistics of the Central Executive Committee of the Nationalist Party was different from the Bureau of Investigation and Statistics of the Military Council was that they were not sneaky. It was this sense of subterfuge that upset the regular departments of the Nationalist Party. However, Ma Hanshan's performance hit the mark by a fluke.

Xu Tieying turned to Secretary Sun again with a sullen face.

Secretary Sun said with extraordinary calmness: "Has Deputy Director Ma finished? May I ask a question now?"

Ma Hanshan dragged his eyes away from the ceiling while waiting for Sun's question. "Who is in charge of the executive team of the Central Bureau of Investigation and Statistics?"

"Don't beat about the bush." With a wave of his hand, Ma Hanshan said: "Just ask a straightforward question."

Secretary Sun continued: "Does the Peking Police Bureau have the right to mobilise the executive team of the Bureau to shoot people?"

"Go on," urged Ma Hanshan through gritted teeth.

"Even if our chief can mobilise the Bureau's executive team on behalf of the Investigation Group of the Ministry of Defence," asked Secretary Sun, "did you ever see Chief Xu assign a task to Deputy Director Ma in person? Or did Deputy Director Ma get a warrant from Chief Xu to shoot Cui Zhongshi?"

Ma Hanshan anxiously retorted: "Then who are you? Who conveyed Chief Xu's order?"

Secretary Sun replied: "I won't defend myself. If a secretary of a chief executive exceeds his duties, then I might as well order you to shoot your executive team head. Will you obey?"

"Just say it!" How could Ma Hanshan have been stumped by him at this moment? "Give me your gun. I will shoot anyone you want me to! Is it necessary to ask your Chief Xu? Just give me the gun!"

Secretary Sun didn't expect Ma to be so arrogant and unreasonable, and he turned to Xu Tieying in shock, refusing to hand over the gun.

To everyone's surprise, Fang Mengwei swiftly took out his gun and handed it to Ma Hanshan, which shocked Xu Tieying, Secretary Sun and everyone else present from the Juntong team, as well as Ma Hanshan who was afraid to take it.

"Why don't you take the gun?" asked Fang Mengwei

Ma Hanshan answered nervously: "Deputy Chief Fang, why should I take it?"

"What kind of a question is that? You asked for a gun a moment ago."

"We've all been deceived, don't you understand?"

Fang Mengwei took back his gun and said: "It's time to dig for answers. Why was Cui Zhongshi shot so quickly? Was he a Communist?"

No one answered. Everyone just stared at one another.

Suddenly, Fang Mengwei fired a shot in the air, shouting: "Who can answer me?"

Ears buzzed as Xu Tieying sought to rein in the situation by prompting Secretary Sun to reply.

Unlike the flustered onlookers, Secretary Sun was calm. "Report to Chief Xu and Deputy Chief Fang. At present, we only have evidence that he was suspected of embezzling public funds, but nothing to say he was a Communist."

"He was executed for embezzlement?!" This time it was Xu Tieying who bellowed."Mengwei, as Cui Zhongshi was the deputy director of the Peking branch of the Central Bank, we have to explain this to the headquarters. Take a word of advice, calm down and we'll discuss it later."

Fang Mengwei looked at him for the first time. "Is there anything to discuss?"

Xu Tieying said sincerely: "I'll tell you later."

He then turned to Ma Hanshan and the others, and said: "Since the whole thing was completely escalated, if anyone arbitrarily identified Cui Zhongshi as a Communist in order to evade responsibility, then there would be other specialised personnel coming to you for investigation. If this information is leaked to Nanking, I'm afraid that your Bureau Chief Mao will not able to give the president an explanation. Just keep it under your hat!"

Although Ma Hanshan and the Bureau team were unconvinced, they remained quiet.

Xu Tieying whispered in Fang Mengwei's ear: "I'm sad too, but the saddest must be Governor Fang and Chief Fang of the Investigation Brigade. We have to calm down and discuss a solution with Assistant Manager Xie. It would be better to keep it secret from your father and older brother for now."

Fang Mengwei strode angrily towards the door with his gun.

After a glance in Secretary Sun's direction, Xu Tieying went out, followed by Secretary Sun.

Ma Hanshan and a dozen Bureau men stood still in the mortuary. It wasn't that they were reluctant to leave. It was that they didn't know why they were standing there.

"Follow me!" yelled Ma Hanshan, walking towards Cui Zhongshi on the bed. After realising what was happening, the Bureau people followed Ma Hanshan over to the bed.

"Mr Cui, every debt has its creditor. Whether you are a Communist or not, it is not us who wanted to kill you. Please tell the person who wants to avenge you through a dream to see clearly who he should kill," said Ma Hanshan.

Finishing his words, Ma made a deep bow towards Cui. The people from the Bureau behind Ma bowed too. "Go!"

Feeling at that moment akin to Cui Zhongshi, Ma Hanshan walked out solemnly, and the people from the Bureau followed him unthinkingly.

Nobody noticed that on Cui Zhongshi's face, an honest and kind smile was just about visible.

Before dawn, two jeeps and a ten-wheel military truck screeched to a halt outside the gate of the main warehouse of the Peking Citizens' Food Distribution Committee.

"Watch the door!" said Fang Meng'ao, jumping down from the smaller vehicle. "No one gets out!"

Fang Meng'ao didn't wait for the others and broke in first.

The soldiers on guard, armed with guns, gave their salutes, whether they knew Fang Meng'ao or not.

Twenty pilots from the Youth Aviation Brigade jumped down from two jeeps one after another and followed Fang in.

A platoon of young soldiers there to escort the Youth Aviation Brigade sat in the military truck. They were all armed with American-style carbines, as was Battalion Commander Zheng. They jumped down one after another. A squad of soldiers went to guard the gate, and the other two squads ran to a street entrance, sealing off the main warehouse.

In the duty room of the warehouse, Fang Meng'ao asked Section Chief Li and Section Chief Wang where Ma Hanshan was. This brought Li and Wang back to reality. They pretended not to hear, looking at each other, waiting for the other to answer.

"Handcuff them," ordered Fang Meng'ao.

Shao Yuangang and Guo Jinyang promptly handcuffed Section Chief Li and Section Chief Wang.

"Take them outside," commanded Fang Meng'ao, "and gather all the people here in the main square."

"Yes sir!" Shao Yuangang and Guo Jinyang led the handcuffed Li and Guo out of the duty room.

Outside, someone blew a harsh-sounding whistle and people shouted and made a racket.

Fang Meng'ao wasn't one for thinking too much before acting. He picked up the phone in the duty room to call the Peking Police Bureau. "Put me through to Chief Xu Tieying," he said. "Wake him up. This is the Investigation Group of the Ministry of Defence." Fang took out a cigar and a lighter. He held the cigar in his mouth, flipped the lighter's cover and lit the cigar. Even Fang Men'gao's hands were trembling a little, a rare sight.

"I am Fang Meng'ao and I'm at the Peking Citizens' Food Distribution Committee," said Fang when the call was connected to the

Peking Police Bureau. "I hope to see Ma Hanshan in half an hour... an hour then... one day. If thirteen thousand people in the Peking Police Bureau cannot find Ma Hanshan, perhaps Chief Xu can find Ma himself."

Hanging up, Fang strode out of the duty room.

It was early morning and dozens of people on the large ground outside the main warehouse of the Citizens' Food Distribution Committee, including the deputy section chief, section members, the two section chiefs in handcuffs and the pilots holding them, had turned into a crowd. No one realised that something serious was about to happen. As Chief Fang Meng'ao strode towards them, the sound died down, and tension was in the air.

"Who can answer me, how should I cope with a person who embezzled a bag of flour from the committee?" asked Fang Meng'ao in a low voice when he came in front of them.

No one answered.

"How should I deal with embezzlement of a sack of rice?" Fang asked again. Still, no one answered.

Fang Meng'ao did not expect an answer, so he answered himself. "It is stipulated in the regulations of the committee that anyone caught embezzling flour or rice from the committee should be shot on the spot."

As Fang emphasised the words "shot on the spot" loaded with sadness, everyone shuddered. Fang balanced his words.

"I hereby announce several new regulations. Those who report embezzlement of a hundred bags of flour or rice will be exempt from the death penalty, and those who report embezzlement of a thousand bags of flour or rice will be exempt from imprisonment. Those who report Ma Hanshan's whereabouts will be rewarded!" added Fang.

When Section Chiefs Li and Wang heard these words, their faces paled, whereas the eyes of everyone else present lit up. They had wanted to speak up but were unsure how.

"You have plenty of time to think about it carefully. Raise your hands if you want to. Guo Jinyang!"

"Yes." Guo Jinyang answered loudly.

"Wait in the duty room. All whistleblowers will be received separately and you must keep their identities secret from each other," said Fang.

"Yes sir!" answered Guo, handing the handcuffed Section Chief Wang to another aviator.

With necks craning like geese, the men watched as Fang Meng'ao strode out of the door to the smaller jeep parked outside.

The gate of the front garden of the Fang mansion was unexpectedly opened.

The sun had risen, shining obliquely on the open door. There was no janitor and there was no one in the front garden.

Fang Meng'ao stopped at the gate and looked at the Western-style building in front of him. He knew who was responsible for the silence, and this person was waiting for him in the building at that moment.

The door of the living room was also opened, and his father's shadow filled the door frame.

Fang Buting sat alone at the dining table, with the warmth of the sunshine on his body blocked by Fang Meng'ao.

Fang Buting carried on with what he was doing. With his head down, he slowly scooped up a sweet dumpling in the bowl with a spoon and popped it in his mouth. He chewed gradually. After finishing the first half, he scooped up the other half, and then chewed and swallowed it.

He wasn't yet sixty but Fang Buting looked like a toothless eighty-year-old eating his last supper. Fang Meng'ao stood at the gate, motionless and silent, waiting for Fang Buting to finish eating.

"That bowl of sweet dumplings is for you," said Fang Buting, with his head down, scooping up the second sweet dumpling. He carried on chewing.

"I made the dumplings myself just as my mother taught me, but they've never been a match for hers," added Fang Buting.

Fang Meng'ao looked around the whole living room and found that all the photos in the room had disappeared, except one! In the photo, a kind-looking old woman sat in the middle of the front row holding a three-year-old child in her arms. Behind her stood a man and a woman, one gentleman-like and one beautiful, recognisable through careful analysis as Fang Buting and Fang Meng'ao's mother when they were still young.

The three-year-old child was obviously Fang Meng'ao, who was now nearly thirty years old.

Fang Meng'ao contemplated the scene from the past. He walked towards the table while Fang Buting was putting the other half of the second sweet dumpling into his mouth.

With Fang Meng'ao sitting opposite, Fang Buting put the bowl of sweet dumplings he had prepared for Fang Meng'ao in front of his son.

Meng'ao did not look at the bowl but instead waited for the old man to swallow. Fang Buting was about to scoop up a third dumpling when he saw what Fang Meng'ao had slid in front of him.

A photograph of two people, Fang Meng'ao in Air Force uniform and Cui Zhongshi in a suit and tie!

"I didn't kill him, but I did have something to do with his death," said Fang Buting, looking at the photo after putting the spoon into the bowl.

"Why was he killed?"

Fang Buting had imagined the first words his eldest son would say to him and in his imagination Fang Meng'ao could have started their dialogue any which way. "Why did you become faithless after you promised?" or "Why are you still the kind of father who is not up to the role even after ten years." However, he did not expect such a brutally simple question.

"Why was he killed?"

Fang Buting thought hard but could not find the answer. Because he was a Communist? Because he should not have been involved in so many things? Because he was a good man who had to die? Because he was a man and he had to die? How can I explain it clearly? Can anyone explain it clearly?"

When Fang Buting raised his head and looked at Fang Meng'ao, he said: "This question should be asked by others, not you."

"Then who?"

"Zeng Keda or his superior," replied Fang Buting.

"Where are the account books?" asked Fang Meng'ao, taking the photo back slowly and putting it in his jacket pocket.

"Locked away."

"Where?"

"Your uncle-in-law keeps them."

"You're wrong if you think that you can just kill a scapegoat and then slurp on dumplings safe and sound while people starve to death because I'm not able to arrest anyone here in this house," said Fang Meng'ao after standing up.

Finishing these words, he took up the bowl of dumplings in front of him, gently placing it next to Fang Buting before turning and walking out the door.

"Put that photograph away," said Fang Meng'ao, stopping at the door. "I don't want to see my grandmother and you in the same photo. I'd prefer you to reflect on what my grandmother taught you, and give some thought to Cui Zhongshi's wife and two children and the two million starving in Peking than to care about a framed image of a lie."

Fang Meng'ao left and the sun reached the western annex connecting the ground floor to the first floor. At the open door of Fang Buting's bedroom on the first floor, Cheng Xiaoyun stood with tears in her eyes, looking blankly at Fang Buting, who sat motionless at the table.

With a scared expression on her face, she rushed to the stairs and called out: "Buting!".

At the dinner table, Fang Buting bent over and put his fingers down his throat, trying to spit out the sweet dumplings he had swallowed.

"Peidong! Peidong!" yelled Cheng Xiaoyun, running downstairs to find Xie Peidong.

Bent over still, Fang Buting pressed his stomach with one hand and held out his other to Cheng Xiaoyun, urging her to stop shouting.

"Fellow students! Compatriots!" cried an impassioned Liang Jinglun, standing under the eaves of the former Princess Hejing's Mansion, a metre above courtyard level. "It has become increasingly clear that the Peking Municipal Council has made the decision to expel the Northeastern students because the Citizens' Food Distribution Committee of Peking embezzled grain due to be distributed to the public! In other words, every last grain is being looted from our Peking people, including our teachers and our students! Nanking has given no explanation of the Fifth of July Incident, and cannot account for either the dead students or those arrested, now languishing in prison! A five-member team dispatched by the government came to Peking by plane and left less than a week later. They have still not released any results or explanations. What does this tell us? It tells that they are deceiving the public. They are more afraid of power than of the public! Without the Youth Aviation Brigade led by Fang Meng'ao, a thousand tons of grain intended for the people of Peking would probably have been sold in Tianjin or elsewhere, turning into dollars and flowing into the pockets of the authorities. And how is the grain for the Fourth Corps of the Nationalist Army connected to the grain of the Citizens' Food Distribution Committee of Peking? The depths of this shady deal are being revealed bit by bit. More than twenty days after the Fifth of July Incident, should we remain silent and let an aviation team of just over twenty people fight the war alone? Is it fair to place all our hope in them?"

Students crowded the grounds, took their places under the eaves and even climbed trees to hear him. All were quiet and looked in Liang Jinglun's direction as he spoke.

But some, standing at vantage points, were there to observe for another master – the spies of the Chiang Kai-shek Student Society.

He Xiaoyun, overwhelmed by the crowd, kept her eyes peeled on Liang Jinglun and Xie Mulan with mixed feelings.

Xie Mulan had eyes for no one but Liang Jinglun, and she was immersed in the scene to the extent that she had forgotten her place in the world! This was obvious to He Xiaoyu!

"There is no such thing as a saviour in this world!" said Liang Jinglun, his voice rising further. "We can only rely on ourselves to change our lives, gain freedom and achieve democracy."

"Fight corruption!" A student shouted out, raising his arm in an agitated fashion. "Fight corruption! Oppose the civil war! Rise up against persecution!" Shouting broke out, as waves of protest started rolling forward.

Liang Jinglun lifted his hands high and brought them down in an attempt to calm the protesters.

As the crowd returned to a quiet state, Liang Jinglun said: "The Youth Aviation Brigade is within the Citizens' Food Distribution Committee of Peking. How can we still sit here, waiting for them to discover more corruption and inform us when we can go for collection?"

As soon as he stopped, someone raised his arms and shouted out: "We must go to the Citizens' Food Distribution Committee!"

"Go to the Peking Municipal Council!"

"Go to the Peking Consultative Council!"

"Go for Fu Zuoyi! Go for Li Zongren!"

The protests grew louder and louder. The crowd was in turmoil and protesters streamed towards the door.

He Xiaoyu was pushed back by the crowd. At that moment, she heard a special voice and looked back over her shoulder.

Xie Mulan was holding Liang Jinglun's arm tightly and shouting: "Protect Mr Liang! Protect Mr Liang!"

Hearing these words, a number of boys encircled Liang Jinglun, protecting the two of them!

Zeng Keda again put on the formal American-style uniform of a major general of the Ministry of Defence and stood at his desk listening to the phone. The voice from the mouthpiece seemed to hang over Peking.

"Do not be afraid of turmoil... Until now, turmoil has only caused minor trouble but if we suppress it, it will ferment and grow... The time has almost come to do battle with the Communist army. We have better solders and better armaments. So why are we defeated by them time and time again? The defeat lies in politics, not military affairs. We must be clear about that. The Communist Party occupies the countryside and has launched an agrarian revolution. Its power has expanded from the countryside to the city. If we cannot even ensure people's wellbeing in the cities, trust in us will vanish. We'll have lost the battle before it's even started."

Zeng Keda was overwhelmed by what he was hearing.

"Are you listening?" Comrade Jianfeng asked.

Zeng Keda paused before replying. "I'm listening, Comrade Jianfeng. Instruct me clearly. What can I do?"

"I suggest we face trouble head-on," Comrade Jianfeng continued. "Rather than leave the Communist Party to rile up the public to target the Nationalist Party, the government and the president, we need to address elements corroding us from inside. If we do this, the Communist Party will have no means left to use to stir up trouble. They need the trust and will of the people even more than we do. The economy of the Nationalist Party and the Republic of China is already on the verge of collapse. We have to get on with currency reform, abolish the old legal tender and roll out a new currency that guarantees our reserves and resources! I will personally promote the reform in Shanghai and you can do the same in Peking. The Central Bank and the people behind it will certainly oppose such reform. You deal with it here while I do the same with issues I encounter in the central government. You must persuade Fang Buting to work with me!"

At this, Comrade Jianfeng stopped.

Zeng Keda replied loudly after waiting a few seconds: "Yes sir! We will definitely carry it out. At present, Fang Buting is not the biggest stumbling block. We have to deal with the shareholders of the Yangtze Construction Company in the political circles of Peking and Tianjin, the Fourth Corps of the Nationalist Army represented by Chen Jicheng, the Central Bureau of Investigation and Statistics represented by Xu Tieying and the Bureau of Investigation and Statistics of the Military Council represented by Ma Hanshan. If things continue to ferment, those parties will join forces to oppose us."

Comrade Jianfeng went on: "They dare not speak out against me or you. However, they will certainly make trouble for us. Xu Tieying is obliged to cooperate with you. You should control him and make him aware of the situation. If the cliques of Chen Jicheng and Ma Hanshan dare to make trouble, you should seek the help of

General Fu Zuoyi and Vice-President Li Zongren. They are on our side. If Chen Jicheng hinders us, you should dismiss him from his post, and if Ma Hanshan makes trouble again, you should put him to death!"

"Understood, Comrade Jianfeng!" Zeng Keda answered loudly this time.

———

A gathering whistle could be heard in the front garden of the Peking Police Bureau. Policemen holding batons and guns rushed to a row of police cars that had already started their engines.

"Where is Deputy Chief Fang?" shouted Deputy Chief Shan Fuming, addressing several captains around him as he struggled to keep control of the situation, sweating as the army was still not making a move. No one had a clue.

Deputy Chief Shan barked an order at one of the captains: "Find Deputy Chief Fang right now. He should be in full command of the Citizens' Food Distribution Committee!"

"I'll try," the captain answered uncertainly.

"You must find him! Otherwise, you take charge!" Shan Fuming shouted with a grim expression that he rarely showed.

"In that case, you had better dismiss me right now."

The captain was not afraid of his ferociousness, but was certain of his failure to find Deputy Chief Fang.

"Excuse me?" said Shan Fuming, drawing his gun. "Even though you will not be dismissed now, you will be shot dead according to wartime law!"

"You have to calm down first!" Ma Hanshan appeared mysteriously with a twenty-bullet gun in his hand. More than two hundred soldiers of the Bureau of Investigation and Statistics of the Military Council behind him strode into the police bureau. With this, Shan Fuming came to his senses.

"All right. The place surrounded by thousands of students is the Citizens' Food Distribution Committee. You have to rein them in. The others follow me to the Peking municipal government and Peking Consultative Council!"

Shan Fuming hesitated no longer and got into a small jeep.

The police cars were beeping and pulling out of the police bureau one by one.

In a second, only Ma Hanshan and more than two hundred soldiers of the Bureau of Investigation and Statistics of the Military Council were left. The bloodthirsty soldiers turned to Ma Hanshan for direction.

Ma Hanshan was at a loss. He thought for a while before saying: "Wait here first. I will make arrangements with Chief Xu. Later, we will use the old method, besieging the place from all sides and shooting the leaders!"

In the police commissioner's office of Peking Police Bureau, Ma Hanshan stood still beside the screen.

"Please listen to me, Chief." Xu Tieying was on the phone. He had never been this anxious before. "This is a Communist Party conspiracy. And people on our side are sabotaging the situation. We are facing enemies on both sides now... Tens of thousands of students are protesting on the streets and Fu Zuoyi explicitly said they would never become scapegoats... Chen Jicheng will not accept my assignment since he is being controlled by the Ministry of Defence... Yes, I await guidance."

"Brother Tieying!" Ma Hanshan seized the chance to break in with a murderous look. "It is time to act soberly. The ones who are genuinely concerned about the destiny of the Nationalist Party and the Republic of China are your Central Bureau of Investigation and Statistics, and us with the Bureau of Investigation and Statistics of the Military Council. Battle-hardened troops, more than two hundred in total, are here in Peking. We are at your service but you have to give the order!"

"All right. All right," said Xu Tieying. "I am just looking for you. I want to have your opinion."

"We face a life-or-death struggle," answered Ma Hanshan. "There is no second choice. The reason why we are at a disadvantage with the Fifth of July Incident is that we were too merciful in killing and arresting people. They burn if we are submissive. This is a sheer affront! Fang Meng'ao led his brigade to occupy the Citizens' Food Distribution Committee and the Communist Party seized the opportunity to incite students by adding fuel to the fire. It wasn't me they were targeting. It was the Nationalist Party and the Republic itself! How come the Nanking authorities still cannot distinguish right from wrong..."

"I hear you," interrupted Xu Tieying impatiently.

"Kill! They will surrender if dozens or hundreds of their companions are killed," replied Ma Hanshan with a murderous look.

Xu Tieying looked at him wryly. "What would you do if faced with the Defence Ministry's Inspection Brigade? To be frank, if Fang Meng'ao and his pilots of the Aviation Brigade were here, would you dare to kill them?"

"We should kill Communist Party members and hidden Communists among the students," replied Ma Hanshan.

"If they are led by Fang Meng'ao, would you dare to kill them? Forget it. I will tell you what has just happened," said Xu Tieying.

"What?" stammered Ma Hanshan.

"Two hours ago, Fang Meng'ao called me, and ordered me to assist him in the name of the Investigation Group of the Ministry of Defence. They will definitely find you no matter how many Peking policemen are deployed. He demanded that you meet him at the Citizens' Food Distribution Committee," explained Xu Tieying.

Ma Hanshan lowered his head in thought. He said to himself: Does he think I'm afraid of him? "Brother, should I go or not, in your opinion?"

Xu Tieying's expression shifted. "It doesn't depend on me but on the Investigation Group of the Ministry of Defence. They think you should be responsible for the Fifth of July Incident and the failings of the Citizens' Food Distribution Committee! Didn't you just warn me to think soberly? I guess the one who should be sober is you. Talk to me when you've washed your face."

Ma Hanshan felt embarrassed. "Chief Xu, you don't need to talk to me like that."

"Why didn't you ask for my opinion before you killed Cui

Zhongshi yesterday evening?"

Xu Tieying slammed the desk. "It's too late now!"

Ma Hanshan's face had turned as red as pork liver. He thought he had been tricked by Xu Tieying last night but he embarrassed him with this thing when something terrible had happened today. Ma Hanshan was anxious to draw his gun so he could die together with Xu Tieying and be free of the torment.

Suddenly, Ma Hanshan felt a sharp pain in his wrist and he bent down.

From behind him, Secretary Sun had reached for Ma Hanshan's wrist and grabbed his twenty-bullet gun from him.

With his head close to the ground and legs unbending, he shouted: "Brother! Xu Tieying! Tell him to free me!"

However, Secretary Sun held on and pressed the gun to the back of Ma's head. "Son of a bitch! I should have shot you dead last night! How dare you murder our chief! Who made you kill Cui Zhongshi?"

Ma Hanshan was desperate but still had the urge to escape being made a scapegoat. So he kept silent.

Secretary Sun flicked off the gun's safety catch with a loud click and was about to fire the Mauser. "Killing you is as easy as stepping on an ant! Tell me the truth or forever hold your peace."

Ma Hanshan struggled to raise his head.

Xu Tieying turned his back, stopped and said: "Tell me the truth. We at Party Headquarters will never wrong a good man, or mistakenly kill a man who is loyal to the Nationalist Party and the Republic of China."

Ma Hanshan closed his eyes, "I killed Cui Zhongshi myself. No one made me do it. Are you satisfied now?"

Xu Tieying knocked the desk again and said to the secretary: "Leave now."

"Yes sir," replied Secretary Sun. With a vigorous thrust of his hand, he grappled with Ma Hanshan's right shoulder which apparently became dislocated with a loud cracking sound.

After all this activity, Secretary Sun left, gun in hand.

Xu Tieying looked at Ma Hanshan who was squatting there and asked: "Do you need me to help you up?"

"No need," replied Ma Hanshan who was still contorted, holding his right arm out due to the dislocation.

Xu Tieying paced back and forth deliberately, saying: "Our party is the party that established the country's first premier after forty years of national revolution and today the Republic of China is one of the four greatest powers in the world. We are under the wise leadership of President Chiang. I cannot imagine that a good-for-nothing like you is a member of this party."

Ma Hanshan was in great pain. Was this being recorded? A tape recorder lay on the desk!

"Chief Xu, I have to admire you. How did you think to use a recorder! How smart," said Ma, in grudging admiration.

"Save your praise," said Xu Tieying. "Now, tell me, how did you end up in this farce? You should be calming the city down instead."

Ma Hanshan was silent again. With great pain, he opened his Zhongshan jacket with his left hand, pulled out an envelope from the belt and handed it to Xu Tieying.

"What is it?" asked Xu Tieying, without accepting the envelope. "Just open it?"

"It's too thin to be a bomb!" remarked Ma Hanshan.

Xu Tieying took the unsealed envelope. He pulled out the folded rice paper but still refrained from unfolding it, asking: "What is it?"

Ma Hanshan looked at the ground and said: "You have already seen it. It is the authentic work of Tang Bohu."

Xu Tieying now opened it slowly and read what was written on the paper. He folded it again, put it back in the envelope and returned it to Ma Hanshan. "You keep it. Send it to Fu Zuoyi or Vice-President Li Zongren. Maybe they can save you."

"There is another box of cultural relics," answered Ma Hanshan. "I have prepared them for Director General Ye and Director Chen. The Party Headquarters cannot be bribed with money. But they might be interested in relics."

"A box of what?" asked Xu Tieying seriously.

"Cultural relics that Minister Chen would be most interested to see," replied Ma Hanshan. "I have hired someone to authenticate some pieces, including those of the Shang and Zhou dynasties. There are inscriptions on them."

Xu Tieying raised his head slowly, sighing. "What an era we are in when a living person has to be saved by the dead."

CHAPTER 5

With the current political situation out of whack, both phones on Xu Tieying's desk in the police commissioner's office of the Peking Police Bureau were ringing simultaneously.

Instead of picking up right away, Xu Tieying gazed at the phones as they clamoured, then shot a glance at Ma Hanshan who was standing off to one side, holding one arm with the other.

"Shall I get out of your hair?" said Ma Hanshan.

"Get out of my hair?" replied the chief. "When every single phone call has something to do with you?" Adept at multi-tasking, Xu Tieying reached out to take both receivers, leaving Ma Hanshan just standing there.

Xu listened to each in turn, holding one up to his left ear, one to his right, and speaking into the one to his left ear. "Speaking. Spill the beans."

The person on the other end of the line cut him off, saying in a hurried, loud voice: "Chief, this is Shan Fuming. The situation is getting out of control. Protesters outside the North China Headquarters for the Suppression of Communist Insurgency, the Peking Municipal Council, the Municipal Government and the Municipal Party Headquarters are being held off as we speak! But over at the Food Distribution Committee there are just too many. They'll start looting before long, chief."

Knowing that Xu Tieying was busy taking another call, the

person on the other end of the line on Xu Tieying's right ear was patient for ten seconds, before bursting out with: "If you're done, mind if I get a few words in?"

Only then did Xu Tieying realise it was Chen Jicheng, deputy commander-in-chief of the North China Headquarters for the Suppression of Communist Insurgency and commanding officer of the Peking Garrison Headquarters. He stared blankly for a moment, then placed the phone with Shan Fuming on the other end of the table, and spoke into the right one: "Commander-in-Chief Chen? I do apologise. That was a duty officer with an urgent report."

Meanwhile, still unaware that the receiver on the other end had been placed on the table, Shan Fuming spoke in an increasingly loud and impatient voice: "Chief! Chief!"

Xu Tieying in turn took the receiver from which Shan Fuming was incessantly shouting, and deliberately held it against the one Commander Chen was calling through, so that the latter could hear.

Naturally, Commander Chen could hear the shouting, and asked: "Could you hang up on that call first?"

"All right," said Xu Tieying, and he placed the receiver back with a click. "I await your instructions, Commander Chen."

As he spoke, Xu shot Ma Hanshan a glance. Ma had been standing by his side, straining to hear the conversation, and once he felt Xu's eyes settle on him, he pretended not to eavesdrop.

Xu motioned for him to come nearer to have a listen. Ma Hanshan was grateful, and came closer.

The aggressiveness in the commander's voice made it all the more thunderous. "You know that the Youth Aviation Brigade of the Ministry of Defence has occupied the Food Distribution Committee?"

"We received reports this morning," Xu Tieying replied. "They mobilised spontaneously."

"How can you call this a sudden mobilisation," replied Commander Chen, "knowing that the Student Union was able to mobilise people from all schools to hit the streets at once? The Ministry of Defence Inspection Brigade and Fang Meng'ao's Aviation Brigade in particular are clearly working with the Communist

Party! As a member of the investigation team, surely you must be aware of this!"

Xu Tieying's gaze happened to cross that of Ma Hanshan, causing both men to remember the scene of the night before, when they were confronted with the sight of Cui Zhongshi's corpse at the morgue. They were still intent on concealing it, with one in the Central Bureau of Investigation and Statistics, the other in the Bureau of Investigation and Statistics of the Military Council – the situation was poised on a razor's edge.

Xu gave Ma a steely-eyed look before replying to the commander: "Sir, I stand behind your assessment. But at the moment we have no proof. It's hard for us, what with links to the Ministry of Defence and especially to the number two special line."

Commander Chen only became angrier. "Nobody has any doubts concerning this line of contact! But none shall be permitted to round up us veterans of the party-state under the pretence of a direct line of contact! Nor shall they be permitted to take advantage of the Communist Party for the sake of jostling for power, and be taken advantage of by the Communist Party to take down the party-state! They've stirred things up enough as it is. Commander-in-Chief Fu is incredibly angry. Orders just came down calling on all parties to make their way to the Bandit Suppression Command Headquarters for an emergency meeting. You need to come immediately. Zeng Keda will also be there. As a representative of the party headquarters and a veteran of the party-state, you should understand that when it comes to people and matters inside the party-state, even when they're in the wrong, they mustn't result in the system being brought down. Please refrain from showing your support for Zeng Keda at the meeting."

"Rest assured, Commander Chen, I understand," replied Xu Tieying in acquiescence.

"Do you know where Ma Hanshan is hiding out?" asked Commander Chen all of a sudden, catching the man off guard as he stared bewildered at Xu Tieying.

"Sir," replied Xu Tieying, "are you implying I should be looking for him?"

"Find him," replied the commander. "Tell him to also sit in on the meeting. Tell him that if he shuts that filthy mouth of his, and doesn't go running all over the place, there'll be no need to worry. As for matters pertaining to the overall situation of the party-state, as long as he doesn't step out of line, we've got his back."

"Understood."

Ma Hanshan, who now looked as emotional as a toddler, said: "I'll make sure I find him right away and bring him along to the meeting."

The commander slammed down the phone and Xu Tieying replaced the receiver. "You got all that?"

Ma Hanshan had completely forgotten about his dislocated right arm, held his left arm up high and chopped down hard from the shoulder, saying: "It's about time we went all out with them!"

Xu Tieying's stern face softened and he suggested: "How about I get a medic to come and take a look at that arm of yours?"

"No need," Ma Hanshan replied. "A bandage'll do the trick."

"Showing up to the meeting with your arm in a sling?"

"Let Commander Chen and the lot of them take a look at the kind of violence the students are getting up to."

Xu Tieying suddenly saw something amiable in Ma Hanshan and couldn't help breaking out into a smile. He went to pick up the painting by Tang Bohu given to him by Ma Hanshan and handed it over.

Ma Hanshan then said: "Chief Xu, this is a genuine work by Tang Bohu. If it doesn't appeal to your taste, take it with you to Nanking and pass it on as a gift to someone else. I'm sure you can find someone willing to take it off your hands."

Xu Tieying took another look at his dislocated shoulder and sighed apologetically. "It's not that I don't like it. It's just that, at present, it'd be more useful to give it to someone else. Take it with you, go to Commander Chen's house, and give the painting to his wife with him present, before heading to the meeting."

Ma Hanshan took the painting with one hand and said: "Brother Xu, once we get over this bump in the road, I'll find a way to get you Wu Daozi's *Scroll of Eighty-Seven Sages* from the residence of Xu Beihong!"

"No need to further harass Xu Beihong and his family." Xu Tieying took his hat and said: "Let's go."

Looking rather panic-stricken, Ma Hanshan followed Xu Tieying out. Thousands of students were gathered outside the gate of the main warehouse of the Peking Municipal Food Distribution Committee.

"Bring us Ma Hanshan!" they yelled in unison.

"Give us Ma Hanshan!" the crowd clamoured.

"Weed out behind-the-scenes corruption!"

"Weed out behind-the-scenes corruption!"

"We want to eat!"

"We want to eat!"

"We want an education!"

"We want an education!"

The sun was high in the sky as students were scattered everywhere. Facing the large gate of the Food Distribution Committee's Main Warehouse hung a giant banner that read: "Northeastern Students Petition Group".

To the east of the road, suspended above the masses supporting the Northeastern students, hung a huge banner that read: "Peking University Solidarity Group", "Tsinghua University Solidarity Group". On the west side of the road, above the masses who came out to show support, another enormous banner read: "Yenching University Solidarity Group" and "Peking Normal University Solidarity Group".

Even more exhortations were written on giant banners, reading: "Down with corruption!"

"Down with persecution!"

"Down with starvation!"

The youth squadron led by Commander Zheng had retreated to the big gate of the Food Distribution Committee, where they lined up, facing the protesting, screaming mob. Although they were worked up, the platoon remained silent and still. And while the street ahead was barricaded, everyone knew this would not suffice to deter the students. If the burgeoning crowds were to stampede towards them, it could lead to a second "Fifth of July Incident"!

At this point, Commander Zheng recalled Zeng Keda's words: "Do not open fire, do not get in the way, do not fear turmoil!"

Although he kept reminding himself of this admonition and was able to calm himself down, Commander Zheng felt unstable. A large number of reinforcements from the Peking Police Bureau had been dispatched to the scene, as had a large number of armed forces from the Peking Garrison Headquarters.

A convoy of police vehicles were parked behind the droves of students, stationed up to the east of the road. In front of the police cars were rows and rows of police officers wielding shields and batons, and in the back were armed policemen.

Fortunately, this police regiment was still showing restraint because who else happened to stand motionless in the convertible jeep commanding the convoy but Fang Mengwei himself!

The situation on the west side was more worrying. Parked behind the students was a string of military vehicles. Mounted atop each of these vehicles was a machine gun pointed at the student masses. In front of the vehicles, droves of military police wearing steel helmets were also pointing the ominous, jet-black muzzles of their guns at the students. And standing atop the command vehicle on this side was that Special Task Battalion commander of the Fourth Corps of the Nationalist Army.

Unlike Fang Mengwei atop the command vehicle across from him, the Special Task Battalion commander had an ominous look on his face, not to say murderous!

Battalion Commander Zheng was unsure as to how long he could keep this up. He now stood on the sandbags behind the road blocks and spurs, from where he could make out Liang Jinglun hidden among the crowd of people over at the "Yenching University Solidarity Group" banner. He wasn't shouting slogans with the rest of them but instead was just quietly surveying the situation. Around him were several stick-in-the-mud male students, some of whose faces looked familiar to Commander Zheng, as he knew them to be "on their side" as members of the Chiang Kai-shek Student Society. Some of their faces were unfamiliar to Commander Zheng but he knew them to be core members of the Peking Students' Union. He was somewhat calmed to see how these Student Union cadres were able to control the situation under Liang Jinglun's command, and that the trusted friends of the

Chiang Kai-shek Student Society would try their hardest to protect Liang Jinglun.

At the same time, Liang Jinglun happened to be looking over at battalion Commander Zheng, and both men's glances met briefly.

Liang Jinglun gave Zheng a nod, then looked downwards, because a pair of hands were resting on his waist, a pair of hands belonging to a woman: Xie Mulan! She was stealthily hidden behind Liang Jinglun, and looked utterly thrilled and trembling with joy. The pushing and shoving of the crowd enabled her to press her face into Liang Jinglun's back and to put both arms around his waist. For love to exist in such a turbulent assembly, with only herself and Liang Jinglun in the know, she deeply wished this day would go on forever.

But she'd forgotten that another pair of eyes was trailing behind her and Liang Jinglun, among the Yenching University students, separated from them by only two to three rows of fellow students, who could watch her and Liang Jinglun, and those eyes belonged to He Xiaoyu!

Amid the swaying masses, Xie Mulan's face and Liang Jinglun's back kept appearing and disappearing in He Xiaoyu's field of vision.

He Xiaoyu didn't want to lay eyes on them any more. She was reminded of someone else, as her piercing gaze fixed on that large gate of the Food Distribution Committee.

As the sunlight flooded her eyes, she laid eyes on another man. The man, of imposing stature, was walking in her direction from the iron gate, seemingly unimpeded by the railings placed in the vicinity of the gate. A sudden realisation made her eyes gleam: the man had disappeared. She didn't understand why, at a time like this, she should see visions of Fang Meng'ao.

―――

A car approached the main gate of the North China Headquarters for the Suppression of Communist Insurgency with unprecedentedly reckless audacity!

Guards at the first security cordon were taken by surprise and, one after another, had to dodge in both directions. Once they'd brushed themselves off, they chased the vehicle, guns at the ready and yelling at the top of their lungs.

The jeep skidded to a halt in front of the iron gates of the second security cordon, the force of the brakes even lifting the vehicle off the ground momentarily.

Next to the iron fencing was a large locked gate, above which loomed a sign that read: "North China Headquarters for the Suppression of Communist Insurgency"!

With guards at the second security cordon having rushed to the scene, all types of guns were now being pointed at the person driving the jeep! "Get out!" bellowed the captain of the guards.

It was Fang Meng'ao!

He turned off the ignition from the driver's seat, pulled out a cigar, flicked open his American cigarette lighter, lit the cigar and started smoking in the vehicle.

He was being stared at by countless guards and guard captains. They got a clear look at the American Air Force officer's cap he was wearing, along with the three stars studded on both epaulettes of his American Air Force military uniform.

As the darling of the National Revolutionary Army, the Air Force lived up to its reputation, and this especially thanks to its high-ranking officers. The guards all stared at their captain. After all, since this was the North China Headquarters for the Suppression of Communist Insurgency, the captain of the guards was still putting on airs.

"Let's see some credentials!"

Fang Meng'ao kept on smoking and held his identification out of the car. The captain of the guards opened up the ID and perused it from top to bottom: it carried a bright red seal that said: "Ministry of Defence Preparatory Bureau".

Under "Duties", it read "Colonel Fang Meng'ao, Chief of the Peking Economic Inspection Brigade, specially appointed by the Ministry of Defence".

One look at the picture was enough to equate the face of the man pictured to that of the man sitting in this vehicle, wearing a standard issue American Air Force uniform. The guard captain was, of course, well aware of the hierarchy of the National Revolutionary Army. But his delusions of grandeur made him reluctant to be trampled on by a man of this rank, in front of the largest military institution of North China.

He held Fang Meng'ao's proof of identification, refusing to give it back to him, and asked sternly: "Have you any idea where you are?"

Fang Meng'ao didn't ask for his identification back, and without looking at the guard, said: "With a sign like that, how could I not?"

"If so, where did you get the nerve to come hurtling in here with screeching tyres?" Get out of the car!" The guard captain turned around and said to the nearby guards: "Bring the vehicle inside and confiscate it."

Fang Meng'ao remained seated calmly in the driver's seat, then looked at the guard captain and said: "Aren't you going to ask me what I'm doing here?"

"Get out of the car and then we'll talk."

Fang Meng'ao flicked the cigar out of the car, a large part of it still unsmoked, then said: "Open the door."

The guard captain was dumbfounded and opened the door with a sullen look on his face. In one swift move, Fang Meng'ao grabbed hold of the guard captain's hand and said: "Open the barrier and the gate."

Having never encountered anyone like this, the guard captain tried to jerk his hand back, only to find that the colonel's fingers were like a steel vice.

"Uphold military discipline!" The guard captain screamed.

Several guards surrounded the vehicle, the dark muzzles of their weapons pointed at Fang Meng'ao seated in the car as they looked at their captain and awaited his orders, for the sake of upholding military discipline.

Fang Meng'ao's hand gripped even tighter.

As the guard captain's hand got wrenched into the car, his body was already pressed tightly against the car door, unable to move.

Fang Meng'ao retorted: "You're going to uphold military discipline by shooting me?"

The guard captain's face was already awfully close to Fang Meng'ao's. He then realised that this guy's eyes shone brightly, which made him dumbstruck.

"If you don't have the balls to open fire, then open the gate. I'm here to carry out the Ministry of Defence's orders to arrest a fugitive criminal. Tell them to open up!"

The guard captain replied: "Sure, sure... I'll need to see that order from the Ministry of Defence."

"It's right there in your hand," Fang Meng'ao replied. "What more do you want?"

"Those are just your credentials," said the guard captain.

"Give them here." Only when the guard raised his other hand, did Fang Meng'ao retrieve his papers.

"See this here. It says I'm chief of the Peking Inspection Brigade, specially appointed by the Ministry of Defence. There's a 'Fifth of July' fugitive hiding in these headquarters. If this fugitive remains on the loose, the people of Peking who objected in the Food Distribution Committee will come looking for your Commander-in-Chief Fu. Do I make myself clear?"

This time it really got through to the guard captain, because that same month the North China Headquarters for the Suppression of Communist Insurgency had been surrounded by droves of protesters several times in the name of the Fifth of July Movement, which gravely annoyed Commander-in-Chief Fu. The guard finally gave Fang Meng'ao a direct answer: "Who's this fugitive? Tell me his full name and position. I have to run this by my superiors."

There was no arguing with this, so Fang Meng'ao looked at him and said: "Ma Hanshan! Deputy chairman of the Food Distribution Committee! He arrived here half an hour ago and is attending a meeting inside. Don't you go claiming he's not here."

The guard captain was being compelled by the look in Fang Meng'ao's eyes. "Even if he's here, I still have to run it by my superiors on the phone. Let go of me now, will you?"

"You need to dial the number of Commander-in-Chief Fu's office directly," said Fang Meng'ao. "I'll be right here waiting."

He let go of the guard's hand.

Outside the gate to the Peking Food Distribution Committee's main warehouse, the crowd continued with their shouting:

"Show us Fu Zuoyi!"

"Show us Li Zongren!" Deafening waves of protest resounded again.

"Give us Ma Hanshan!"

"Weed out corrupt cliques!"

"No more famine!"

"No more persecution!"

"No more corruption!"

"No more civil war!" The crowds began to swarm in the direction of the Food Distribution Committee's main warehouse gate!

At the west gate, the Special Task Battalion commander on top of his military vehicle threw his hand up in the air! Atop the other military vehicles, machine gun bolts were being pulled back, preparing to put a round in the chamber. Rows and rows of helmeted military police clicked back the bolts of their carbines.

He Xiaoyu, who'd been fretfully wishing for Fang Meng'ao to appear, was already very wound up, worried that bloodshed would ensue yet again. She threw her hand up as well but was unable to utter anything.

There was one person in the bustling crowd who felt even more on edge than her. Yan Chunming's face was covered in sweat, his eyes filled with dread. The voice of old Comrade Liu echoed sharply in his ears: "Control the situation, detect secret enemy agents, conceal elites, protect the students!"

This was by no means a coordinated action by the Peking Student Committee of the Communist Party. Even a rock would be driven to bloodshed in the face of these countless indignant masses, as well as the countless steel helmets, firearms, police caps and batons. How do you control a situation like this? How do you identify who the secret enemy agents are? How do you conceal elites? How do you protect the students?

While looking at the banner that said "Yenching University Solidarity Group", Yan Chunming faintly saw Liang Jinglun standing beneath it, then threw caution to the wind and squeezed his way forward.

Suddenly a hand tugged at Yan in the dark.

Looking back, Yan recognised the person pulling at him as Comrade Liu. He had actually showed up!

Yan Chunming saw a light flash by as Comrade Liu looked the

other way. Yan followed Liu's line of sight, only to realise that there were a large number of plainclothes agents of the National Bureau of Investigation and Statistics among the masses. These undercover agents were the same people who had prepared to go on a killing spree with Hanshan in front of the Peking Police Bureau! The crowds were still surging when a loud roar resounded from the loudspeakers: "Hold your fire!"

The swaying crowds came to a standstill, as did Yan Chunming, and they all looked in the direction of the amplified sound. On the police command vehicle to the west, Fang Mengwei was yelling into a megaphone: "Everyone, hold your fire!"

The police regiment was obviously still formed up in its original formation, but across from them the military police still had the muzzles of their guns pointing towards the students! Because that Special Task Battalion commander still held his hand up high in the air!

"Give me a rifle!" Fang Mengwei yelled angrily into the device!

A sergeant immediately handed him a sniper rifle. Under the prying gaze of the masses, he used his right hand to hold up the sniper rifle parallel to the horn he had in his left hand, taking aim at the commander on the vehicle across from him, saying: "I order all of you to lower your weapons!"

The commander never expected Fang Mengwei to act in this way. He looked stupefied while his hand was still in the air, then seemed to remember that Fang Mengwei concurrently held the post of deputy chief of the Investigation Department of the Garrison Headquarters, and had no choice but to slowly lower his hand. The servicemen clutching their machine guns and carbines let go of their triggers.

It wasn't until then that Fang Mengwei lowered his sniper rifle and announced to the masses: "Fellow students, the Ministry of Defence's investigation team is currently looking into the 'Fifth of July Incident'. The team is combing through the Food Distribution Committee as we speak! What's more, a meeting at the Bandit Suppression Headquarters is under way, after which Commander-in-Chief Fu will provide everyone with a response. I urge you all not to do anything rash! Avoid any further bloodshed!"

For a brief moment, the crowd was quiet.

One pair of eyes finally awoke amid the incomparable excitement and euphoria: Xie Mulan let go of Liang Jinglun, moved her face away from him and sheepishly looked over at her elder cousin on the vehicle.

Suddenly she was overcome with inexplicable panic. Another person was looking at Fang Mengwei abstrusely; it was He Xiaoyu.

Yan Chunming took advantage of the masses quietening down to look sharply at Liang Jinglun underneath the Yenching University banner.

Liang Jinglun was whispering something in the ear of a student beside him. That student then cried out: "Fellow students! Everyone sit down! We're going to wait until they give us a clear-cut answer! If we don't get an answer, we'll find Fu Zuoyi!"

Right away, students under the various streamers cooperated: "That's right! Everyone sit down!"

"Everyone please sit down!"

Group by group, the masses sat down under the scorching sun. Yan Chunming sat down along with them and by the time he looked again, he'd lost sight of old Comrade Liu.

In the conference room of the Peking Headquarters for the Suppression of Communist Insurgency, Fu Zuoyi had convened an emergency meeting, which he himself was absent from. But the high-level nature of the meeting could be felt at a glance. The three people seated in front of the long table covered in a white tablecloth placed up against the podium were all lieutenant generals.

Zeng Keda unexpectedly was assigned to sit in the seat furthest to the right. Having been in Peking for nearly a month, this was the first time Zeng Keda had sat in on a meeting of the North China Headquarters for the Suppression of Communist Insurgency. As a major general, Zeng Keda wouldn't have had any reason to feel wronged sitting in this position, were it not for the fact that in this meeting he was representing the Ministry of Defence, as well as Comrade Jianfeng!

Something he was even less able to accept was the presence of Ma Hanshan, who was assigned a seat in the same row as him, specifically, in the seat furthest to the left. Seeing how he, Zeng Keda, who'd been ordered to come to Peking to investigate the case, was sitting at the opposite end of the same row as the prime subject of investigation, made him realise they would truly be going head to head in this meeting.

But he was playing it cool, surreptitiously looking at the three men sitting by the podium. The person in the middle was the moderator of today's meeting, as well as the one scheming against him today, namely, Chen Jicheng, the deputy commander-in-chief of the North China Headquarters for the Suppression of Communist Insurgency and commanding officer of the Peking Garrison Headquarters. He had a sombre, ghastly pale look on his face. The man sitting to Chen's right, despite donning his lieutenant general uniform, was looking down poker-faced at the table surface. It was Wang Kejun, secretary-general of the Bandit Suppression Headquarters, who was at the meeting in lieu of Fu Zuoyi. Since Chen Jicheng was deputy commander-in-chief, he had no choice but to sit in the 'deputy's seat'.

The lieutenant general sitting to the left of Chen Jicheng had a tranquil facial expression and his demeanour was slightly aloof, owing to his exceptional status, given that he held the post of adjutant-general of the Rear Office of the Military Affairs Commission Peking Field Headquarters of the Nationalist Government. In May 1948, this commission in various places had already begun to be merely nominal institutions. But the Peking Field Headquarters was different, since Li Zongren, the current vice-president, had been a former chairman of the Field Headquarters. Hence, this adjutant-general was representing Li Zongren, automatically giving him superior status by proxy. This man, adjutant-general of the Peking Field Headquarters of the Military Affairs Commission of the Nationalist Government, was Li Yuqing.

Sitting beside Zeng Keda was Xu Tieying. In his capacity as representative of the Defence Ministry's investigation team, he was merely a facilitator, meaning he ought to have been seated to the right of Zeng Keda. Now, however, he was sitting to his left, which showed that he was evidently attending today's session in his role of Peking Police commissioner and chief of the Investigation Department of the Garrison Headquarters. Further down the line were the seats at the centre. Seated next to Xu Tieying was a man in his fifties with a pasty, ill-looking complexion, dressed in a Zhongshan suit. This person was the reason why the Peking Fifth of July

Incident had occurred in the first place. It was Xu Huidong, the Peking Municipal Council speaker.

Sitting right in the middle, next to Xu Huidong, was also a man in his early fifties, looking refined in his long tunic, with a dignified expression on his face. In terms of executive position, this man was Peking's *de facto* highest chief executive, namely, the distinguished Mr Liu Yaozhang, mayor of Peking. But given that it was currently wartime, with military affairs above all else, the role of the so-called mayor had been reduced to observing formalities, putting out fires and getting walked over.

This current mayor had once been famous in journalistic circles and concurrently held the post of member of the Central Executive Committee of the Kuomintang, having been brought on to take up this onerous task after He Siyuan's resignation. Sitting beside Liu Yaozhang was Fang Buting, perhaps the man who felt he had the hardest task among all of the attendees.

Following the sudden murder of Cui Zhongshi, Fang Buting's own elder son Meng'ao was frantically trying to get to the bottom of the scandal, setting the great fire of the party-state ablaze in his own backyard. His wrecked home was a harbinger of the peril the nation was in. Here he was, this well-connected veteran of the party-state, forced into having a showdown with his own unseasoned son, who had got himself up to his neck in this mess.

He closed his eyes and waited for the first blood to be drawn.

Most strikingly, Ma Hanshan was sitting beside Fang Buting. The Defence Ministry's Inspection Brigade had searched all over for him, and the Food Distribution Committee he was in charge of had already been surrounded by hordes of people.

At this point, he had shown up with his right arm in a sling and a fearless look on his face, that fickle and protean face of his, looking both obstinate and wronged, as if he was the biggest victim in all of this.

"Shall we kick off the meeting?" Chen Jicheng asked Wang Kejun and Li Yuqing as he looked to his left and right respectively.

Both men nodded. "Let's begin!" Chen Jicheng spoke in a sombre tone when addressing the others.

Immediately after being declared open, the meeting was interrupted by a voice by the door shouting: "Report!"

Chen Jicheng was about to lose his temper but as he looked up, he was unable to.

A colonel was standing upright in the doorway. It was Fu Zuoyi's confidential aide-de-camp.

"Come in," said Wang Kejun.

"Aye aye, sir."

The aide-de-camp entered the conference room and made a beeline for Wang Kejun, the secretary-general in charge of the proceedings, leaned over and whispered a few words in his ear.

Wang Kejun's expression remained dignified as he said to the aide: "Go and report back to Commander-in-Chief Fu that we will handle it in an appropriate fashion."

"Aye aye, sir."

The aide brought his leg back to attention and exited the premises with great strides. Everyone was now looking in the direction of Wang Kejun, who leaned over and whispered into Chen Jicheng's ear: "All the protesters have convened at the Food Distribution Committee. They are demanding to see Ma Hanshan. The chief of the Defence Ministry's Inspection Brigade, that Fang guy, he's there demanding to take Ma Hanshan into custody, to answer to the grievances of the public."

Chen Jicheng's complexion became more ashen and he couldn't help but ask: "What does Commander-in-Chief Fu advise?"

"Commander-in-Chief Fu told us to come up with a view on it," replied Wang Kejun.

"My view is: not on your life!" The loudness of Chen Jicheng's voice made everyone's eyes widen. He suddenly stood up and exclaimed: "What 'Fifth of July' incident?" It's nothing more than a reactionary deed plotted by the Communist Party to overthrow the party-state and throw Peking into disarray! It's been almost a month and they've been causing mayhem daily under the pretence of this incident. Their objective is to discredit the party-state and to negatively impact the 'operational deployments' of the Bandit Suppression Headquarters against the Communist Army. Its properties are so obvious, whereas the party-state internally is unable to cooperate in good faith against external forces."

At this point he shot a glance at Zeng Keda, who reciprocated. Chen Jicheng then said: "Inspector-General Zeng, how's the investigation of the Defence Ministry's Inspection Brigade coming along?"

"It's coming along," replied Zeng Keda.

Chen Jicheng continued: "Are you investigating the Communist Party or our own people?"

"Our task is clear," said Zeng Keda. "To investigate the causes of the 'Fifth of July Incident'. We'll aim to uproot all of those in the Communist Party who are involved. Likewise, those involved from inside the party-state will be dealt with severely."

"Resolutely going against the party with one hand and going against corruption with the other, is that it?" asked Chen Jicheng reprovingly, without letting him answer. "What sort of inspection brigade is this? You've been in Peking a month without apprehending anyone in the party, nor have you ferreted out any Communist organisations. Yet in your daily probings you never relax your grip on the interior of the party-state. Especially that Youth Service Department of the Ministry of Defence, who've been conspiring with the peripheral student organisations of the Communist Party, even looting the provisions of the Fourth Regiment of the National Revolutionary Army. What are you up to? You won't stop until you've helped the Communist Party occupy Peking, Tianjin and the whole of northern China, is that it? Today, at this very moment, that Youth Aviation Brigade of yours is arresting people from the Peking Food Distribution Committee left and right, thereby playing into the hands of the Peking Students' Union, who've all gone to the Food Distribution Committee, ready to loot provisions. How well you've been cooperating. Do you know what Commander-in-Chief Fu's private aide has just reported to us?"

Zeng Keda was in no hurry to reply.

The others weren't looking at Chen Jicheng either, as they waited for him to finish his rant.

"An Air Force colonel," Chen Jicheng continued in his loud voice. "It's one thing not to punish a suspicious character with

Communist leanings who openly defies the highest military orders on the frontline, but it's another to appoint such a character to come to Peking to cause trouble. I'm talking about Fang Meng'ao. He charged into the Bandit Suppression Headquarters looking to arrest people. Inspector-General Zeng, please inform me, by whose orders does he think he can go about making arrests?"

Ma Hanshan, impulsively, was about to stand up, but Chen Jicheng's gaze stopped him in his tracks. Chen Jicheng then looked over at Fang Buting. Fang Buting, who had had his eyes closed the whole time, now opened them and looked straight ahead into the void.

"What's more," said Chen Jicheng, quick to change the topic in his lead-up to exonerating Ma Hanshan, "the president has consistently and solemnly taught us to 'show piety and kind-heartedness'.

"At a time when national affairs are becoming troublesome, Governor Fang Buting has been painstakingly providing us with generous economic support. What's wrong with that? And people still deliberately use his son to get to him! As if their disloyalty to the party-state weren't enough, they had to go and jostle his son into behaving unfilially towards his father. Esteemed Governor Fang."

Fang Buting could hardly stay seated.

Chen Jicheng continued: "Waging war with the Communist troops in northern China, protecting the people of Peking and Tianjin, the burden placed on your shoulders is considerable. Your domestic issues are equal to those of the state. We're all here, feel free to vent whatever grievances you may have."

"I'm grateful for your concern, Commander-in-Chief Chen," replied Fang Buting. "But there's something I need to declare. Both my sons are enlisted in the Revolutionary Army, and I therefore understand their inability to frequently observe their filial duties. I don't feel any grievances in this respect. As for what you said about Fang Meng'ao wanting to arrest Deputy Chairman Ma, and all kinds of suspicion surrounding Fang Meng'ao, as his father, I request to be withdrawn from this line of questioning."

Chen Jicheng's attempt to sow discord was fruitless. He had forgotten the old maxim that "blood is thicker than water". He had been put on the spot by Fang Buting's stern refusal.

"Deputy Commander-in-Chief Chen!" said Ma Hanshan, standing up heroically. "Deputy Commander-in-Chief Chen! I, Hanshan, am grateful to the party-state, to the senior officials. Having acted in a way that's brought suffering to the Food Distribution Committee, of my own accord and with no behind-the-scenes backers, I deserve to be torn to pieces! This morning, on the way here, my arm was already broken by the Communist students. And now Brigade Chief Fang is out to arrest me. Let him do it and I, Ma Hanshan, will comply."

"Sit down," barked Chen Jicheng, reprimanding him in a seemingly stern voice.

With his left hand, Ma Hanshan was holding his right arm that was in a sling. He sat down haplessly. "Mayor Liu."

Since his speech hadn't had the intended effect on Fang Buting, Chen Jicheng now sought out another target, this time looking at Liu Yaozhang.

"You are the mayor of Peking and a member of the Central Executive Committee of the Kuomintang, as well as the chairman of the Peking Food Distribution Committee. Today's issues are mainly geared towards the Food Distribution Committee. In the face of the Communist Party stirring up trouble, and people inside the party-state adding fuel to the fire by ignoring the bigger picture, you must let your voice be heard!"

"Commander Chen is putting me in a difficult position," said, Liu Yaozhang who, by virtue of his seniority, could afford to remain seated. "Is it really me who needs to speak out on this issue?"

Still highly reverently, Chen Jicheng went on to say: "You are representatives of the party-state. In the face of a crisis, of course, it's you who should speak out."

"OK, then I'll just say a quick word."

"Even just one word will do, go ahead and speak."

Liu Yaozhang stretched his tunic's fabric before slowly standing up, then said: "I request my resignation from the post of mayor of Peking and chairman of the Peking Food Distribution Committee."

Chen Jicheng was met with refusal from not one, but two people in the meeting. The notoriously overbearing man had no choice but to face off with either Fang Buting, a favourite of the

Song and Kong families, or with Liu Yaozhang, a big shot of the party-state. Despite feeling like a balloon about to pop, he couldn't vent his anger at them. It just turned his face sour. "Mayor Liu, at this point in time, you should refrain from this type of statement."

"I had no intention of saying this here," replied Liu Yaozhang, "but you left me no choice, so I came out and said it anyway. Around two months ago, Mr He Siyuan resigned from his mayoral office, why was that? It was because more than 1.7 million mouths in Peking weren't being fed and people were dying of hunger by the day. He was also chairman of the Peking Food Distribution Committee but had trouble overseeing its accounts. The esteemed mayor had merely been able to take the initiative to receive American aid of rice and flour. Yet as soon as he signalled he would take serious charge of the Food Distribution Committee's affairs, someone sent him a bullet in the mail. Under such circumstances, anyone would be excused for bungling their mayoral duties, or those of the Food Distribution Committee chairman for that matter. I've been in office for two months now, so go ahead and ask Deputy Chairman Ma, in charge of all of this, when's the Food Distribution Committee going to debrief me? I know my position is merely for show, but I have to speak up now. If you ask me to speak, I can only say these two words: I resign!"

"Why don't you all just resign!" said Chen Jicheng, finally giving vent to his frustration. "Hundreds of thousands of Communist troops are garrisoned outside Peking, a decisive battle is imminent, yet all those on the inside of the party-state keep passing the buck and shirking their responsibility, to the point of sawing off the branch they're sitting on! I was asked to convene today's meeting by Commander-in-Chief Fu. I've only one thing to say. No matter what department you're in, or how well connected you are, you all need to commit to the cause. Right now, students controlled by the Communist Party are running amok in front of the Food Distribution Committee. The Suppression Headquarters is suggesting we strike out at them, and ferret out and arrest members of the Communist Party, including the leaders of the student unions under Communist control! All so-called investigations aimed at the party-state must cease this instant. None of our own people can be arrested, whatever mistakes they may have made. Inspector-General, you go first in stating your position."

Zeng Keda was aware that a fight was on the way. He stood up and said: "I'd like to give my opinion on something Deputy Commander-in-Chief Chen just said."

"Your opinion is exactly what I'm here for," said Chen Jicheng.

"When Deputy Commander-in-Chief Chen just mentioned the solemn instructions given to us by the president, he left something out. There were two parts to the instructions given to us by the president, the first being 'Show piety and kind-heartedness'. The other half was as follows: 'Have a sense of propriety'. The reason the party-state has devolved the way it has, is because too many of us have forgotten this part of the president's admonition! The Defence Ministry's Inspection Brigade has come to Peking on the basis of this guideline."

"Who are you referring to?" asked a now furious Chen Jicheng. "Stop beating around the bush and get to the point!"

"Our investigation is still ongoing," Zeng Keda replied. "When the time comes, we'll convey our point clearly to Deputy Commander-in-Chief Chen, Commander-in-Chief Fu and the central government in Nanking."

"So be it!" replied Chen Jicheng. "Enough harming the country with all this empty talk. Regarding the aforementioned, the disturbances caused by the Communist Party and the students, state your position loud and clear!"

"I have no right to take a stand on this," opined Zeng Keda.

"You can't take a stand on arresting Communist Party members, but you have the right to round up your own?"

"I don't have the authority to round up anyone," said Zeng Keda. "Just now, you, Deputy Commander-in-Chief Chen, said that it was the Bandit Suppression Headquarters' suggestion to use force in dealing with the student unrest at the Food Distribution Committee. I'd like to briefly clarify whether or not the Bandit Suppression Headquarters has put out a formal notice to this effect. After clarification, I'll ask Nanking and Comrade Jian Feng of the Defence Ministry for further instructions. As far as authority goes, that's all I'm authorised to do."

"You've all heard it. He's brought the Ministry of Defence into this," said Chen Jicheng, trembling with rage. "Brother Yuqing, you represent Vice-President Li Zongren. Secretary-General Kejun, you represent Commander-in-Chief Fu. Peking and Tianjin rely on us for their defence. We shall fight the battle on behalf of northern China. Surely we must take a clear stance."

Seated on both sides of Chen Jicheng, who stood erect in their midst, Li Yuqing and Wang Kejun exchanged glances, then both men stood up at the same time.

"A decision of this magnitude requires that I ring Vice-President Li for instructions," insisted Li Yuqing.

"I too need to consult with Commander-in-Chief Fu," said Wang Kejun.

"Then consult with them at once," said Chen Jicheng. "We will suspend the proceedings for a quarter of an hour. After that, a decision must be made. The Communist Party-controlled students shall not be permitted to sow further unrest!" Outside the gate of the Peking Food Distribution Committee's main storage warehouse, the sun was shining fiercely and the students were covered in summer sweat as they endured hunger. The authorities still owed them a clear response. The Northeastern students in the centre were still sitting in the same spot.

With dry throats and in unison, all of them were singing the song that had fuelled their resentment:

> *My home is on the Songhua River in the northeast,*
> *There are forests, coal mines, fields of soybeans and sorghum*
> *All over the mountains.*
>
> *My home is on the Songhua River in the northeast.*
> *That is where my fellow countrymen and aged parents are...*

All over the place, Peking students all stood up in support. Sweat and tears ran across countless faces. The choked sound of singing resounded near and far:

> *The eighteenth of September, the eighteenth of September,*
> *Since that miserable day,*
> *The eighteenth of September, the eighteenth of September.*

Since that miserable day,
I've wandered my homeland, discarding endless treasures.
Roam, roam, the whole day I roam inside the Great Wall...

Her face covered in tears, He Xiaoyu had never experienced such an emotional release as at this very moment. She was known for having the best singing voice in the school but only now did she have a deep sense of why it was that people sang such things in the first place. Who would have known that ideals and beliefs would be so inseparable from emotions? The one thing she wasn't able to distinguish clearly at this point was whether the ardour and grief she was feeling were to do with those Northeastern students or with herself! Tearful, she was still able to see Xie Mulan singing excitedly behind Liang Jinglun. Amid the singing, they were unaware of the danger that was drawing nearer. Many students began holding hands, singing at the top of their lungs.

He Xiaoyu noticed that a large hand had taken hold of her own and she gripped it while singing, her face covered in tears: *"When can I go home?"*

Suddenly, she noticed there was something unusual about this hand that was gripping hers. She looked at it, teary-eyed, and was utterly surprised to see the person next to her holding her hand was Comrade Liu!

He Xiaoyu quietened down, but Comrade Liu motioned her to keep on singing. She looked away, then resumed her singing. She felt him loosen his grip on her hand and turn the palm of her hand upward. He then used his index finger to write the word 'leave' on the palm of her hand!

A Communist!

Lower ranks must obey the orders of higher ranks! Despite still being carried away by a surge of passion, she had to abide by the solicitous instructions Comrade Liu had given her in this unusual way. But worming her way out of this swarming mass of people was easier said than done. Immediately, two unfamiliar male students showed up alongside He Xiaoyu, one in front of her and one behind, and with some difficulty shielded her as she inched her way forward through the crowd. She jerked her head back but Old Liu was nowhere to be seen.

In the heat of the moment, she remembered the prologue to the *Communist Manifesto*, which she piously recited to herself: "A spectre is haunting Europe – the spectre of Communism. All the powers of old Europe have entered into a holy alliance to exorcise this spectre: the Pope and the Tsar, Metternich and Guizot, French radicals and German police-spies."

He Xiaoyu, shielded by this pair of male students, kept turning her head, searching. This time she wasn't searching the crowds for Old Liu, nor did she cast her gaze toward the Yenching University banner, unwilling to witness the shenanigans of Liang Jinglun and Xie Mulan any longer. Instead, she stared intently at the gate of the Food Distribution Committee. She was hoping to catch a glimpse of that other 'spectre', Fang Meng'ao! Meanwhile, in the meeting room of the North China Headquarters for the Suppression of Communist Insurgency, the fifteen-minute recess was almost over and all the attendees had returned to their seats.

"Let's continue the meeting."

Chen Jicheng still had the same vexed expression, a stubborn stick-in-the-mud, obstinately self-assured. "Next up, let's listen to Adjutant-General Li Yuqing proclaim President Li Zongren's instructions, and Secretary-General Wang Kejun proclaim those of Commander-in-Chief Fu!"

The six people in the front row held their breath as they looked at Li Yuqing and Wang Kejun sitting beside Chen Jicheng. They could feel at once that Li Yuqing and Wang Kejun had come to a tacit understanding, as both men had looked past Chen Jicheng and exchanged glances.

Li Yuqing then said: "I'd like Wang Kejun to read out Commander-in-Chief Fu's instructions first."

"All right." Wang Kejun opened the briefcase on the table in front of him and pulled out an official notice written in formal script. The densely written sheet had over a thousand characters on it. This didn't look like a document that had been drafted on the fly during the fifteen-minute recess. The atmosphere in the room became solemn. Even Chen Jicheng, who was standing beside Wang Kejun, had a hunch about what was to come as he glanced over at the document Wang Kejun was holding.

Wang Kejun was already standing up, and out of habit cleared his throat. "Dear sirs. By order of Commander-in-Chief Fu Zuoyi, I have been asked to read the following handwritten communiqué of Commander Fu! If you would all rise to your feet!"

Everyone had a premonition and they all stood up as they looked at Wang Kejun. "To esteemed President Chiang and Vice-President Li!"

Wang Kejun read out these two names in a heavy, ponderous tone of voice.

Those who occupied an official post in the army, including Ma Hanshan, all stood at attention. Only after those who weren't in the military, namely, Liu Yaozhang and Xu Huidong, as well as Fang Buting, stood upright along with them, as did Wang Kejun, who began reading the main part of the communiqué:

"I, Zuoyi, humbly address Mr President and Mr Vice-President: Your humble servant has been charged with the important post of commander-in-chief of the Bandit Suppression Headquarters and shoulders the great burden of defending northern China and guarding Peking and Tianjin. Since the beginning of this year, we've been conducting military operations on all fronts against the Communist armed forces. Transport to Peking and Tianjin has been blocked and we've been losing ground in various places of strategic importance in the Shanxi-Chahar-Hebei region. At the expense of our troops who have performed their duties conscientiously, our line of defence at Peking and Tianjin has been breached while Shijiazhuang, Pingshan and Fuping have fallen into the hands of the Communist armed forces. In the past few days, enemy troops have pressed on towards Baoding, Langfang and Fangshan, where fierce battles have been fought. Only by sending five hundred thousand troops to their deaths in the bloody battle against the Communist Army were we able to recapture lost territory and to perform our duty of defending our territory. However, what has become of our country's defenders? In the city of Peking alone, hundreds of thousands of National Revolutionary Army troops are running low on military supplies while two million civilians are famished; there's a general sense of unrest while student uprisings are occurring with great frequency! I, Zuoyi, genuinely don't know what is the point of defending this famine-stricken city and these turmoil-stricken regions any further. What eludes my understanding in particular is the decision by the Peking Municipal Council on 5 July to drive out fifteen thousand Northeastern students and have the 4th Regiment of the Nationalist Revolutionary Army shoot down the remaining petitioners for calling for more grain from the Food Distribution Committee! Those fifteen thousand Northeastern students had been evacuated by the Nationalist government. How come the current measures by Peking's political circles are so blatantly inconsistent with the Nationalist government's compensatory policies aimed at the people? Since the 'Fifth of July Incident', the Northeastern students, teachers and students alike hailing from Peking's institutes of higher learning, and people from all walks of life from all over the country, are all bellowing in protest and condemning and reviling me! I, Fu Zuoyi, am willing to lay down my life on the battlefield for the sake of the servicemen of the party-state but am unwilling to be insulted by each and every bureaucratic faction of officialdom. The morale of the troops on the one hand, and the will of the people on the other, have driven me to a place of injustice. Having to consider both military supplies and food for civilians has put me between a rock and a hard place, so that even without war I am facing defeat! I hereby plead with Mr President and Mr Vice-President to strip me of my title of commander-in-chief of the North China Headquarters for the Suppression of Communist Insurgency, and to select another virtuous individual to fulfil this role, someone who may help resolve the current domestic and international issues, and who can live up to the trust of the party-state! I, Fu Zuoyi, submit this confession on 3 August in the thirty-seventh year of the Republic of China."

The message bordered on being resentful and all those who'd heard it were dumbstruck. Chen Jicheng was, of course, the most flustered of all. Fu Zuoyi was the highest-ranking military commander in all of northern China, and with him ranking the second highest,

Chen shared his superior's responsibility of defending Peking and taking command of the war effort in the region. He had been completely in the dark about this pre-written resignation letter. Now it was being read out in this meeting and the primary person singled out for criticism in it was he himself! He couldn't help but feel disgraced and enraged. The only one whose eyes lit up, was Zeng Keda.

He remembered what Comrade Jianfeng had told him over the phone: "If Chen Jicheng, Ma Hanshan and the like dare to stir the pot, you'd better get in touch with General Fu Zuoyi. Or you could reach out to Vice-President Li Zongren. They'll have our back when push comes to shove."

He knew he had won today's stand-off but Chen Jicheng and his acolytes would not admit defeat. He scanned the others for a reaction as they all awaited the impending confrontation. After Wang Kejun had finished reading the letter of resignation, he handed it with both hands past Chen Jicheng to Li Yuqing. It was deadly silent in the meeting room, and the chirping of cicadas in the trees outside sounded deafening.

"Brother Kejun."

With a grave countenance, Li Yuqing cast an eye on the resignation letter that was being held in front of him. "I'm afraid I'm hesitant to accept this resignation letter of Commander Fu's."

"Well then how about I take it back with me and make Commander Fu present it to the president and vice-president in person?"

Right away, Wang Kejun put the resignation letter in the briefcase on the table in front of him.

"I guess it's my turn to convey the instructions given to me by Vice-President Li," said Li Yuqing.

He then glanced over at Wang Kejun. "After hearing Vice-President Li's statement, we hope that Commander Fu may retract this resignation letter of his."

Zeng Keda's eyes twinkled even more, as he knew what to expect. Ma Hanshan no longer had his usually bold expression on his face. Xu Tieying, who had been stone-faced the entire time, continued to show no emotion, but his eyes widened considerably. He had begun brooding on how to rise to the emergency.

Fang Buting was also waiting contemplatively, but his expression didn't give away what exactly he was waiting for.

Li Yuqing went on to relay the message of Vice-President Li:

"The Nationalist government remains a government of all civilians, and all civilians remain dedicated to the Nationalist government. At present, there are fifteen thousand students from the Northeast who, due to wartime chaos, were relocated to study in Peking. This shows the government does not shun its responsibility towards its citizens. The Peking municipal government and various government branches of the party-state located in Peking all had to, without exception, make appropriate arrangements. On 4 July, the motion submitted by the Peking Municipal Council making arrangements to send them away was highly inappropriate and resulted in a conflict between the students and the government which erupted the next day. There's a sense of apprehension among the people, aggravating the entire country, which has damaged the government's image and fed the rumour mill regarding an impending attack by the Communist Party. In recent days, the Nationalist government has already issued explicit orders to placate the students but its agencies haven't taken the slightest bit of notice, resulting in ever more violent student upheavals. The object of most hatred is indeed Commander-in-Chief Fu Zuoyi, who they hold responsible for conflict in the Northeast. I, Zongren, in my capacity as vice-president of the Nationalist government, as well as former chairman of the Military Affairs Commission Peking Field Headquarters, can bear this no longer. I order Li Yuqing, adjutant-general of the Rear Office of the Military Affairs Commission Peking Field Headquarters to be present at the meeting in my stead and to placate the masses. We must endeavour to give assurances regarding the wholly reasonable demands and legitimate conditions of the people. Those who bear direct responsibility for the Fifth of July Incident must step up and face the public. They must admit responsibility for their mistakes. From the desk of Li Zongren, vice-president of the central government of the Republic of China, 3 August, in the thirty-seventh year of the Republic."

The expression on Chen Jicheng's face changed completely! As did that of Ma Hanshan, and Xu Huidong, who had been silent all along.

"Were those the actual directives of Vice-President Li and Commander-in-Chief Fu?" shouted Chen Jicheng, coming to his senses.

Li Yuqing was the first to vent his dissatisfaction: "Deputy Commander-in-Chief Chen, would I dare falsify the word of Vice-President Li?"

Chen Jicheng then looked over at Wang Kejun and said: "Secretary-General Wang, Commander Fu is the commander-in-chief of the North China Headquarters for the Suppression of Communist Insurgency, and I, Chen Jicheng, am the deputy commander-in-chief. Shouldn't Commander Fu have consulted with me first before taking such a stance regarding the Communist Party and the rioting students who are under its manipulative control?"

Wang Kejun replied in a faint voice: "As far as matters regarding Deputy Commander Chen are concerned, you ought to report to Commander Fu yourself. I'm not suited to act as a middle man in this respect."

"So be it!" Chen Jicheng was already blue in the face. "I too can hand in my resignation to Nanking, and I can even do it over the telephone directly to President Chiang himself!"

After saying this, he rose from his seat and stormed out of the meeting. "Go ahead and carry out Vice-President Li's instructions."

Li Yuqing took charge of the meeting: "Mayor Liu, Speaker of the Council Xu, please consult with one another and see whether the motion brought before the Municipal Council on the fourth of July can be revoked. Then draft a relief plan for the Northeastern students. Take stock of the food distribution and livelihood resources that have been supplied in Peking over the last few months."

Xu Huidong, looking dismal, replied: "I'll convene the council and relay Vice-President Li's opinion on these matters."

"I've already drafted three relief plans for the Northeastern students," noted Liu Yaozhang. "If needed, I can put together another one. As for taking stock of the food distribution and means of livelihood supplied in Peking over the last few months, there's nothing I can do. The Defence Ministry's Investigation Team is in Peking. They should and can take stock."

Li Yuqing immediately looked at Zeng Keda. "Inspector General Zeng."

"We'll put together an inventory! We'll get to the bottom of it! The Chief of the Defence Ministry's Inspection Brigade is still waiting outside for Deputy Chairman Ma. It appears Deputy Chairman Ma had better be cooperative."

Ma Hanshan looked at Zeng Keda, as well as Xu Tieying who was standing beside him. Xu Tieying was looking straight ahead, avoiding his gaze. Ma Hanshan snapped at them: "Talk of cooperation, do you? You'd better get the handcuffs if you're planning to make a scapegoat of me."

Outside the gate of the Peking Food Distribution Committee's main warehouse, the crowd was getting agitated. He Xiaoyu had already squeezed her way to the edge of the crowd under the protection of the two male students. Looking back, her eyes lit up like never before! There was virtually no need for the military police to keep the peace. The excited students, of their own volition, freed up a path. All she could see was a convertible jeep with Ma Hanshan standing on the back seat, one hand held up high, handcuffs attached to it, the other in a sling!

The crowds of students were cheering! Many of them were jumping up and down!

He Xiaoyu was dying to see who was driving the jeep but only the students clearing the path could see him and, of course, it was Fang Meng'ao! She found herself making an unprecedented request from one of the male students escorting her: "Lift me up, let me see."

The male student nodded, with a hint of a smile. He Xiaoyu stayed put and refused to go any further. She just had to wait until she could see the person in the driver's seat. Through the students' coordinated effort, it wasn't long before the jeep reached the big gate. He Xiaoyu finally could see the person jumping down from the vehicle: there was nothing affected about Fang Meng'ao's behaviour. Without greeting anyone, he merely hoisted Ma Hanshan up from the back seat. He Xiaoyu could now see Fang

Meng'ao more clearly, as he led Ma Hanshan in through the gate of the Food Distribution Committee.

In the crowd, almost simultaneously, another person was looking at the sky, lit up by the scorching sun.

Slowly, Comrade Liu could discern the rolling hills in the distance. Appearing in the sunlight were the Taihang Mountains, stretching for over four hundred kilometres from Shanxi into Hebei and then Henan. From Hebei's Pingshan County, you could only just see the main ridge of the Taihang Mountains as it meandered nonchalantly yet majestically southward like a snake, leaving in its wake a stretch of mountains fifty kilometres wide. At the northern end of the range were the vast North China plains, dotted with hubs of human activity, while to the south there was nothing but wilderness, a true no-man's land.

Out of nowhere, the beckoning call of history could be heard, reverberating over these mountain ranges: Two hundred kilometres northwest of Peking, in the year 1948, in Pingshan County in Hebei Province, on these ridges of the Taihang Mountains, a village named Xibaipo cemented its name in the history books. In May of that year, this was the place where Mao Zedong, Zhou Enlai and Ren Bishi had led the Central Committee and core organs of the CPC. They were biding their time, hidden deep in the labyrinthine mountains during a barrage of search raids and bombing by Nationalist Air Force planes. They were to emerge from their lair and, in the blink of an eye, launch the Liaoxi-Shenyang Campaign, the Huai-Hai Campaign and the Peking-Tianjin Campaign, all of which would decide the fate of China. In one or two days' time, they made incredible strides like dragons and tigers, and Peking was chosen as the site of their future capital.

This sunlit scene came to a sudden stop as vaguely discernible courtyards suddenly emerged from dense clusters of mountains. These courtyards were located in Xibaipo, the seat of the Central

Committee of the CPC. The vague sound of horses galloping could be heard as five horsemen riding in Indian file traversed the mountain passes and galloped past the dwellings scattered along the mountain passes. Small, scattered plots of farmland in the distance were being tilled by villagers, apparently unfazed by the familiar sound of galloping horses. They merely lowered their hoes, smiled and waved at the five horsemen clad in grey military uniforms, then continued farming the fields. Next to a small road in the shade of a towering tree stood a bunch of soldiers on guard, the sight of whom caused the horsemen to rein in their horses. The first soldier on horseback came to a halt and dismounted. It was Liu Yun, head of the North China Municipal Works Department. The four other horsemen dismounted too. Liu Yun handed the reins of his horse to one of the soldiers, then did the same with his pistol.

"Wait here," he said.

"Sir. Yes sir."

Liu Yun walked over to the tree on his own. One soldier with a pistol tucked under his belt moved towards him, flanked by two gun-carrying soldiers.

"Are you Department Head Liu Yun?"

"Affirmative. Liu Yun, head of the North China Urban Works Department, reporting on my work!"

The soldier with the gun under his belt replied: "Vice-Chairman Zhou is waiting for you. Follow me."

"Aye, aye." Liu Yun followed the soldier to the gate of the compound in the distance.

CHAPTER 6

A large crowd of people were standing on the large open ground in front of the general storage warehouse of the Peking Citizens' Food Distribution Committee. The twenty pilots of the Youth Aviation Brigade stood in two lines while the staff of the Citizens' Food Distribution Committee, including section chiefs Li and Wang, stood among the pilots. The sun seemed to be even more scorching after three in the afternoon. The students outside the gate were starving and thirsty. The pilots decided not to drink water, while naturally those working for the Citizens' Food Distribution Committee were given no water to drink. As a result, they appeared so dehydrated that their lips were chapped and their eyes looked dim. What they could see vaguely was the back of the army officer standing on top of the sandbags outside the big iron gate. There were also banners with characters that they could not read clearly and the huge crowd of people that had gathered around them.

From outside the iron gate, the voice of Vice-President Li's adjutant continued to come through the loudspeaker, though intermittently. Li was standing on top of the sandbags. The pilots listened intently while those with the Citizens' Food Distribution Committee listened nervously.

"...Therefore, students and my fellow compatriots, please understand the dire situation and challenges facing the government. Please, abide by the Constitution and obey the laws. Go back to your campuses. Regarding how to arrange the accommodation of students from the Northeast, and how to distribute the food, oil and coal on a timely basis for the teachers, students and residents in Peking, please rest assured that Vice-President Li will consult closely with the Peking municipal government and other relevant departments to resolve the problem as soon as possible."

Again, there was a short silence.

"Citizens' food rations have been embezzled. What can Vice-President Li do to solve the problem?" More than a dozen students shouted out almost simultaneously the same question which obviously had been a common concern of the students present at the rally.

"Students..." as soon as he spoke again through the loudspeaker, Li Yuqing was interrupted by a dozen students.

"When will corrupt officials be punished?! When will the students be released?! Why are we fighting a civil war in the middle of an economic depression?! Can Vice-President Li give a clear answer?"

Then came the chanting of countless protesters: "Oppose corruption! Oppose hunger! Oppose persecution! Oppose Civil War..."

"Students, students..." Li's voice was quickly drowned out by the students' screaming.

The general storage warehouse of the Peking Citizens' Food Distribution Committee was quite empty except for just one table and one chair for the bookkeepers. Strangely enough, the presence of Fang Meng'ao and Ma Hanshan added even more of a sense of emptiness to the warehouse as both of them were listening to the clamour from outside.

"Do you hear all that?" said Fang Meng'ao.

"It's quite over the top, isn't it?" replied a handcuffed and bandaged Ma Hanshan.

Although the door of the warehouse was locked from the inside, the small one set in the door was left open. Fang Meng'ao went over and kicked the door closed. This immediately lowered the noise level from outside the entrance. Fang Meng'ao came back to Ma Hanshan again: "Then don't listen. Let's talk."

"About what?"

"About the grain, the money to purchase the grain, the accounting of the purchase, as well as those starved to death and those who were killed!" With that, Fang Meng'ao suddenly interrupted what he was saying. Meanwhile, the sharp look in his eyes was gone, yet the mirth on his face returned. "Let's forget about those things today. What do you think?"

Ma Hanshan appeared momentarily confused, then retorted with a mischievous smile: "Is that because Captain Fang wants to talk about wine and women?"

"That's it. Let's talk about what kind of liquor we like, what kind of women we like and what kind of antique calligraphy and paintings we like, anything except the Citizens' Food Distribution Committee case. Let's make a bet, just the two of us. Whoever talks about the case, loses."

"What shall I do if I lose?" Ma Hanshan's smile disappeared.

"Whoever loses will treat us to dinner tonight. If I lose, I'll invite you and your people to dinner. If you lose, you invite my brigade to dinner."

"Just bet on a dinner?" Ma Hanshan couldn't believe it.

"Too little? Then let's raise the stakes. Whoever loses, buy them dinner. If they amount to ten thousand, pay for them all. If they amount to twenty thousand, count them in."

Ma Hanshan forced another smile. "Captain Fang, there isn't such a big restaurant in all of Peking, is that right?"

"Then give everyone cash and let them buy themselves dinner."

Ma Hanshan knew that Fang Meng'ao would not let him get away with it. In fact, he had been on edge for over a month. Like it or not, Fang Meng'ao was the man he had to reckon with. With that in mind, he put one foot on the chair and claimed desperately: "No, I won't take this bet."

"Can't afford to lose or loathe to give up?"

"Come to think of it, one *dan* of rice costs seventeen million *fabi*, one dan of rice for each person, one meal for ten thousand people will cost a billion *fabi*, and two billion for twenty thousand people. Plus the cost of the dishes, it would come to more than three billion *fabi*. Captain Fang, there is only one person in Peking who can bet so much money with you. If you want such a bet, you should go to him," he said with a wicked smirk on his face.

Fang Meng'ao seemed to be expecting his evil smile: "Well, whoever loses, we'll go to this person for the money wagered. Tell me, who is this man?"

Ma Hanshan smiled a little unnaturally. "Captain Fang, you can go to him for the money if you lose the bet. But I can't."

"Say it, who is this man?"

"Captain Fang, who else can this person be? The governor of the Central Bank's Peking branch!"

Fang Meng'ao thought about punching out his blackened teeth! Yet he held his arms to his chest with an even more vicious smile on his face. "How come the governor of the Peking branch of the Central Bank can treat me with the bank's money?"

"Of course, it's not appropriate to spend public money for personal use. Nevertheless, it's safe to forge an item and cook the books."

Slowly, Fang Meng'ao's eyes swept Ma Hanshan's face and his leg on the chair when suddenly he kicked the chair away with a mighty kick. With his foot missing the supporting chair, Ma Hanshan's body fell forward. Luckily, Fang Meng'ao anticipated what was about to happen and seized his broken arm. Although his forward fall was caught by Fang Meng'ao, Ma Hanshan felt an excruciating pain in the arm. It was so painful that he could not even breathe. Nevertheless, he gritted his teeth and said: "Thank you…"

Fang Meng'ao surreptitiously applied his strength to hold Ma's broken arm. "No thanks required. Sit, please sit down and tell me what I should forge and how to withdraw so much money from the bank. Because if I lose, I'd go to the Peking branch for the money."

Although he told Ma Hanshan to sit down, Fang Meng'ao still held his broken arm firmly. Ma Hanshan was sweating profusely because of the sharp pain, and the sweat on the top of Ma Hanshan's head kept dripping down his cheeks. Surprisingly, he managed to force a smile. "You used to ask Cui Zhongshi about such things... Now I'm afraid you'll have to ask Governor Fang himself..."

"Fair enough, take me and ask either of them!" Fang Meng'ao grabbed his broken arm and pulled him to the door.

Ma Hanshan's remark touched a sore spot with Fang Meng'ao who Ma Hanshan forgot was actually a fierce tiger. A fierce tiger shouldn't be provoked. As he was being roughly dragged out by Fang Meng'ao, Ma Hanshan realised that he could not fight him and instinctively went limp. Fang Meng'ao exerted so much force that he dragged him to the door with his feet sliding on the ground. Ma Hanshan held his right arm with his left hand but it didn't help alleviate the sharp pain that shot through his arm. He had no choice but to shout at the top of his lungs: "I didn't kill Cui Zhongshi!"

Ma's painful whining caused Fang Meng'ao to pause. When he turned around and looked at him again, there was no smile on his face and his eyes were red with indignation.

"Captain Fang, I know you are avenging Cui Zhongshi today, who was in charge of the accounts of the Citizens' Food Distribution Committee. But I'm not capable of murdering someone who is supposed to be a witness!"

Fang Meng'ao looked at him for a long time and smiled again. But it was a frightening smile. "When we made that bet, we agreed not to mention the Citizens' Food Distribution Committee or the murder case. You really shouldn't talk about it. Since you lost the bet, you should buy them dinner. They haven't eaten all day. C'mon."

Ma Hanshan closed his eyes and said: "Let go of me, I'll go with you anyway."

When Fang Meng'ao opened the small door of the warehouse, they heard the thunderous singing of the protesters outside the main entrance.

In unity, there's strength. In unity there's strength.

Under the burning sun outside the warehouse, many students and their professors were brave enough to sing the song which was banned outright by the KMT government although they were starving and indignant. Meanwhile, both the Kuomintang officials present on the site as well as the undercover agents of the CPC's Urban Works Department were shocked to realise that the situation had got out of control, especially when they found that the soldiers of the Fourth Corps deployed to the east side of the crowd had set up their machine guns on top of the trucks again and were pointing their rifles at the students who continued singing enthusiastically.

This strength is iron, this strength is steel.

On the command vehicle to the west side, Fang Mengwei, whose face was drenched with sweat, looked nervously at Li Yuqing standing on the sandbags next to the warehouse gate.

This strength is iron, this strength is steel.

Clad in his lieutenant general's uniform, Li Yuqing found himself soaked in sweat, more so than Fang Mengwei.

Fire on the fascists, all undemocratic institutions shall perish!

Liang Jinglun was also in the crowd that had gathered. For a moment, he almost forgot whether he belonged to the Communist Party or the Kuomintang. Xie Mulan stood beside him, holding his arm while singing loudly with tear-filled eyes!

Towards the sun, towards freedom, towards the New China which will shine in all its splendour.

Suddenly, Liang Jinglun felt a hand on his shoulder! Just as he was about to turn round, he heard a tense voice speaking sternly in his ear: "Stop singing! Protect the students!" It was Yan Chunming! He had completely ignored the fact that he might have his identity blown by squeezing his way through the crowd to where Liang Jinglun was so he could give him the instructions!

"Yes..." replied Liang Jinglun.

...This strength is steel, harder than iron, stronger than steel...

The anger had turned their inner turmoil into a volcanic eruption of soulful passion. It was like an upsurge that was a long time coming, with no one able to stop it.

Yan Chunming spoke into Liang Jinglun's ear amid the huge wave of protest: "Let's squeeze our way out, you and I, let's go to the gate to control the situation!" Liang Jinglun had no choice but to comply. "But we can't afford to get you exposed. I'll go with you. Move!" Liang Jinglun elbowed his way out of the madly singing throng. Meanwhile, several male students formed a guardrail around the two while pushing their way forward. Among them were some progressive students of the Peking Students' Union, as well as the spy students of Chiang Kai-shek Student Society.

"Don't follow me!" Liang Jinglun tried to shake off Xie Mulan's hands tightly holding his arm as he squeezed his way out. Xie Mulan, however, held him even closer with both of her hands, her eyes gleaming with passion while she belted out the iconic lyrics:

Towards the New China which will shine in all its splendour......

Liang Jinglun had no choice but to take her and push forward together. Suddenly, the voice became weaker, and the crowd also became quiet. Liang Jinglun immediately became alert. He grasped Xie Mulan's hand and halted where they were. The student guards around him also stopped. They followed the surging crowd and looked out towards the big iron gate of the warehouse. It turned out that Li Yuqing had stepped down from the top of the sandbags, to be replaced by Fang Meng'ao and Ma Hanshan! The singing crowd was stunned into silence as Fang Meng'ao was seen standing side by side with Ma Hanshan by countless eyes. Fang Meng'ao reached his hand out to Li Yuqing standing on the ground.

"Sir, please give me the loudspeaker."

"OK, OK." Li Yuqing, whose cap was held by his adjutant, was busy wiping the sweat from his brow with a handkerchief with one hand, but he managed to hand the loudspeaker over to Fang Meng'ao.

"My dear students!" Fang Meng'ao's voice emanated from the

loudspeaker into the void. He was greeted by countless pairs of expectant eyes, as well as vacant eyes. Lastly, several pairs of eyes reflecting complex emotions.

Liang Jinglun!

Xie Mulan!

Fang Mengwei!

As well as the special task battalion commander!

Yet none of the eyes were as complicated to decipher as those of He Xiaoyu who was looking at Fang Meng'ao from a distance. Fang Meng'ao held the loudspeaker in his left hand, with his right hand clutching Ma Hanshan's left hand. "Now, Deputy Director Ma of the Citizens' Food Distribution Committee has something to say to all of you." He shoved the loudspeaker into Ma Hanshan's left hand. Ma Hanshan, who had been completely subdued, asked in a low voice: "Now, with so many people, what do you want me to say? Huh, you tell me..."

"Just tell them about the treat!"

Ma Hanshan had to put the loudspeaker close to his mouth: "Students, officers. Just now... just now, I made a bet with Captain Fang." Everyone was surprised, yet the crowd became even quieter. Even Li Yuqing, who was wiping the sweat from his face, couldn't help looking at Ma Hanshan.

"I lost... I'm here to tell you I lost," Ma Hanshan shouted into the loudspeaker.

Then he put down the loudspeaker again and turned to Fang Meng'ao. "What do you want me to say next?"

"Go on."

Ma Hanshan spoke into the loudspeaker again: "Captain Fang said that whoever lost today, should invite all the students here to dinner..."

There was a little commotion in the crowd again. Ma Hanshan was quite aware of the dire situation he was facing today with the presence of Fang Meng'ao and so many students, plus the officers representing the Peking Field Headquarters. So he resorted to talking nonsense which he believed might help him muddle through. "I told Captain Fang that there is no restaurant in Peking large enough for so many people to eat dinner. Captain Fang told me to do a cash handout instead so that each and every one of you can pay for your dinner. So, I did some calculation. For instance, one student would have to spend a hundred and fifty thousand *fabi* for a meal, since we have so many people, it would cost us more than three billion *fabi*. More than three billion yuan, my dear students! I swear I don't have that much money. But I lost, I'm willing to admit my loss. So, you can eat me instead!"

The crowd, which had been in some sort of commotion before, fell silent again, baffled by Ma Hanshan's nonsense. However, it took them no longer than a second before they burst out loud: "Stop fooling around!"

Once again, the clamour began: "Oppose fooling around!"

"Oppose oppression!"

"Oppose hunger!"

"Oppose corruption!"

"Oppose civil war!"

At this point, Ma Hanshan attempted to jump off from the top of the sandbags. Fang Meng'ao was quick to seize him again, and yelled into his ear: "Appease the students!"

Ma Hanshan had to put the speaker to his mouth again: "Please calm down! Please calm down..."

His appeal was met with a loud roar.

Li Yuqing's face, which was already pale with anger, now looked even more pale! He had been ordered to come and appease the students that day. Yet he had failed to fulfil his promise. He was feeling rather frustrated when all of a sudden, Ma Hanshan appeared to pour fuel on the fire so inexplicably that he couldn't help but shiver with indignation. He said to the guard captain beside him: "Go and bust the mad bastard!" The captain of the guard waved his hand, two guards jumped on top of the sandbags and tried to hold him down, with one on each side of him. Ma Hanshan had to save himself and he struggled hard to keep his mouth close to the loudspeaker.

"Captain Fang! It's Captain Fang who forced me to say all these words! Students, now Captain Fang has important instructions. Hurry! Let's give him a warm welcome."

These words really worked. First of all, the two guards stopped dragging him. Instead, they just tried to hold him down and looked at Fang Meng'ao. And the students gradually became quiet again, with their eyes turning to Fang Meng'ao. Fang Meng'ao's grief, heightened by fear and despair, agony and loneliness, had reached its peak since Cui Zhongshi was brutally murdered. He knew that people from his organisation were in the crowd amounting to ten to twenty thousand people. From the moment when Cui Zhongshi denied that he was his CPC contact point, he had been expecting the organisation to connect with him in other ways, but his impatience prevented him from waiting. Today, on behalf of the investigation team of the Ministry of Defence, he not only forced the Kuomintang corruption group to confess to the people, but also sent a signal to his own organisation that he would be left to do whatever he decided to do on his own terms if he could not connect with the organisation or get specific instructions from it.

Fang Meng'ao grabbed the loudspeaker from Ma Hanshan, but nobody knew what he would say. He Xiaoyu looked particularly nervous. Because in her eyes stood the lonely Fang Meng'ao! She imagined seeing herself walking by Fang Meng'ao's side, standing shoulder to shoulder with him! But when she came around, she found Fang Meng'ao so far away from her as he was standing on top of the sandbags in front of the gate.

Hidden among the crowd of teachers, Old Liu managed to hide his nervousness. He appeared like a bystander, whereas Yan Chunming had been so keyed up that he became fatigued with the commotion. However, he was thinking more about how to survive the punishment of the organisation.

Fang Mengwei, who was standing on top of his police command car, was the first to know the double identity of his elder brother. But he chose to close his eyes at the moment when he was supposed to alert in order to keep the situation under control. There was also a pair of eyes that looked very perplexed and gloomy. These were the eyes of Liang Jinglun who tried to get the students out of his way so that he could look straight into Fang Meng'ao's eyes, and wait for Fang Meng'ao's eyes to meet his; he intended that Fang Meng'ao would recognise him as the comrade representing the Communist Party he had been searching for!

"Just now," said Fang Meng'ao through the loudspeaker, "Deputy Director Ma said two things. One is that I made a bet with him to invite you all to dinner, while the other is that I'm going to give important instructions in my capacity as captain of the Youth Aviation Brigade. I don't understand that. How can a person give important instructions to tens of thousands of people while gambling with another person? I guess there are only two possibilities: one is that I am a madman, the other is that he is a liar! Now that the representative of the vice-president, Officer Li Yuqing, is here, I want to ask why the Investigation Group of the Ministry of Defence sent me to Peking to investigate the case knowing I am a lunatic! If Deputy Director Ma is a liar, why does the national government put him in charge of distributing food and grain to two million residents? It's a life-saving job, isn't it?"

The closely-packed ranks of the crowd had a hard time responding to Captain Fang's sudden confession, having only just tried digesting Ma Hanshan's irresponsible talk. But after a short while there was a reaction from the crowd gathered on the concourse.

"Spot on!"

"Well said!"

"Carry on!"

All of a sudden, the students who had been angry and anxious for the whole day became animated again, some even began to cheer followed by thunderous applause. Fang Meng'ao, however, as if in a no-man's land, stood there alone with the loudspeaker in his hand. He waited until the crowd fell silent again.

He looked into the distant void and spoke also as if into the void through his loudspeaker. "I'm sorry, my dear students, especially those from the Northeast, for I just said something I didn't understand myself. But one thing I do understand is that I share the same feeling as you do, which is of abandonment. Without family, no one cares about you as children! You, my compatriots from the Northeast, you lost your homes after the Eighteenth of September Incident... I lost mine after the thirteenth of August. But as recently as three years ago, we won the War of Resistance Against Japanese Aggression and we, the Republic of China, have also ratified our own constitution. Why are so many people still left homeless?"

Xie Mulan's eyes glistened with tears while it was hard to see Fang Mengwei's eyes as they were hidden under the brim of his police cap. Many familiar scenes appeared before He Xiaoyu's eyes, including the first time when Fang Meng'ao had asked her about the Communist Party in Xie Mulan's room; when Fang Meng'ao was having fried bread slices in her home for the first time; when she saw Fang Meng'ao's laundry in a bucket in his separate bedroom in the barracks; when Fang Meng'ao sang *The Virgin Mary* and when Fang Meng'ao helped Fang Buting walk out of the drawing room.

Nobody had any idea when Fang Buting's car had arrived at the scene of the protest and parked behind the Army Fourth Corps' convoys. Fang Buting was sitting quietly in the back seat. Sitting next to him was Zeng Keda. Fang Meng'ao's words were echoing in Fang Buting's ears and sounded like a nightmare. "You don't have a home... I don't have one either..." He turned to look out of the window from which he saw the soldiers and military vehicles of the Fourth Corps.

Zeng Keda put his hand on the back of Fang Buting's hand. He was waiting for him to turn around and understood that he was meant to comfort him. But instead, Fang Buting slowly took Zeng's hand off his. "General Zeng, you may get out of the car now. I'm going home."

The look of consolation in Zeng Keda's eyes disappeared. He sat there motionless.

"Open the door and help General Zeng out," Fang Buting told the driver.

"Don't bother." Zeng Keda opened the door himself, got out of the car and closed the door behind him.

Fang Meng'ao's voice emanated from the loudspeaker again. "Students, don't wait here, this is not your home."

"Home!" demanded Fang Buting. The car reversed, then turned around and headed homeward.

Fang Meng'ao was still speaking, but Fang Buting couldn't hear a word.

Fang Buting entered his living room as if he was venturing into the wilderness. As usual, the servants shunned him, except for Cheng Xiaoyun who was watching him with concern. Fang Buting ignored her. Nor did he walk to the washstand to wash his face first, as usual. Neither did he go over to sit on the sofa, as he did when he was tired. Instead, he walked over to the piano, which had been moved into the living room a few days before, and sat down on the bench. Strangely, he just sat there without lifting the cover. Cheng Xiaoyun walked over gently. Knowing that she should not say anything at that moment, she stretched her hand to the piano cover and looked at Fang Buting. She was about to open it when Fang Buting gently pressed down the piano cover from which Cheng Xiaoyun had to withdraw her hand.

"I've fixed you some congee. I'll go and get it for you."

She turned around and was about to go to the kitchen when Fang Buting asked from behind her: "Where's Peidong?"

"He went to negotiate with the two companies. He said he'd try to secure more grain in a couple of days. You want me to call him back?"

"Don't." Fang Buting looked away from her and continued: "At present, he is the only one who can really help me in this family."

"You're right. Apart from you, only Peidong in this family can help you, plus your two sons." Cheng Xiaoyun still had her back to him.

Fang Buting didn't utter a word.

"I know," said Cheng Xiaoyun, sounding a little hesitant. "I've never been a member of this family. Neither has Mulan. There should never be a place for women in Fang Buting's house."

Fang Buting raised his head sadly and looked at her. "Come."

Cheng Xiaoyun didn't turn around. Fang Buting sighed and held her hands from behind her.

"You haven't answered me yet." Cheng Xiaoyun tried to pull her hands back. Fang Buting held them tightly.

"Look at me, I'll answer you." Cheng Xiaoyun had to turn around slowly.

The cicadas were chirping loudly outside the living room and the house looked even more serene.

"Do you hear it?" Fang Buting asked, obviously not referring to the cicadas' chirping.

"Hear what?"

"Meng'ao speaking..."

Cheng Xiaoyun looked into this tough old man's eyes and found them sparkling with tears. Fang Buting turned his face to the door. "The students from the Northeast took to the streets again. It was quite a scene. Vice-President Li's deputy spoke to appease them but to no avail. But when Meng'ao spoke, all the students fell silent. In fact, he hasn't engaged in public speaking since he was a child..."

Sensing Fang Buting's anguish, Cheng Xiaoyun asked him softly: "What did he end up saying?"

"It doesn't matter what he said," replied Fang Buting. "Darling, listen to me. The Republic of China has come to an end. Our family has come to an end. My career has come to an end. My two sons will be stranded here. Peidong has to stay and help me clean up the mess. Only you can leave. Take Mulan with you to Hong Kong in a few days..."

Cheng Xiaoyun took back her hands and suddenly cradled Fang Buting's head in her arms as if he were a child, something Cheng Xiaoyun had never dared to do since they were married. Fang Buting instinctively tried to keep his usual reserve but Cheng Xiaoyun held his head so tightly that he was not able to move. He just let her have her way. Both of them were listening to the chirping of cicadas in the garden.

"You haven't promised me yet."

Fang Buting gently held Cheng Xiaoyun's hands and moved his head away from her chest.

"Promised you what?" A smile appeared at the corner of Cheng Xiaoyun's mouth as tears welled up in her eyes. "Meng'ao and Mengwei, those two rebellious sons of yours, now call me mum but they have no terms of endearment for you or their uncle. What a shame for you two old buddies! You can't even control your own children, so how can you tell me to leave at this critical moment? Are you still thinking I married you for your money, as Mengwei suggested?"

Fang Buting looked at her for a while and a smile lit up his face. "Even the most virtuous stepmother would hold a grudge." Quickly, he opened the piano cover. "I haven't accompanied you on the piano since we left Chongqing. Come on, please sing our favourite before the two boys get home. Too bad they recognise you as their mother but not me as their father."

Cheng Xiaoyun took his hand and said: "Perhaps, it'd be better to find out where Peidong is first. Maybe he has secured a better deal on more grain. At least, we'll be in a better position to talk to Meng'ao when he confronts you."

"Grain is planted, not spirited up out of thin air," retorted Fang Buting. "He's not Plutus." He raised his hands stubbornly and pressed down on the keys. From the piano keys flowed the interlude of *"Blooming Flowers, Full Moon."*

As the music of *Blooming Flowers, Full Moon* on the piano echoed through the soulless Mao'er Hutong neighbourhood, a rickshaw entered an alleyway in a different neighbourhood and stopped in front of a courtyard house. Xie Peidong was in the rickshaw covered by a parasol. He was wearing his tunic and sunglasses. He picked up his bag, closed his fan and got out of the rickshaw. The gate of the courtyard opened for him then instantly closed behind him.

"Comrade Peidong!" Just as Xie Peidong took off his sunglasses, someone inside the courtyard shook his hand warmly. "Comrade Yueyin!" Xie Peidong immediately went up to him, his bag in his right hand, and held the man's hands warmly in his.

From the living room on the ground floor of Fang's house came the music played by Fang Buting on the piano and Cheng Xiaoyun singing:

> *The floating scattered clouds,*
> *The bright moon shines on the arriving people.*
> *Today is the happiest reunion.*

The piano and the song, both seemed to be performed for the

reunion of Xie Peidong and Comrade Yueyin. Comrade Yueyin, who was in his late twenties, held Xie Peidong's hands tightly with one hand and used the other to take Xie Peidong's briefcase. Comrade Yueyin, whose full name was Zhang Yueyin, was head of the CPC's Urban Works Department in Peking.

"Regarding the death of Comrade Zhongshi, your situation and that of Comrade Fang Meng'ao, Comrade Liu has reported to me and my supervisors. Let's go inside and talk." Zhang Yueyin walked side by side with Xie Peidong to the north wing room.

The sound of Fang Buting's piano playing and Cheng Xiaoyun's singing continued to emanate from the living room on the ground floor of Fang's house:

> *In pairs, the spouses share a mutual love.*
> *This soft wind blows upon the beautiful flowers,*
> *Blowing on the good flowers,*
> *Full of the warmth and affection between the people.*

Before the singing came to an end, the piano playing had stopped. Silence fell again.

"Wash your face, please," said Cheng Xiaoyun. "I'll go and get you some congee."

"Indeed, it's time to eat!" Fang Buting stood up quickly. "My eldest son is sure to come and question me any time soon. I must conserve some strength to confront him." With that, he moved to the table.

In the north room of the courtyard house in Mao'er Hutong, there was a square table. While there were no chairs on the side facing the door, there were three chairs arranged at both ends and opposite the table. Instead of taking the head seat, Zhang Yueyin sat in the one on the west side, facing Xie Peidong. From the next room came what vaguely sounded like a radio transmitter. Zhang Yueyin bent over with his arms on the table to get as close as possible to Xie Peidong. His voice soft and powerful, he said: "Comrade Fang Meng'ao's aviation brigade and underground resistance in the banking sector in Peking under your leadership are more important than ever to us. The CPC North China Bureau and even the CPC Central Committee have been following your work very closely." He paused for a moment. "My higher-ups are very upset about Comrade Zhongshi's death..."

"I hold myself accountable for his death." Xie Peidong, who had never been emotional, could no longer hide his agony before Comrade Yueyin.

"Let's not talk about who is responsible now," said Zhang Yueyin, interrupting him. "We've lost Comrade Zhongshi but we can't afford to have similar tragic accidents happen again, not to you or Comrade Fang Meng'ao. Today, I'm going to discuss with you two important issues which are closely related to you and Comrade Fang. One is how to deal with the new currency system the Kuomintang is likely to launch very soon. The other is how to reconnect with Comrade Fang Meng'ao who is supposed to coordinate a concerted revolt by his brigade at a critical time in the near future."

Nobody knew when the guards had taken Ma Hanshan down from the sandbags in front of the gate of the general storage warehouse of the Peking Citizens' Food Distribution Committee, leaving Fang Meng'ao and Li Yuqing standing on top of the sandbags. With the loudspeaker in his hands, Li Yuqing was addressing the last question: "On behalf of Vice-President Li and Commander-in-Chief Fu, I also promise to solve the fifth question you raised."

With Li Yuqing's promise, the student protesters, who had been suffering hunger and thirst from early morning to late afternoon, began to feel excited about their hard-earned victory. Some in the crowd started to cheer but were quickly stopped by other students. By then, they had accepted Li Yuqing by association with Fang Meng'ao. Li Yuqing continued: "The accounts of the committee will be checked thoroughly by the government authorities. They're also subject to public supervision during the process. Therefore, on behalf of Vice-President Li and Commander-in-Chief Fu, I agree that all universities should send their representatives to form a joint inspection team to cooperate with Captain Fang and his Youth Aviation Brigade!"

"Hail!" Some cheered in the crowd.

"Hail!"

"Hail!"

The loud cheering for victory resounded through the Peking dusk. Li Yuqing also became excited but the initial excitement was soon replaced by nervousness. He shouted: "Be quiet! Please be quiet..." The cheering died down.

"Now, let me invite Captain Fang to announce the list of the joint team members." Thunderous applause broke out from the crowd as the loudspeaker was passed to Fang Meng'ao. Surprisingly, Fang Meng'ao appeared so timid that he remained silent for a while. The excited eyes remained excited. The nervous eyes still remained tense.

It was a different kind of tension in Liang Jinglun's eyes as there were several male students hanging around, waiting for him to give instructions. Liang Jinglun stretched out his hand and many hands immediately stretched out and were folded onto his palm. Liang Jinglun pushed away some students' hands with his other hand, with four pairs of hands left on his palm. Two of them belonged to the backbone students of the Peking Students' Union, while the other two were those of the spy students of the Chiang Kai-shek Student Society!

There was a strong sense of anxiety in Xie Mulan's eyes. While holding Liang Jinglun's arm, she tugged hard on his sleeve but Liang Jinglun did not respond. Xie Mulan looked anxiously into He Xiaoyu's eyes which looked equally anxious. She switched her gaze to Fang Meng'ao and began to look at the two strange male students who were supposed to protect her. The two students exchanged a look and one of them nodded firmly. The one who was assigned to protect He Xiaoyu whispered in her ear: "Let's move."

He Xiaoyu did not dare look back but heard Fang Meng'ao's voice from the loudspeaker: "I'd like to know which one of you are economics majors..."

Countless students responded by raising their hands from under the banners of Peking University, Tsinghua University, Yenching University and Peking Normal University. While under the banner of the Northeast student petition groups, almost all the students raised their hands!

Fang Meng'ao looked at Li Yuqing who immediately whispered: "How many people do you need at most?"

"There are twenty people in my brigade. Give me one person for each of them."

"Then we'll need twenty people," replied Li Yuqing.

Fang Meng'ao put the loudspeaker to his mouth again: "We only need twenty people. Please recommend four students each from Northeast China, Peking University, Tsinghua University, Yenching University and Peking Normal University." The crowd immediately became excited!

"Let me join them!" pleaded Xie Mulan to Liang Jinglun under the banner of Yenching University, holding his arm tightly. Liang Jinglun gave her an angry look, then stared at her hands. Xie Mulan timidly let go of him. Liang Jinglun turned to a member of the students' union. "Hurry up, find He Xiaoyu."

The students' union guy turned round, looked up and squeezed into the crowd. His eyes swept over the crowd but He Xiaoyu was nowhere to be found.

Nobody knew when Zeng Keda took the passenger seat of a truck parked to the east side of the garrison headquarters after he got out of Fang Buting's car. At first, he sat huddled in the cab before sitting up straight as he saw Liang Jinglun and Xie Mulan under the Yenching University banner and several other students of the Chiang Kai-shek Student Society who had once escorted him by bike. A casual smile crossed his face.

Meanwhile, in the north room of the courtyard house in Mao'er Hutong, the silence was broken by the following words: "The documents you've submitted are very important."

The blue-headed document had four big characters printed on it in bold traditional style, "Central Bank", while the top right corner of the letterhead bore the two characters "Top Secret", printed in black ink with imitation Song Dynasty-style typeface.

"Xiao Wang!" Zhang Yueyin called out to the room next door. The door opened and out came a young man who, though dressed casually, raised his hand politely to Xie Peidong.

"Hello, sir!" he said and then went over to Zhang Yueyin.

Zhang Yueyin handed the document to him and said: "Send the full text to the headquarters of the Urban Works Department of the North China Bureau."

"Yes sir." Wang quickly walked back into the room with the papers and closed the door behind him.

"The state coffers are almost empty, prices are spiralling out of control and speculation is rampant!" Zhang Yueyin repeated these words written in the document from rote memory. "Zhang Gongquan best summed up the reasons why Chiang Kai-shek was eager to issue the gold yuan notes and correctly pointed to the fact that it was impossible to issue these notes now. By the way, Mr Xie." He suddenly switched from Xie Peidong to Mr Xie, apparently needing his advice on some particular financial issues. "With all due respect, when do you predict the gold yuan notes will be issued at the soonest, according to this document?"

"It could happen within a month or two weeks at the latest," replied Xie Peidong.

Zhang Yueyin nodded. "Since Zhang Gongquan is opposed to the issuance of gold yuan notes, why did Chiang Kai-shek seek his advice at this sensitive moment? And circulate his opinions among those at all branches of the Central Bank? Zhang was the former governor, anyway."

"Chiang Kai-shek is sending a signal to the United States that he has a dilemma. His goal is to secure American assistance. Without USAID as a reserve fund, it would be suicidal for them to issue the gold yuan notes," noted Xie Peidong authoritatively.

"Brilliant. What actions do you think they will take in Peking to help secure the USAID?"

"Yenching University, John Leighton Stuart. The White House and Congress are deeply divided over whether to aid the Chiang Kai-shek regime or not. In China, Ambassador Stuart's attitude is crucial. They are doing all they can to get Stuart's support."

"Who can influence Leighton Stuart?"

"Professor He Qicang."

"And who can influence Professor He Qicang?"

"Fang Buting should be the one."

Zhang Yueyin interrupted Xie Peidong for the first time during their conversation. He stood up abruptly. "There is another person whose identity seems to be so well guarded that we'll have to talk about him today!"

Meanwhile, outside the gate of the general storage warehouse of the Peking Citizens' Food Distribution Committee, Xie Mulan shouted: "Liang Jinglun!" She didn't know how she'd plucked up the courage to call out his name so loudly. She became nervous as soon as she'd done it and looked timidly at Liang Jinglun. The crowd was still surging forward but Liang Jinglun slowly pushed aside Xie Mulan's hands.

"Permit me to join them. I know more than they do about the inner workings of the system," said Xie Mulan.

Liang Jinglun looked towards the gate of the warehouse where Fang Meng'ao and his twenty pilots were lined up in front of the sandbags, while on top of the sandbags stood the twenty student candidates. They stood in a row on the sandbags, each raising their clenched fists.

"And me!" Xie Mulan had already pushed her way through the crowd and rushed towards the gate! Fang Mengwei was the first to see her, his eyes filled with astonishment. He looked at Xie Mulan, who was running to her cousin Fang Meng'ao, and immediately turned his eyes to Liang Jinglun who was standing under the banner of Yenching University! With a surprised look on his face, Liang Jinglun looked at Xie Mulan's back. Fang Meng'ao also saw her approaching. With mixed feelings in his eyes, he looked at Guo Jinyang beside him and then immediately turned to Shao Yuangang and barked: "Stop her." Shao Yuangang, who was as tall as a giraffe, strode towards Xie Mulan.

"What did Comrade Liu tell you about Liang Jinglun?" asked Zhang Yueyin calmly in the north room of the courtyard house in Mao'er Hutong. But Xie Peidong had discerned Liu's concern from his tone of voice. Zhang was equally concerned with Old Liu's approach to his job!

With a solemn expression on his face, Xie Peidong asked: "Comrade Liu only conveyed the instructions of the higher-ups. He told me to persuade He Xiaoyu to listen to Liang Jinglun and to approach Fang Meng'ao as a member of the Student Union. As for why the organisation has made such arrangements, Comrade Liu didn't tell me, and it wouldn't have been right for me to enquire further."

Zhang Yueyin nodded and looked even more solemn.

"It's not that the organisation doesn't trust you, it's that Comrade Liu doesn't have the authority. Comrade Peidong, on behalf of the Urban Works Department, I want to tell you an inconvenient truth, namely, that Liang Jinglun is probably an undercover agent of the Kuomintang who has infiltrated our party! He's also a core member of the Iron and Blood Congress and poses the greatest threat to you and Comrade Meng'ao!"

Xie Peidong was so shocked to learn this that he almost got up from his seat. He stared at Zhang Yueyin in total astonishment. He wanted to ask but all he could do was wait for Zhang Yueyin to tell him what he was entitled to know.

However, Zhang Yueyin fell silent again and asked: "Do you happen to have any cigarettes on you?"

Xie Peidong was struggling to adjust his state of mind but managed to reply: "I don't smoke."

Zhang Yueyin smiled apologetically. "Sorry, I don't smoke either." Then he picked up the teapot on the table and topped up Xie Peidong's cup. "Perhaps I shouldn't say this but it's a matter of life and death, so I must tell you. Mr Xie, I trust that you're well prepared to handle it."

Xie Peidong felt compelled to respond with a calm smile. "You're my superior, I can't very well ask you when you joined the party. I joined the CPC in 1927 when our party was caught in a time of crisis. Trust me, please."

The respect in Zhang Yueyin's eyes proved to be true and

sincere. "Let me report to you as a junior member of the party. We found out about Liang Jinglun too late. In fact, we didn't become alarmed until after Zeng Keda and Comrade Fang Meng'ao's aviation brigade had arrived in Peking. The CPC Student Committee at Yenching should be held largely responsible for the mistake. Thanks to our vigilance, we launched a covert investigation through Comrade Liu. His identity was confirmed a few days ago. Actually it was confirmed on the very night Comrade Cui Zhongshi was murdered."

"Was he behind Comrade Zhongshi's death?" Xie Peidong finally asked.

"No, he wasn't," confirmed Zhang Yueyin. Then, without looking at Xie Peidong, he said: "That night, when Fang Mengwei rushed to save Cui Zhongshi from He Xiaoyu's place, your daughter went to Liang Jinglun's place."

Xie Peidong jumped to his feet.

Zhang Yueyin stood up. "Comrade Zhongshi's death has nothing to do with your daughter. But Mulan was with Liang Jinglun the whole night."

Xie Peidong closed his eyes. Zhang Yueyin tried to remain calm. "According to those sent by Comrade Liu to keep watch over them, Liang Jinglun and Mulan have been lovers." Xie Peidong suddenly opened his eyes again. This time, he did not look at Zhang Yueyin but stared blankly ahead.

"Liang Jinglun was supposed to be in love with Comrade He Xiaoyu," Zhang Yueyin continued, "but after He Xiaoyu was sent to contact Comrade Fang Meng'ao, he quickly developed a romantic relationship with Mulan. Absolutely, members of the party in charge of the Student Union should never do such a thing! How confused Comrade Yan Chunming was! Although Liang Jinglun reported to him afterwards, explaining that the relationship with Mulan was a cover, namely, the romantic relationship with Mulan was to assist He Xiaoyu who was working on Fang Meng'ao. It's ridiculous that Comrade Yan Chunming believed it, while knowing that it was without the prior approval of the organisation. It actually seriously violates the principles of the organisation."

"I'm also very confused," murmured Xie Peidong,

"Well, none of this has anything to do with you, Mr Xie.

Anyway, I have more important oral instructions for you. Please sit down and have some tea first." Zhang Yueyin picked up the tea cup in front of him and handed it over to him across the table. Xie Peidong took the cup with both hands and sat down slowly. Then he put it back on the table and looked at Zhang Yueyin intently.

Zhang Yueyin was still standing.

"There's plenty of room left for self-criticism of our performance at the Urban Works Department. For example, Comrade Liu asked you to contact He Xiaoyu. The Peking Student Committee under the CPC did not fully implement the spirit of Comrade Peng Zhen's speech on the sixth of July. We were still struck by inertia, we didn't try to evacuate the progressive students to the liberated area, nor did we control the students' extreme actions during this period, resulting in senseless loss of life among the students. The reason was that many of us were carried away by the fact that our troops had won one strategic victory after another in the front line. To put it mildly, it's an excess of revolutionary zeal or, to put it harshly, it's the fanaticism of the petty bourgeoisie. They want to outperform themselves before the upcoming final victory and take more credit after our takeover. Both Yan Chunming and Old Liu are standouts with this kind of thinking, which is very dangerous. Not long ago, Chairman Mao said: 'I'm never afraid of failure, but I'm afraid of victory!' What he said is quite true. Vice-Chairman Zhou Enlai and other central leaders also elaborated on this issue, the most important of which is that we have only experience in rural revolution but lack experience in urban development, especially in building and managing cities after taking them over. Comrade Peidong, comrades like you, including a large number of progressive students, are valuable assets for us to build and manage cities after taking them over. Next, there are two main tasks for you. The first is to closely follow the implementation of gold yuan notes by the Kuomintang through the Peking branch. The second is to assist Comrade He Xiaoyu in contacting Comrade Fang Meng'ao. Specifically, according to the organisation's instructions, you should continue to secure the implicit trust of Fang Buting in order to better conceal your identity as well as the identities of Comrade He Xiaoyu and Fang Meng'ao. Fang Buting may ask you to do what Comrade Cui Zhongshi used to do in the past. The organisation fully understands this. As for other related matters, including your personal matters, we'll make separate arrangements. Don't be distracted by your daughter getting mixed up with Liang Jinglun. The student committee will have her transferred to the liberated areas at the right time when they see fit."

Xie Peidong heard him out quietly, stood up and said gratefully: "I will comply with the organisation's decision and thank you for all you've done on my behalf."

It was starting to get dark both inside and outside the room.

"Now, you'll have to excuse me as I'm scheduled to meet with Comrade Liu." Zhang Yueyin held out his hand across the table. "You can't stay here long. Regarding the grain transported by the two companies to Peking, the North China Field Army Headquarters has ordered the PLA not to intercept them. You can tell Fang Buting subtly that they are due to arrive tomorrow."

Xie Peidong was stunned as soon as he entered the gate.

"It's my freedom, you have no right to interfere with it!" shouted Xie Mulan from the living room of the house. There was no response.

Xie Peidong looked at the gatekeeper who lowered his head slightly and said softly: "Your daughter and the second young master are bickering. Assistant Manager, the master and his wife are waiting for you in the bamboo grove."

Xie Peidong looked east toward the bamboo grove where he found that the lights along the path were on and the bamboo cast a deep and serene shadow.

"Uncle Peidong!" Cheng Xiaoyun greeted him warmly. She took Xie Peidong's bag and looked at his face. Xie Peidong, as usual, politely bowed his head and walked over to Fang Buting sitting on the stone bench. Fang Buting didn't get up. Although the light was dim, Xie Peidong could still clearly see the bitter smile on his face.

"Did you hear that? They are quarrelling again."

"They laugh here, they cry here and they gather as family here," replied Xie Peidong with a faint smile. "How can we not quarrel with such a large family under the same roof?"

159

"Times are changing. Do you happen to know why Mulan and Mengwei are quarrelling?" Fang Buting didn't smile.

Xie Peidong didn't either. He had to wait for him to say it.

Fang Buting looked at the top of the bamboo above the lamp and said: "Meng'ao's managed to put together some twenty students from several universities to set up a task force to help with the investigation. Now, of course, their target is the Citizens' Food Distribution Committee, but eventually it will come to investigate me at the Peking branch. Mulan also wants to join in. My son and your daughter, they will come to investigate us. Peidong, are you doing OK with the accounts?"

Xie Peidong was shocked to learn this, and that particular name immediately came to his mind. It was Liang Jinglun. This time, however, he smiled while looking at Cheng Xiaoyun. "The governor is getting old."

Fang Buting turned to look at him.

"Even those economics professors from Peking University wouldn't be able to find anything wrong with the accounts of the Peking branch, let alone Meng'ao and Mulan. In addition, Governor, what Meng'ao intends to check are accounts concerning the grain to be allocated by the Citizens' Food Distribution Committee. By the way, the nine hundred tons which the committee is supposed to distribute and the six thousand tons for the next two weeks will be delivered tomorrow."

Fang Buting jumped to his feet. "Tomorrow? Via the Peking-Tianjin railway only?"

"Of course not."

Fang Buting immediately became alert and asked: "Did you contact the CPC through your personal network?"

"There was no need for me to personally contact anybody. There are more than a million people in Peking, including so many celebrities and students. As long as we plant the banner 'Citizens' Food' on it, the Communist troops will not stop us delivering it."

Fang Buting thought for a while and said: "It can't be that simple, can it?"

"It shouldn't be that complicated," countered Xie Peidong.

"You know little about politics. If the six thousand tons of grain can be transported to Peking from the regions controlled by the

Communist troops, someone must have made a secret deal with the Communist Party! I guess the CPC is doing Li Zongren a favour. The president, the vice-president; the troops he favours and those he doesn't; from Li Zongren and Fu Zuoyi to a mere air force colonel, the agents of the Communist Party, they are wrestling hard for it. Chiang Kai-shek can't fight Mao Zedong and the Iron and Blood Congress can't fight the forces of the Communist underground. That stubborn son of mine has been so deeply involved; Peidong, you can't allow Mulan to get mixed up in this. I've spoiled her and Mengwei can't persuade her. Go and tell her that she must remain in her room from today on."

Xie Peidong hadn't expected to get support from Fang Buting to solve the problem that his organisation couldn't. He replied: "It's about time. I'm going to go and discipline her. But Governor, please don't interfere by playing nice."

"Let's go and visit Cui Zhongshi's wife and children first. Tonight, we will stay in your courtyard house."

Xie Peidong stopped there on his toes just as he was walking into the living room. He was struck by what he saw as his daughter was standing in front of the stairs, with Mengwei hugging her from behind. Xie Mulan was motionless, neither resisting nor accepting Mengwei. Fang Mengwei did not make any move either. A view of his back allowed Xie Peidong to see that he was almost in despair.

A hesitant Xie Peidong also looked quite gloomy and forlorn.

"Dad." Xie Mulan actually knew that his father was at the door. "Tell my cousin to let go of me."

Fang Mengwei had released his hands but was still standing there numbly.

Xie Mulan went up the stairs. Xie Peidong slowly walked up to Fang Mengwei from behind. "What does she want?"

"She just won't stay at home any more. Uncle, let her go," replied Fang Mengwei, without turning back.

"Go where?" asked Xie Peidong, raising his voice. "No, she's going nowhere!"

Fang Mengwei turned around with an unusual look in his eyes which Xie Peidong had never seen before. "Really, I'm not speaking to her today on behalf of the Kuomintang against the Communist Party. But what I know is that the man Mulan is falling for is evil."

Fang Mengwei was shocked by the horrified look in Xie Peidong's eyes. "Uncle, Liang Jinglun is a very sinister man, you have to believe me."

"Both of you are really underhand!" yelled Xie Mulan, suddenly rushing out of the room with some clothes in her hand. She stood beside the railing on the first floor, looking very emotional. "Deputy Commissioner Fang, you have a police force under your command. You also have troops at your disposal from the garrison headquarters. Just fix Professor Liang with a crime and put him behind bars on the charge of his affiliation with the Communist Party. If that happens, I won't see him any more. Go and bust him!"

Xie Peidong reacted harshly. "What nonsense! When did Mengwei do such a thing? There is no Communist Party or Kuomintang in this house. And no room for dirty politics under this roof!"

"Then what makes my cousin say he's a bad guy? What did he do wrong? Is he a murderer, or is he involved in corruption like some people are?" It was amazing to see Xie Mulan talk back to her father today. Previously, she had always been afraid of him.

"If he didn't kill or embezzle, then why do you have to defend him like this?" Xie Peidong asked.

"He is my teacher," said Xie Mulan, freezing momentarily.

"He is still Professor He's student and the future son-in-law that Professor He has longed for! Girl, you have been wilful since childhood, which I don't care for. But this time, if you continue down this road, the first person you will hurt is Xiaoyu! God forbid!"

"What did I do?" replied Xie Mulan instinctively, but sounding so flimsy that she was aware that what she was saying was indefensible. Her face turned pale and she trembled a little. The words emanating from her father's mouth pierced her heart like a dagger. Her mind went blank, her vision blurred. Suddenly, she collapsed beside the railing on the first floor.

"Mulan!" Fang Mengwei ran up the stairs.

"Leave her!" Xie Peidong called out, resentfully. "She deserves it."

CHAPTER 7

It was just getting dark. Yan Chunming had never felt so exhausted as he did today. Yet he walked all the way from the reading room to the door of the rare books section without turning on the light.

The reading room doors in the library had built-in circular locks, except for the door to the rare books room which had an additional steel padlock. Yan Chunming first fumbled to open the padlock but when he inserted another key into the round dormant lock, he suddenly had a premonition and became alerted to something unusual. His instinct was accurate. As he turned the key gently, the door opened with a crack through which multiple rays of light shot out. Someone must be inside. No matter who was inside, he had no choice but to open the door. "This is the rare books section. How did you get in? Who told you to go in?"

The 15-Watt light bulb was turned on and the clock hand on the wall pointed to 8.14 pm. The man viewed from behind was busy sorting out and dusting books in front of the bookshelf. Yan Chunming was so shortsighted that he still didn't recognise the man.

"Professor Yan," said the man eventually.

Yan Chunming recognised the man's voice, which made him even more surprised not to have recognised him until now. The man turned around, it was Old Liu. Although the light was not that bright, his eyes were brighter than the light. Yan Chunming did not know how he closed the door but found his hands were shaking. He did his best to compose himself, which he managed to do when he turned round. "Comrade Liu…"

"Why! Did I make you feel more nervous than when seeing the Kuomintang military agents? Were you calling me Master Five again in your mind?"

"No, no… You shouldn't be here. It's too dangerous." Yan Chunming went over to pour tea for him.

"Sit down, please, and have some tea." Liu had already picked up the porcelain pot on the table and poured tea for him first. "Even if they did come, the Kuomintang special agents wouldn't arrive at this hour of the night."

Yan Chunming was more nervous. He didn't sit. He didn't dare to sit.

"First, allow me to make a suggestion to you on behalf of the organisation and, of course, also on behalf of myself. Don't call me Master Five! I'm a member of the CPC. Our party is a vanguard of the proletariat, not a secret society of gangsters. I'm not the Master Five under the red flag." Old Liu wiped the table slowly.

"Comrade Liu… Some comrades have made such jokes occasionally behind your back. But let me assure you that no such thing will happen again."

"Then get on with today's thing!" Indeed, Old Liu did look like the five revolutionary leaders whose faces were stern and scary. "Joking with the lives of tens of thousands of students and the revolutionary cause of the party!"

Yan Chunming's face was whiter than ever.

"The revolutionary situation is indeed developing towards victory day by day. Yet it is hard-earned because countless numbers of our comrades at the front have shed their blood for us. Many of our comrades in the enemy-occupied areas have sacrificed their lives for us. Lastly, countless workers and peasants, including those progressive students today, have supported us. So don't get carried away by the victories we've achieved so far. If you want to have a career as an official after we win the war, don't join the Communist Party!"

"I wasn't even thinking about it…"

"I bet you weren't!" Old Liu pressed on with his criticism. "What

I said to you just now is what my superiors said when criticising me today. Do you want to know what I thought then?"

Yan Chunming fell silent.

After a short while, he replied: "I don't think you had such a thought."

"I said I had just now," Old Liu continued. "Why did you say I hadn't? It sounds a little embarrassing but it is perfectly normal for a revolutionary to join the ranks of officialdom to contribute more once we become the ruling party of the country. I'm no match for you in this regard, so I admit that, and I quote, I don't know who said that a soldier who doesn't want to be a marshal isn't a good one. Nevertheless, my superior was much more knowledgeable than I am. He didn't say what I quoted was wrong. Instead, he just told me that Napoleon said it. He also told me that he was quoting Vice-Chairman Zhou who recently criticised the senior leaders within the party for their selfish thoughts. That's what he told me, and I immediately made a self-criticism. It wasn't something I faked but something from the bottom of my heart. I reiterated my commitment to the liberation of the whole of China. If I am still alive on that day, I will ask the organisation's permission to let me go home and be a farmer. Now what do you think about that?"

"I know nothing about farming. I can continue teaching."

"You forget the premise of what I said, which is that you'll be able to survive the war!" Comrade Liu's tone suddenly became harsher. "You and Comrade Liang Jinglun were almost on top of the sandbags today. Do you think that was an act of heroism? It wasn't, that was a Napoleonic act of individualism. The Communist Party always acts collectively, one person can't make a hero! The Peking Student Committee of the CPC came within an ace of being exposed, so many progressive young people have been exposed! Did you worry about the safety of the organisation? Were you ever worried about the safety of the students? Many Kuomintang agents from the Bureau of Investigation were mixed up in the crowd. We had no idea who among our comrades or the young people of the students' union have been exposed. Do you worry about it? Now tell me, was it an act of spontaneity on the part of the students today or was it organised by members of the party?"

Yan Chunming kept his head down and then took out his handkerchief to wipe his sweat-covered head.

"As far as I know, the students from the Northeast quickly gathered when news broke of Fang Meng'ao's aviation brigade announcing their intention to take over the headquarters of the Citizens' Food Distribution Committee. They were very excited and students from various universities spontaneously rushed to support them."

"What were you thinking, all of you," asked Old Liu, "including Comrade Liang Jinglun and the members of the Student Committee's Yenching branch?"

"It happened so suddenly," replied Yan Chunming, sounding a little emotional, "that we felt it was our responsibility to control the situation and protect the students. Comrade Liang Jinglun was in a better position than us due to his relationship with He Qicang, so he went to Princess Hejing's mansion first. As you well know, we all went to the Citizens' Food Distribution Committee headquarters. The instructions you gave me at that time were to 'control the situation, to seek out the traitors, and to cover and protect the students'. Except for the second instruction, this is what was going through our minds beforehand and what guided our actions afterwards. As for today's incident, let me personally reassure you, it was purely an isolated incident. I really didn't find any hidden traitors inciting from within the organisation."

"How is Comrade Liang Jinglun doing now?" Old Liu asked.

"Does the organisation suspect Comrade Liang Jinglun?" Yan Chunming was shocked.

"I'm asking you how Comrade Liang Jinglun is doing now?" repeated Old Liu, raising his eyebrows. "Is he in some kind of danger?"

"Comrade Liang Jinglun is not in any danger, I can assure you," answered Yan Chunming, slowly regaining his composure.

"How can he not be in danger? How can you be so sure?" said Old Liu with his eyes blazing.

"So far, he has never exposed his identity. The Kuomintang authorities also remain wary of him being the favourite student and assistant to Professor He Qicang. They wouldn't upset Leighton Stuart by seizing him."

This time, Old Liu fell silent. With the stern look in his eyes slowly dissipating, he actually appeared quite concerned. "Comrade Peng Zhen's 'Sixth of July instruction' has been made known to us for nearly a month, the spirit of it being to conceal those who are the most capable and protect the students. Today, the leaders of the CPC North China Bureau have issued new instructions. They are calling a halt to all actions that may cause loss of life. Of course, it's very challenging to develop and suddenly reduce or even suspend the student movement. You and I have witnessed what happened today. Even if the Peking Student Committee had intended to stop organising things, it still would have been difficult to prevent the escalation of the student protests, given the students' spontaneous urge for political protest and the possibility that the corrupt forces and anti-corruption faction within the Kuomintang might use it to their advantage. As a result, more student lives would have been lost. After careful deliberation, we've come to our final decision, and that is to agree to the proposal made by Comrade Liang Jinglun to the party branch of Yenching University."

"To win Fang Meng'ao over to our side?" asked Yan Chunming, becoming excited again.

"Yes," confirmed Liu. "Fang Meng'ao and his aviation brigade's anti-corruption efforts have profoundly influenced the majority of the student body yet their endeavours have largely blurred their understanding of the reactionary nature of the Kuomintang regime, and thus shifted the direction of our struggle. Comrade Liang Jinglun saw this a fortnight ago, which shows that he is quite experienced and capable of revolutionary vigilance. Now the party has decided to adopt his suggestion and agreed to let He Xiaoyu contact Fang Meng'ao on his behalf. If it's possible, let's get Fang Meng'ao on our side. At the very least, let Fang Meng'ao understand that they are welcome to fight corruption but not at the expense of students' lives."

"I see," said Yan Chunming, leaping to his feet. "I'll go and share this message from the higher-ups with Comrade Liang Jinglun."

Comrade Liu stretched out his hand and held Yan's in a sincere grasp. He looked quizzically at his muddle-headed comrade-in-arms. "Comrade Chunming, at any time, especially now, don't just focus on the assignment, but also pay attention to your safety and protect yourself... Don't come back here after meeting with Comrade Jinglun tonight. Find a safe place to hide for a few days. Let Comrade Jinglun know that it'd be better to stay at Professor He's house these days."

———

"Our determination to fight corruption has worked through your actions today in Peking." Comrade Jianfeng's voice on the phone echoed in Zeng Keda's ears as he took the call in his room in Gu Weijun's residence, just like the voice in the microphone in the conference hall.

"Yes. I'm listening, Comrade Jianfeng," affirmed Zeng Keda, trying to suppress his excitement.

"I have just returned from the presidential residence. Ambassador Leighton Stuart has promised us US$170 million in immediate aid to the Nationalist government on behalf of the US government. Therefore, the president has promptly made a final decision and will soon carry out the reform of the new currency system."

Zeng Keda's mood turned from excitement to being emotional. "The president is wise. Comrade Jianfeng is wise!"

"When will you come to realise that there is only one wise man and he's always second to none?" Although Comrade Jianfeng still sounded calm over the phone, he went on to offer the following criticism: "As a matter of fact, all our actions have been carried out under the wise leadership of the president. However, Li Yuqing announced the five commitments of the government on behalf of Vice-President Li Zongren without mentioning the president. Today's evening papers have already given the vice-president credit for reassuring the people and tomorrow more newspaper stories will give Li the credit. Although the president didn't blame me for this, I couldn't help but blame myself. In Peking, we should try to win Li Zongren's support but we shouldn't be used by him. It's a matter of principle, so make sure you make no mistake in this matter." Zeng Keda felt beads of sweat standing out on his forehead. "I failed to live up to the teachings of Comrade Jianfeng. 'Penny wise, pound foolish', I'm willing to accept any punishment."

There was a brief silence over the phone, then came Jianfeng's voice: "Improper use of words means that you're still confused."

"Yes," was all that Zeng Keda could manage in response.

Comrade Jianfeng continued to enlighten him tirelessly on the phone. "Don't confuse small gains with big priorities. The president is the paramount leader of the party and the state, and the fact that some people covet that office doesn't change the facts. Now, the top priority is to save the nation by suppressing the Communist insurgency. To that end, the only way out is to put in place a new currency to stabilise our urban economy and win our allies' support to turn the tide of the war on the front. I am in Shanghai and you are in Peking, Nanking, Guangzhou and Wuhan. For all of us in the five major cities, the top priority now is to fight corruption, to fight hoarding and to push forward the new currency reform. Only we can accomplish this task. Li Zongren has no such ability. So, it won't make any difference for them to try and buy off the masses. In the afternoon, Chen Jicheng also called the president's residence and complained about Li Zongren and Fu Zuoyi. Incidentally, he also complained about you. In fact, he was complaining about me. Is that a big deal? Maybe, maybe not. When we do great things, many complicated problems follow. The key is to have our own perspective and determination. Heaven is about to place a great responsibility on this great man. I hope that members of the Iron and Blood Congress will measure up to the expectations of 'this great man' as well. In Peking, you are the man, and Comrade Liang Jinglun is the man. By the way, how is Comrade Liang Jinglun doing these days?"

"Comrade Jianfeng, I've received a report that the Student Committee of the CPC's Urban Works Department in Peking has just summoned Comrade Liang Jinglun. I'm waiting for a further report. I'm also ready to meet with Comrade Liang Jinglun tonight to learn about the CPC's response to our actions today, to ensure that the new currency system will be introduced." Zeng Keda rose in high spirits.

"Our understanding of the CPC's response should be based on observation and analysis. The CPC will definitely react strongly to the action taken by Fang Meng'ao and his brigade today. There must be plenty of speculation and even doubts about Comrade

Liang Jinglun. Don't expect to learn from the conversation what the CPC really thinks. Try to analyse their true reaction from every detail of their meeting with Comrade Liang Jinglun. We should carefully examine the whole process of their meeting with Comrade Liang Jinglun. Analyse the rhythm, tone and attitude when he speaks. People's mouths can tell lies but their emotions can't."

"I'll remember that, Comrade Jianfeng," noted Zeng Keda, committing his advice to memory as he gently brought his legs to attention with his body upright.

After gently opening the locked door, the first thing He Xiaoyu saw was the grandfather clock in the drawing room on the ground floor of the house. It was a unique clock with a peculiar pendulum swinging from side to side without making any noise, yet both the long and short hands were pointing to the number eleven on the clock face, signifying 10.55 pm. At that moment, the pendulum had stopped. He Xiaoyu, leaning against the door, did not hurry to step inside, but still looked at the glass door of the large clock, on which appeared the smiling eyes of Comrade Liu when he met her not long ago.

In Peking, Comrade Liu served as a liaison person on different levels of the party organisation but also as the underground agent in charge of executing Kuomintang spies. Because of his rich experience in fighting the Kuomintang, his name had become the most feared by both the Military Bureau of Investigation and the Central Bureau of Investigation. Even a senior party member such as Yan Chunming was quite in awe of him, hence the inappropriate analogy of 'the Fifth Master' invoked by a few comrades behind his back. The Fifth Master was the head of the Torture Hall within the secret society known as the Green Gang. His guild number was Red Flag Five, meaning that Old Liu enjoyed similar status to the Red Flag Five. In fact, there were essential differences between the two. Comrade Liu was far more imposing than the former in terms of prestige. The only exception was that when Comrade Liu communicated with special members of the party, such as He Xiaoyu, he was more like a caring elderly gentleman.

"Comrade Xiaoyu, besides being your superior, you can regard me as your uncle. In addition to our day-to-day work, you can also talk about personal life to me, of course, if you are willing to..."

He Xiaoyu cried when she saw herself in the glass door. The reflection of her image had reminded her of the conversation with Old Liu that had taken place just an hour before. Typical of his father, Comrade Liu deliberately looked elsewhere and said softly: "Comrade Liang Jinglun is carrying out the decision of the party organisation. He is trying to accomplish the mission assigned by the student committee. Therefore, all he's doing is assigned by the party organisation. You should fully understand him, especially when it comes to your personal feelings. Well, how should I put it? You need to understand him in your heart although you can always pretend not to understand him because your identity, especially that of Comrade Fang Meng'ao, is unknown to anyone except me and Comrade Xie Peidong. At present, Comrade Liang Jinglun only knows that you are a progressive youth outside the party organisation. It is also painful for him to let you contact Comrade Fang Meng'ao. Therefore, you can only report to him as a progressive youth. As for how to report to him and what to report to him, Comrade Xie Peidong will discuss that with you in detail. Your real task is to replace the comrade who originally contacted Fang Meng'ao. In the future, it'll be a one-way contact with Comrade Fang Meng'ao. After you take over, you're only responsible to Comrade Xie Peidong and me for all your actions. You're not allowed to disclose to anyone the true identity of Comrade Fang Meng'ao. In this way, we can ensure your safety and that of Comrade Fang Meng'ao. It is the cruelty of the struggle and the complexity of the situation that has compelled the organisation to make such a decision. You have never done this before, yet you've been given such a daunting task. Are you willing to accept it or can you accomplish it? I'm ready to hear your own opinions."

Back in the present, He Xiaoyu wiped away her tears and replied firmly: "I understand, I accept."

The scene of the day's general protest in front of the Citizens' Food Distribution Committee headquarters replayed itself vaguely on the glass door of the large clock with the shadowy figures of countless students swaying in the distance. Then Comrade Liu disappeared like a spectre.

Looking up at her father's bedroom door on the first floor, He Xiaoyu stepped into the living room. Unconsciously, she went straight to the countertop in the kitchen and glanced at the bag of flour given by Fang Meng'ao through the care of Fang Mengwei. She picked up a knife on the kitchen table and reached for the unopened bag. She hesitated again and looked nervously up the stairs at her father's closed bedroom door.

"Never accept anything from the Fangs, no matter who it is, not even a single grain of rice." Her father's voice was echoing in her head. But her hand refused to do what she directed it to do and neither did her knife. The tip of the knife pierced the flap and broke the bag's seal.

Strangely enough, He Xiaoyu began to read to herself the two lines of a poem that seemed to be quite irrelevant:

> With her whole heart she's sewing and sewing.
> For fear I'll ne'er be roving and roving....

She cut open the bag, picked up the bowl and scooped a bowlful of flour out of the bag, poured it into a basin, picked up some chopsticks and slowly poured in the right amount of water and began to mix the dough. It would not be possible for her to sleep tonight anyway because she had to knead the dough, make steamed buns and fry the slices for her father's breakfast the next day. She would not be able to finish all the chores until daybreak.

But just then the phone began to ring. He Xiaoyu was startled and rushed to answer it although she did not forget to look back at the door of her father's bedroom.

"Who is it? It's so late."

"It's me... Xiaoyu..." Surprisingly, it was Xie Mulan's voice on the other end.

The look in He Xiaoyu's eyes immediately became vexed but she calmed herself down and asked softly: "What's the matter? Are you crying?"

"Xiaoyu." It was obvious that Xie Mulan sounded even more upset over the phone. "Is Mr Liang home now?"

Of course, He Xiaoyu understood what was on Xie Mulan's mind at that moment. During the day, she had been holding Liang Jinglun from behind his back and publicly walking arm-in-arm with him. Obviously, she would have been quite aware of the fact that He Xiaoyu might have noticed them. Despite the rowdy crowd, He Xiaoyu was also keen enough to observe Xie Mulan's eyes twinkling with feeling. Those eyes did not see hers but Xie Mulan clearly felt them behind her back.

"It's so late but do you want to see Professor Liang?" He Xiaoyu asked as calmly as she could.

"Don't get me wrong, Xiaoyu." Xie Mulan sounded so guilty over the phone. "I just want to join the student audit group."

"Then you should go and talk to your older brother."

Xie Mulan's voice sounded even more anxious on the phone: "It's just that my older brother won't allow me to join. It's also so annoying that my father won't allow me go out of the house again. My younger cousin locked me in my room. Please do me a favour. I want to go to your place."

"What can I do?" asked He Xiaoyu. "I can't go and pick you up now."

Xie Mulan was silent for a moment. "If Professor Liang can put in a good word for me, my older brother will allow me to participate."

"Professor Liang has been away for quite a few days. He's not supposed to be here tonight."

"Can you go and talk to him at the bookstore?"

He Xiaoyu sensed that she dared to say these words not just to make her affair with Liang Jinglun open but to force her to speak on her behalf. He Xiaoyu could not speak about feelings of the heart but tried to calm herself down for a second, then replied: "Professor Liang is very busy. It's inappropriate for me to go and talk to him at this hour of the night."

"He has a phone in his office. Can't you ring him on my behalf?" Although she tried to sound very gentle, she simply could not hide her excitement. Xie Mulan would not let it go at that and was pushing her luck!

Why don't you call him yourself? He Xiaoyu thought to herself but she managed to hold it back. Instead, she replied: "It's too late for me to call him."

"Please, call my elder brother, I'm begging you. Ask him to get me out. He should listen to you." Xie Mulan was quite desperate.

"OK," replied He Xiaoyu, very straightforwardly this time. "I'll call him."

"It's awfully kind of you, Xiaoyu."

He Xiaoyu hung up the phone. She closed her eyes and felt the breeze wafting from Liang Jinglun's long gown which drifted away along with the wind. She opened her eyes again and began to make the call. Now her eyes were limpid.

In the woods beside the highway that led to Yenching University in Peking's northwestern suburbs, one could see the sky spangled with stars but only a glimmer of light from the Yenching campus in the distance. It was rather dark but the six student agents of the Chiang Kai-shek Student Society still parked their bicycles off the road. In fact, they laid all six bicycles on the slope beside it. Crouched down, they were watching vigilantly in every direction.

The six student agents were specially assigned to protect the safety of Zeng Keda and Liang Jinglun. Therefore, their mission was supposed to be even more important than that assigned to the agents affiliated with the Military Council's Bureau of Investigation and Central Bureau of Investigation. Now, in the depths of the night, they were surrounded by small trees behind which Liang Jinglun and Zeng Keda were sitting.

"You should believe me, Comrade Keda." Liang Jinglun could barely believe what he was saying, even as he said it. "Based on the content of Yan Chunming's remarks and his attitude towards me, I don't see any sign that they suspect me."

"Does that mean I can report to Comrade Jianfeng that you are safe now and our action plan can be carried out as scheduled?" asked Zeng Keda while staring into Liang Jinglun's face, the features of which he could barely make out in the darkness. On a subconscious level, he was practising what Comrade Jianfeng had just taught him during their phone conversation, namely, trying to tell whether Liang Jinglun was lying based on his mood.

"You're right not to believe me." Liang Jinglun, whose intuition was far more acute than Zeng Keda's, had realised that Zeng Keda had been observing him and trying to make sense of the truth behind his appearance and beyond his words. However, he knew Zeng Keda well enough. As a returned scholar with a doctoral degree earned in the US, he had studied Arthur Schopenhauer's *The World as Will and Representation* that dissected the world far better than the spy textbooks did. Besides, he was the one who had maintained long-term contact with the Communist Party, while Zeng Keda, at most, was only a professional soldier who had received some limited military and political training in southern Jiangxi Province and Nanking. However, it was hard to subconsciously avoid a tone that was inappropriate for a subordinate to adopt when conversing with their superior.

"What do you mean by 'not to believe' you?" asked Zeng Keda, who was gifted and intelligent enough to sense the 'contempt' behind the tone.

Liang Jinglun came closer to him and said sincerely and seriously: "Comrade Keda, I understand you and Comrade Jianfeng are concerned because the new currency system reform is about to be launched and I've been assigned the arduous task of facilitating it. The Communist underground insurgents are well organised and well equipped and it is proving to be a daunting task. During the day, I did feel that someone was trying to manipulate the situation behind Yan Chunming. Unfortunately, with so many of us from the Military Bureau of Investigation, the Central Bureau of Investigation as well as the students from the Chiang Kai-shek Student Society, none of us were able to identify the guy. Yan Chunming came to me just now to offer his criticism or concern but his attitude was so sincere that I can safely assume that the Communist underground leadership doesn't have the slightest doubt about me. Furthermore, it all happened so naturally when he communicated to me the higher-ups' instructions. But if it is too natural, then it may not be normal. I'm worried about the invisible master behind Yan Chunming."

"Who is it?" asked Zeng Keda, immediately turning serious.

"If I knew who he was, he'd surely be disqualified as a master. But I can provide some clues that will hopefully alert our organisation."

"Tell me in detail," said Zeng Keda.

"It's impossible to give details. Only occasionally have I heard of him from the underground party members in Peking. His nickname is 'Master Five'. He is the chief liaison with all divisions of the underground organisation of the CPC in Peking and the person who secretly oversees everyone in all the divisions. I presume Yan Chunming had met up with him before he met me."

"Then arrest Yan Chunming immediately and secretly," said Zeng Keda, jumping to his feet. "Catch this man through Yan Chunming!"

Liang Jinglun still sat on the ground and made no response.

Zeng Keda, finding himself losing his composure, sat down slowly. "Tell me your ideas."

"Comrade Keda, according to the regulations of the CPC, Master Five can contact Yan Chunming at any time but Yan Chunming can't initiate a meeting with him. If you have Yan Chunming arrested now, that'll surely blow my cover."

Zeng Keda was embarrassed but the darkness of the night helped conceal his embarrassment. "I know. I will assign some of our agents of the Military Bureau of Investigation through the Ministry of Defence to keep Yan Chunming and others under strict surveillance. We must catch this man. Today, Chen Jicheng made a complaint about us to the president, alleging that we just had it in for those within the party-state but have never uncovered any individual members of the underground Communist Party organisations in Peking. So let us make the arrest and tell them to cooperate with us. The idea is to ensure your safety, to ensure that Fang Meng'ao will no longer be used by the Communists and to ensure that the new currency system will be implemented in Peking."

"Thanks, Comrade Keda, for your attention to this. It's almost twelve o'clock. I'll have to go and meet He Xiaoyu and tell her how to contact Fang Meng'ao. I have a hunch that the Communist Party underground agents in Peking will outwardly use me to let He Xiaoyu contact Fang Meng'ao while arranging for someone else to connect Fang Meng'ao. Please consider that possibility, too."

In the sitting room at He Qicang's house, Yannan Garden, He Xiaoyu asked in a low voice: "Why did you come?" As she spoke, she tried her best to indicate that it was not her idea to call him while, at the same time, she also tried to show that she did not intend to embarrass him by asking.

"Didn't you ring me just now?" Fang Meng'ao looked closely at He Xiaoyu, as if he was smiling, yet he was actually examining her response.

He Xiaoyu avoided any eye contact with him and instead looked up at the first floor and then at the large clock. "Mulan asked me to call you to get her out of your house."

"It's late. She is supposed to be in her own room at home. Is there any special reason why she asked me to pick her up?" retorted Fang Meng'ao.

"You know, she wanted to join the joint investigation team to help you with the auditing."

"Do you think she should join the investigation team?" Once again, He Xiaoyu found herself being cornered. And the rules of engagement, according to Comrade Liu, had made it very clear that she must meet with Liang Jinglun first, then contact Fang Meng'ao in the name of the Peking Students' Union and engage him secretly on behalf of the Communist Party. Fang Meng'ao's unexpected arrival before Liang Jinglun threw the party organisation's plan into disarray. Until then, He Xiaoyu had realised that it wasn't Xie Mulan's call that was wrong, it was she who had made the wrong call.

"No, she can't join the joint investigation team." Fang Meng'ao stared at her with such sharp eyes that he quickly detected He Xiaoyu's predicament. He immediately answered the question he had asked her. "I'll allow only one person to work against my father or against my family. No second person shall be allowed to do that."

"I shouldn't have called." It was such an inappropriate reply which He Xiaoyu herself felt embarrassed about. Conversely, it was only natural for her to try to cover that up with a smile. "Your brigade and twenty other classmates should be checking the accounts round the clock. You are the team leader, perhaps you need to get back now, because I need to fix some breakfast for my father." With that, she looked at the bowl for kneading dough and the bag of flour. "By the way, thanks for the flour."

Then she went over to the living room door, ready to open it so that Fang Meng'ao could exit. But Fang Meng'ao stood still. "Don't you want to ask me why I came?" He Xiaoyu immediately became nervous again and stopped where she was, not knowing what to do.

When approaching He Qicang's house from the campus of Yenching University, Liang Jinglun suddenly stopped about three hundred metres from the free-standing house which was quite familiar to him. He soon recognised the small military jeep, Fang Meng'ao's vehicle, parked beside the road. He then looked towards the house.

There was no light in the window on the first floor, yet there was a light glimmering in the living room on the ground floor. "Hesitation." Liang Jinglun developed a peculiar feeling for this word for the first time. To go or not to go? He turned around and walked back to the campus, his long gown floating like his shadow on the ground. But he halted after a few steps, turned around again and walked towards the house in which he belonged. It was the middle of the night as the hem of his long gown fluttered, the leaves on the roadside swaying beside it.

Back in the sitting room of He Qicang's house, Fang Meng'ao said: "You should know why I came."

"You didn't say, so how would I know?"

"Can we talk about something else first? I'll let you know when I leave."

He Xiaoyu instinctively looked towards the door of the living room. She worried that Liang Jinglun might return at any time. Meanwhile, she felt that Fang Meng'ao was looking at her so she turned her eyes to the first floor. "Please, it's one o'clock in the morning. My father is sick and he's a light sleeper. I will soon need to fix some breakfast for him. I need time to leaven the dough. If it's delayed, I won't be able to make the steamed bread." With that, she went over to the bowl and continued to knead the dough so that Fang Meng'ao would feel compelled to leave.

Fang Meng'ao, however, refused to leave; instead his tall figure came up to her side. He Xiaoyu didn't know whether she was frustrated or nervous but it was only her heartbeat she heard at that moment. She squinted to see that the tap was turned on and a thin stream of water was coming out. Fang Meng'ao tried to minimise the noise of the running water. He was washing his hands there.

"What are you up to, anyway?" asked He Xiaoyu in an effort to calm her nerves.

"Out of the way, please," Fang Meng'ao whispered in her ear.

He Xiaoyu took a step back and looked him in the eye, as if to beg him.

"I promise I won't wake up your father and his breakfast will be fixed on time. Give me an hour. Now, go and wash your hands. Go on." As he said that, Fang Meng'ao moved to resume her position in front of the bowl. He Xiaoyu didn't know why she did as she was told. She went on to wash her hands as if the tap water was running for her.

"Add another bowl of flour."

"My father can't eat that much."

"For you and Mulan tomorrow morning," said Fang Meng'ao.

He Xiaoyu became really desperate and went to scoop a bowl of flour from the bag, this time with a smaller bowl. "Do you want me to add to it?"

"What are you saying?" Fang Meng'ao moved his hands away.

He Xiaoyu felt that she was the silliest person of all as she emptied the flour into the bowl.

"Go and get the hot water bottle, use a large bowl, pour in one-third of the boiling water and add two-thirds of the cold water."

Once again, He Xiaoyu obediently did as she was told.

Fang Meng'ao took the bowl, poured the water evenly into the flour bowl with one hand and stirred it quickly and skilfully with the other. He Xiaoyu looked at him from the side of the door, not knowing whether she was entranced or fascinated.

Meanwhile, outside, on the doorstep of the living room of He Qicang's house, Liang Jinglun was still waiting. For many nights, he had stood on the same spot near the door, either expecting his professor to come back from meetings, or just enjoying a moment to himself away from his own small room. He enjoyed standing there to feel the bond with the two people closest to him. Tonight, Liang Jinglun was standing almost on the same spot, not knowing where he was.

"Vinegar." It was the voice of Fang Meng'ao.

"Yes." He Xiaoyu's voice was light but audible. Then Liang Jinglun imagined that He Xiaoyu took out the vinegar bottle from the cupboard.

"Pour fifty millilitres."

"Will do," replied He Xiaoyu.

Again, Liang Jinglun imagined He Xiaoyu carefully pouring vinegar into the flour bowl.

"Enough."

The hem of Liang Jinglun's gown stirred gently again. It was inappropriate for him to stand there eavesdropping. So he walked out of the small porch but stopped again after walking down two stone steps. It was fair to say that it was the ideal position to gaze at the stars in the sky or the setting crescent moon.

"Have you got any baking soda?" Fang Meng'ao began to knead. Instead of looking at the living room door or that of her father's bedroom, He Xiaoyu was stunned by Fang Meng'ao's skilful kneading.

"According to the proportion of five hundred grams of flour, fifty millilitres of vinegar and three hundred and fifty millilitres of warm water, leaven the dough for ten minutes. Then add five grams of baking soda and knead again. This way, you don't need to ferment it but the steamed bread is still soft." As he leavened the dough, Fang Meng'ao instructed her gently: "If you don't have enough time to leaven the dough in future, use this method."

"Where did you learn this?" asked He Xiaoyu, fascinated.

"In the Air Force, from the Flying Tigers."

"In the Air Force? Did you have to make your own steamed bread?"

"The Yankees wouldn't let us touch the planes in the first year. So we helped them do the laundry and cooking, and polished their shoes. Chennault, the old man, liked me. So he went on to give me hands-on skills himself the next year." He Xiaoyu suddenly felt her heart ache. She no longer wanted to compel Fang Meng'ao to leave.

Outside, Liang Jinglun was sitting down on the stone steps in front of the porch. He knew when to leave, not because of what he saw or heard, but because of what he felt. He could pick the right moment to avoid embarrassment but what he couldn't control was his strong feelings at that moment. So keen were his feelings that they flashed through his eyes. Unfortunately, when he looked up, he could not see the pair of eyes looking down from the bedroom window on the first floor.

As quietly and quickly as he could, he rose again and walked silently towards the gate. He tried to look back at the window on the first floor but he didn't make it. He knew that He Qicang was not asleep yet, or at least that he was awake now. He went out of the gate and stood by the tree on the side of the road. Liang Jinglun was right. Actually, He Qicang was wide awake although he didn't know when he woke up. To keep his daughter from knowing that he was awake, he sat on the edge of the bed, leaning on his cane in the dark and listened to what was going on in the drawing room downstairs. Due to his back ache, he remained seated in his chair by the window.

In fact, He Qicang was very perceptive for a man some years past the allotted span. He could see and hear what was going on downstairs but he chose not to interfere simply because he thought he was not entitled to intrude on others' privacy, an idea he picked up while studying abroad many years ago. With a family well versed in traditional learning, he chose to give up his right to manage family affairs even though he was neither blind nor deaf. Instead, with a sensible and obedient daughter, he pretended to be aloof after she began to attend middle school, leaving her enough space for her to grow up and communicate freely with classmates and, more importantly, to reduce her concern for him. As for now, he heard every word of the whispered conversation between his daughter and Fang Meng'ao on the ground floor.

"Now, you can tell me why you came, can't you?" It was his daughter's voice, which seemed to be louder than before. He Qicang understood his daughter's intention. There was a saying in his hometown in Jiangsu Province, roughly to the effect that one needs to 'clarify' what one has just said.

"If I do, don't be disappointed or get angry." It was Fang Meng'ao's answer to which his daughter didn't reply.

"I just want you to help me about today. Right in front of the gate of the Citizens' Food Distribution Committee headquarters, Ma Hanshan claimed that I made a bet with him. I said I didn't. Do you think he was lying or I was?"

Sure enough, it came back to the subject of the Citizens' Food Distribution Committee. Ironically, Fang Meng'ao used such teasing words. He Qicang felt that he was trying to cover up something and immediately became alert. How would his daughter respond?

"Did you come to ask me about this?"

"Of course, I want to ask you more. But this is mainly what I wanted to ask you tonight."

"Then all I can say is that, of course, he is lying."

"You're partially right. He was lying and so was I."

He Qicang frowned with disgust. "How could you both be lying?"

"Because he is bad and so am I."

He Qicang stood up slowly with his walking stick.

"I see. You can go now."

There was a short silence, then Fang Meng'ao continued: "I'm joking. Do you want to know the real purpose of my coming here tonight?"

He Qicang pricked up his ears. But his daughter didn't answer.

"To see you." Finally, Fang Meng'ao said what He Qicang was worried about all along. His daughter didn't answer, and what Fang Meng'ao said next left He Qicang even more astonished. "I also want to see if Professor Liang is here or not."

"Are you finished? Thank you for coaching me how to make steamed bread your way. Professor Liang is not here tonight. Let's call it a night now."

The tone of his daughter's voice sounded a little cross. He Qicang moved to the window in his traditional-style cloth shoes. He wanted to see Fang Buting's eldest son leave his home, the sooner the better, but was unable to when he looked down at the courtyard gate. He did not even see Fang Meng'ao's jeep which was supposed to be parked outside his gate. Although the street light was on, it only cast a dim light. So he looked further down the street, only to find Fang Meng'ao's jeep parked under another street lamp. He Qicang's gaze scanned along the street until he was momentarily surprised at what he was seeing; it was the figure of a man walking all alone, amazingly that man was Liang Jinglun. Apparently he had just left his courtyard.

Fang Meng'ao was standing in front of the drawing room door. "Please pass on my words to Professor Liang." Hearing this, He Xiaoyu changed her mind and took her hand off the door knob.

"Professor Liang is a man I admire and our inspection team is looking forward to his help."

"Certainly, I'll tell him."

"One more important thing," said Fang Meng'ao. "Mulan's fallen in love with him but she mustn't."

He Xiaoyu turned around and looked intensely at Fang Meng'ao.

"I have no other family, only one younger brother. He is now the deputy chief of the police bureau. In fact, he is a very pitiful man. He loves Mulan very much."

He Xiaoyu was again confused at what she saw with her own eyes. He didn't seem at all like a special party member recruited by the organisation. Meanwhile, in front of the window of his bedroom, He Qicang's face was lit up by two headlights that had been switched on about three hundred metres away from the courtyard gate. He couldn't believe what happened next. He saw Liang Jinglun walking up to the car, about five metres in front of the headlights, when two people jumped out of the car and twisted his arms behind his back, one from the left, the other from the right!

Liang Jinglun's limp body was dragged and thrust into the car roughly. The car backed up so savagely that the wheels crushed the bushes planted by the gardeners on the side of the road. Without slowing down, the car made a 180-degree turn and sped towards the university gate. He Qicang could see clearly that it was a police car.

"Uncle He." It was Fang Meng'ao who first heard the footsteps from the first floor and spotted He Qicang standing at the entrance to the ground floor stairs.

"Dad." He Xiaoyu looked at her father in surprise.

The look on He Qicang's face was one of horror. Holding the stairs, he walked down rapidly as fast as his feet would carry him. He Xiaoyu rushed up and held him by the arm but failed to slow him down. Fang Meng'ao also noticed something amiss with He Qicang who went straight to the phone. He picked up the receiver and dialled, his hands trembling slightly.

"Dad, what's the matter? Who are you calling?" He Xiaoyu panicked even more. He Qicang ignored her and put the phone closer to his ear.

He Xiaoyu and Fang Meng'ao both had their eyes fixed on the phone receiver jammed against He Qicang's ear! Because it was late at night, the voice over the phone sounded very clear and one could discern the arrogance of the voice on the other end of the line. "The Rear Office of the Peking Military Affairs Commission. Who is it and why are you calling at this hour of the night?"

"I need to talk to Li Zongren!" snapped He Qicang. "Wake him up and get him to take my call!"

Fang Meng'ao and He Xiaoyu's eyes met. Both were surprised.

"May I know who is speaking, please?" The voice on the other end softened at this point.

"This is He Qicang, the economic adviser of the national government!" He Qicang's voice was still very loud.

"It's Chancellor He. Respectfully, could you please call back at six tomorrow morning if it's not very urgent?"

"I wouldn't bother to call him if it was'nt urgent."

"Chancellor He, do you mind if I ask what the issue is?" said the voice on the other end of the line. "I need to ask for permission."

He Qicang had managed to curb his emotions, yet his tone of voice was still angry. "Just now, at my doorstep, my assistant was taken away by the police!"

He Xiaoyu's eyes were wide with astonishment. Fang Meng'ao's expression immediately became tense and concerned!

"Chancellor He, please tell me the name of your assistant. What's his title?"

"Liang Jinglun, Professor, Department of Economics, Yenching University."

"I see. Chancellor He, how about if I report this to Adjutant-General of the Rear Office Li Yuqing first? I'll ask General Li to answer your call"

He Qicang pondered for a moment before giving his consent.

Fang Meng'ao turned on the tap and washed his hands. "Chancellor He, did you see clearly that it was a police car?"

With the phone in his hand, He Qicang didn't even bother to look at him. Of course, he didn't reply. Fang Meng'ao was not embarrassed and asked He Xiaoyu: "Did Mulan say she was being kept at home by Mengwei?" He Xiaoyu looked at her father and just nodded her head. At that, Fang Meng'ao strode out of the house.

The Kuomintang Garrison headquarters in Peking was the most spacious government office in the municipality. Located in a gated compound, it was symbolically guarded by two real stone lions, illuminated by multiple iodine tungsten lamps and searchlights, and last but not least, by the blue helmets and the blue carbines. Formerly the presidential palace of Yuan Shikai, it later became the seat of the Duan Qirui government. After the victory of the Chinese People's War of Resistance Against Japanese Aggression, the Kuomintang government took over Peking and located its commanders' headquarters of the 11th Theatre Command and the Peking Garrison Headquarters in the compound. With the abolition of the 11th Command, the Rear Office of the Peking Military Affairs Commission was established. Li Zongren, however, was unwilling to share the office compound with Chiang Kai-shek's police headquarters and set up his command centre in the Zhongnanhai compound. Therefore, the garrison command had the whole executive government compound to itself. It was the middle of the night now, yet military vehicles, police cars and motorcycles were still driving in and out.

The office, with a ceiling height of five metres and around a hundred square metres of floor area, had been where Duan Qirui, Yuan Shikai's minister of war, ran state affairs. With Chen Jicheng in office, he set his large desk against the wall opposite the door, facing an expanse of long and short sofas backed by a circle of seats with backrests. The seat with the highest back was, of course, the one in front of his desk. He liked to sit here for meetings, calling in those who had the power to arrest and execute, listened to them from a commanding position and told them who should be busted and killed. In this way, he seemed to have developed the same sort of sick pleasure as Yuan Shikai or Duan Qirui.

For nearly a month, Chen Jicheng had been fretting in the cluttered suite of offices here. To the west of his headquarters was the Princess Hejing's former residence which was officially reserved for the Inspection Brigade of the Cadre Reserve Bureau of the Ministry of Defence. However, Fang Meng'ao's aviation brigade gave it up for the Northeast students without his prior approval. The noise made by the neighbouring student residents had been very disturbing day in and day out, yet he was not able to take any action against them. He had tried to put up with it over the past few days but had found himself unable to do so today. Right here in the afternoon, he complained bitterly to Chiang Kai-shek about the suspicious actions and interactions between Vice-President Li, Commander-in-Chief Fu and the investigation team sent by the Ministry of Defence. Unfortunately, he discovered that the president had sounded so ambiguous on the phone that he responded only occasionally with an 'OK' in his thick Fenghua accent from Ningbo. What gave him satisfaction, however, was Chiang Kai-shek's signature curse "Goddammit" when he reported that the CPC was behind the student protests. The presidential instructions were crystal clear: the Communists must be put behind bars!

The operation was scheduled to commence after dark. For the sake of secrecy, he didn't call those affiliated with the Rear Office, nor did he summon anyone with the North China Headquarters for the Suppression of Communist Insurgency. Therefore, almost all the sofas in front of him remained empty. As a result, Chen appeared less enthusiastic and sat in the high chair with his eyes closed, mulling over his phone call to the president that afternoon. The ringing of the telephone on the desk caught his attention. He recognised that it was the second of the five phones, so he deliberately waited. The attendees who had been sitting with him in the large office looked at the phone and there were only two people who were qualified to sit on the sofas in the front.

One of them was Xu Tieying, chief commissioner of the Peking Municipal Police Bureau and the Garrison Headquarters Investigation Department. He had another important title as director of the Peking chapter of the Central Bureau of Investigation. Whichever titles he had, he was obliged to participate in today's meeting. The other person wore a grey summer-cloth Zhongshan suit, about forty years of age, with a face so white as to give the initial impression of an overcautious clerk. But the stature of this man was very eye-catching. Sitting there, he appeared half a head taller than Xu Tieying. His fingers resting on the armrest of the sofa were thin and long. This was Wang Puchen, head of the Peking station of the State Secrecy Bureau under the Ministry of Defence.

The five people sitting in the seats along the walls were of lower rank. There were two familiar faces, one was the group leader of the Peking station of the Military Bureau of Investigation, the other was the Special Task Battalion Commander of the Fourth Corps of the Nationalist Army. The other three were colleagues of theirs.

The phone had been ringing, non-stop. The words on the paper slip attached to the phone read: "The Peking Field Headquarters of the Nationalist government". Chen Jicheng was not ignoring the phone but was disdainful of the Rear Office of the Military Affairs Commission of the Peking Field Headquarters. There were four other telephones besides the one which was ringing.

The first phone: "Nanking, the president".

The second: "The North China Headquarters for the Suppression of Communist Insurgency".

The third: "The Garrison Station of the Army Corps".

The fourth: "The Military and Central Bureau of Investigation and Statistics".

"Commander-in-Chief Chen, it might be Vice-President Li. You'd better answer it." Xu Tieying was a little worried, looking at Chen Jicheng.

"Li Zongren would not call me at this moment but Li Yuqing might." Chen Jizhen picked up the phone.

All eyes in unison were on the phone next to his face but mainly on his face.

"Adjutant-General Li?" As Chen Jicheng had anticipated, it was Li Yuqing who had made the call. "After a hard day's work," said Chen, "it's time to call it a day now, perhaps?" Not everyone could hear what Li Yuqing was saying over the phone.

"Whose aide?" Chen Jicheng asked unnecessarily loudly. "What do you mean by the economic adviser's aide? Yes, we do have an operation tonight... Do we have to inform the Rear Office when we want to make some arrests? To bust members of the Communist Party...? Yes, the police chief of Peking Municipality and comrades of the military and central bureaus of investigation are all here. You can come and ask for yourself who made the arrest!"

With that, he just hung up the phone.

"Who is Liang Jinglun, the guy from Yenching University? Is he an aide to the economic adviser of the national government?" Chen glanced at Xu Tieying and Wang Puchen.

"I think so," Wang Puchen replied cautiously yet politely. "I told you that he is the assistant of He Qicang, Vice-Chancellor of Yenching University, and He Qicang is economic adviser to the national government."

"What sort of fucking economic adviser?" Chen Jicheng was trying to demonstrate his seniority when he chose to use foul language. "They used the investigation team of the Ministry of Defence as a shield. Now, again, they are using the economic adviser as an excuse. Why not tell us to stop busting the Commies altogether? Goddammit!"

Xu Tieying and Wang Puchen exchanged looks.

Everyone knew that he was one of the eight King Kongs of Whampoa Military Academy, the president's most trusted henchman. But it was too much for a Jiangsu person to swear with the president's Zhejiang accent and he thought he was being cool by cursing the president's son.

Chen stared at Wang Puchen and demanded: "Who was watching Liang Jinglun during the day?"

Wang Puchen coughed gently, then looked back at the leader of the executive group of the Military Bureau of Investigation. "Now, report to Commander Chen..."

Chen's face fell, as he said: "I'm asking you. You're the head of the Peking station, why don't you report to me yourself?"

Wang rose respectfully but his white face was whiter than ever. "It wasn't that I didn't want to report to you, sir, but that they're better informed than I am."

Chen Jicheng thought there must have been an insinuation in that remark and insisted that he explain the reason.

"I don't think I can." Wang Puchen coughed again twice. "Ma Hanshan, Director Ma, is my predecessor. He is a very responsible man. After I took over as head of the Peking station, he continued to run the bureau's business. Besides, all the brothers at the station are his former staff. As a junior, I couldn't very well compete against him."

At this point, Chen Jicheng became even more agitated with all the nagging issues. He banged the table and barked out an order: "I'll leave Liang Jinglun to you at the Military Bureau of Investigation, and you will interrogate him yourself, Chief Commissioner Xu."

Xu Tieying also stood up.

"Tell Ma Hanshan, the party and the state are not secret societies like the Green Gang. If he is transferred to another department, tell him not to interfere in the affairs of the Military Council's Bureau of Investigation and Statistics."

"Yes sir," replied Xu Tieying. "But Director Ma is now being detained by the Inspection Brigade of the Ministry of Defence. If they release him, I will convey your instructions, Commander-in-Chief Chen."

Chen Jicheng suddenly recalled that Ma Hanshan had been detained by Fang Meng'ao's brigade to assist in auditing the accounts. "Interrogate Liang Jinglun overnight. Besides that, have you had Yan Chunming of the Yenching library and other Communist suspects arrested yet?"

This time round, Xu Tieying did not make things difficult for Wang Puchen and he replied: "We sent our men at eleven only to find Yan Chunming had not returned to the library, so we're waiting and keeping watch. We've seized several others from various universities, though they're not necessarily Commies."

"It all depends on the results of the investigation. Interrogate

Liang Jinglun straight away. The point is to find out if there are any members of the Communist Party among the twenty students who are helping Fang Meng'ao to audit the accounts. If you can identify one of them, you can go and bust Fang Meng'ao immediately! That Goddamned son of a bitch!"

CHAPTER 8

In the living room on the ground floor of He Qicang's house, He Xiaoyu sat next to her father's sofa. Her eyes were fixed on the phone receiver pressed to her father's ear but the look in her eyes was far away from it. Right now, there were two men who made her extremely anxious. One of them was in police custody while the other was in danger of getting himself into trouble. And what made her even more anxious was that she had to take care of her angry and sick father.

It was so silent that night that she could vaguely hear a persistent beeping sound, whether far away or close by, it was hard to tell. He Xiaoyu quickly returned to her senses, only to find that it was the engaged tone from the phone near her father's ear. The man on the other end of the line had already hung up but her father still held the receiver tightly to his ear.

"Dad?" He Xiaoyu held her father's hand in panic.

While He Qicang's phone was taken away from him by his daughter, he looked at her, feeling lost and alone.

"They... made you angry?" He Xiaoyu put the phone back with one hand and clasped her father's with the other.

"No." He Qicang looked deep into his daughter's eyes. "They are making China angry. A bunch of scum who bring disaster to the country. They make China suffer. They are a national disgrace."

He Xiaoyu discovered that her father's hands were shaking as he spoke. "Dad, who on earth arrested Mr Liang? What exactly did Adjutant-General Li say to you?"

"The distinguished vice-president of the Republic of China could not protect a university professor and asked me to call John Leighton Stuart."

"Dad, you don't want to call Uncle John."

"Don't call him Uncle John again."

He Xiaoyu was shocked. She knew of her father's personal relationship with Ambassador Stuart and of his respect for him. The pain in his voice and the reason she must have known made her stare at him.

The expression in He Qicang's eyes had never been so fraught when looking at his daughter. "You could call him 'uncle' when he was teaching at Yenching. Now he serves in this post as the US ambassador to China, so he represents the United States. Who's your father then? A professor in China. Economic adviser to the Nationalist government; bullshit, total bullshit."

He Xiaoyu was even more surprised. Her father had never been abusive. She could see that his head and neck were trembling slightly as he spoke. So she quickly clasped her father's hands. "Dad..."

"Li Yuqing just told me about it on the phone. It was Chen Jicheng's backchat. Good for him! What's the use of an economic adviser for an autocratic and corrupt government? It's just that I could have a word with the US ambassador to China and beg for some US aid. What does Chen Jicheng add up to? Nothing but a small-time warlord from Huangpu Military Academy. Why did he dare to scold me? Why did Li Yuqing pass on the backchat? This is the government of the Republic of China, with one faction arresting my assistant and the other telling me to complain to the Americans. Do you think I should make the call?"

For the first time, she had a real feel for her father's predicament. "Then don't make the call," she said. "We'll try another way to save Mr Liang."

The expression in He Qicang's eyes changed again as he watched his daughter. "I know my students. Jinglun can't be a Communist. It's just that he's more radical in his discontent with the authorities. Isn't Fang Meng'ao also approaching them to rescue him? He's been dispatched by the Ministry of Defence. Let's wait for his news."

"It's no use." He Xiaoyu didn't agree with her father's expectation. "I joined the protest at the Citizens' Food Distribution Committee today. The arrest tonight has nothing to do with the Communist Party. They did this simply to cover up their corruption and other crimes. If Fang Meng'ao hadn't been sent by the Ministry of Defence, they would have placed him under arrest."

Hearing his daughter speak of Fang Meng'ao in such a manner, He Qicang's eyes turned to the bag of flour. "Why didn't you return it? Who opened it?"

He Xiaoyu was quite astonished by her father's words. She became so sensitive that she had to avoid confronting him because she also had the same sad feelings and the same troubled thoughts. "There's nothing left to eat at home," she explained.

"I won't have you opening it, though."

"Dad, I understand you don't like those in the military, but you watched Fang Meng'ao grow up," said He Xiaoyu. "He was also a war hero in the second world war."

"That war has been over for three years. Look at the way he acts. It's like the words displayed on this bag: 'Made in the USA'! What's the point of pretending to be American?"

"Dad, aren't you also a returned scholar from the US?" countered He Xiaoyu. "Mr Liang also studied in the US. Wasn't it you who appealed to the US for the flour? Why do you despise Fang Meng'ao so much?"

He Qicang's eyes were fixed on his daughter's face. She seemed to have confirmed his hunch, that his daughter had fallen for Fang Meng'ao. This was absolutely impossible. "I was educated in the US, so was Liang Jinglun. But when do you see us act like Americans? The reason why I regard Leighton Stuart as a friend is because he's more like a Chinese. You know the kind of Americans your father despises the most, don't you? It's warmongers like Patton and, more recently, MacArthur, who's lording it over Japan as if he owns the place. He lost to the Japanese but later became a conqueror and now he desperately wants to help Japan, pretending to be the saviour with a gun. Don't you think Fang Meng'ao is learning from them?"

He Xiaoyu's face paled a little. "Dad, Fang Meng'ao has just been castigated by a military court for refusing to bomb the ancient city of Kaifeng and for that he was almost sentenced to death. How come he pretends to be a saviour when he can't even save himself?"

"If he can't save himself, why did he go and save Liang Jinglun?" He Qicang had never had such an argument with his daughter but today he decided not to spare her feelings. "You just said that Fang Meng'ao might have been arrested as well. Let me ask you this: if both Liang Jinglun and Fang Meng'ao were put in prison but I could only rescue one of them, which one would you prefer me to save?"

He Xiaoyu was overwhelmed. She wanted to control her feelings but her eyes were already full of tears. He Qicang immediately regretted what he had said. His daughter had lost her mother in her early teens. For that reason, He Qicang had never sought to remarry after the death of his wife because he loved his daughter so much. His daughter took care of him, taking on the full responsibility of her mother. Why did he hurt his daughter like that today? He was confused and felt at a loss. He stared blankly for quite a while then suddenly turned and said: "I'll call Leighton Stuart."

He Qicang reached out for the phone but He Xiaoyu quickly reached out to press down on her father's hand. "Dad, don't feel bad about yourself. Don't do anything that might make people despise you." He Qicang's hand rested feebly on the phone. What his daughter had just said seemed to be a wake-up call. Why was he losing control of his emotions? It was all because he had no one to talk to about his grievances for so long.

"Your dad has been looked down upon by others for a long time. I'm not referring to scumbags like Chen Jicheng but to professors from various universities, they despise me. On the seventeenth of June, they signed *The Declaration by One Hundred and Ten Teachers*, which I trust all of you can recite. Me, I can also recite it."

He Xiaoyu obviously did not want to see her father suffer. She stood up and walked over to him, holding his arm in her hands.

"Dad, you're ill, you should go and lie down in bed. I'll wait for the call here. Whether he can rescue Mr Liang or not, Fang Meng'ao will surely call us."

"Listen to me, I'll recite the last paragraph of that statement first, OK?" He Qicang continued to sit there stubbornly.

He Xiaoyu had to stop walking her father up the stairs. Instead all she could do was to support him with her hands.

He Qicang suddenly started to recite loudly: "'In order to show the dignity and integrity of the Chinese people, we categorically reject all donations, whether purchased from or given by the US, which are meant to buy us off. It is hereby declared that the following colleagues agree to refuse to purchase cheap flour from the US and are unanimous about returning the ration cards...' I didn't recite it wrong, did I?"

"Dad," He Xiaoyu's voice was so low that only her father could hear it. "It's my fault, I shouldn't have opened this bag of flour. We won't eat it, we'll sew it up and return it tomorrow, OK?"

"If it has been opened, don't return it." He Qicang still didn't dare to look at his daughter. "We aren't hypocrites but we can't pretend not to be starving. Professor Zhu Ziqing and his family of nine have been starving and had no coal to heat themselves last winter. He has an advanced stomach illness but he has signed the statement. It's true that they don't want to accept charity from the Americans. It's also true that your father has helped to ask for charity from the Americans. But the truth is, I'm not doing this for myself. What caused the sudden outbreak of the massive student protest on the fifth of July? It's because more than ten thousand students from the Northeast have no food to eat and two million residents in Peking are starving. The government refuses to engage in economic reconstruction. Instead it's bent on fighting a civil war. When it runs out of money, it turns to the US for assistance and they go all-out to embezzle US money, which is why Leighton Stuart and William Cadbury have made statements that have hurt the feelings of the Chinese people. But, come to think of it, it's what you did that breeds contempt. Still, I have to help the government reach out and beg for aid. Today, the Americans have promised a hundred and seventy million dollars' worth of aid, but more than half of it is surplus weapons from the second world war. Only a fraction of the aid is life-saving material. If I make the call, Leighton Stuart will surely get angry and report to the US government, then the aid could run aground again. It'd be better if it does run aground, we can survive without such aid! I'll join the professors who are starving and sign the statement."

He Xiaoyu could sense the tears filling her father's eyes from behind his back. "I will listen to you and won't call Leighton Stuart. Unless Fang Meng'ao can't rescue Liang Jinglun and they are both arrested." Tears welled up in He Xiaoyu's eyes and streamed down her cheeks. In her tearful eyes, her father was still as tall and noble as ever.

On the shore of Beihai's Houhai Lake, Colonel Zheng of the Youth Army was confused again because Fang Meng'ao had ordered the platoon that was to escort Ma Hanshan and the two section chiefs Li and Wang of the Citizens' Food Distribution Committee to go there at night and to guard them so that no one could approach them. He wanted to interrogate these three men on that very night and in the same spot where he interrogated Cui Zhongshi.

The lights from Zhongnanhai could be seen shining in the distance. After deploying his platoon of young soldiers to their posts, Commander Zheng could not help looking back to the spot on Houhai Lake. From a distance, he saw the water sparkling on the surface of the lake and could vaguely see that Captain Fang had taken off his Air Force uniform while Ma Hanshan and the two section chiefs stood there like zombies. Zheng remembered that night, at the very same spot here, when Fang Meng'ao pulled a soaked Cui Zhongshi out of the water onto the lake shore. He instantly became nervous. Tonight, these three men might be forced to jump into the lake again. Would Captain Fang be able to get them all out of the water? If someone happened to drown, he must be held responsible.

"Who can swim?" whispered Colonel Zheng. At that, several of the soldiers raised their hands.

"Take off your clothes and get ready," ordered Zheng under his breath.

"Yes sir!" answered the young men who had raised their hands. They began to undress.

On the shore, Fang Meng'ao had taken off his uniform.

Stripped down to just his vest and a pair of shorts, he looked more like a basketball player. He looked straight at Ma Hanshan, Li and Wang. Ma Hanshan's shoulder, which had been dislocated by Secretary Sun, had apparently been fixed. And although the arm was still weak, there was no more sling. He was fully dressed and pretended to be enjoying the night view of Zhongnanhai in the distance.

"Captain Fang, I really can't swim. Once I'm down there, I can't get my ass out of it." Although he was afraid of Ma Hanshan, Wang just couldn't care that much now. With that anxious look on his face and that flabby body of his, he didn't seem to be lying now.

"I've told you everything I was supposed to during the day. If you find out anything I didn't, you can throw me into the lake anyway, why don't you?"

Section Chief Li didn't take off his clothes or say anything.

"I didn't ask you to go into the water. I just asked Director Ma to do it," Fang Meng'ao said, seriously. "You told me the truth and wrote it down but Director Ma didn't. He didn't even bother to admit it. Surely, I don't expect him to admit it. I just want to have a fair fight with Director Ma and you two are my witnesses. Don't side with me or him. If he loses, he has to come with me tonight. If I lose, I'll never interrogate you people at the Citizens' Food Distribution Committee again, neither about the money you've embezzled nor the murder you've committed."

Section Chief Wang dared not speak, nor did he dare to look at Ma Hanshan. Instead, he looked only at Li. Chief Li couldn't keep silent any longer.

"Captain Fang, you are the ace flyer in our air force, while our director is in his early fifties. He will lose even if you fight him with one finger. It's not fair."

At that moment, Ma Hanshan turned around from enjoying the night scene. He looked at Section Chief Li appreciatively and nodded his head. Then he turned to Fang Meng'ao to see how he would reply.

"I didn't say I want to fight him. If I did, I could fight ten of you, Director Ma included," said Fang Meng'ao with a wry smile. "What I mean is I'll make a bet with him in the lake. Isn't Director Ma an excellent swimmer? I heard that no one in the Military Bureau of

Investigation and Statistics can match him. So I'll challenge him in the water. That's fair, isn't it?"

Ma Hanshan had been a rogue all his life. He had experienced all kinds of situations, be it when he was with the Military Bureau of Investigation and Statistics or the criminal underworld. Early in the morning when Fang Meng'ao had him detained, he heard him speak of a 'murder case'. He surmised that Fang Meng'ao was referring to Cui Zhongshi's death, something that he considered daunting to get over. Still, he smiled and said to Fang Meng'ao: "Captain Fang, even if you put aside the issue of my age, my shoulder joint has only just been fixed. I couldn't compete against you even if I was in my prime. As for the corruption and murder case you referred to, let's say, if you want to settle this officially, you have the full power to send me to the Special Criminal Court because you represent the Ministry of Defence. If you want to settle this privately, you've a gun in your hand. You can blow my head off right now. Then you will end up in the Special Criminal Court. Beat your brains out to have me killed or drowned, huh? What kind of fair fight is that?"

If it had not been for the fact that he had killed Cui Zhongshi and the people behind him had arrested Liang Jinglun tonight, Fang Meng'ao would not have hated Ma Hanshan. Hearing his rebuttal, he turned to Wang and Li: "You two, come over here."

At this moment, they seemed rooted to the spot. How did they have the guts to go up to him?

"Listen carefully. Just now, Director Ma claimed that I tried by every means to drown him. Now, both of you! Open your eyes and watch if I drown him or not. I won't compete with him for who is the better swimmer. Instead, we will go into the water together and hold our breath. Whoever surfaces first will lose." After he was done talking with the two men, he turned to Ma Hanshan. "You said you were older and your arm's just been reconnected. I'll let you breathe one more time after you submerge. But if you come up first after the second breath, then the two of us will need to talk." With that, he yelled to his three captives: "Is this fair?"

In the distance, Colonel Zheng and his Youth Army soldiers couldn't help looking this way. As for Chief Li and Wang, they looked at each other, and nodded in agreement.

Not knowing whether he was really confident or he felt that he should make the final move since Fang Meng'ao had hurt his pride so badly, Ma Hanshan barked at Li and Wang: "I can't use my hands. Help me remove my clothes!"

Both Wang and Li were notorious for being cunning and stubborn but neither had ever been involved in such a ridiculous situation. Both of them hesitated and looked at Fang Meng'ao in frustration. Fang Meng'ao cast a quick glance at the buttons on their clothes. Of course, they understood the implication of this glance. If they didn't help Ma Hanshan take off his clothes, they would have to take off their own clothes.

"Let's give Director Ma some help," said Chief Li. One after the other, the two walked over, one helping Ma Hanshan with his jacket, the other with his trousers.

Fang Meng'ao went into the water first followed by Ma Hanshan in his shorts.

"It's shallow here. Go in further." Fang Meng'ao moved a few metres further. Ma Hanshan really was a good swimmer. Not being able to paddle with his hands, Ma Hanshan unexpectedly managed to swim over using just his feet to paddle with. Fang Meng'ao, also paddling with his feet, stopped there waiting for him. Ma Hanshan stopped paddling about a metre away.

"Keep your eyes wide open while down there. Cui Zhongshi is waiting for us underneath."

Ma Hanshan's blood froze at the demand. He hesitated again.

"Get under the water!" Fang Meng'ao bellowed, his head about to submerge.

Ma Hanshan took a deep breath and submerged unwillingly as it took him a few more seconds to do so.

"Secretary Wang? Is Comrade Jianfeng back yet?" asked an increasingly irate Zeng Keda from his room in Gu Weijun's compound. He pressed the phone closer to his ear for an answer.

"Not yet."

Zeng Keda, who was silent for about two seconds, was almost begging him: "Could you please connect the call to special line one and report to Comrade Jianfeng that there is an emergency in Peking? I must report to him immediately!"

"There is no way to put you through to the number tonight no matter how urgent the situation is. In fact, except for those from major military commands, no calls should be connected to the special number."

Zeng Keda fell silent again. He replied after a split second: "As soon as Comrade Jianfeng comes back, please inform me immediately."

"Yes sir."

Zeng Keda slowly replaced the receiver and stared blankly when suddenly the phone rang. He picked up the phone. "Secretary Wang? Is this Secretary Wang speaking?"

"Excuse me, Chief Inspector Zeng. This is Secretary Sun of the Peking Municipal Police Bureau."

Zeng Keda was somewhat disappointed but forced himself to stand up. "Chief Commissioner Xu is back, please answer the phone."

"Commissioner Xu? Where are you keeping He Qicang's assistant now?"

"Whose assistant? Who is He Qicang?" asked Xu Tieying at the other end of the line.

"Vice-chancellor of Yenching University, economics adviser of the Nationalist government and a good friend of US Ambassador Leighton Stuart! Now you know who he is, don't you?" snapped Zeng Keda through gritted teeth.

"Are you referring to Liang Jinglun, the professor of Yenching University who stirred up trouble among the students today?"

"Mr Xu, you're responsible for cooperating with my team dispatched by the Ministry of Defence to investigate the case. The purpose of our investigation is to raise money to support soldiers in fighting the war on the front line and to feed people in major cities who are suffering from famine. That's why we have to rely on aid from the US. Liang is He Qicang's right-hand man. It is imperative we coordinate the arrest. Why did you not inform us in advance?!"

"Inform you in advance? I didn't know myself until I got to the garrison headquarters. What I can tell you is that tonight's operation was coordinated by Commander-in-Chief Chen and the arrest was carried out by the Military Bureau of Investigation and Statistics. None of us at the police bureau was involved." Xu Tieying did not take offence.

"Where are you confining him?"

"We'll need to check with the Military Bureau of Investigation and Statistics. You can check with them yourself or I can do it for you."

Zeng Keda was so furious that he slammed down the phone.

Back on the shore of Houhai Lake, Fang Meng'ao had already put on his trousers. He tied his belt and demanded: "Go to the car. I'll help Director Ma put his clothes on."

Section chiefs Li and Wang were watching Ma Hanshan sitting on the bank gasping for breath. They were definitely at a loss. On hearing Fang Meng'ao's instruction, they quietly turned around. As if pardoned by the emperor, they sprinted away with gratitude to Colonel Zheng who was standing guard some two hundred metres away. Meanwhile, Fang Meng'ao put on his Air Force jacket, picked Ma Hanshan's clothes up off the ground and walked over to him.

"Kill me or not, it's up to you," said Ma Hanshan, barely managing to control his breathing.

"Put them on yourself, I'll help you with your jacket." Fang Meng'ao handed him his trousers. Ma Hanshan took his trousers and sat down on the ground to put them on. With his good left hand, he pulled the trouser legs over his knees and stood up. Then he pulled the trousers up to his waist.

Fang Meng'ao was holding his jacket and was considerate enough to lower the sleeves for him. "Put your hands in."

Ma Hanshan had no idea what it would be like. He put his hands into his sleeves while Fang Meng'ao gently lifted them up. This was how he got his jacket on.

"Did you see Cui Zhongshi underneath the water?" Fang Meng'ao's voice sounded like a harsh, cold wind howling in his ears.

"I can't say for sure. In fact, I can't be bothered to tell you. Just make it quick. Let me know what you're going to do to me!"

"I don't want you to tell me anything. Just take me to the spot where Cui Zhongshi was murdered."

"Then let me take you to the Caishikou neighbourhood. Go and take a look at the spot. Historically it's known as the execution ground where most of Peking's capital punishments were carried out during the Qing Dynasty. With so many people executed, no one went after the executioners."

Fang Meng'ao nodded. "If it weren't for this reason, someone would have been chasing you like mad. As I said just now, if you lose, you should do something for me. You're the one who can do it. If you do it, you may be able to atone for your crime."

"What is it?" said Ma Hanshan, tempted by the proposal.

"The Military Bureau of Investigation and Statistics has busted someone they shouldn't have. Now I want them to release him. Take me to him."

"Who is it that they've arrested?"

"Professor Liang Jinglun, personal assistant to the economics adviser of the Nationalist government."

The interrogation room in the secret prison of the Military Bureau of Investigation and Statistics in the Western Hills was obviously not an ordinary one. It had a small iron door and an iron window mounted high above with empty walls on all sides. A lamp was hanging from the middle of the ceiling, under which there were two wooden chairs with backs.

The man sitting in one of the wooden chairs was a real intellectual while Wang Puchen, sitting opposite, looked the same. Wang Puchen quietly observed a calm Liang Jinglun as if the two were officially discussing some academic issue. Liang Jinglun, however, didn't have to pretend to be calm, because he was certain that those who had arrested him belonged to the Military Bureau of Investigation and Statistics and the local police. But as he looked at the soft-spoken, genteel man sitting opposite him, who appeared not to be in very good health, an unspeakable foreboding came over him.

This man was either a member of the Military Bureau of Investigation or the Central Bureau of Investigation, and most likely in a high-ranking position. By now, he realised he had been caught as a real Communist.

As if hallucinating, the man in front of Liang Jinglun was transformed into Yan Chunming. "Comrade Jinglun, the protest we organised today has drawn the Kuomintang's attention. You must stay at Professor He's house tonight. It's relatively safe there."

The feeling of indescribable sorrow he felt just now had gradually become clear. It was a warm feeling, to be sure, a feeling of Yan sharing weal and woe with him. The Communists were proving to care more about him than those with the Iron and Blood Congress. But since he was not a member of the Communist Party, he should not have been in a position to have developed such sentiments. In light of the subsequent interrogation, he could not admit his secret identity as a Communist Party member, nor could he reveal his true identity as a member of the Iron and Blood Congress. For this, he could very possibly be tortured. All of a sudden, an idea occurred to him. He thought that perhaps he should undergo torture like a true member of the Communist Party. The idea made his heart swell with strong emotions. Given the choice, would he really choose the Communist Party or the Kuomintang?

"Thinking about choosing sides?" Wang Puchen suddenly opened his mouth but was still soft-spoken.

Liang Jinglun was also startled at first but quickly calmed down again, knowing that this was the so-called 'expert investigator' either with the Military Bureau or the Central Bureau of Investigation. Of course, he would not respond to the question. Wang Puchen didn't mind at all. He coughed and took out two packs of cigarettes from the big pocket attached to his Zhongshan suit. One pack was open, the other was not. He put the unopened one back in his pocket. Liang Jinglun found that both packs were *Frontline*, specially reserved for those in the upper echelons of the Kuomintang.

Wang Puchen took one out and handed it to Liang Jinglun. "Do you care to smoke?"

"Thank you. No, I don't smoke." Liang Jinglun suddenly realised that the man had very delicate fingers, thin and long.

Wang Puchen put the cigarette gently into his mouth and put the pack back in his pocket. He lit the cigarette, took a puff and then blew out the match, saying: "I know I shouldn't smoke but I can't help it. It's a human weakness. Everyone has weaknesses, Mr Liang, don't you think?"

"There are people without weaknesses." Liang Jinglun had to talk to him now.

"Really?" asked Wang Puchen, no longer coughing.

"Of course."

"I'd like to hear more." Wang Puchen looked at him very earnestly.

"One is not born, the other is dead."

"You've shown your weakness." Wang took another deep puff but didn't cough any more, nor did the smoke he inhaled appear to come out again. "This is what Mr Mao Zedong said of the CPC during the Rectification Movement in Yan'an. Originally, that 'there are only two kinds of people in the world who can't make mistakes. One refers to those who are not yet born, the other to those who are dead.' Mr Liang, did I remember that correctly? Mr Mao is quite right. Don't be afraid of making mistakes. Just admit it and correct them. So tell me, when did you join the CPC?"

There was a look of disappointment in Liang Jinglun's eyes, which Wang Puchen saw as a kind of contempt, actually a contempt for his professionalism! The cigarette, which had only half left, was burning in Wang's hand.

"What's the date today?"

"August the fourth, the thirty-seventh year of the Republic of China." Wang Puchen braced himself with high spirits.

"Remember it was on this day I joined the Communist Party."

Wang jumped to his feet suddenly and dropped his cigarette on the ground. "Surely, I'm your sponsor, aren't I?"

"You said it yourself, didn't you?"

Wang Puchen burst into violent coughing again. Obviously he had been trying hard to suppress it, yet without success. All of a sudden, the iron gate was pushed open from outside and the head of the Military Bureau's executive group rushed in with two members of the group.

The head watched Wang Puchen closely, who was slowly recovering from his violent coughing fit. "Sir, are you OK?"

Wang Puchen took out the same pack of cigarettes from his pocket and put another one in his mouth. Then he took out a match.

"Sir, please don't."

Wang Puchen struck a match and lit the cigarette. "Can't stay away from it. Cuff him and take him to the interrogation room."

Then he coughed loudly again.

The headman waved, two of his stooges walked across to Liang Jinglun, one grabbing him by the arm and pulling him up, the other slapping the handcuffs on his wrists and escorting him out.

The head, who stood there waiting for Wang's cough to ease a little, asked: "Sir, what degree of torture shall we subject him to?"

"Let him see it first. " Wang stopped coughing. "Let him watch how the others suffer and when it's his turn, I will do it myself."

"Yes sir." The head moved to the door, turned around and repeated what he had said just a moment before: "Sir, please don't smoke any more."

The confidential room of the secret prison of the Military Bureau of Investigation in the Western Hills had an iron door with integral sound insulation. It contained a secret radio, a direct line to the Kuomintang higher authorities and multiple large safes placed against the wall. The room had no windows but was lit by a lamp that was on day and night. It was a dark room with access restricted to anyone except him. Wang Puchen opened the thick iron door. But before stepping inside, he stamped out his cigarette and shook his long fingers, evidently unwilling to bring the bad smell into the room. Then he entered the room, closing the heavy door firmly behind him. There was an electric fan in the room but he didn't turn it on. Instead, he went straight over to dial a number on the phone. It didn't take long for the operator to put him through.

"Secretary Wang, this is Wang Puchen."

Actually, from the other end of the line came the voice of Wang, Comrade Jianfeng's secretary. "Hello, Comrade Puchen. Comrade Jianfeng has been waiting for your call. Please let me transfer you immediately."

Comrade Jianfeng, who had a heavy Ningbo accent, spoke loudly enough to echo throughout the room.

"Permission to report to Comrade Jianfeng. This is Wang Puchen." Wang Puchen brought his legs to attention, even though he was still sick with his cough.

Jianfeng's voice reverberated on the telephone. "How is the interrogation going?"

"Report to Comrade Jianfeng that I've just interrogated him in accordance with your instructions."

"How did Comrade Liang Jinglun react?"

"He was very normal, very tactful when answering my questions."

"Perhaps you were too kind to him?"

"I'm afraid I wasn't, Comrade Jianfeng. I comply with all the procedures for interrogating CPC underground agents. The crux of the matter is what to do next. He Qicang called Li Zongren, and Li Yuqing personally intervened, but Chen Jicheng is rather defiant. He doesn't buy it. He insisted that Comrade Liang Jinglun be interrogated and tortured to establish whether he is a CPC agent. In addition, the twenty student auditors should also be tortured so that we can identify the CPC agents among them, which is a bit challenging. Would it be possible to ask Nanking to call Chen Jicheng and tell him to give He Qicang some face and release Liang Jinglun?"

There was a brief silence on the phone.

Trying to avoid coughing when speaking with Comrade Jianfeng, Wang Puchen clamped the phone to his shoulder, struck a match and immediately put it out. A wisp of phosphorous smoke came from the end of the match. He put the match close to his nostrils and sucked in the wisp of phosphorous smoke.

Miraculously, it worked, and he stopped coughing.

"It's not as simple as you think." Jianfeng's voice reverberated down the line once more. "He Qicang shouldn't call Li Zongren. Chen Jicheng called to complain to the president before anyone else, saying that he would resign if he couldn't arrest any Communists this time. I learned from a presidential aide that the president hung up the phone with a simple answer: 'I see.' So it was impossible for Nanking to put pressure on Chen Jicheng."

"Do we really need to torture Comrade Liang Jinglun?"

Suddenly, Jianfeng's voice lost its echo over the phone, as if he had appeared in person to speak directly into his ears.

Wang Puchen was quite nervous, yet even in the dog days of summer he was not sweating. He wiped his forehead with his hand but was obviously not wiping away sweat. "It's hard to know the proper limits, Comrade Jianfeng, which is not to say that I'm concerned about Chen Jichen's dissatisfaction with lighter torture but that it is likely to arouse the suspicion of the Communists. But if we use harsher torture, will Comrade Jinglun be able to stand it? May I suggest we ask Comrade Zeng Keda to find a way to get Comrade Liang Jinglun released through his connections?"

"On what grounds?" Now, Comrade Jianfeng was sounding quite stern. "Zeng Keda is tasked to deal with corruption, while you're tasked to deal with the Communist Party. You and Zeng Keda are supposed to work along parallel lines that never intersect! Your identity is confidential within the organisation. Do you want to undermine the principles of the organisation by passing the buck and pushing it onto Zeng Keda?"

"I accept your criticism, Comrade Jianfeng." Wang Puchen had to make a firm statement now. "I'll take care of it alone and personally, and report to you as soon as possible."

"How will you handle it personally? Give me the details." Jianfeng's voice had calmed down a little.

It was time to put him to the test, as he thought sharply and had to answer promptly. "Yes, Comrade Jianfeng. Here's my take. First, I'll personally torture him, though I'll try my best not to hurt Comrade Liang Jinglun too much. Meanwhile, I'll see to it that no one suspects him as well. Second, my first idea must be based on the second, that is, Comrade Liang Jinglun should be able to withstand the torture I subject him to without revealing anything. It's hard for me to rule out the possibility that Comrade Liang Jinglun won't be able to stand the torture and might say something he shouldn't." At this point, he stopped intentionally.

'Go on," said Jianfeng.

"Yes, I will make him stop talking in time but Comrade Liang Jinglun may perhaps withdraw from the organisation. It's a pity, it might even disrupt Comrade Jianfeng's overall arrangement."

"Don't you think you have too many ideas?"

Wang Puchen was startled.

"Reconsider your first comment and withdraw your second!" With that, Comrade Jianfeng hung up the phone.

Wang Puchen heard a confused noise when the telephone at the other end was put back on its stand. He sensed that Comrade Jianfeng must be in a very bad mood. Wang Puchen was also in a bad mood by then. Finally, he wasn't able to hold back any longer and burst into a violent coughing fit when suddenly the ear-piercing sound of the electric bell installed by the iron door began to ring. Knowing that this was an emergency, Wang Puchen tried to suppress his cough and walked to the heavy iron door.

The secret prison of the Military Bureau of Investigation in the Western Hills contained a yard inside its huge compound where Fang Mengwei had driven to rescue Cui Zhongshi that night. There was still the same two-storey building in the compound. Wang Puchen stopped before reaching the doorstep near the entrance. Through the window, he could see Ma Hanshan standing in the open yard, with Fang Meng'ao next to him. Behind them was a platoon of Youth Army soldiers.

The number of agents affiliated with the Military Bureau of Investigation was fewer than that of the Youth Army. All of them were standing in front of the stairs outside the building. Pistols in hand, they stood in a row, trying to block the entrance.

"Why the guns? Are you going to fight me? Are we going to be fighting among ourselves?" Ma Hanshan looked sharply at the executive group leader.

"Sir, they didn't force you to come, did they?" the head of the group asked Ma Hanshan, doubtfully.

"Who forced me? Who would dare force me?"

Ma Hanshan threw a quick glance at all the agents of the Military Bureau of Investigation and said: "Put away your pistols!"

Exactly as Wang Puchen had said before, Ma Hanshan was still quite capable of controlling the situation. At his command, all of the agents affiliated with the Peking station of the Military Council's Bureau of Investigation and Statistics put their guns in their holsters.

Wang Puchen took in the disorder through the window. "Did you arrest a guy by the name of Liang Jinglun?" Ma Hanshan asked the executive group leader again. The latter did not immediately answer this time and instead glanced at Fang Meng'ao standing behind Ma Hanshan, whom he suspected was being held at gun point.

"What are you looking at him for? He's with me. Are you keeping Liang Jinglun here?" Ma Hanshan did not seem to be under duress.

"Yes sir. Mr Wang is also here. He's interrogating him in person," replied the head of the group.

"Is he a member of the CPC?" asked Ma Hanshan, intently. Fang Meng'ao's eyes, incandescent with rage, also stared at the group leader.

"Not that I know."

"Why did you arrest him if he is not a Communist? It makes things messier, doesn't it?" Ma Hanshan looked back at Fang Meng'ao.

"Let the brothers take a rest outside. I will take you to have him released."

"Director Ma." The door on the ground floor opened and out came Wang Puchen, shutting the door behind him.

"I'm looking for you, Puchen." Ma Hanshan obviously regarded him as his junior. When he saw Wang Puchen sizing up Fang Meng'ao at the door, he added: "Haven't you two met before? Let me introduce you. This is Station Chief Wang, my successor, very talented, even though he is in poor health. This is Colonel Fang Meng'ao, head of the Inspection Brigade sent by the Ministry of Defence."

"Pleased to meet you. I've heard so much about you." Wang Puchen stood still at the entrance.

Seeing him blocking the entrance, Fang Meng'ao did not greet him in return. Instead, he turned to Ma Hanshan who seemed to be able to sense where the problem was. He went straight over to Wang Puchen and whispered in his ear: "Let Liang Jinglun go. He is He Qicang's assistant and has lots of connections in the US. The

Ministry of Defence's investigation team is giving me a hard time. Don't mess around on this issue."

Wang Puchen replied in his signature weak voice: "I'm quite aware of the fact that Liang Jinglun is He Qicang's assistant and that he has connections in America. But he has nothing to do with the investigation mission of the Ministry of Defence. Why did Colonel Fang tell us to free the suspect?"

"The Fangs and Hes are close family friends." Ma Hanshan was still patient but his tone had become much more grave. "As long as he is not a Commie, you should let him go, just do the chancellor this honour."

In fact, countless thoughts had already crossed Wang's mind. Both Fang Meng'ao's unexpected appearance and Ma Hanshan's inconceivable intervention on Liang's behalf could help him solve the pressing issue at hand. The key was to report to Comrade Jianfeng in advance.

"Sir, we didn't arrest Liang Jinglun," said Wang Puchen whose attitude today was neither hostile nor friendly.

"But the guy is being kept inside the building. How come you say you didn't bust him?"

"Commander-in-Chief Chen personally ordered me to arrest him. I'm in no position to let him go."

Ma Hanshan's eyeballs began to roll. He looked back at Fang Meng'ao and then turned to Wang Puchen. "I know Commander-in-Chief Chen ordered the arrest but he would not name who he wanted to make the arrest. We can decide who to release, can't we?"

Looking at Ma Hanshan, Wang Puchen's eyes sparkled and his voice was low and ambiguous. "Liang Jinglun was busted because Commander-in-Chief Chen personally mentioned him by name, mainly because he has been such a trouble-maker. Besides, you've also been detained for this. Commander-in-Chief Chen believes it's the Communist Party that has been the instigator behind the scenes, that's why he put the finger on Liang Jinglun. Director Ma, you really shouldn't have brought him here."

Ma Hanshan stood there motionless but quickly exclaimed: "Then you'll have to ask Commander Chen for instructions. In short, if there is no proof that he is a Commie, you should let him go."

This was evidently addressed to Fang Meng'ao who, of course, heard it and went over to them, extending his hand to Wang Puchen. It was a gesture to defuse the situation via a handshake. Wang Puchen had to extend his hand with his long, thin fingers while Fang's was big and bony. Ma Hanshan looked at their hands with childlike wonder, seemingly oblivious to all that was going on around him.

Fang Meng'ao gently clasped Wang Puchen's hand, as if holding a small bunch of spring onions. Wang Puchen quickly realised that he could not withdraw his hand because the moment he thought about doing so, Fang Meng'ao tightened his grip. He had just lost control of his own hand. Meanwhile, Ma Hanshan also felt that one of his arms was in Fang Meng'ao's firm grasp. Ironically, one was a former stationmaster while the other was the current stationmaster of the Military Council's Bureau of Investigation. Both men were entirely in Fang Meng'ao's control.

"Director Wang, can you call for instructions? Meanwhile Director Ma, can you take me to check out the detainee first?"

The officers on both sides went in, with no instructions left for Colonel Zheng and his Youth Army. They continued to stay in the yard, as did the agents of the Bureau of Investigation and Statistics. Colonel Zheng walked over to the head of the group. "Can I use the direct line in the guard's room?"

"Yes, please do."

"Take me there."

"How come you're calling me to report this late?" asked Zeng Keda in his room in Gu Weijun's residence.

"I didn't have access to a telephone on the way, nor did I know what he was planning to do," answered Colonel Zheng, nervously.

"Listen up!" snapped Zeng Keda. "Make sure Captain Fang and Professor Liang are safe, and try not to have a confrontation with the agents of the Military Council's Bureau of Investigation and Statistics."

Without waiting for Zheng's response, Zeng Keda hung up and began to dial another number.

"Secretary Wang? I've got a situation here. Is Comrade Jianfeng back yet?"

"No, not yet."

"Secretary Wang." To his great surprise, the person at the other end quickly hung up. Zeng Keda stood there, frozen, like a woman abandoned by her lover.

Inside the confidential room of the secret prison of the Bureau of Investigation and Statistics of the Military Council in the Western Hills, Wang Puchen was reporting on the phone: "Yes, Comrade Jianfeng." Much of the politeness, as well as the dread, had vanished and what was now so clearly visible was the deep-seated fighting spirit that was actually tantamount to a kind of murderous spirit. "I understand your great thinking and the calculated move. One should be suspicious when using people and one should also use them even if one is suspicious of them. Using Fang Meng'ao is a risky move. I've just got to know him today. Once again, Duke Zeng Wenzheng puts it best: 'Dead men can be used. The key is to use them to our advantage.' Please correct me if I'm wrong, Comrade Jianfeng."

"Your understanding of the issue is much deeper than Comrade Keda's," commended Comrade Jianfeng on the phone. "I agree with what you just said. Tell Ma Hanshan to give Liang Jinglun and the few students to Fang Meng'ao. As for Ma Hanshan, tell him to explain himself to Chen Jicheng. From now on, use your men and keep a close watch on Fang Meng'ao. The Communist Party will surely send someone other than Comrade Liang Jinglun to contact him. Your task is not only to cut the Communist Party off from Fang Meng'ao but also to follow the clues to the Communist Party's core underground organisation in Peking. The idea is to ensure that the Nationalist Army can fight the Communist insurgents in the Peking-Tianjin region without fear of an attack from the rear and that the currency reform should be carried out."

"Yes, Comrade Jianfeng." Wang Puchen answered in a way that didn't sound remotely like the response of a sick man.

"Also, regarding the man you mentioned just now, the man by the name of Master Five, the underground Communist Party agent in Peking, I got a detailed report from Bureau Chief Mao today. This man, who has a labour movement background, is now in charge of the Communist Party's underground organisation in Peking. He's extremely dangerous. Try everything possible to catch him first. If you can't capture him alive, shoot to kill him on the spot!"

"Hello Professor and Xiaoyu," said Liang Jinglun as he pushed open the door to the living room in He Qicang's house. He stood at the door with the first light of the morning shining from behind his back. He Qicang sat upright on the sofa in amazement while He Xiaoyu jumped to her feet from the chair beside her father.

"How did you manage to get out?" asked He Qicang after regaining his composure.

Liang was surprised to see He Xiaoyu looking at the half-open door behind him, so he coughed slightly to clear his throat before replying to his professor: "Captain Fang drove me back. He's outside waiting for permission to come in."

"Come on in!" He Qicang quickly stood up with aid of his walking stick.

But Liang glanced at He Xiaoyu and saw that she was still standing there with no intention of going to open the door. He turned and opened it himself.

"Captain Fang, Professor Liang would like to invite you in."

As Fang Meng'ao came in, the sky outside was even brighter. He Qicang stood very straight with his eyes looking at Fang Meng'ao as he entered. His daughter was the first to feel the change of heart, followed by Liang Jinglun. It was not just about welcoming a special guest, it was also about being baptised in an aura with which Fang Meng'ao should be seen as a good influence by his daughter and his favourite student.

In this way, He Xiaoyu was able to look at Fang Meng'ao with great respect. Fang Meng'ao had also changed dramatically since his departure the night before: first, he was not wearing his air force cap, and second, standing side by side with Liang Jinglun at the door, he no longer appeared like a professional soldier. He Qicang, who was still standing there very straight, looked at Fang Meng'ao kindly and appreciatively.

Only then did Liang Jinglun realise what he should do. He said to Fang Meng'ao: "Captain Fang, please come in."

Fang Meng'ao, in a particularly humble manner, nodded politely to Liang Jinglun and then walked in.

All of a sudden, He Qicang bowed gratefully to Fang Meng'ao as he stepped inside the living room.

"Uncle He!" Fang Meng'ao had never been so embarrassed. He hurriedly raised his hand to salute He Qicang, only to find that he was not wearing his military cap, so he bent his body to perform a standard ninety-degree bow. To show his respect, he remained in that posture. He Xiaoyu helped support her father but Fang Meng'ao was still bowing and remained where he was. At that moment, she deliberately avoided eye contact with Liang Jinglun and instead kept her eyes on Fang Meng'ao.

Unexpectedly, He Qicang also fastened his eyes on Fang Meng'ao now that he was standing upright while Liang Jinglun felt rather overshadowed. When he came up to Fang Meng'ao, his gown, rather than fluttering, almost tripped him up.

"Captain Fang, please have a seat." Liang Jinglun helped Fang Meng'ao up, and his tone was very modest and polite.

Fang Meng'ao walked over to the sofa.

He Qicang smiled and stretched out his hand towards the sofa but Fang Meng'ao remained standing.

"Dad, you sit down first." He Xiaoyu helped her father sit down.

"Mr Liang." Fang Meng'ao still did not sit, looking at Liang Jinglun, obviously waiting for him to sit first.

The look in He Qicang's eyes grew softer and softer. He sensed Fang Meng'ao's respect for Liang Jinglun. At the same time, he could not restrain the desire to see his daughter's reaction. However, He Xiaoyu's eyes were already directed at the floor.

He Qicang's voice last night was echoing almost simultaneously in the ears of the father and daughter: "He has a gun and pretends to be a saviour... Don't you think Fang Meng'ao is learning from them?"

"Sir, if you need to talk with Captain Fang alone, Xiaoyu and I can wait outside," suggested Liang Jinglun, thoughtfully.

He Qicang nodded and then looked at Fang Meng'ao. "Please, sit down," he said.

Fang Meng'ao did as he was told. Liang Jinglun stepped back first, then turned to walk out of the living room. But He Xiaoyu looked at the aluminium pot with steamed bread on the kitchen stove.

"I'll take care of it," said He Qicang.

He Xiaoyu then looked at Fang Meng'ao, nodded her head and went over to the living room door.

For several days, he had not returned to his one-bedroom bungalow in He Qicang's courtyard. But he didn't even bother to look around when he sat down. He Xiaoyu remained standing without taking a seat. The table and chair in the room were neat and tidy, as was the bedroom inside. Liang Jinglun, however, felt out of place, as if it was not his residence.

"They didn't hurt you, did they?" asked He Xiaoyu softly.

"I was already in the torture room when Fang Meng'ao arrived. Just in time. He was so fast."

Liang Jinglun looked at He Xiaoyu.

"Anything wrong with him coming in time to save you?" He Xiaoyu sensed something strange from Liang Jinglun's manner and tone.

"All the students who were caught simultaneously were tortured. I did have a feeling that the Kuomintang's Bureau of Investigation of the Military Council was deliberately waiting for Fang Meng'ao to rescue me." Liang Jinglun did not conceal the questioning look in his eyes but he was looking at He Xiaoyu.

"My father called Li Zongren as soon as you were arrested. Li Yuqing answered the call." He Xiaoyu explained it so briefly that Liang Jinglun felt very embarrassed about what he had just said.

"Then Fang Meng'ao came to my rescue? It makes sense. It's such a complicated struggle we're having with the Kuomintang, isn't it?"

Liang Jinglun sat by the window through which he could see the courtyard and several Youth Army soldiers standing guard at the closed gate. "I should have talked with you about the decision of the Students' Union the night before. Unfortunately, Fang Meng'ao came... Time is tight. Please sit down."

He Xiaoyu didn't know whether to feel sorry for Liang Jinglun or pity him. After all, she had accepted the assignment given to her by the party organisation and now she still had to accept the instructions that she was pretending to follow. She went over to him and looked across the table at his still solemn face. As she sat down, she unconsciously straightened her skirt to cover her legs below the knee and crossed her feet.

Being aware of her self-consciousness, Liang Jinglun said: "Through our investigation, the union decided that in order to win the final struggle, we must immediately win over Fang Meng'ao and his Youth Aviation Brigade."

"It must have been eleven years, huh?" asked He Qicang.

"More like thirteen since we last met, Uncle He," said Fang Meng'ao. "You've been teaching here at Yenching since 1935 while Aunt He and Xiaoyu were staying in Shanghai."

"My mistake. Indeed, it's been thirteen years," lamented He Qicang. "'A general dies in a hundredth battle, a valiant warrior returns triumphantly in the tenth year'. It has been three years since victory in the War of Resistance Against Japanese Aggression. You, however, have a home and a country you can't return to, am I right?"

Fang Meng'ao was shocked but did not answer. He looked carefully and listened attentively. "I like the way you are now, including the way you came in this morning." He Qicang began to recollect the past again. "You were a teenager at the time. You liked to eavesdrop on my conversations with your father while pretending to be asleep. But we decided not to expose your trick. When you were a child, you were afraid of nothing but two people. One was your father, the other was your Uncle He." Fang Meng'ao tried to hide his mixed feelings with a forced smile.

"Now let's talk but, of course, you don't have to if you don't want to. Just listen instead like you did when you were a kid," said He Qicang solemnly. "I said just now that you have a country you cannot return to. Actually, that's not accurate. During the eight years of the War Against Japanese Aggression, we were all fighting to save our nation. But to date, the Republic of China is still not a unified state. Some are smug enough to claim that we are one of the

Four Great Powers. Take a look at the bag of flour you gave me. Which powerful country depends on the charity of another to maintain its day-to-day governance? A failed state in need of rescue can be bossed around all the time!"

Fang Meng'ao sat upright and looked in Uncle He's eyes, sparkling with tears. He Qicang pointed to the bag of flour. "Made in the US! Which country on earth has ever been *made* by another?"

"Well said!" replied Fang Meng'ao appreciatively. "Indulge me, Uncle He, please go on."

Leaning on his cane with both hands, He Qicang also sat upright. "You've been in Peking for a month, you must have seen a lot of what is going on. You've intercepted the grain for the Army Fourth Corps, checked the accounts of the Citizens' Food Distribution Committee and those of the Peking branch. Many people are clapping their hands and thinking you're doing something really great – fighting corruption! But is it really about fighting corruption?"

"I'm listening."

"Are you capable of fighting against corruption? If you are, it is truly anti-corruption. If you aren't, it's fake!"

"I planned to come here to ask Professor Liang about these things. But thank you for trusting me, Uncle He. Could you please tell me what is corruption from the perspective of economics?" His eyes were full of anticipation.

He Qicang gave a wry smile. "Your father studied economics in the US for six years, I studied for eight years. But even now, I don't know what economics is. Especially back in China, there is no such thing as economics at all. What you're doing now has less to do with economics and more to do with politics. You're involved in politics. If you really want me to teach you, let me be honest: not a thing I learned in America applies. To describe what you're doing, I can share with you an old Chinese saying that can be summed up in eight characters."

"Uncle He, please tell me."

"To cut off one's source of wealth is tantamount to killing one's parents."

Fang Meng'ao was stunned for a moment and then laughed.

"Don't laugh," beseeched He Qicang, becoming even more serious. "The Bureau of Reserve Cadres of the Ministry of Defence has so many confidants whom they don't use. Why do they just use you? Because you are rightfully willing to 'kill their parents'! Because you even dare to kill your own parent!"

"Uncle He, are you trying to advise me against something?"

"No, I'm not. I've never tried to advise your father before, so I will not advise you either. Just remember, they seized Liang Jinglun last night. Later they might also arrest you and perhaps kill you. Do you think Chen Jicheng and so many others will be willing to let you go on like this? You're now heading the investigation team of the Ministry of Defence, that's because they need to use you for a bigger agenda. A big storm is brewing. Many people will die in this storm, including those who are corrupt and those who fight against corruption!"

"Of course, I am one of those who will die in the storm. But it's not so easy to have me killed."

"It's easy, they can always trump up a charge. After all, you're a member of the CPC!" He Qicang shook his head and looked at Fang Meng'ao as if he was looking at his own son.

CHAPTER 9

The large desk in Governor Fang's office was piled high with account books left by Cui Zhongshi. Xie Peidong's had his head buried in the accounts. Seemingly all night long, he had been doing something that seemed incomprehensible to a casual observer. On his left was an open account book, in the middle an open book, on the right an open notebook.

On the left side of the account book were lines of neat numbers, while at the bottom of the page was the signature of Cui Zhongshi, three characters that Xie Peidong was very familiar with. Xie Peidong looked sequentially in the ledger for the numbers that had occasionally been written in red ink. By putting three red characters in a group, Xie Peidong opened the book in front of him on the page number according to the first red character; then counted to the line on that same page based on the second red character. Finally, he located the character in that line corresponding with the third character.

His eyes were sharp, his hands were quick and a number came out fast. Xie Peidong wrote quickly in the notebook on the right!

As the nib of the pen slid along, a line of the following characters appeared:

On 24 June, the Yangtze Construction Company and Fuzhong Company arbitraged US$12 million worth of cheap rice and sold it to the Citizens' Food Distribution Committee at a price five times higher than the black market price.

Xie Peidong repeated the previous procedure. First, he looked for the red numbers in Cui Zhongshi's account book, then looked through the book to find the characters, and then wrote the following words in his notebook:

Peking and Tianjin (Pingjin) embezzled US$10 million in profits, with the Yangtze Construction Company and Fu Zhong Company embezzling sixty per cent, the military twenty per cent and the Citizens' Food Distribution Committee the remaining twenty percent.

As the day dawned, Xie Peidong could not help but look at the signatures on the account books signed by Cui Zhongshi, especially when looking at the hard evidence that Cui Zhongshi had collected while putting his life at stake. The notebook contained details of corruption since the Citizens' Food Distribution Committee was founded in April.

"Cui Zhongshi", the three characters slowly and magically transformed into a mirage that morphed into his loyal and honest face!

Xie Peidong's eyes were wet with tears.

A shrill telephone ring woke him up! Xie Peidong closed his notebook, put it in his inside pocket and picked up the receiver. There was urgency in the voice at the other end. "Is this Governor Fang? Governor Fang, this is Wang Benquan speaking."

It was an early call, the tone of which had a strong sense of urgency, from the chief secretary of the Central Bank in Nanking. It must have been of great significance!

Xie Peidong replied humbly: "Chief Secretary Wang? This is Xie Peidong. The governor is not available at the moment."

Wang Benquan's voice sounded even more urgent. "When do you think he'll be available?"

"In about half an hour," said Xie Peidong.

"That might be too late!" snapped Wang Benquan, full of nervousness and anxiety. "The Rear Office of the Military Affairs Commission of the Peking Field Headquarters will soon inform him of a meeting he should attend. This is a heads-up! You must tell him in detail before his meeting."

"Tell me," said Xie Peidong. "I'll take notes."

Wang Benquan sounded more frustrated as he said: "Don't take notes, just remember it!"

"Go on, please tell me."

"It's me, Keda, Comrade Jianfeng," said Zeng Keda, holding the phone tightly in his hand in his room in Gu Weijun's residence. He had been waiting all night for Comrade Jianfeng's call.

"Something went terribly wrong, did you know that?" Jianfeng's voice on the phone bordered on grief and indignation.

"What is it? Comrade Jianfeng, does it have anything to do with our job performance?" Zeng Keda looked horrified.

"Generally speaking, yes. Technically, no. You are not responsible. The truth is that the Americans suddenly sent a note that they would stop delivering the first batch of a hundred and seventy million dollars of aid material and leave them on the high seas without entering the harbour. It was Leighton Stuart who reported to the US government last night!" The voice of Comrade Jianfeng on the phone was like a shrill wind blowing in from the sea.

Zeng Keda's face turned white. "I was just about to report to you. Chen Jicheng ordered the arrest of Liang Jinglun and his students last night. Did He Qicang make a complaint to Leighton Stuart?"

"Even worse. It was Li Zongren who disclosed the news to the Americans."

"That old fart! Does he want to replace the president?" Zeng Keda cursed with grief and anger.

"Leighton Stuart and his ilk in America have been trying to support Li Zongren for a long time. When our own men fail, they take advantage of our failure..." Jianfeng's voice on the phone turned gloomy and forlorn. "Our anti-corruption efforts have met with considerable approval by the US government but were totally compromised by Chen Jicheng's operation last night when he arrested the students as well as our own agent. Li and his stooges must have taken advantage of it! Just now, Li Zongren proposed to the president to convene an emergency anti-corruption meeting and the president had to agree. Remember, you are on the list of attendees. On behalf of the investigation team of the Ministry of Defence, make a firm statement and let them know that we will intensify our efforts to investigate corruption cases involving the Peking Citizens' Food Distribution Committee!"

"Comrade Jianfeng, may I ask how?"

Jianfeng's voice on the phone revealed a cold-blooded toughness. "Arrest Ma Hanshan and others involved in the corruption cases of the Citizens' Food Distribution Committee and audit the accounts of the Peking branch! Tell Fang Meng'ao and his inspection brigade to do it immediately after you're done with the meeting. Then, in my name, call Xu Tieying and Wang Puchen, the stationmaster of the Peking station of the State Secrecy Bureau, to meet with you and order the Central Bureau of Investigation and Statistics, and the Military Council's Bureau of Investigation and Statistics to secretly investigate the Rear Office of the Military Affairs Commission Peking Field Headquarters. Two things: one is to find out whether Li Zongren and his people have conducted secret peace talks with the Communist Party. The other is to conduct a thorough investigation of Li Zongren's subordinates. If they are involved in any corruption cases, report to me directly."

"Yes sir!" replied Zeng Keda loudly, followed by one last question. "Comrade Jianfeng, according to our investigation, Xu Tieying and the party headquarters of the Kuomintang are possibly colluding with those involved in the corruption case at the Peking Citizens' Food Distribution Committee. If they are involved, will I be able to investigate them? And if so, how?"

Obviously, Jianfeng had a solution in mind since he replied straight away: "First of all, corruption within the party has been something that I now find impossible to reverse. Therefore, cases pertaining to corruption of party property can only be tolerated for the time being while we fight the Communists. But they should not do it for personal gain in the name of the party! Xu Tieying works for personal gain! Warn him on my behalf, let him understand our resolve to stamp out corruption. Tell him to stop immediately and cooperate with us. If he continues working against us, he might be the next one to be arrested."

"Understood."

Xie Peidong opened the office door as soon as he was done talking on the phone. As he went to the stairs he found Fang Mengwei sitting in the living room. Fang Mengwei was wearing a trim police uniform with a large suitcase and a rattan box beside him, looking as if he was about to move out of the house!

Obviously, Fang Mengwei was waiting for Xie Peidong to say goodbye. He stood up immediately after seeing Xie Peidong coming his way. Xie Peidong glanced at the two suitcases at his feet and then looked at him with a grim expression on his face. "Come upstairs." He turned around and walked into the office.

"Do you want to move out?" Xie Peidong looked at Fang Mengwei at the door of the office.

Fang Mengwei nodded.

"Because of Mulan?"

Fang Mengwei was silent for a while, then he nodded his head gently.

"Listen up," said Xie Peidong, looking him in the eye. "Your elder brother has put a lot of pressure on your father and it will get even more intense. So you can't put any more pressure on him. Now, leave the cases behind, drive to your stepmother's place and pick up the governor so that he can attend a meeting at the Rear Office of the Military Affairs Commission Peking Field Headquarters."

"What's up?" asked Fang Mengwei, raising his head.

"I got two phone calls just now, one from the Central Bank in Nanking, the other from the Rear Office of the Military Affairs Commission Peking Field Headquarters. The Americans suddenly presented a note calling an immediate halt to their one hundred and seventy million dollars in aid. The incident started in Peking because it accused the government of continuing to embezzle their aid."

"How could such a thing have happened just last night?" Fang Mengwei sensed the seriousness of the situation.

"It's said that last night Chen Jicheng arrested the students who protested at the Peking Citizens' Food Distribution Committee and also the personal assistant of Chancellor He, Liang Jinglun. Vice-President Li himself intervened but did not solve the problem. Eventually, someone leaked it to the US Embassy."

"Who the hell is Liang Jinglun?" Hearing this, Fang Mengwei had quite mixed feelings.

"Don't worry about Liang Jinglun any more. I'll stay put and talk some sense into Mulan. By the way, try to look relaxed when you pick up the governor."

"OK, Uncle Xie." Fang Mengwei turned around to the stairway, looking so lonely from behind.

Xie Peidong watched Fang Mengwei walk out of the living room. Then his eyes turned to his daughter's room on the first floor.

At Liang Jinglun's place in He Qicang's residence, Liang Jinglun pleaded with He Xiaoyu: "So we won't talk about Xie Mulan today, then?"

"If Fang Meng'ao asks me out again, how do I answer him?"

"Tell him that Mr Liang is celibate," responded Liang Jinglun hard-heartedly as he looked out of the window.

He Xiaoyu lifted her gaze and looked affectionately at Liang Jinglun whose gaze moved back from the window to meet hers. "Can you recite Chen Mengjia's *A Wild Flower*?"

He Xiaoyu's eyes filled with tears; even though she could recite it, she shook her head.

"I'll recite the first paragraph, then you recite the second. Just do it to keep me company."

Without looking at He Xiaoyu, Liang Jinglun stood up and slowly paced up and down in the small space which he had to himself, his gown beginning to flutter again. With his uniquely deep and rich voice, and a soft southern accent, Liang Jinglun began to recite the poem that they had both enjoyed tremendously once before.

> *A wild flower bloomed and withered in the wilderness.*
> *Unexpectedly, the little life laughed at the sun*
> *God gave him wisdom, and he knew it.*
> *His joy, his poetry, fluttered softly in the breeze.*

He Xiaoyu remained silent. Liang Jinglun's gown was still fluttering. But in He Xiaoyu's eyes, the long gown would soon vanish without a trace. She was so afraid that she began to recite the second stanza in a low voice.

> *A wild flower bloomed and withered in the wilderness.*
> *He could not see his own smallness when he saw the spring.*
> *He was so used to the softness and howling of the wind that even*
> *His own dreams were easily forgotten.*

The gown stopped fluttering, with Liang Jinglun very much alive, still standing in front of her.

"The poem will belong to Fang Meng'ao later." Liang Jinglun's voice seemed to He Xiaoyu to come from afar.

"Is that also the decision of the party organisation?" He Xiaoyu suddenly jumped to her feet.

Liang Jinglun looked at her again, very intensely. "No, but it's my suggestion."

"What do you mean by your suggestion? Do you mind explaining yourself?"

Liang Jinglun looked away again. "The struggle the Students' Union is engaged in needs Fang Meng'ao, as does the survival of the people in Peking. The Fang Meng'ao you come into contact with must be the real Fang Meng'ao. You must know what he likes and dislikes."

"That you don't have to tell me, I know what he likes."

"What does he like?"

"He likes drinking, smoking, he has all the bad habits of a man."

Liang Jinglun gently shook his head. "Any merits? Why do you exclude his strong points?"

"He likes music, he likes Western *bel canto* and sings very well."

"What else?" Liang Jinglun closed his eyes.

"He also likes to sing folk songs, such as *Blooming Flowers, Full Moon*. His singing would move you to tears."

"What else?" Liang Jinglun's eyes were still closed.

"He also likes to drive his jeep as fast as an airplane. It is liable to hit people or objects at any time." He Xiaoyu bit her lip.

"Anything else?" Liang Jinglun opened his eyes.

"I don't know. I'll tell you when I know more."

Liang Jinglun was silent for a moment. "I'll tell you what. He also likes poetry. He likes Tagore and lately he's taken to the poems of the Crescent Moon School. He particularly likes the one we recited just now, *A Wild Flower*, Xu Zhimo's *Saying Goodbye to Cambridge Again* and Bian Zhilin's *Fragment*. Xiaoyu, you should practice reciting all the poems of the Crescent Moon School."

"Any more instructions?"

"What's more, he doesn't like being humoured."

"Anything else?"

"That's all I can tell you."

"I see. Can I make a request to you, too?"

"Of course."

"In the future, in addition to things related to my job, can I choose not to tell you what Fang Meng'ao likes or dislikes?"

Liang Jinglun had such a strong desire to look at He Xiaoyu at that moment. But when he turned round, he chose to look out of the window and a single word burst out of his mouth: "Yes."

With that, he strode out of the room, his gown still fluttering. Finally, He Xiaoyu was aware of tears streaming down her cheeks. She stood there for a moment when suddenly she heard her father calling in the garden: "Where's Xiaoyu?" She quickly took out her handkerchief, dried her tears and looked out of the window.

Her father, Fang Meng'ao and Liang Jinglun were all standing in the garden. She took a deep breath and walked out of the door of the small room.

Outside the gate of He Qicang's house, the Youth Army soldiers, who were supposed to be guarding Fang Meng'ao, were all standing upright as they saw an approaching Buick car flying a small national flag of the Republic of China on the front of its bonnet!

Almost everyone in Peking could recognise the car. It was Vice-President Li Zongren's presidential limo! Liang Jinglun was standing beside He Qicang and He Xiaoyu had also come to join them. They all saw the car.

"Sometimes I wish my predictions were wrong," He Qicang told Fang Meng'ao.

Fang Meng'ao seemed to understand him and nodded his head.

Then, He Qicang turned to Liang Jinglun. "It looks as though no one dares to catch you today, at least. Get some rest and help me sort out that pile of waste paper again."

"Is that the economic reform plan you are talking about? Do you need to bring it to the meeting?"

"It's not a plan, it's waste paper. What the Nanking government wants is just waste paper. Today's meeting has nothing to do with a pile of waste paper. I'm going because I heard that Chen Jicheng will also attend the meeting. I need an explanation from him. If he can't explain to me what happened last night, I will have them burnt when I come back!"

With a wave of his hand, he went to the gate.

"Dad!" yelled He Xiaoyu behind his back. "You haven't eaten your breakfast yet!"

"I'll eat at Vice-President Li's!"

He Qicang had walked out of the courtyard with his stick. The soldiers saluted him in unison. He walked to the rear seat of the Buick where Li Zongren's adjutant, the colonel, had been waiting for him, with one hand on the door frame, the other helping him into the limo.

The adjutant moved quickly to sit in the front passenger seat. The car was escorted by two motorcycles in front and one mid-sized military jeep behind.

"It's been a whole night and I don't know how they have progressed in auditing the accounts. I'll have to go, too," said Fang Meng'ao, looking at Liang Jinglun and He Xiaoyu.

"Can you give me a lift? I'm going to check on Mulan."

Fang Meng'ao turned to Liang Jinglun who held out his hand to him. "Thank you, Captain Fang, for rescuing the students and me. If you don't mind, please give Xiaoyu a lift."

With that, he gratefully shook Fang Meng'ao's hand.

Fang Meng'ao became quite aware of the hidden meaning of the handshake and saw the resolute look on He Xiaoyu's face.

"Good. Let's get into the jeep."

The Youth Army soldiers saluted him again. Fang Meng'ao went to his jeep, hesitated for a moment and opened the rear door. Liang Jinglun was still standing at the gate watching He Xiaoyu getting into the jeep while Fang Meng'ao took the hat handed to him by one of the soldiers. After putting on his hat, Fang Meng'ao waved to salute Liang Jinglun from a distance before sitting in the driver's seat. Colonel Zheng rushed to his jeep at the back of the convoy. Some of his Youth Army soldiers got into the jeep but the majority boarded the ten-wheeler. All three vehicles started moving. Liang Jinglun was still standing at the gate of the courtyard even though he was not able to see He Xiaoyu sitting in Fang Meng'ao's jeep.

In the back of the jeep, He Xiaoyu looked at Fang Meng'ao in the front while Fang Meng'ao looked at her in the rearview mirror.

"I've been told that I look better when viewed from behind. Is that true?" As always, Fang Meng'ao's words and actions had a tendency to catch people off guard.

He Xiaoyu was stunned for a moment and replied: "Does anyone like to see you from behind your back?"

"Like it or not, they all look at my back. In fact, countless pairs of eyes look at me from behind but I can't see them."

Fang Meng'ao apparently said these words wilfully but He Xiaoyu felt her heart miss a beat. She understood it to signify his loneliness and state of crisis but it sounded like the Crescent Moon school of poetry. A recent remark made by Liang Jinglun echoed in her ears. "He also likes poetry. He likes Tagore and lately he's taken to the poems of the Crescent Moon school."

He Xiaoyu had no idea whether it was Liang Jinglun behind her or Fang Meng'ao in front of her who was making her heart beat so fast.

"You're afraid people will look at you from behind, aren't you?"

"I'm afraid so."

"Well, I can see you're not afraid at all."

"They can't see it either. You know why?"

"Nope," replied He Xiaoyu.

"I run faster than they do, so they can't see my back."

"Who are they?"

"Everyone."

"Including me?"

"All of you."

"Is that why you drove so fast that day?" asked He Xiaoyu.

"Which day?"

"The day Mulan and I rode in your car."

"What about today?"

He Xiaoyu became aware of the fact that today he was driving much more smoothly and steadily. She looked back through the rear window only to find that the driver of the mid-sized jeep behind them was impatient to be going so slowly.

"Do you hate the jeep behind you?" asked Fang Meng'ao.

He Xiaoyu immediately turned her head. "Can you see me?"

Fang Meng'ao didn't answer but looked in the rearview mirror above the seat.

"You can see me but I can't see you. That's not fair."

"Is it fair for you all to hide behind me and look at me," replied Fang Meng'ao, "but in front I can't see any of you?"

He Xiaoyu knew the time had come. "Then you'd better go faster and get rid of those people behind us."

Fang Meng'ao's back inadvertently stiffened and He Xiaoyu's heart missed a beat.

"Will you run with me?" asked Fang Meng'ao, his voice not as calm as it had been.

"Yes."

"Who told you to come?" Fang Meng'ao asked suddenly, switching the subject of conversation.

He Xiaoyu was a bit surprised, then replied firmly: "The organisation."

"I don't know anything about any organisation. Tell me names, names of people I can trust."

He Xiaoyu intuitively grasped the handrail beside her seat, then settled down and gave him a name: "Cui Zhongshi!"

"Say it again, speak more clearly!" Fang Meng'ao's hand clenched the steering wheel.

"Comrade Cui Zhongshi!" said He Xiaoyu, raising her voice.

The jeep suddenly accelerated and darted forward. He Xiaoyu's body was thrown heavily into the back of her seat.

"Attention! Salute!" The young platoon leader inside the main warehouse stood bolt upright, taking the lead to salute Zeng Keda. The line of Youth Army soldiers stood at attention, saluting simultaneously. Zeng Keda, followed by his adjutant, entered the gate. The platoon leader of the Youth Army followed closely behind.

"Where's Captain Fang?" asked Zeng Keda, walking fast.

"Report to General Zeng, Captain Fang went out last night and hasn't come back yet."

"Where did he go?"

"Report to General Zeng, Colonel Zheng went with him. I've no idea where."

"Where are the rest of the Inspection Brigade and Director Ma?"

"Report to General Zeng, Director Ma went out with the captain last night but was escorted back before dawn. The inspectors and staff of the Citizens' Food Distribution Committee are all inside."

Zeng Keda looked at Wang, his adjutant, and the two exchanged a puzzled look.

"Find Colonel Zheng. Tell him to come back with Captain Fang immediately."

"Aye-aye, sir." Adjutant Wang walked to the guard office at the gate.

Zeng Keda went inside the compound again and said: "Blow the whistle for assembly!"

"Yes sir!"

The whistle blew sharply.

Ma Hanshan was slumped over his desk in the director's office, asleep with furrowed brow. Outside the window, the whistle kept blowing. With his eyelids flickering, he felt the whistle coming from a long way off and closed his eyes again. But the heavy footsteps and running startled him and this time he opened his eyes and leaned over the table to listen.

"Stop auditing, now!" It turned out to be Zeng Keda's voice. Ma Hanshan raised his head and pricked up his ears.

"Seize them all! As soon as Captain Fang is back, bring them all back to the barracks for interrogation!" Zeng Keda's voice was certainly less pleasant to listen to than Fang Meng'ao's. Ma Hanshan clenched his teeth at every word.

Then came the sound of heels clicking in unison. Apparently, many soldiers were clicking their heels and saluting. When Ma Hanshan listened again, the noise from outside the window was quite disturbing.

"Anyone above the level of section chief will be taken to the duty room and anyone below to the warehouse. Move it!"

"Get a move on! Go, go!"

Ma Hanshan subconsciously looked at the door and, sure enough, soon heard footsteps approaching. It was Chen Changwu, a member of the Youth Aviation Brigade, who came in with a pair of handcuffs.

"Deputy Director Ma, please stand up." Chen Changwu looked him straight in the eyes. Ma Hanshan was still sitting there and asked: "Cuff me? What will your captain say?"

"Captain Fang hasn't come back yet. This is an order from Chief Inspector Zeng. Thank you for your cooperation."

"Come here." Ma Hanshan lowered his voice and raised his head in a slightly mysterious way.

"If you have anything to say, please say it." Chen Changwu stood his ground.

"I had an agreement with your captain last night. Whether you handcuff me or not, you will know as soon as he comes back."

Chen Changwu hesitated and thought for a moment. "OK, I won't handcuff you for the time being." He sat down in the chair opposite him.

Adjutant Wang walked briskly from the guard room over to Zeng Keda, who was standing at the gate of the warehouse. Zeng Keda looked at him.

"Yes, Colonel Zheng called you at Ambassador Gu's residence not long ago," whispered Adjutant Wang, "saying they are now in the barracks of the 309th Division based in the northwestern suburbs. According to him, Captain Fang drove with He Xiaoyu and gave them the slip. They were headed to the Great Wall area in the northwestern suburbs where the troops were looking for them."

Zeng Keda frowned. He understood that He Xiaoyu had begun to engage Fang Meng'ao as instructed by Liang Jinglun but not at this particular moment!

"What a bunch of idiots!" cursed Zeng Keda, striding out of the premises to the vehicle outside the gate. "I have a meeting with Chief Commissioner Xu and Wang of the Bureau of Investigation and Statistics of the Military Council at the residence. You wait here. As soon as Captain Fang arrives, tell him it's a direct order from the Ministry of Defence!"

"Yes sir!"

At the foot of a section of the Great Wall in the northwestern suburbs of Peking, there were no roads originally, so it was less travelled and more remote. It was a place thickly forested with trees of different species and heights. No one knew how Fang Meng'ao managed to drive into the woods and park his jeep on a grassland clearing among the trees.

High above behind Fang Meng'ao loomed the Great Wall. He sat on a slope at the foot of a hill where he could scan any action in the surrounding area from a one hundred and eighty degree angle. He Xiaoyu was standing on the grass at a lower spot where she needed to raise her head slightly to meet Fang Meng'ao's eyes. The sun was shining all over the green grass behind He Xiaoyu and on the Great Wall behind Fang Meng'ao. There were birds singing and insects chirping but Fang Meng'ao and He Xiaoyu looked at each other in silence.

"I think I understand," said Fang Meng'ao: "You are a member of the Students Union and it sent you to engage with me hoping to recruit me to help you fight corruption and persecution?"

He Xiaoyu gently nodded in agreement.

"And you're also an underground member of the Communist

Party. Did the Peking underground organisation send you to meet me?"

"Yes."

"I don't follow." Fang Meng'ao stared at her in disbelief. "Since I arrived in Peking I, along with the Investigation Brigade under my command, have been committed to investigating corruption and protecting the students. Is it necessary for the Students' Union to engage with me like this?"

"As I said just now, representing the Students' Union is just a cover. My task is to meet with you as a representative of the party organisation."

"Don't even talk about it," snapped Fang Meng'ao. "I'm not a Communist. I assume you're not either. I won't tell anyone else if you are. You'd better not share this with anyone else."

"Yes, you are a member of the Communist Party. Comrade Cui Zhongshi was your sponsor. I know the whole process."

Fang Meng'ao sat still on the rocky slope.

"How come you know what I don't? Indulge me."

He Xiaoyu was fully aware of his state of mind at that moment, so she changed tack. "Now, forget the Communist Party or the organisation and show some respect for women. Can you come down and talk to me on an equal footing?"

Quite unexpectedly, Fang Meng'ao stood up, walked down the slope, went to the flat grass and sat down one metre away from her.

"Now you're in a higher spot than me. I respect you. Go ahead."

"Can I also sit down?" He Xiaoyu felt flatly offended by his manner but she had to be patient.

Fang Meng'ao looked up at her while his body remained still. There was a scrutinising look in his eyes which was almost frightening.

He Xiaoyu overcame her fear and said: "I know it all happened on the evening of the Mid-Autumn Festival on the fifteenth day of the eighth month of the lunar calendar in 1946. Cui Zhongshi came to visit you at the Air Force's Jianqiao Central Aviation School on behalf of your family. You walked with him on the lawn of the airport runway. Then you sat down and he stood still, pacing back and forth beside you, explaining the Communist Party's vision of China's future.

"You assumed that I didn't know the details, didn't you? I'm not used to walking up and down in front of you the way he did. I want to sit down."

Fang Meng'ao sat cross-legged, his body still did not move. There was no sign of him being shocked except that he looked at He Xiaoyu with eyes that radiated a more complex quality.

"It's not natural to stand to tell a story, is it? Please sit down. I can hear you well enough whether you are closer or further away from me."

"Then I'll sit behind you. You're not running away today, anyway." He Xiaoyu tried her best to make herself acceptable with relaxed language.

"Is there a better reason?" Fang Meng'ao asked.

"Of course, you'll see." He Xiaoyu moved closer and sat down about a metre behind him. She began to recite in a soft voice:

> *When you watch the scenery from the bridge,*
> *The sightseer watches you from the balcony.*
> *The bright moon adorns your window,*
> *While you adorn another's dream.*

"Is it a good reason?"

Fang Meng'ao, who appeared as broad as a mountain from behind, was still sitting there motionless. Looking at his thick, powerful back, He Xiaoyu felt quite frustrated. She couldn't sense Fang Meng'ao's mood and wondered loudly why he was rejecting her flatly like this. In fact, Fang Meng'ao, with his eyes closed, had conjured up almost every scene of the past in his mind's eye.

Cui Zhongshi and he walked side by side on the lawn of Jianqiao airbase in Hangzhou. They were gently reciting Wen Yiduo's *Prayer* and *Stagnant Water*.

Over the Hangzhou Bay Estuary, Fang Meng'ao flew a plane at a low altitude of a thousand metres. Sitting beside him, Cui Zhongshi looked at the estuary and the endless sea down below, his face full of excitement.

"Isn't it nice?" Fang Meng'ao said to Cui Zhongshi, sitting next to him.

"It's magnificent!"

"Can I ask you a question? If I fly the plane to Yan'an, may I offer a ride to Chairman Mao and Vice-Chairman Zhou?"

"I think so, they would be very happy to fly in your plane."

"In that case, shall we go now?"

"Not now."

Day turned to night and the vast sea of Hangzhou Bay turned into Houhai in Shichahai, Peking. Cui Zhongshi stood beside him silently.

"I am not an underground member of the CPC and neither are you," said Cui Zhongshi. "But that's not important. When you were willing to join the CPC, you didn't do it for my sake. You're willing to follow the Communist Party not because you believe in me but because you choose the Communist Party in the first place, because you want to do your bit to save China and are willing to do anything for your compatriots. Don't believe in me, believe in yourself."

When Fang Meng'ao opened his eyes, Cui Zhongshi had disappeared. What was left behind was the dappled shade of the trees and He Xiaoyu behind him, who was expecting an answer from him.

"Will you sit in front of me?" Fang Meng'ao's voice delighted He Xiaoyu.

"OK." He Xiaoyu came in front of Fang Meng'ao, smoothed her skirt and was ready to sit down.

"Come closer to me." He stretched out his hand.

He Xiaoyu's heart was pounding wildly. She shouldn't have been afraid but she was. Slowly she extended her hand to Fang Meng'ao who gently tugged at her fingertips. He Xiaoyu took a small step forward and sat down. It was too close.

Fang Meng'ao released her hands. "I am not directing my question at you. So just feel free to answer me. Don't be afraid."

He Xiaoyu could only nod lightly.

"What did Cui Zhongshi die for?"

"He died for the revolution."

"My question is why did he die?"

He Xiaoyu saw the agony in his eyes and didn't know how to answer, nor was she able to.

"There are many reasons but I don't know much about it. A lot of things remain secrets of the organisation."

"Don't tell me about the organisation." Fang Meng'ao's voice suddenly became harsh. "Go and tell Mr Liang and the Students' Union that my team and I are under the command of the Investigation Brigade of the Ministry of Defence. It's my task to investigate corruption and ensure the rations are distributed among the residents of Peking. You don't need to win me over."

"I will tell them the truth," assured He Xiaoyu, nodding her head.

"Also, I never knew whether Cui Zhongshi was a Communist or not. I didn't join the Kuomintang or the Communist Party. I don't care whether you are a Communist or not. So, don't talk about engaging with me any more."

He Xiaoyu was really flustered and anxious. "Comrade Cui Zhongshi protected you and worked hard to recruit you by putting his life on the line. How can you play down all his work for the party and for you like this?"

"Why do you have to impose all this on me?" Fang Meng'ao's unfeeling response made He Xiaoyu bitterly disappointed.

"Cui Zhongshi and I were friends," continued Fang Meng'ao. "He was like my big brother. No matter how he died and who he died for, I will try my best to catch them. I won't let them get away with it! Now, get in the jeep." With that he strode to his jeep.

He Xiaoyu was so stunned that she found herself unable to take a step. Fang Meng'ao looked back only to find that He Xiaoyu was sniffing back a tear but to no avail. Tears were streaming down her cheeks.

"Still want to look over my shoulder?" Fang Meng'ao was so inhuman that He Xiaoyu had to swallow her tears.

"Just go yourself. I'll find my own way home."

"I brought you here, so I must take you back." Fang Meng'ao strode towards her.

"You didn't bring me. I've nothing to do with you." He Xiaoyu was bewildered and worried. She wanted to bypass him and walked in another direction.

Fang Meng'ao's figure flashed right in front of her and blocked her way. "You and I have nothing to do with each other, that's quite correct. I'll take you back this time. Don't try to look for me again."

Suddenly, He Xiaoyu seemed to come to a realisation about something. She was no longer flustered, even though she felt quite empty. Although they were so close to each other, she was not daunted any more and neither would she try to avoid him. Her eyes looked into his.

All she needed was an answer.

Fang Meng'ao sounded in very low spirits. "I have never shared my secret with anyone but I will do so now, with you. I'm a lone wolf, I can only go it alone. During the second world war, every pilot I was paired with in the Air Force, whether it was my leader or my wingman, they were all shot down. Twenty-seven men, not one of them made it back alive. Before I came to Peking, I was tried by the Nanking Military Court together with two others. Of the three of us, one was a Communist, the other a Kuomintang member. Both of them were sentenced to death. Only I survived. Cui Zhongshi was my only family and he's dead now. Tell those who sent you not to send another man to his death. I will always fight alone."

When He Xiaoyu heard this, it chilled her heart.

"Let's go." Fang Meng'ao didn't mean to force her at all this time. He turned and walked to his jeep.

He Xiaoyu followed him. Fang Meng'ao opened the door to the back seat and then got into the driver's seat himself. He Xiaoyu got into the jeep and closed the door. Fang Meng'ao turned the rearview mirror to his right. "Now, I can't see you," he said. "You can lie down and get some sleep. When you wake up, you will forget everything."

The jeep started. The road was rugged but the ride was smooth and stable. He Xiaoyu looked out of the window at the Great Wall that extended to the sky. Then she said: "There has never been a saviour, and no one can control the life and death of others. I'll find you again. You can run but you can never hide from me."

Fang Meng'ao did not make any response but looked straight ahead. The jeep slowly proceeded onto the highway, then accelerated toward Peking.

An emergency meeting was convened at Zeng Keda's place. "I must solemnly declare," said Zeng Keda, evidently having interrupted either Xu Tieying's or Wang Puchen's conversation. "There are no dilemmas. There is no contradiction between the president and the vice-president, or between the commander-in-chief and the deputy commander-in-chief, nor can there be any. In China, between the president and the vice-president there is absolute obedience to the president. In Peking, we should not listen to Li Zongren just because he used to be in charge of the Rear Office of the Military Affairs Commission Peking Field Headquarters. As for military affairs, Deputy Commander-in-Chief Chen Jicheng must obey Commander-in-Chief Fu Zuoyi's command. This is not my opinion, this is the consensus reached among Comrade Jianfeng, Minister Chen of the Kuomintang Party Headquarters and Director Mao of the State Secrecy Bureau. After the meeting, you can make phone calls for confirmation."

The telephone rang. "Excuse me," said Zeng Keda to Xu Tieying and Wang Puchen who were on the sofa opposite the tea table. He then got to his feet from a high-backed chair to answer the phone.

"Report to General Zeng. We've located Captain Fang," Colonel Zheng said at the other end of the phone.

"How did you find him? Where has he been?"

"Sir, he has been to the Great Wall."

"The Great Wall is so long, which section did he go to?" yelled Zeng Keda.

"Sir, allow me to report." Colonel Zheng knew that Zeng Keda would not put up with such a vague description. "It's about a dozen *li* from the barracks of the 309th Division. It's almost no man's land, yet it was a place thickly forested with trees. According to my humble observation, Captain Fang shook us off for a secret rendezvous with He Xiaoyu. Permission to seek your instructions, General. Should I avoid such pursuits in the future?"

"Escort Captain Fang back to the city and straight to the Citizens' Food Distribution Committee headquarters!" Zeng Keda put down the phone and sat down, only to find that both Xu Tieying and Wang Puchen were looking gloomy and a little out of sorts.

"I'd like to first make a statement on behalf of the Kuomintang Party headquarters," said Xu Tieying. "The president is not only the president of the Republic of China but also the supreme leader of the party. I was sent to Peking by the party headquarters and have full responsibility to uphold the leader's image and authority without being challenged by anyone. It's the president's vision that we never compromise with the Communists. I can guarantee that we at the Peking Police Bureau will firmly oppose any attempt to contact or even negotiate with the Communist Party. In addition to the leadership of the president, we will also accept the command of Comrade Jianfeng, because only Comrade Jianfeng can represent the president. On this point, I find that deputy Commander-in-Chief Chen Jicheng is also very firm. Therefore, those affiliated with our party headquarters should support Deputy Commander-in-Chief Chen in Peking. I endorse Comrade Jianfeng's anti-corruption action and agree to arrest Ma Hanshan and those involved in the Citizens' Food Distribution Committee's corruption case. But in the process of combating corruption, it is necessary to maintain the image of the party-state, and to ensure our anti-corruption effort will not be taken advantage of by the Communist Party. The abrupt suspension of American aid just proves that someone has played the card of peace talks with the Communist Party by hijacking our anti-corruption action. We should prioritise the anti-Communist agenda, instead of that of anti-corruption. I can only obey Comrade Jianfeng's decision to reinstate the dismissed Fang Meng'ao but I am minded to reserve my opinion of him. The man has developed some bad habits while serving in the Air Force. He disobeyed his superiors and acted recklessly. Last night, he made an unexpected visit to the bureau's secret prison and managed to have the Communist suspect released. I can't go through this without taking into account what Inspector Zeng has said, the man has probably been used by the Communist Party. What's more, Ma Hanshan is absolutely hopeless. Last night, he coordinated on Fang Meng'ao's behalf the release of the Communist suspect. Are there any kind of secret deals going on between them? I think so. Therefore, can we ask Inspector Zeng to suggest to Comrade Jianfeng that those involved in the case, including Ma Hanshan, be transferred to our Peking

Police Bureau? At the same time, I'm also committed to cooperating with the investigation brigade of the Ministry of Defence to look at the case. I will absolutely hold myself responsible to Comrade Jianfeng by interrogating Ma Hanshan and auditing the accounts of the Citizens' Food Distribution Committee."

Zeng Keda knew Xu Tieying very well. From his lengthy speech, he was able to discern his motive. The instructions of Comrade Jianfeng reverberated in his ears.

"Xu Tieying is a piece of work! Give him a dire warning on my behalf. Tell him to stop being corrupt and work with us honestly. If he continues to work against us, he might be the next to be arrested!"

"I can suggest to Comrade Jianfeng," said Zeng Keda, starting to think about how to issue the warning. "The Citizens' Food Distribution Committee has been so corrupt under Ma Hanshan that popular discontent has been running high, which led to the Fifth of July Incident. Now it is having a direct impact on US aid policy to China. I'd like to hear how Commissioner Xu interrogates them and what your desired outcome will be. With that, I can report to Comrade Jianfeng in detail."

"First, we should understand Comrade Jianfeng's intended purpose. In my opinion, it should be twofold. The first should be a long-term one, namely, to thoroughly eliminate corruption within the party-state. As I said, this is the long-term goal, it's time-consuming and will be based on the total defeat of the Communist Party. The other is of immediate urgency, namely, to seize and even execute some of the corrupt officials, to encourage those who are still corrupt to be more scrupulous. Meanwhile we should strengthen economic control in our territory and gain the confidence of our allies to assist us in order to facilitate the president's command of the national army to roundly defeat the Communists in various battlefields across the country."

Zeng Keda stared inquisitively at Xu Tieying. "Who should be arrested? Who should be executed? Will it be like killing Hou Juntang? Once he is executed, the money will be gone with him, never to be recovered again?"

Xu Tieying was put on the spot, and his eyes rolled as if he was in deep thought. "I'll need to think about that."

Zeng Keda cast a quick glance at Wang Pucheng who pleaded: "Old habits die hard, I'd like to take a drag. Can I go out for a puff? I know you hate the smell of smoke."

"It doesn't matter. Feel free to smoke here." Zeng Keda meant to humiliate Xu Tieying in front of someone else. "We need to think deeply about the issue raised by Commissioner Xu just now because it involves your former stationmaster of the Military Council's Bureau of Investigation and Statistics. Stationmaster Wang, what's your take on the issue?"

Wang nodded cautiously. Having pulled out a pack of cigarettes and a box of matches with his long fingers, he lit one, took a drag on it and began to cough again.

With one stakeholder rolling his eyes pretending to be deep in thought and the other coughing in a deliberate attempt to delay, Zeng Keda frowned in contempt.

Zeng Keda waited until Wang Puchen was done coughing. He said gloomily: "You can't indulge yourselves in this kind of deep thinking all the time, can you? You have to talk about your thinking and share it, which I must report to Comrade Jianfeng in detail."

"You damn son of a bitch!" cursed Xu Tieying, seething with hatred, but he had to concur, so he began to explain: "To recover the booty! Especially what was embezzled by Ma Hanshan and others. I will intensify my interrogation efforts and try my best to recover the stolen money."

"What do you mean by your best effort?" queried Zeng Keda who, as the host of the meeting, was no longer inclined to give Xu Tieying any face. "The people working for American intelligence are not amateurs. There are also secret agents working for the Communists. They have more accurate information than we do and, even if we can't, they are able to find out how much you've embezzled and who is involved. Supposedly, it amounts to ten million dollars, but all we recover is barely a million dollars. Commissioner Xu, I'm afraid you can't account for that to your superiors? Let me put it this way, on behalf of Comrade Jianfeng, I agree to let you interrogate those affiliated with the Citizens' Food Distribution Committee. How much money do you think you can recover?"

"Chief Inspector Zeng," said Xu Tieying, unable to stand it any longer. "Just give me a number."

"Ten million dollars!" answered Zeng unequivocally. "It's a number the Americans should be able to accept."

Xu Tieying laughed without the least attempt to conceal his confrontational attitude. "Go ahead and conduct the interrogations. I'll fully cooperate with you."

"Of course, you should, you must!" stressed Zeng Keda. "These are Comrade Jianfeng's exact words. Mr Wang, in my opinion, we should continue to assign Fang Meng'ao to conduct a thorough investigation of the committee in order to find out who is behind it. We should cooperate with each other on whatever level and in whichever department. What do you think?"

Wang Pucheng tried to extinguish his cigarette but found no ashtray on the table. He took his tea cover, poured a little water into it, and extinguished the cigarette in it. Then he replied: "I'll cooperate in your anti-corruption action and, more importantly, the anti-Communist effort. It's what the investigation group of the Ministry of Defence expects of Fang Meng'ao and his brigade to come up with the desired results. To that end, I propose putting together a squad from the Peking station on behalf of the State Secrets Protection Bureau of the Ministry of Defence. This new squad will temporarily be reassigned to join the Youth Army and be embedded into Colonel Zheng's platoon. The idea is to supervise Fang Meng'ao and his brigade, not only to check corruption, but also to guard against Communist infiltration."

"I agree. I'll report it to Comrade Jianfeng for approval." Zeng Keda looked at Xu Tieying. "Does Commissioner Xu object to the motion to commit Fang Meng'ao's inspection brigade to conduct the investigation?"

"What I object to is not the ministry's inspection brigade but the Communist suspect! Liang Jinglun clearly is the Communist suspect who instigated the student protests! By joining hands with Ma Hanshan, Fang Meng'ao forced Mr Wang to release the suspect. Did you report this to the Nanking authorities? On behalf of the Communications Bureau of the Kuomintang Central Committee members, I'm strongly opposed to appointing Fang Meng'ao to interrogate Ma Hanshan. I will report my opinions to Director Ye and Minister Chen."

Zeng Keda knew that this was going to involve a lot of political infighting. However, he was not quite sure what Fang Meng'ao had done in terms of releasing Liang Jinglun. It was likely to cause disagreement among the upper echelons unless Comrade Jianfeng was firm on this.

He looked at Wang Puchen and asked: "Does Mr Wang also want to consult Director Mao to determine who will interrogate members of the Citizens' Food Distribution Committee?"

Wang pulled out another cigarette but this time he left the matches in his pocket. "There's no need for me to ask for his instructions separately. I'll cooperate with whomever is here to conduct the interrogation."

"Commissioner Xu, why don't you consult your higher-ups for instructions now?" suggested Zeng Keda, standing up. "Fang Meng'ao is scheduled to arrive at the Citizens' Food Distribution Committee's headquarters very soon. I will go and join him at the Inspection Brigade's barracks and arrange to take Ma Hanshan and all those involved into custody. Nanking has given us only three days. If anyone deliberately interferes with the investigation and prevents us from giving Nanking a satisfactory answer within three days, so that the Americans can resume their assistance, then they will be the next to be arrested!"

Xu Tieying stood up, straightened the hem of his uniform and strode straight out.

Never before had Xu Tieying's car been driven so fast in Peking. The driver, who was exceptionally skilful, turned the steering wheel hard and drove fast from the main street into the narrow alleyway where Fang Buting's house was located.

The car stopped abruptly. Xu Tieying in the back seat stared at the driver who slammed on the brakes. Without waiting for him to open the door, he got out of the car himself, then froze. There was a vehicle parked outside the gate of the Fang household, a small jeep. To his surprise, Fang Meng'ao was standing beside the jeep. Xu

Tieying could not return to his car because Fang Meng'ao had spotted him. However, Fang Meng'ao didn't seem to be interested, so instead he opened the back door of his jeep with only a quick glance at Xu Tieying who happened to hear him say: "It's time to wake up. Here we are at the Fangs' house."

"Can I use your kettle, please?" asked He Xiaoyu, who had dozed off in the car.

Fang Meng'ao was startled for a moment. As if he had just realised something, he grabbed his military kettle from the front seat, removed the lid and handed it to He Xiaoyu who reached out of the car and took the kettle. She then poured some water from the kettle onto a handkerchief. Xu Tieying could not very well watch them but had to look over to the entrance of the alleyway.

He Xiaoyu dampened her handkerchief, wiped her face in the car, combed her hair and put on a hairband. Then she got out of the car and went to the gate without looking at Fang Meng'ao again.

"Good morning, Commissioner Xu." Fang Meng'ao's greeting came from behind him. Xu Tieying turned around and pretended to smile like an elderly gentleman.

"All work and no play, that's not the way things should be. It's time to think about your personal life."

"Perhaps you can get your car backed up and let me out."

"Captain Fang, don't you want to go in?" Xu Tieying asked in a seemingly friendly manner, then said to the driver: "Back her up!"

In the living room on the ground floor of the Fangs' house, Cai Ma greeted her and shouted to the first floor: "Master, Madam, Miss He is visiting."

Xie Mulan, who had lost all her desire for food or drink, sat up in bed in her room. Her hair wasn't even combed. She walked to the door, her hand reaching out for the handle but surprisingly withdrew it. She stood there for a moment, confused, turned around and retreated into the bathroom.

Fang Buting was undressed again and was lying on the bed in the bedroom with multiple cupping jars on his back.

Cheng Xiaoyun stood by the bed and looked at Xie Peidong.

"Xiaoyu is here to visit Mulan. Peidong, go ahead and unlock the door."

"Alas!" sighed Xie Peidong, before going out.

"Good morning, Uncle Xie." He Xiaoyu looked at Xie Peidong coming down the stairs.

"Are you here to see Mulan?"

"Yes." With Xie Peidong coming up to her, He Xiaoyu whispered: "Fang Meng'ao drove me here."

Xie Peidong looked at her, a flicker of excitement in his eyes. But He Xiaoyu's depressed look immediately weakened the light in Xie Peidong's eyes. "I'll go and see Mulan first," she said.

Xie Peidong nodded and handed her the key.

As she went upstairs, He Xiaoyu brushed past Xie Peidong and she said in a low voice: "Xu Tieying is arriving."

He Xiaoyu went upstairs.

Xu Tieying appeared at the door of the living room and said with a smile: "Good morning, Mr Xie. Is the governor at home?" As he was speaking, he had already stepped inside.

Nevertheless, Xie Peidong went over to greet him: "He's in a cupping session."

'Is he sick?" asked Xu Tieying, looking around. "He looked quite well at the meeting just now."

"It's heatstroke. If it's not something urgent, can you possibly reschedule it, Commissioner Xu?"

Xu Tieying looked very serious. "It's always about time. Sometimes a person can get killed within ten minutes. I must see the governor now."

"Mr Xu, please take a seat and wait." Xie Peidong motioned Xu to sit down. "Cai Ma, tea for Commissioner Xu, please!"

Xie Mulan hurriedly washed and changed. She looked at He Xiaoyu and smiled awkwardly, standing at the door to her room, but she actually felt nervous and uneasy.

He Xiaoyu entered the room, gently closing the door behind her. Seeing that she was still standing in the same spot, she said with a faint smile: "What's the secret you are keeping from me?"

Xie Mulan had no choice but to greet her and stepped aside, revealing her untouched breakfast under a screen covering on the table beside the window. "I've got a stomach ache. I don't want to eat anything."

"I didn't have my breakfast either. Please eat with me," said He Xiaoyu, then went to the table and sat down.

Xie Mulan thought she was covering up her embarrassment. "Do you know what time it is now? You haven't had breakfast yet?"

"Your elder brother took me out for a ride before seven o'clock. He wasn't hungry but he guessed I wasn't either. May I eat?" He Xiaoyu had removed the gauze cover.

"Go ahead. I'll eat with you." Xie Mulan's face immediately brightened up and she sat down on the other side. "Was it my elder brother who drove you here?"

"That's correct," replied He Xiaoyu, taking a sip of milk.

Xie Mulan also took a sip of milk, then they were speechless again.

Xu Tieying stood up in the living room and looked out onto the first-floor corridor. Fang Buting was still well dressed and his hair was neat. His face had obviously been dried with a hot towel, so he didn't look sick at all. He gave Xu Tieying a seemingly defiant look and moved slowly to the stairs in front of the office. He stood still and said to Xu Tieying: "Please come to the office and talk."

Xu Tieying nodded his head in a slightly reserved manner and walked slowly to the stairs.

Inside the governor's office on the first floor, Fang Buting stopped by a rattan chair beside a round table by the window and looked at another one without a word of invitation to Xu Tieying to sit.

Xu Tieying stood in the room, trying to maintain a bit of reserve, but soon realised that the effort was in vain.

Fang Buting was still looking at the chair, however, with a vague expression in his eyes; instead, he seemed to be looking at the person sitting in it. But, actually, nobody was sitting in that chair. Suddenly, Xu Tieying's eyes brightened. The image of Cui Zhongshi, who was sitting on this chair that day, flashed past his eyes!

Fang Buting was merciless, but not in the same way as the Central Bureau of Investigation and Statistics. As such, he was seen walking away from the rattan chair that had been solely reserved for himself and went to the one in which Cui Zhongshi once sat. Then he said: "Just now Mr Xie said that Commissioner Xu wanted to see me about something urgent. Please sit down and speak."

Xu Tieying walked over and took the chair he used to sit in. But the person opposite him this time around was Fang Buting. "Governor Fang, I came here in violation of party discipline. Just now, on behalf of the Investigation Group of the Ministry of Defence, Zeng Keda summoned Wang Puchen of the Military Bureau of Investigation and Statistics and I to convey the secret instructions of the Iron and Blood Congress. What a malicious move! You're the first one to be involved! I should have reported it to Director Ye Xiufeng and Minister Chen Lifu first but I felt I had to tell you first."

"Don't tell me if it involves me."

"Not just you," said Xu Tieying. "There are too many people involved, including those at the Central Bank, and the Song and Kong families. Governor Fang, this is not for our personal gain. This is for our superiors, our friends, because many people's lives are at stake. We can no longer be humiliated like this. We're all in the same boat."

"Both the boats of the Central Bank and my home have been broken by you," said Fang Buting with a faint sneer hanging on his lips. "Tell me how we can help each other in the same boat?"

"Everyone's boat is broken. The only way out is to fix it! Does Governor Fang agree with me?"

"Since it's your opinion, I can't stop you from saying it."

"They're going to arrest and kill people. The breakthrough was Ma Hanshan. Fang Meng'ao, your eldest son, is in charge of his interrogation! Cui Zhongshi was executed by Ma Hanshan. Meng'ao has already lost his head. He would seize and kill anyone. He has completely abandoned Confucian ethics, namely, the three cardinal principles and five constancies. They're gone…"

"Are you worried about what's going to happen to my family, morally and ethically?" asked Fang Buting, interrupting him. "On the thirteenth of August, I abandoned my wife and children in order to save other people's wealth, violating the ancient ethics. Now, if my son really wants to catch and kill me, that's my karma.

Commissioner Xu, if you've finished expressing your view, it's time to report to your superiors." He stood up.

Xu Tieying also stood up. "OK, I'll refrain from stating my own opinion. Permit me to make a suggestion that I believe will work. I will take over the interrogation of Ma Hanshan and others with the Citizens' Food Distribution Committee in order to stop the situation from deteriorating. I can persuade Director Ye and Minister Chen. Can I ask Governor Fang to consider reporting to Mr Song and Mr Kong? If we work together, we can hold down the Iron and Blood Congress so that they can no longer use Meng'ao. It's not just for our good but also for Meng'ao's."

Fang Buting was lost in thought. Xu Tieying looked at him eagerly and finally saw him sit down again.

While the two adults were negotiating, the younger ones were also negotiating. Xie Mulan looked at He Xiaoyu. "I won't be impulsive but I can't be locked up at home like this. I have to be with my classmates, just to be with them."

He Xiaoyu looked at her, trying to appear calm and understanding so as to help her cover up the twinkle in her eyes. Not daring to look at He Xiaoyu directly, Xie Mulan complained in a low voice: "Mostly my dad. They say Uncle Fang is powerful, but my dad, actually, is the most powerful one in our family. You're the only one who can convince him now. Tell him I'm with you and he will say yes."

"I can help you with that but Uncle Xie won't necessarily listen to me."

"Thank you, Xiaoyu!" Xie Mulan jumped with joy. "Go and talk to him now!"

As He Xiaoyu looked at her, a burst of pity welled up in her heart. Was she taking pity on Xie Mulan or on herself? She could not tell.

CHAPTER 10

In the bamboo groves in the back garden of Fang Buting's house, it had been still the night before and for a quite a while there was peace and quiet. However, all of a sudden, the wind began to blow.

He Xiaoyu sounded a little erratic. "He said in the end 'I've told no one my secret and, believe it or not, I've told you.'"

"Let me think about it," said Xie Peidong as he stood up from the stone bench.

What was there to think about? He Xiaoyu followed Xie Peidong with an inquisitive look and then stood up. Xie Peidong walked to a bamboo pole near him and broke off a branch of bamboo. "In my hometown," he said, "if my son was disobedient, I would teach him a lesson by hitting him with this. Unfortunately, I had a daughter and her mother died when she was a child. I couldn't hit her or scold her. Besides, she was grown up already." Then he handed the bamboo branch to He Xiaoyu and exchanged a quick, frustrated look. Clearly, he was referring to Fang Meng'ao with reference to Xie Mulan. He Xiaoyu took the bamboo branch with a knowing look. Xie Peidong's eyes turned to the bamboo branch in He Xiaoyu's hand. He Xiaoyu also looked at the bamboo branch in her hand and noticed that the wind was blowing the bamboo branch towards the house.

"When we speak here, can they hear us up at the house?" She understood Xie Peidong's hidden meaning and asked softly.

"Come on," urged Xie Peidong, walking slowly downwind. He Xiaoyu followed him.

"Well, remember, to do our job well, we should make sure to check the direction of the wind and always be on the leeward side," said Xie Peidong.

"When you speak, stay upwind. The idea is that you will enable others to hear you, while speaking downwind you don't want those upwind to hear you."

He Xiaoyu, though a little puzzled, somehow understood that he was teaching her by example. Looking at Xie Peidong sitting on another stone bench, she felt that the man was indeed her superior as well as a father figure.

"Sit down, and let's continue where we left off. Tell me what Fang Meng'ao's original words were."

He Xiaoyu only nodded. She stood still, thinking, and answered gently: "He said he was tough enough to fight alone. Also, 'during the second world war, every pilot I was paired with in the Air Force, no matter who it was, my leader or my wingman, they were all shot down. Twenty-seven men, not one of them made it back alive.'"

As the wind grew stronger, He Xiaoyu felt as if what she had relayed about Fang Meng'ao was echoing in the sky over the Great Wall.

"Go on, I can hear you," said Xie Peidong.

"He said, 'Before I came to Peking, I was tried by the Nanking Military Court together with two others. Of the three of us, one was a Communist, the other a Kuomintang member. Both of them were sentenced to death. Only I survived. Cui Zhongshi was my only family and he's dead now. Tell those who sent you not to send another man to his death. I will always fight alone.'"

Xie Peidong looked up at He Xiaoyu, who also looked back at Xie Peidong, indicating that she had finished her report. The two fell silent. As the wind was blowing through the bamboo grove, He Xiaoyu felt the chill in the air, but continued to wait for the response of Xie Peidong who was sitting on the stone bench.

Xie Peidong noticed it but did not rush to comment on the

issue. Instead, he moved further along the bench. "The chill wind before the rain, come and sit here."

The leeward side of the long stone bench was left vacant for He Xiaoyu who went to sit on it. This way, Xie Peidong could shield her from the chill wind.

"You've done a good job today."

He Xiaoyu was a little taken aback by his comment.

Xie Peidong began to speak fast. "Since Fang Meng'ao did not admit to being a member of the Communist Party, you should not talk about getting him re-connected to the party organisation in the future."

"Then is it necessary for me to contact him again?" asked He Xiaoyu, confused.

"Of course, it's necessary. The Students' Union will continue to send you to contact him."

He Xiaoyu was puzzled.

"I've told him that my affiliation with the Students' Union was just a cover. My true identity and real mission is to replace Comrade Cui Zhongshi as his contact point and get him re-connected with the organisation. Without re-connecting him to the organisation, I have no reason to meet him again."

As Xie Peidong looked at this subordinate of his, whom he treated like his daughter, he developed quite mixed feelings which swelled up in his mind. He had to explain everything to her but he couldn't.

"Now you've told him everything, he's already convinced of your true identity. The reason why he had second thoughts is probably that he is worried the situation is too complicated and hesitated to get you mixed up in it. What he hoped for, perhaps, is that the organisation might send another person to contact him. However, only you are eligible for the next task. First, you have been sent to contact him by the Students' Union, which is a peripheral organisation. It's normal to persuade him to fight on their side in the capacity of the Students' Union, which means, if you continue to contact Fang Meng'ao in this capacity, both of you are relatively safe. Second, as long as you continue to engage with him, he will understand that you are acting on behalf of the party organisation, knowing and acquiescing in what he does."

"What the Kuomintang ordered him to do, the organisation will also acquiesce in?"

"Yes. He has to do what the Ministry of Defence orders him to do now. That way, he will be able to accomplish the important task assigned to him by the party! To keep in touch with him is to make him always feel recognised and valued by the party. The purpose of not giving him any task is to protect him so that the Kuomintang won't find any evidence to suspect him. Comrade Cui Zhongshi had been in contact with him for three years, until his death, and that was how he did it. He never talked to him about any mission, never interfered with his actions."

He Xiaoyu held her breath in the wind.

"Nevertheless, something unexpected happened. Comrade Fang Meng'ao was suddenly court-martialled by the Kuomintang military authorities, followed by a new appointment by a core department at the upper level of the Kuomintang and sent to Peking. Things were getting very complicated and the party organisation was also caught a little off guard. In the end, Comrade Cui Zhongshi had to sacrifice himself to protect Meng'ao and the organisation as well. It was too difficult for him then."

He Xiaoyu felt the agony in Xie Peidong's voice when talking about Cui Zhongshi. At the same time she was also reminded of the painful moment when Fang Meng'ao talked about Cui Zhongshi. It was the second time she had found it so heartbreaking to hear Cui Zhongshi's name mentioned to her that day.

A sacred sense of mission rose in her. "Uncle Xie, I can do the same. I will protect Fang Meng'ao and protect the organisation at any time."

Xie Peidong looked at her with gratification, encouragement and solemnity. "You should also protect yourself! The higher-ups have clear instructions to protect Fang Meng'ao and you. From now on, you must cooperate with him in accomplishing any given task. Both of you have to hold out until the end, until we are victorious. This is going to be tough for you, for the organisation may not be able to share the weight. You can only rely on yourselves. You must be well prepared mentally."

He Xiaoyu suddenly came to realise that Uncle Xie, the father of her classmate, from whom she had always kept a certain distance, and who she later found out was her current superior, had been so close to her own heart. His situation was more difficult than anyone else's, which is why he understood Cui Zhongshi's and her own difficulties in this way!

"I can handle it, Uncle," said He Xiaoyu, looking at Xie Peidong sincerely.

When Xie Peidong looked backed again he also felt like-minded. "You should go and see Professor Liang immediately and tell him exactly what Fang Meng'ao said in reply to the Students' Union, including the last part of Fang Meng'ao's words you relayed to me."

"Can I also tell Professor Liang the section that involves Comrade Cui Zhongshi?" He Xiaoyu wanted so much to know Liang Jinglun's true identity in the organisation but she couldn't ask; only in this way she thought she could get a positive or negative answer.

"Except for your true identity and the content of your conversation with Fang Meng'ao on behalf of the organisation, you should tell Professor Liang everything truthfully."

Xie Peidong was absolutely positive. "To the Students' Union and Professor Liang Jinglun, your principle should be like this: don't tell all the truth, and don't tell any lies."

Up in the sky, the wind had gathered the dark clouds that loomed large over the bamboo groves, and a hard rain was going to fall at any moment. He Xiaoyu felt the light shining in front of her and had become quite enlightened. However, what she did not know was that Xie Peidong was treating her with a similar principle: he did not tell her that Liang Jinglun was a member of the Iron and Blood Congress, yet the rest of what he said was all true. In this way, Liang Jinglun could not detect the CPC suspicions about him from He Xiaoyu, nor could he find out about He Xiaoyu's identity as a member of the party.

"It's going to rain. Xiaoyu, Uncle Xie needs your help, too. Let's talk about Mulan." Xie Peidong then changed back into a father and an elder.

Back at the governor's office on the first floor of Fang's house, the wind was passing through the balcony, through the open French windows, and was blowing directly in the face of everyone in the room. Xu Tieying, who was talking, stood up and closed the window.

"Don't close it." Although he had been very cold to Xu Tieying, Fang Buting's voice was adamant yet calm. "Even if you close it, you can't stop the wind coming from all directions. Commissioner Xu, please continue. Besides Cui Zhongshi, who else is a Communist at the Peking branch?"

Xu Tieying had no choice but to leave the window open. He sat back with Fang Buting, both of them caught in the draught. "I did not identify any alleged Communists at the Peking branch but I'm sure that the Communists will pop up from the Peking branch because they want to get their hands on Cui Zhongshi's account books!"

This time, as if in token of approval, Fang Buting nodded and cast a glance at the safe by the wall, along with some of the books piled high on the desk. "Commissioner Xu, do you mean to say that the people with the Citizens' Food Distribution Committee should be audited by you and that the accounts of the Central Bank should be transferred to the Peking Police Bureau to be kept and checked by you?"

"That's right." Xu immediately defended himself. "I know the rules and I know that no department can take the books away from the Central Bank without authorisation."

"Then, you're concerned that the Communists will take the account books away from me!"

"That's what we have to prevent from happening. I didn't know before I came to Peking. That's why I sent people to keep an eye on Cui Zhongshi's home and the man himself twenty-four hours after I arrived in Peking. The accounts of the Central Bank are the accounts of the party and the state. The party headquarters sent me here and it's my duty not to let the Communists take a page out of my account books during my stay in Peking!"

"You needn't worry about that, Mr Xu. My assistant, Xie, has been checking all the account books left behind by Cui Zhongshi. He can assure you not one page is missing."

Fang Buting's voice was neither loud nor quiet, which made it hard for Xu to hear him clearly against the passing draught. To hear Fang more clearly, Xu Tieying had to move his body closer to him as he folded his arms on the table.

"Please allow me to ask you a question. Governor Fang, please, if you don't mind. Who has access to the account books in your office?"

"Me, as well as Xie, and occasionally Mengwei. Of the three of us, which one do you worry about the most? Who do you think is most prone to give the account books to the Communists?"

In the bamboo grove in the back garden, Xie Peidong's eyes were sad. "Actually, Xiaoyu, you know what Mulan said are all excuses. She won't spend time with you. Your present duties will not allow you to do so. Perhaps I am selfish and unwilling to let my daughter participate in the movement for fear that she might be in danger. But the reality is that the party's organisation in Peking is facing a major test and the ensuing struggle will be more complex and intense. With my responsibilities within the party, Mulan's actions at this point could have serious consequences for the organisation. That's the real reason why I can't let her out, which you should understand."

"I understand, Uncle Xie. But I can't tell Mulan this is the reason why she's being locked up. With no one to help her, she'll think that we are purposefully preventing her from pursuing progressive causes." Speaking of this, the scene of students protesting before the Citizens' Food Distribution Committee headquarters suddenly came to her mind, including the one in which Xie Mulan held Liang Jinglun tightly from behind in the crowd. "...she will hate you and won't forgive me..."

"Let her hate me. The party organisation has a clear understanding of her situation and that of the vast majority of progressive students as well. In fact, the party authorities also have clear instructions that affirm their enthusiasm for the progressive cause but do not encourage them to act on blind impulse. Unlike you, they can't be recruited by our organisation," said Xie Peidong with a wave of his hand.

"Then, how shall I answer her?" He Xiaoyu became quite unsettled.

"You don't have to answer her, I will."

Finally, raindrops began to fall.

Xie Peidong stood up and He Xiaoyu rose with him. Xie Peidong strode out of the bamboo grove. "Xiao Li!" Fang Buting's driver, who was sitting chatting with the gatekeeper under the eaves of the front garden gate, turned around and saw Xie and He in the rain.

"Ah!" he called out, picking up an umbrella for them to use and dashing towards them. He opened the umbrella to cover Xie Peidong and He Xiaoyu, and walked them to the gate.

"Drive Miss He home."

"Yes sir!"

"It's raining hard. Drive slowly and safely."

"Don't worry." He Xiaoyu walked out of the gate under the driver's umbrella as Xie Peidong stood there watching her.

As the raindrops kept beating down on the umbrella, they quickly walked to the car parked outside the gate. The moment the back door opened, He Xiaoyu glanced back. She saw Xie Peidong still standing at the gate waving his hands. For some reason, she felt her heart ache as she saw Xie Peidong waving to her and signalling for her to get into the car quickly. He Xiaoyu could not bear to look back again, turned around and got into the car. The rear door closed and the umbrella, like a boat, floated to the driver's door in the pouring rain. Indeed, the car in the rainstorm was like a boat, slowly reversing towards the entrance of the alleyway and disappeared in an instant.

Xie Peidong was still standing under the eaves of the gate.

"Mr Manager, the governor wants to see you." Xie Peidong turned his head, only to find that Cai Ma was standing behind him, holding an umbrella in her hand.

"Governor, did you ask for me?" Xie Peidong stamped his wet shoes when he entered the office. Then he felt the wind blowing against his face from outside the window. To his great surprise, he found the window and the door still open with the storm raging outside.

Xu Tieying got to his feet with a grin on his face.

"Commissioner Xu needs to discuss something with you." Fang Buting remained seated.

Xie Peidong nodded to Xu Tieying half-heartedly, then walked quickly across to the window.

He glared at Fang Buting and said: "Why are you still sitting in the draught? You were just done with the cupping session, weren't you?" With that, Xie Peidong closed the windows. To his amusement, Xu Tieying found Fang Buting sitting there like a poor child who had been chastised for some unknown mistake he had made. He became more polite to Xie Peidong as he turned around.

"Governor Fang is not to blame. It's my fault. Manager Xie, please have a seat."

Xie Peidong was meticulous in carrying out family rules. He went up to hold Fang Buting's arm. "Governor, please sit in your own chair."

Fang Buting was obedient enough and sat back down in his own chair. Xie Peidong stood next to the chair which Fang Buting had just taken. Then he turned to Xu Tieying.

"Mr Xu, please take a seat."

Xu Tieying nodded, but did not sit until Xie Peidong was seated.

"May I?" Xu Tieying cast a glance at Fang Buting who acquiesced, he then turned to Xie Peidong.

"Manager Xie, you know as I do, it's very urgent. Just a moment ago, I reached a consensus with Governor Fang that Meng'ao should no longer be manipulated by anyone. Therefore, I myself must handle the case of the Citizens' Food Distribution Committee and you must take care of the accounts of the Peking branch. We must bust certain suspects and punish them, recover some embezzled money and deliver the results to the Nanking authorities so that the Americans can quickly resume their aid. The key for us is to remain consistent in the way we talk."

Xu Tieying paused at this point as Fang Buting looked back at Xie Peidong. Fang understood that what was said next would be crucial, so with a nod of his head, he said to Xu Tieying: "I'm listening, please, go ahead."

"The truth about this whole case is that Cui Zhongshi was bought off by Ma Hanshan and his like-minded corrupt members of the Citizens' Food Distribution Committee, and those scumbags like Hou Juntang of the Air Force. He smuggled and sold American aid materials through black market trading and embezzled illegal profits. Governor Fang informed me after he detected Cui Zhongshi's wrongdoing. I made the arrest. However, Ma Hanshan and his former subordinates took him by force to the secret prison in the Western Hills and murdered him to prevent divulgence of the secret. Fortunately, the account books Cui Zhongshi had been in charge of were seized in time. Based on Manager Xie's thorough examination, the embezzlement was three million two hundred thousand dollars."

"Three million two hundred thousand?" Xie Peidong looked at Fang Buting in disbelief. "How did you come to that figure? Not to mention the difficulty of cooking the books, who do we collect the cash from?"

"Don't interrupt," snapped Fang Buting. "Let Mr Xu finish."

"Zeng Keda demanded that we recover ten million!" Xu Tieying continued, looking almost indignant. "It would be expensive to pay a thousand dollars to buy one's life. How many lives are ten million dollars worth? He himself refused to check the books but asked Meng'ao to do the job instead. Out there, at least ten thousand people are waiting to fight Meng'ao to the death! In order to compete for favours, they kill their rivals by proxy, but causing destruction to both sides. In the end they would sit back and enjoy their success! We don't even need the Communist Party to defeat us, just Zeng Keda and his brigands of the same stripe can terminate the party-state!"

Suddenly lightning flashed across the dark sky outside the window, followed by a series of thunder claps rolling over the horizon. It was raining even harder.

The downpour continued throughout the night and the sound of the storm shook the ground. On the larger ground of the Inspection Brigade's barracks in the northwestern suburbs, twenty pilots of the inspection teams were standing in line in the rain, two metres apart from one another. They were stripped to the waist but wore military trousers and leather boots. Opposite each pilot stood a staff member of the Citizens' Food Distribution Committee, some in Western-style jackets and others in Zhongshan suits. They were all soaking wet with their clothes stuck to their bodies. This kind of one-to-one interrogation could only have been conceived by Fang Meng'ao.

"How much? Ten thousand dollars?" Guo Jinyang asked Section Chief Wang in a loud voice.

"One thousand! Mr Guo, I said one thousand!" Section Chief Wang was soaking wet all over due to the rain but was anxious to defend himself against the allegation.

"What? Did you say a hundred thousand?" Guo Jinyang immediately increased the number by ten times.

"No." Section Chief Wang choked on a big mouthful of rain water.

"A million?" Guo Jinyang suggested.

"I didn't say that." Wang just could not bear it any more.

"You said yes?" Guo Jinyang burst out in praise of Wang.

"Shoot, shoot me." Section Chief Wang couldn't stand his ground any longer. He slumped down on the ground in the rain with his head in his hands. Except for death, there could have been no greater misfortune.

Guo Jinyang was still standing firm in the rain, his body unmoved.

"What are you talking about? Five hundred and six hundred? Dollars or silver dollars?"

"You just said twenty thousand, how come it's nineteen thousand again?"

"Say it again, is it three thousand or four thousand?"

The pilots barked out their questions to the officials being interrogated in the heavy rain and the committee staff members were about to break down.

After turning on all the lights in the office, Xie Peidong produced several account books that he put on the round table, selected one of them and read carefully. "According to Commissioner Xu, three million two hundred thousand dollars means three thousand two hundred embezzlers. Whichever way we look at it, we can't locate the corresponding numbers."

Xu Tieying patiently squeezed out a smile. "That's one way to characterise it. But different people at different levels can embezzle different amounts. While Ma Hanshan can embezzle five hundred thousand dollars, a section chief in the committee can do fifty thousand. And folks affiliated with some other departments in Peking Municipality, the military, some can do ten thousand, twenty thousand or a hundred thousand, it all depends on what position they hold. If we pin them down to death, we'll be able to recover the three million two hundred thousand dollars once and for all."

"Why does it have to be three million two hundred thousand dollars?" Xu Tieying did not answer this time. Instead, he looked at Fang Buting and invited him to answer.

Fang Buting said with a sigh: "I have just checked with the Central Bank, only to find out that there is another important reason for the US to stop their aid this time. These people were so greedy that they swallowed up more than seventeen million dollars of profits that American companies based in China deserved! The US companies in Shanghai just seized the chance presented by the Fifth of July Incident and nailed Peking Municipality, claiming that the Peking Citizens' Food Distribution Committee had embezzled three million two hundred thousand of their profits. Now, with the accusations made by American companies in China, Leighton Stuart will surely report to Washington, plus he is already deeply prejudiced against the Nationalist government. It's likely that the US government will stop providing aid. If there is a fire at both ends, put out the big one first. We've got no choice but to recover the three million two hundred thousand dollars for the American companies in China."

Xie Peidong listened attentively. As usual, he did not respond instantly but tended to think about what was going on before Fang Buting told him his real intentions. Fang Buting waited while he pondered the issue.

Xie Peidong was utterly clear that there was ten million dollars' worth of everyday materials and goods embezzled by the Peking authorities. Among them, Kong's Yangtze Construction Company and Song's Fuzhong Company accounted for six million, and Xu Tieying secretly skimmed off eighty thousand dollars from Hou Juntang. Now they were only supposed to recover three million two hundred thousand dollars which would be used to compensate the American companies. So, as it happened, there was not even any need to recover the six million eight hundred thousand dollars stolen by the Kong and Song families, and Xu Tieying. As an undercover agent of the CPC lurking in the financial sector, he didn't believe in destiny. However, this coincidence made him feel amazed at the fact that the days of the Kuomintang regime were indeed numbered.

Xie Peidong seemed to have straightened out his thoughts and was ready to share his concerns with some trepidation. "I can cook three million two hundred thousand on the account books here but the auditing group of the Ministry of Defence has specifically demanded the figure of ten million. They were so specific, they must have acted on accurate economic intelligence. If they continue to press us hard, how do we reply about the remaining six million eight hundred thousand?"

"A ship carrying US aid materials jointly owned by the Yangtze and Fuzhong companies sank on the high seas. The Air Force had two planes that had been flying smuggling missions which also crashed. Natural and man-made disasters inflicted further losses on us of six million eight hundred thousand. Therefore, we were only able to recover three million two hundred thousand."

Xie Peidong looked at Fang Buting who nodded.

"Then I'll make an account entry of three million two hundred thousand dollars but it'll be the responsibility of Commissioner Xu to recover the money."

"Good. I'll go back and convey our profound concern to Director-General Ye and Minister Chen. Meanwhile, Governor Fang, please help explain the situation to Mr Song and Mr Kong through the Central Bank headquarters right away. If both of us report to the president at the same time, he will naturally judge, weigh the advantages and disadvantages, and prevent the Ministry of Defence from investigating the case. That way, Meng'ao will be freed from his responsibilities as an investigator. I'll transfer the suspects to the police bureau for interrogation as soon as the order from Nanking arrives. The crux of the matter is that Manager Xie should balance the three million two hundred thousand dollars on the account books as soon as possible."

Fang Buting didn't immediately have anything to say this time. Instead, he looked at Xu Tieying and asked a seemingly irrelevant question. "Who will be doing the interrogation at the police bureau?"

Xu Tieying had already been expecting this question.

"Governor Fang, please rest assured. I won't involve Mengwei in this case. I have made proper adjustments to his work schedule. He'll only be responsible for the field work of the bureau of Peking Municipality which means I won't get him involved in busting troublemakers among the university protestors."

Xu Tieying's plan changed Fang Buting's view of him. Finally, a satisfied expression appeared on his cold face. Although this man had been greedy, he knew after all how to help others in the same boat. His desire to release Meng'ao from his investigative duties might be outright lies but it was quite human for him to take the initiative to extricate Mengwei.

"Thank you for taking the trouble to make the plans." It was the first time Fang Buting had uttered such kind words to Xu Tieying that day. With that, all three men stood up. Fang Buting glanced at Xie Peidong, then looked at Xu Tieying. "Just follow Mr Xu's advice."

"I'm all for the idea of helping each other when we're all in the same boat," said Xu Tieying, picking up his hat and putting it on. "Time is tight. I must be going."

With that, he saluted Fang Buting. Fang Buting was unprepared, so he was quite taken aback by the act of courtesy but quickly responded by bowing slightly. Xu Tieying reached out to Xie Peidong again and shook hands with him tightly, then departed.

"Peidong, why don't you walk him out," said Fang Buting.

"It's raining outside, Governor. Stay inside, please." Xie Peidong went out alone.

Fang Buting followed them out of the office door and watched Xie Peidong walk Xu Tieying down the stairs. He still wanted to follow him but suddenly he felt dizzy again and quickly clung to the railing of the stairway. "Commissioner Xu, Peidong will see you off, I won't..."

The heavy rain outside the house had drowned Fang Buting's weak voice when Xie Peidong accompanied Xu Tieying out of the living room. The bedroom door at the far end of the corridor opened immediately. Obviously, Cheng Xiaoyun had heard Fang Buting. She was surprised at the way he looked, so she rushed over to him, holding him at the railing. "Are you OK?"

"I'm OK."

"Let's go to the bedroom, shall we?" Cheng Xiaoyun suggested.

Fang Buting saw the anxiety in Cheng Xiaoyun's eyes. "What's the matter? Is Mulan crying again?"

Cheng Xiaoyun shook her head. "It's Mengwei. He's leaving. I've been talking to him for a while. I couldn't very well interrupt you while you were talking business."

"Alas!" Fang Buting let out a long, heavy sigh. He then walked to the bedroom with Cheng Xiaoyun supporting him. After entering the bedroom Fang Buting stopped, only to feel a burst of heartache. Standing by the chair near the window, he saw his little son had changed into a student uniform with two suitcases beside him. Wasn't he about to move out? Was he going to travel to some distant place?

"What's going on? Where do you want to go?" Fang Buting asked in a stern voice.

"First to Hong Kong, then to France," replied Fang Mengwei.

"What will you do in France?"

"Study, work, whatever..."

"What will you study? What kind of work will you do? Do you think you're one of them?"

"Why are you so loud?" Cheng Xiaoyun quickly interposed. "Mengwei is expecting to discuss this with you."

"What is there to discuss with me? He is a staff member of the Nationalist government and a military officer on active service. If he deserts his post without permission during the period of National Mobilisation in Suppression of the Communist Insurgency, he could be court-martialled!"

"Dad." Fang Mengwei's voice was not aggrieved but desolate. "My brother also serves in the military. Are you working to get him transferred to the US?"

Mengwei's question stumped him. After a long moment of silence, Fang Buting's tone softened. "You know what's going on. Why is it necessary to make me speechless? Between the two sons, you have been the obedient one since you were a child. Although you've been around with me for all those years, you've never been a source of worry. If you really want to leave, give me a reason. I will ask for help on your behalf."

"Sit down. Sit down and talk." Cheng Xiaoyun found that Fang Buting could not stand any longer, so she helped him sit down on the edge of the bed. Fang Mengwei moved a little. He wanted to help but when he saw his stepmother half perched on the bed, holding his father's back firmly, he stopped.

"Mengwei, say it nicely."

Fang Mengwei bowed his head in silence. Finally he made up his mind to speak what was on his mind. "After finishing junior high school in Chongqing, I wanted to go on to high school, but you insisted on sending me to attend the Three Youth League training class offered by the central government. I really didn't want to go. You dropped your glass in anger. That night, I could only shed tears in my room alone. I think that if my mother had still been around, she would have supported my wish to go to high school until after I had finished my studies there, then she would have sent me to study abroad. Who made me a motherless child later?"

Fang Buting's body shook and Cheng Xiaoyun behind him also trembled. She held Fang Buting tightly, supporting him with both hands.

Fang Mengwei's feet moved a little but he didn't step forward. He lowered his voice as he said: "Stepmother, I didn't say this to disturb you. Don't take it personally."

"I know." There were tears in Cheng Xiaoyun's eyes. "Go ahead, speak up, your father will understand."

Fang Mengwei, however, became reticent. Fang Buting had just closed his eyes before slowly opening them. "I was wrong at that time. Go on, say it. If I made the decision on your mother's behalf then it's up to you to decide what to do now, OK?"

Cheng Xiaoyun felt acutely that Fang Buting had shivered a little when he was speaking. So she quickly sat down close to Fang Buting. With this, she'd be able to support him with her body, and at the same time prevent Mengwei from seeing her tear-filled eyes.

"I didn't say you were wrong." Fang Mengwei held back his

tears. "After our family was separated and lost touch with each other in Shanghai, you did everything possible to look for us. At that time, my brother didn't want to see you again but he insisted that I come to you. I still remember when I left, he said he would die in battle to avenge my mother. He repeatedly told me to work as hard as I could, to be a learned man and strive to win credit for our country."

"Don't say it. I'll atone for it." Fang straightened up again and stood up.

"Dad…"

"Buting…"

Fang Buting no longer asked Cheng Xiaoyun to help but looked at her affectionately. "Follow me, let Mengwei take Mulan to France."

"I'll go and tell Mulan," said Cheng Xiaoyun.

"Let me do it instead," said Fang Buting.

"Uncle?" Xie Mulan, who had been waiting for He Xiaoyu in the room, had not expected Fang Buting to come in. Seeing him gently close the door behind him, she was quite startled.

Fang Buting said with a smile: "What's wrong? Why are you looking at me like that? Aren't you going to invite me to sit down?"

"Sit down, please." Xie Mulan quickly straightened the chair by the window and came to help Fang Buting.

Fang Buting tried his best to look pleasantly warm and said: "I'm alone."

"Where's Xiaoyu?"

"Has Xiaoyu been here?"

"Maybe she's talking to my dad. Sit down, Uncle."

"OK." Fang Buting sat down and said: "I wasn't home last night and was in a meeting the whole morning. I just learned your father has locked you in your room, which is quite unreasonable. How could he do that?"

Nevertheless, Xie Mulan had been fiendishly smart, knowing that her uncle was coaxing her. She responded by saying: "Now that you're back, he dare not lock me up any more. Uncle, would you please let me and Xiaoyu go back to school in your car?"

Fang Buting laughed. "When the daughter grows up, she should be set free like a bird to fly far and high. I'll support you. Not only will I let you go out but I'll also let you fly higher and farther. How does that sound to you?"

Xie Mulan looked at him, pondered his words and suggested: "Uncle, you wouldn't lie to me, would you?"

"Of course not. When did I ever lie to you?"

Xie Mulan thought in the blink of an eye and said coquettishly: "Not really. I'm wrong."

Fang Buting nodded with a smile. "It's good that you admit you're at fault." Then he pretended to relax, thought for a moment and asked: "Did you have a chance to discuss with your classmates which country's customs and scenic spots in the world you most want to see?"

Xie Mulan became a little wary. But Uncle Fang's demeanour did not suggest that he intended to force her into anything. "We've had lots of discussions," she replied. "Are you going to tell me about America again?"

"America, there's nothing to talk about. It's just a country with a history of a hundred years or so. Nothing but a country of skyscrapers. I spent six years in the US. But, honestly, the city in Europe I wanted to visit the most was Paris where there is the Louvre Museum and the Eiffel Tower. Did you share anything about those places?"

"Of course we did." Xie Mulan purposefully appeared to be quite aloof. "But China is so backward that even if we go there, we'll be looked down upon."

"You've got a point but you're only partially right. Madame Chiang is also a Chinese, and her speech in the US Congress earned her a long standing ovation, applauded by all the members of the assembly. After that, wherever she travelled she was respected all over the US. Why? Because she has studied overseas, she has knowledge and she has experience. Mulan, I want you to become an accomplished woman like her."

Xie Mulan seemed to understand what he was driving at. "Uncle, do you want to send me to study abroad?"

Fang Buting looked at her. "Doesn't it sound like a good idea for you?"

"No, it doesn't," replied Xie Mulan but she quickly modified her response. "It wouldn't be that bad. I haven't graduated from college yet, so now is not the right time, even if I want to go at some point."

"That's not a problem. I've a classmate in charge of academic affairs at the University of Paris. They can transfer you there where you can finish college, then continue your graduate studies."

"Are you colluding to get rid of me?" Xie Mulan got so angry that she shouted: "You don't need to kick me out. I'll do it myself."

Xie Mulan immediately went to pick up the suitcase she had already prepared.

"Mulan." Fang Buting got to his feet and said: "Don't do this."

Xie Mulan still had great respect for Fang Buting, so she softened her tone. "Uncle, I just want to live on campus. If you allow me to stay on campus, I promise to come back and visit you."

Suddenly, the door was pushed open and Xie Peidong barged in with a long face. "Don't reason with her any more, Governor. You're still quite ill. Go and get some rest, please."

"Say it nicely, nicely." Fang Buting still looked genial.

"I've got nothing nice to say? It's the middle of the summer break, where are you supposed to stay on campus? Running wild and causing a disturbance to make a fool of yourself! Can you step outside? I need to lock the door now."

Xie Mulan's face turned white. "I'd like to stay at Xiaoyu's house. Why am I making a fool of myself? Where's Xiaoyu?" As she was speaking, she looked out of the door, as a glimmer of hope remained in her heart.

"She's back already. I sent her home by car. Governor, shall we step outside?"

"If you lock the door and leave, I'll jump out of the window!" Xie Mulan, who had never been defiant, finally exploded, wild with anger.

"You're not my father, I've never had a father, only feudal parents! I will never be oppressed by you again!" Xie Peidong had never anticipated that his daughter would suddenly do this to him. Although looking calm, he felt a chill in his heart.

"Mulan!" This time it was Fang Buting who was scolding her. "How can you speak to your father like this!"

Xie Mulan did not give in and stood there with her suitcase. "Now, I'm done talking with both of you. Let me go, will you?"

Fang Buting once again seemed so helpless that he had no choice but to turn to Xie Peidong.

Xie Peidong also realised that he could never give in. "I should renounce you as my daughter! You want to go out? Go anywhere you like, except Peking. Take your suitcase, go!"

"Where?" Xie Mulan's voice was almost shaking.

"To the railway station. I'll send someone to take you wherever you want to go."

Xie Mulan slowly put her luggage down on the floor.

"Girl," said Fang Buting, having become aware that she might do something silly.

Sure enough, Xie Mulan turned round, got on the chair and stepped onto the windowsill. Fang Buting felt so terrified that he was at a loss when suddenly a figure flashed in front of him. Xie Peidong had already taken a sudden big stride forward to the window. He grabbed Xie Mulan, then firmly clamped her arm under his. "Are you nuts?! Someone's got to bring you under control!"

Xie Mulan was caged by her father like a bird. She felt so weak and so desperate that she closed her eyes and wept but she no longer struggled.

"Peidong!" Fang Buting could do nothing about the situation. "You don't have to be like this…"

"Governor, will you stop talking?" said Xie Peidong, lifting the suitcase with his other hand and preparing to depart.

"Uncle, put Mulan down." Fang Mengwei's voice was suddenly heard at the door.

Xie Peidong stood there, stunned and startled, as was Fang Buting on finding his son at the door. Fang Mengwei was dressed in his neat police uniform and he looked extremely pale but he was very calm. "Mulan is a student, students should attend school. There is no reason for you not to let her go. Uncle, give me the suitcase."

Fang Mengwei went over and reached out to Xie Peidong.

Xie Peidong didn't give him the suitcase: "Mengwei, you don't want to mess around in the affairs of elders."

Fang Mengwei stood firm in front of Xie Peidong and slowly looked at Xie Mulan, who was still being held horizontally under her father's arm. Without making a move, she turned her tearful face away. Obviously, she did not want him to see her. His heart felt a chill.

Fang Mengwei stared at Xie Peidong. "Uncle, I'm begging you, my elder now. Please don't deprive your children of their freedom. You don't expect me to be rough with you, do you? Please give me the suitcase and put Mulan down."

Xie Peidong did not enjoy the churning in his stomach and found himself in a quandary.

"Peidong, shall we leave it to Mengwei?"

Xie Peidong handed the suitcase over to Fang Mengwei and released his daughter. Fang Buting reached out and took Xie Mulan by the arm. Without looking at Xie Mulan, Fang Mengwei said to her: "Go and wash your face. I'll drive you to school."

Xie Mulan was still rooted to the spot, as if in a trance.

"Don't worry", remarked Fang Mengwei. "I'll drop you at the gate of Yenching University. I didn't mean that..."

Xie Mulan wiped away her tears and looked at Fang Mengwei. "Thank you, cousin."

"Let's hit the road," replied Fang Mengwei with a smile at the corner of his mouth

Then he took her suitcase and walked quietly between the two old men to the door. As if sleepwalking, Xie Mulan followed him to the door. Fang Buting and Xie Peidong watched the two of them walk out of the doorway. Both Xie Peidong and Fang Buting, left alone by their respective son and daughter, listened to their retreating footsteps, scarcely realising what had happened, their eyes filled with profound sadness.

Outside the building, it was not raining as hard any more. The jeep engine could be heard in the distance as it departed. Fang Buting sat back on the sofa specially reserved for him while Xie Peidong took a seat beside him. Both stared blankly into the void ahead of them.

Cheng Xiaoyun appeared at the door, folded the umbrella and hung it on the umbrella stand before walking in quietly.

"What did Mengwei say after I left?" asked Fang Buting.

Cheng Xiaoyun walked over and sat down. "He heard you arguing, so he went back to his room and changed into his police uniform. It seems that he only spoke a few words."

She was about to speak, and then hesitated.

"Out with it!" said Fang Buting, who had been waiting most anxiously.

Cheng Xiaoyun lowered her head. "He was in a fit of anger. He said that the country might perish, families are being destroyed and that people are being forced into terrible scrapes, so there's no way out."

"Peidong!" Fang Buting suddenly got to his feet.

Xie Peidong slowly stood up.

"Call Mr Kong and Mr Song's office right away!"

It was about 4 pm when the wind and rain stopped. Although the ground was all muddy, the wheels still rolled violently on the muddy surface.

On the large open ground of the Inspection Brigade barracks, twenty pilots, who were still standing naked to the waist, were looking vigilantly at the gate. Dozens of Citizens' Food Distribution Committee employees were also looking wide-eyed at the gate, sitting on the muddy ground, all covered with mud and exhausted.

There were two mid-sized American military jeeps and two small ones, followed by three ten-wheeled trucks. Without reducing speed, they drove straight onto the large open ground after entering the gate.

Recognising them as Chen Jicheng's troops, Chen Changwu barked an order at Guo Jinyang by his side. "Report to the captain immediately!" Guo Jinyang strode back to the barracks right away. The motorcade drove straight up to the pilots before stopping abruptly a few metres away.

From the front seat of the first mid-sized jeep, the Special Task Battalion commander of the Nationalist Army's Fourth Corps jumped out, followed by ten elite troopers. From the front seat of the second jeep, out came the executive group leader of the Military Council's Bureau of Investigation, followed by ten members of the group.

Secretary Sun stepped out of the front seat of the first jeep. He opened the rear door for Xu Tieying to get out of the vehicle, while the rear door of the second jeep opened by itself as Wang Puchen got out.

All those who jumped off the three ten-wheeled trucks were gendarmes from the Peking Department of the Garrison Headquarters, wearing steel helmets and big leather boots, and armed to the teeth with carbines and submachine guns. The gendarmes were running around the compound and taking up their positions stretching from the gate to encompass the whole barracks.

Xu Tieying and Wang Puchen walked in front, followed by the Special Task Battalion commander and the execution group leader of the bureau, together with his special agents and other members of the action team. They walked up to Chen Changwu.

The Special Task Battalion commander and the executive group leader yelled at the committee staff who were still sitting on the ground: "Get up! All of you, stand up!"

"Don't move!" Chen Changwu shouted to stop those intending to stand up. The Special Task Battalion commander and the execution group leader and the troopers they commanded immediately stepped forward to confront him.

Chen Changwu and the pilots showed no sign of weakness. A clash was about to ensue.

"Don't!" said Xu Tieying, in an attempt to stop the people on his side. "Where's Captain Fang?"

"Listening to the report inside," replied Chen Changwu.

Xu Tieying again glanced at the committee staff members being forced to sit on the ground. There was mud on their bodies and faces. Each of them only had their eyes exposed, which made them quite difficult to identify. Nevertheless, Xu Tieying found that Ma Hanshan was not among the subdued crowd.

"Where's Director Ma?" Xu Tieying asked Chen Changwu again.

"He's been with our captain."

Guo Jinyang came out of the barracks and strode over to Chen Changwu. "The captain asked who these people are and what they're up to. Have they got any orders from the Ministry of Defence?"

Chen Changwu looked at Xu Tieying.

Of course, Xu Tieying knew that he had to face it by himself but he could not go it alone, so he turned to Wang Puchen. "Our orders are from Nanking. But the State Secrecy Bureau can represent the Ministry of Defence. Station Chief Wang, let's go and arrest Ma Hanshan."

Wang Puchen started smoking again and his smoking triggered a coughing fit. He coughed a few times before replying: "Let's do it."

"We're authorised by Nanking," said Xu Tieying to Chen Changwu. "Take us to see Captain Fang."

Chen Changwu, Guo Jinyang and Shao Yuangang quickly reached an agreement.

"Please take Commissioner Xu and this officer to see our captain," Chen Changwu said to Guo Jinyang.

"Gentlemen, please follow me." Guo Jinyang took Xu Tieying and Wang Puchen to the barracks. The Special Task Battalion commander and the execution group leader followed closely behind.

"What's your business anyway? It's the senior officers' meeting." Chen Changwu and Shao Yuangang immediately stopped them.

"They're here on orders from Nanking. Follow us," Xu Tieying explained.

"Well, let's go with you then."

Chen Changwu and Shao Yuangang exchanged a look of agreement. All six of them headed to the barracks.

―――――

In his room in the residential compound of Gu Weijun in Peking, Zeng Keda found that the situation changed multiple times a day like the weather, yet he had no idea how to cope with it.

Holding the phone, he was anxious to speak but had to be patient. "Secretary Wang, what's going on here?" he asked. "They received direct orders from Nanking but I didn't get any instructions from Comrade Jianfeng. Soon, Fang Meng'ao will ask me if those suspects should be taken away. How should I reply?"

Secretary Wang also sounded a little anxious as he said: "Comrade Jianfeng also just got the information and went straight to consult the president at his residence. When he left, he asked me to tell you to stay calm if you called. He may phone you directly after his meeting with the president."

"Did he say I should turn the people over to them?"

"He's given no specific instructions. According to his tone, I guess Comrade Jianfeng wants you to delay them in the first instance."

"I see."

Now he understood the situation but what should he do? Zeng Keda put down the phone and stood there thinking.

―――

There was not the slightest indication of tension in Fang Meng'ao's room in the rear of the Inspection Brigade barracks. On the contrary, what made Xu Tieying feel both embarrassed and angry, though in a concealed manner, was that Fang Meng'ao and Ma Hanshan were properly seated in chairs while he and Wang Puchen were left standing. As Fang Meng'ao was examining the arrest warrant, Ma Hanshan was looking out of the window. Neither of them bothered to look at him or Wang Puchen. Wang Puchen, on the other hand, was expressionless. His slender fingers took out another cigarette and lit it using his previous cigarette. Again, he coughed like mad once he started smoking.

―――

The Special Task Battalion commander and the execution group leader were blocked in the doorway by Chen Changwu and Shao Yuangang. They were also standing, impatient and trying to assess the situation in the room, only to find that their view was being blocked by two tall, heavily-built men standing side by side.

"Finished?" Xu Tieying asked Fang Meng'ao.

Fang Meng'ao didn't answer Xu Tieying directly. Instead he put the military warrant on his lap and called out to the door: "Chen Changwu."

"Yes sir!" replied Chen Changwu from outside the door.

"Bring in two chairs for the officers," instructed Fang Meng'ao.

"Yes sir!"

Chen Changwu came in with a chair in each hand and put them in the room. "Please sit down." Then he went out again.

Finally, Xu Tieying and Wang Puchen got their seats and sat down.

"This order is for you. It doesn't work for me." Only then did Fang Meng'ao get to the point.

"Absolutely, this military order from the Ministry of Defence is for you. It clearly stipulates that the people involved in the Citizens' Food Distribution Committee should be handed over to my bureau for interrogation. Why doesn't it work for you?"

Ma Hanshan, who had been pretending to look out of the window, fidgeted a little and couldn't help looking at Fang Meng'ao.

"We are the auditing team under the Inspection Brigade of the Ministry of Defence. Not a word of this military warrant was meant for our investigation brigade which, of course, doesn't work."

"Who are you affiliated with? Who commands your Ministry of Defence investigation team? Must the military orders of the Ministry of Defence be issued to you specifically?"

"That's a good question. The Investigation Brigade of the Ministry of Defence was set up by the ministry. Therefore, military orders from the Ministry of Defence must be issued to me specifically. Perhaps you don't like what you hear, Commissioner Xu. Do you follow orders that are not meant for you?"

"You said so."

Fang Meng'ao handed the command back to him. "This military order is fake."

"Captain Fang, you're not kidding, are you!" Xu Tieying abruptly stood up. "Who would dare to forge a military order from the Ministry of Defence. You'll be court-marshalled, won't you?"

Fang Meng'ao did not take offense. "There are daredevils!

Maybe your military order really carries the seal of the Ministry of Defence but it could be a false one."

Xu Tieying felt so frustrated at Fang Meng'ao's response but he managed to keep his temper under control and say: "The phone is right beside you. You can call Inspector-General Zeng now to confirm the order."

"I never ask before I do my job. My superior will inform me of all the details."

"Well, if you don't call, I will."

There were two phones on Zeng Keda's desk. What was more, there was a threadbound book beside the phone in a conspicuous position. The book, which was closed, had the impressively printed title *The Complete Works of Duke Zeng Wenzheng* on its cover. At the moment, Zeng Keda was sitting right in front of the virtual Duke of Zeng Wenzheng, his eyes closed, waiting for the phone. He needed the *jingqi*, the vital energy to bring him peace of mind. The phone rang! Zeng Keda's eyelids moved for a second but he was in no hurry to answer it. He said to himself: calm yourself, keep calm.

Then he opened his eyes but quickly lost his cool. He found that it was an interior Peking line. To answer or not to answer? He was hesitant. Slowly, he raised the phone and put it to his ear without saying a word.

"Is that Inspector-General Zeng? This is Xu Tieying." The voice at the other end was deafening but Zeng Keda remained silent.

"Inspector-General Zeng? Please speak, speak!" The voice became even louder.

Zeng Keda pressed the button with his other hand and was just about to hang up the phone when he stopped. Instead, he put it on the table. That way, the line would remain busy.

Back in his private room in the barracks, Fang Meng'ao, whose hearing was fairly keen, immediately knew that the person at the other end had not answered Xu Tieying's call. Nevertheless, he asked: "What did Inspector-General Zeng say?"

Xu Tieying put down the phone. Knowing that he could not vent his anger on Fang Meng'ao, no matter how angry he was, he replied: "I asked just for the sake of saving his face. In fact, we can ignore him completely according to the rules. The military order contains both the official seal of the Ministry of Defence and the written approval of Vice-Minister Qin in charge. Captain Fang, it's not our intention to give you a hard time. I hope you won't make our job difficult."

"Then tell me how I can make your job easy."

Xu Tieying glanced at Wang Puchen.

"Station Chief Wang has also received an order from the Secrecy Bureau of the Ministry of Defence. Please hand over Director Ma, as well as the committee members outside."

Fang Meng'ao looked at Ma Hanshan. Only now did Ma Hanshan really turn his eyes towards Xu Tieying who had already been in the room for quite a while. He also glanced at Wang Puchen but he remained seated on the chair without any intention of getting up.

Fang Meng'ao seemed to be consulting Ma Hanshan. "Deputy Director Ma, Director-General Ma, are you willing to go with them?"

"My family name is Ma, which means 'horse' but I am not a horse or a mule to be led away by anyone."

"Director Ma!" barked Xu Tieying, beginning to sound more aggressive. "It's not our intention to take you away but this is a military order from the Ministry of Defence. Perhaps you may want to have a look, too?"

"It's not for me. I'm affiliated with the Ministry of Civil Affairs. Why should I take a look?"

Xu Tieying handed the order to him aggressively. "Of course, it's not for you but it has your name on it. You are the person to be interrogated."

"Puchen, is that what it says on it?" asked Ma Hanshan, turning to look at Wang Puchen.

Wang Puchen just stamped out his cigarette and took out another one. "Old Station Chief, I'll tell you what, I'll never get you into trouble but your name is indeed written on the military order. As for the pending investigation, it won't do you any harm."

"Puchen!" Ma Hanshan called out as if he was an old traveller in the underworld of politics. "You are still young. Even though you've succeeded me, I will teach you one last lesson, that is, if they can do this to me today, they will do so to you tomorrow."

"Ma Hanshan, I want to remind you that you should put away

that set of old rules prevailing in the underworld. If you continue to defy the party-state today with these rules, you'll be subjected to severe punishment by the Nanking authorities, even if we want to help you!"

"Xu Tieying!" Ma Hanshan continued to defy him by calling his name. "You are not the party-state. Nanking is so big, which part of the city is your jurisdiction? Wang Jingwei used to be the chairman of the puppet regime in Nanking, did he ever say Nanking was his jurisdiction? Don't scare me with your authorities in Nanking. I'll tell you what, I'm not Hou Juntang, nor Cui Zhongshi! Stabbing people in the back after taking their money away! You'll be despised not just by the party-state but also by folks in the underworld. What are you looking at me for? Do you want to eat me alive? Captain Fang is here. Who killed Hou Juntang and Cui Zhongshi? He's very clear about it."

"Guards!" roared Xu Tieying.

Outside the door, the Special Task Battalion commander and the executive group leader wanted to break in. "We're carrying out our duties. Please get out of the way!"

Chen Changwu and Shao Yuangang stood next to one another, their shoulders wider than the door. The two men pulled out their guns. Chen Changwu and Shao Yuangang were ready to seize their guns.

"Let them in!" ordered Fang Meng'ao.

Chen Changwu and Shao Yuangang hesitated for a moment, then reluctantly made way for them with a small gap through which the two officers could only squeeze through sideways. After entering the room, the Special Task Battalion commander pointed his gun at Ma Hanshan but the gun in the executive group leader's hand was still facing downward. After all, Ma Hanshan was his former superior.

Looking furious, Xu Tieying intended to make the arrest. But he appeared to calm down a little after the unintended episode. He said to Fang Meng'ao: "Captain Fang, we must take Ma Hanshan. Please forgive us, we are just doing our job."

Fang Meng'ao stood up slowly, his body blocking Ma Hanshan from being approached. "Now, it's not that I won't allow you to bust him but that Director Ma doesn't believe you and won't go with you. Director Ma, what are you doing with my gun?"

Although Fang Meng'ao had left his gun at the head of his bed behind the chair, Ma Hanshan didn't actually take it. However, with Fang Meng'ao's reminder, what else could prompt him to pick it up? Knowing that Fang Meng'ao was there for him, Ma Hanshan became so assured that he grabbed the gun from the head of the bed, loaded it and stood up. He jumped from behind Fang Meng'ao to the front, just facing Xu Tieying, sticking the muzzle of the gun in Xu Tieying's ribs. Although he was a veteran agent with the Central Bureau of Investigation and Statistics, Xu Tieying was no match for Ma Hanshan in using a gun. Having been a civil servant for a long time, he would normally miss nine out of ten targets when doing shooting practice. At the moment, with the muzzle of Ma's pistol sticking into his waist and his other hand clutching his chest, he couldn't move a muscle because once he did, he would be most definitely be shot on the spot.

"Ma Hanshan, are you aware of the consequences of your actions?" After all, Xu Tieying was a seasoned policeman. At the moment, he remained unmoved but spoke without the least sign of being intimidated.

"Puchen! People know the consequences but guns don't. There's nothing we can do if the gun goes off!"

"Old Station Chief, you don't have to do this."

Wang Puchen was still standing calmly but he did not light the cigarette in his hand. Hearing Ma Hanshan call him, he replied: "What the hell do you know?" Ma Hanshan did not scold but meant to teach him a lesson. "These guys from the Communications Bureau never treat our people like their equals! If I don't do this today, I'll be dead meat, the second Cui Zhongshi before evening arrives! Wait till you get to the morgue and get me my body. Listen to me, take those two out of the room."

"OK, OK. I'll take them out. Old Station Chief, please, don't do anything stupid. Now, get out."

Wang Puchen motioned with the cigarette held in his slender fingers and walked out slowly. The executive group leader followed him out hastily. Only the Special Task Battalion commander hesitated with his gun in his hand but when Fang Meng'ao stared at him with flashing eyes, he had to withdraw his gun and exited.

"Changwu, Yuangang, go and lock the doors of the barracks!" ordered Fang Meng'ao.

"Yes sir!" answered Chen Changwu and Shao Yuangang in unison at the door.

There were only three people left in Fang Meng'ao's room.

"Director Ma, you can put the gun away. The three of us can clarify lots of things among ourselves."

"No, I don't think so, Captain Fang."

Ma Hanshan was still grabbing Xu Tieying by the chest but the muzzle of his gun was pointing at his heart now.

"Xu, you know this bullet I'm going to fire is aimed at your heart. I've been drinking and having too much sex lately, my hands are shaking, and I'm not sure when I might pull the trigger. Now, tell us how you managed to set him up that night and how you had Cui Zhongshi murdered!"

Fang Meng'ao glared at Xu Tieying, who remained motionless, with his eyes closed.

Once again, the phone rang. It was the interior loop line within Peking municipality. Zeng Keda simply would not answer it. He opened the *Complete Works of Duke Zeng Wenzheng* even if he could hardly read it. But the caller was so stubborn that it continued to ring. Zeng Keda held the book in one hand and picked up the phone with the other. He tried to hang up but changed his mind and put the phone to his ear.

"Inspector-General Zeng, this is Puchen." In the microphone, Wang Puchen's voice was not loud but he enunciated his words very clearly. His tone did not sound urgent but managed to convey a level of urgency with the non-stop ringing.

"I know it's hard for you, but it's hard for us too because things are out of our control now. If you're listening, just answer me."

"I'm listening. Please go ahead, Mr Wang."

"Captain Fang wouldn't let us take Ma Hanshan with us. Director Ma has gone mad, pointing his gun at Commissioner Xu.

It's loaded. I'm not sure if it will go off or not. Who is authorised to arrest and interrogate the staff of the Citizens' Food Distribution Committee? Please call for instructions from the Bureau of Reserve Cadres of the Ministry of Defence."

Zeng Keda was shocked. After thinking for a moment, he said: "It's not reasonable for Commissioner Xu to make the arrest. I really don't want to comment on that. However, since you're there, please stabilise the situation since you also belong to the Ministry of Defence. It's better to have the situation under your control. I'll call the bureau right now."

"Good. I'll wait for your call, Inspector-General Zeng. Please call me back at the guard room."

Zeng Keda hung up the phone, then dropped the *Complete Works of Duke Zeng Wenzheng* in frustration. He turned to look at the special line two with which he could make the direct call but he hesitated. Who could he call when Comrade Jianfeng was not available? Zeng Keda became so restless with anxiety that he just opened the door and went out. It was already dusk. The garden looked luxuriantly green after the rain. The adjutant, Wang, who lived in the little room opposite him along the corridor, came out as soon as he saw him. "Inspector-General, the air is so fresh after the rain, why not go for a jog before supper?" he asked.

"Indeed, now would be a great time to go for a run." Zeng Keda gave a long sigh. "Tell the chef not to cook until he's told to."

"Yes sir." He went back to shut the door of his room, then went down the stone steps, turned right and headed for the kitchen.

Taking a deep breath, Zeng Keda crouched down and began to do quick push-ups on the brick floor of the porch. After a dozen push-ups, he heard the phone ring in the room.

"It's me, Keda, Comrade Jianfeng!" Zeng Keda couldn't restrain the excitement in his voice.

"I'm calling you on special line one. Just listen, you don't have to say anything." The voice of Comrade Jianfeng down the line echoed in his ear.

"Yes," said Zeng Keda.

"It's always hard to make revolution, especially now. They have completely disregarded the fact that the very existence of the party-state is at stake, and will do anything for their own personal gain.

Today, the two major forces have floated around the president, charging that the Investigation Group of the Ministry of Defence was being used by the Communist Party. This led to the issuance of the military order of the Ministry of Defence that would endanger the party-state. I've been in conversation with the president for two hours. The president's instruction is that we should not be used by the Communist Party at any time. The Communist Party member they referred to was none other than Fang Meng'ao. Let me ask you now, how is Comrade Liang Jinglun? Is he making any progress? Has the person from the Students' Union contacted Fang Meng'ao? Has Fang Meng'ao completely cut off his ties with the Communist Party? Don't answer me now. I'll give you half an hour to clarify the above questions and transfer the call to special line one through line two. Give me a clear and definite answer, so that I can reassure the president that we will conduct a thorough investigation of the corruption cases in Peking and let the US immediately resume its assistance."

"Yes. I will go and find out at once, Comrade Jianfeng!" replied Zeng Keda loudly.

Special line one hung up.

"Adjutant Wang!" Zeng Keda called out but immediately remembered that he had gone to the kitchen, so he stopped calling and thought fast. Finally, he made up his mind and began to dial the number of the Peking interior loop line.

In the living room on the ground floor of He's house, Xie Mulan, who was sitting in silence, was startled when the phone began to ring. Confused, she looked at He Xiaoyu, sitting opposite, and asked timidly: "Could it be from my home?"

"It doesn't matter if it's for you. But it should be for my dad." With that, she picked up the phone.

To He Xiaoyu, it was a stranger's voice at the other end of the line. In fact, it was the voice of Zeng Keda: "Is that Chancellor He's residence?"

"Yes. Who's speaking, please?" replied He Xiaoyu.

"This is Zeng speaking. I'm a professor in the economics department at Tsinghua University. May I speak to Professor Liang Jinglun?"

He Xiaoyu covered the phone and whispered to Xie Mulan: "Professor Zeng from Tsinghua University, he wants to speak to Professor Liang." Xie Mulan sighed with relief and her eyes brightened with joy.

"Hello, Professor Zeng, Professor Liang is here but he's busy working on a very urgent plan with Chancellor He. If it's not important, can you call later?"

"I'm really sorry. It is very urgent. It'll only take a few minutes of Mr Liang's time. Please ask him to answer the phone."

He Xiaoyu held the phone in her hand and, without looking at Xie Mulan, called upstairs: "Professor Liang, it's for you from Professor Zeng of Tsinghua University."

There was the sound of chairs moving followed by footsteps from He Qicang's room on the first floor. Xie Mulan could no longer restrain her excitement. She looked at the door with great anticipation and her eyes glistened with excitement.

CHAPTER 11

He Qicang's bedroom was always clean and tidy. But tonight, it looked very disorderly, as disorderly as the city of Peking. Stacks of reference books and materials were piled up on the floor. Those were the books he had read in order to provide guidance for the Nationalist government to issue gold yuan notes. Over the books one could see the cover page of the manuscript on the desk right under the table lamp, entitled *On the Feasibility of Immediate Abolition of the Old Currency and Implementation of the New Currency System.*

Removing the wooden chair, Liang Jinglun left his desk buried under a surprising amount of books and reference materials, and moved to the tea table against the wall to get the thermos bottle. With his back towards He Qicang, one could read the solemnity in his countenance, as solemn as the title of the report on the table. By placing the call to He Qicang's residence, Zeng Keda had seriously violated the rules of mutual contact. That made it difficult for Liang Jinglun to do his job and, because of that, Liang Jinglun became rather nervous. In fact, his top priority at the moment was to assist He Qicang to bring about the golden yuan reform. But once he chose to answer the call, it would be very likely to arouse He's suspicion. Why was it that aggressive superiors never consider the difficulties of their subordinates? Liang Jinglun picked up the thermos bottle and went back to the desk. He removed the lid of He

Qicang's cup, added some hot water and looked at his mentor across the table. He Qicang understood his dilemma since he knew Liang as well as if he was his own son.

"Go and answer the phone," said He as he leaned back on the wicker chair and began to read the manuscript himself.

"Professor Zeng of Tsinghua University is about to publish a paper in which he borrows one of my arguments. I'm afraid I can't explain myself clearly over the phone…"

"Then you've got to do your best to explain it." He Qicang was still reading his manuscript as he replied. "As for our report, I may not be able to submit it tomorrow even though the Nanking government needs it badly."

"Perhaps we should submit it to Minister Wang Yunwu on time. You promised him you would. I'll come up and continue to do the transcription as soon as I'm done talking with him."

Rays of light came flooding down to the living room on the ground floor as He Qicang opened his bedroom door. Xie Mulan's eyes looked up to the first floor. Like a wild horse without reins, she had completely forgotten that He Xiaoyu was standing beside her. He Xiaoyu held the phone in her hand but could not help looking up also. However, she didn't want to look at Liang Jinglun, nor did she bother to see Xie Mulan's state of emotional excitement.

At long last, Liang Jinglun appeared from behind the bedroom door which he gently closed behind him. He walked along the corridor to the stairs. Liang's stride appeared irresistibly charming to Xie Mulan who was looking up at him in adulation.

His hair styled like Wen Yiduo, a dashing contemporary poet and freedom fighter, made him more romantically appealing than ever! His face was gaunt but his eyes were limpid. His body was exhausted but still standing firm in his long gown. His footsteps were light and slow, and the hem of his gown flowed elegantly. Reminiscent of classical poets, scholars and statesmen like Qu Yuan or Jia Yi, and a little bit like Li Bai!

He resembled them slightly but was not exactly like any of them. Rather, he was more like a Xu Zhimo waving goodbye to Cambridge University or a wandering Lu Xun about to howl in protest! Xie Mulan's heart began thumping and as Liang Jinglun stepped down the stairs her heartbeat became louder and louder. What He Xiaoyu could feel through her sense of hearing was the cool breeze after the rain. As his steps slowed, Liang Jinglun repeated quietly to himself some of the key points written in *The Code of Offence and Defence for Spies – The Psychological Chapter*, which read: "Completely forget your own identity, make yourself understandable, make yourself agreeable and make yourself admirable." But with the presence of the two girls who loved him and needed him, both of whom he loved and needed, these tips sounded so useless.

"Hi, Mulan." When he made it to the last step, Liang Jinglun looked at Xie Mulan first and greeted her.

Xie Mulan stood up and watched her idol adoringly. She was so in love that she could barely restrain her tears. Looking at He Xiaoyu with the phone in her hand, she said: "Hi, I'll stay here with Xiaoyu for a few days."

Liang Jinglun reached out for the phone in He Xiaoyu's hand and his eyes also turned to He Xiaoyu.

"Professor Zeng of Tsinghua University, it's rude of you to have kept him waiting," said He Xiaoyu, handing over the phone.

Liang Jinglun reached out to take the phone. "Professor Zeng? I'm sorry, I've been busy helping Chancellor He sort out his report upstairs. My apologies to have kept you waiting for so long."

Zeng Keda was deeply disturbed. Holding the phone, he looked at his watch while thinking fast how to get the words out.

"Professor Liang, I've got a report to submit to the school authorities immediately. The chancellor urged me to hand it over in half an hour. Unfortunately, there's a problem I can't resolve. I must get your thoughts on it. Is it convenient for you to talk now?"

Liang Jinglun laughed awkwardly and spoke into the receiver. "Why is it that you people at Tsinghua always attach so much importance to some academic problems? Is it OK for me to know your research results? I'm afraid it won't be OK. I've got two students here, actually they're my own students, I guess it should be OK."

With this, Liang Jinglun looked at He Xiaoyu and Xie Mulan. Immediately, He Xiaoyu turned to Xie Mulan.

"Let's go and take a walk in the garden, shall we?"

"OK," concurred Xie Mulan, obligingly making her way towards the door.

He Xiaoyu followed her out of the living room. Liang Jinglun lowered his voice. "I am alone, Professor Zeng, please go ahead."

Zeng Keda asked right away: "Did your student set up the meeting with Mr Fang?"

"Yes, she did."Liang Jinglun tried to keep his tone calm.

"Tell me the results right now!" There was a sparkle in Zeng Keda's eyes.

"I'll tell you what, I've been working on the economic reform plan drafted by Chancellor He all day. So I haven't had any time to check with her about that," replied Liang Jinglun.

"What do you mean by 'haven't had any time'? Why?"

There was a trace of petulance in his voice and his tone became stern.

"You refuse to follow my advice because you are not willing to let Miss He engage with Mr Fang, is that it? Now, listen up. It's not me who's dying to know the result, it's special line number two! Are you still fighting me?"

Although his heart was repeatedly gripped by a numbing pain caused by Zeng Keda, Liang Jinglun understood that the situation could actually be serious and felt frustrated that he could not explain himself.

"I'm in the middle of formulating this economic reform plan with Chancellor He, which has to take priority. Time is strictly limited and we must present it to Nanking tomorrow."

Zeng Keda was speechless for a while. Feeling desperate, he relinquished the use of the secret code. He lowered his tone and began to speak in rapid-fire Mandarin. "Stop explaining yourself. Special line number two has just called me from special line number one. Our opponents in Peking have already slandered us in front of the president via their upper echelons in Nanking. Special line number one's confidence in us has been seriously undermined and he has switched his trust to them. He's accused us of being used by the Communist Party and told us to hand over the power of investigation as well as all other tasks to our opponents. Special line number two is distressed, indignant and gravely concerned. I was instructed to report the result to him today in half an hour because whether or not Mr Fang was used by the Communist Party has become the critical issue. If he is really being used by the Communist Party, it means all our previous efforts were in vain. If not, special line number two will be able to reassure special line number one, thereby disrupting their plot and taking back the power of investigation!"

As he was speaking, Zeng Keda took another look at his watch. "We've only got twenty-five minutes to go now. I'll give you twenty minutes. Find out about the situation within fifteen minutes. Call me directly in fifteen minutes and report the result to me clearly."

He hung up the phone with a loud bang, only to find that his face and his whole body were soaked with sweat although he was only wearing his short-sleeved summer military uniform. Impatiently, as he unbuttoned his shirt, he went to the door and opened it. A cool breeze swept over his face. The tops of the trees in Gu's compound rippled in the breeze after the rain, while the street lamps emitted a bright light. In fact, it turned out to be the coolest night since his arrival in Peking.

"Adjutant Wang!" Zeng Keda was more concerned about the situation with Fang Meng'ao's brigade.

"Yes!" Wang appeared from behind the shadow of the roadside trees, and asked: "Time for dinner?"

"What do you mean by 'dinner'? Call Colonel Zheng to check out the situation in the barracks there."

"Yes sir," replied Wang, immediately returning to his room.

All the iodine tungsten lamps on the walls in the four corners of the barracks of the inspection brigade were turned on, illuminating the barracks as if it were broad daylight. Without new orders, the gendarmes from the Garrison Headquarters were still standing like nails around the walls. Wang Puchen stood not far from the guard room by the gate. With Xu Tieying locked in the barracks, he became the most powerful person there, but he never uttered a word. Nor did he move. He did nothing but smoke. The Special Task Battalion commander and his ten soldiers, together with the executive group leader and his ten team members, were all standing idle beside him. They were already quite burnt out.

Only Xu Tieying's secretary, Sun, was standing outside the barracks, trying with great concern to hear what was going on inside the locked barracks, only to be disturbed by the sounds of troops running. He was deeply worried but his face was as expressionless as ever. It turned out that the people running on the terrace were the pilots of the inspection brigade. Although naked to the waist, and without having had dinner, they were still full of energy. They surrounded the people of the Citizens' Food Distribution Committee and ran circles around them in which section chiefs Li and Wang and their subordinates were lolling around. They were starving. Some were squatting, others were sitting. All were exhausted.

When Wang Puchen finished his cigarette, he pulled out another from his pocket. Following his slender fingers, one could see that the two lower pockets of his Zhongshan suit were bulging with at least seven or eight packs. It looked like he was ready for an all-night session. But his subordinates didn't think so.

He heard a yawn. At first, one person yawned then, as if infected, several others began to yawn. He looked at who was yawning and it turned out to be the members of the executive group with the Military Council's Bureau of Investigation and Statistics. He pulled out a handful of cigarettes at a time from the Frontline pack. There were more than a dozen of them.

"Just go ahead. Smoke while you wait."

Every one of the executive group smoked besides its leader. Yet normally no one would smoke on duty in front of the stationmaster. Now, at Wang's call, all of them came over and picked up the cigarettes that might help to keep them awake. For a moment, people struck matches and used their lighters. Everyone with a craving for tobacco was satisfied and smoke began to fill the air.

Wang Puchen was also striking his own long, thin match when suddenly he saw Lieutenant Colonel Zheng running from the guard room.

"Mr Wang!" shouted Zheng, saluting, "there's a call for you."

Still, Wang Puchen lit his Frontline and strode over to the guard room in a crane-like, carefree manner.

"Who is it?"

"Deputy Commander-in-Chief Chen." Lieutenant Colonel Zheng followed him, as if he was dissatisfied with his carefree manner.

Wang Puchen instantly stopped his carefree, crane-like steps. "Why didn't you tell me earlier?" He quickened his pace and walked into the guard room. Secretary Sun, who was standing outside the barracks gate, looked over attentively.

"Commissioner Xu is negotiating with Captain Fang," recounted Wang Puchen, speaking into the phone in the barracks guard room.

"What he meant is that it involves the Bureau of Reserve Cadres of the Ministry of Defence. Try not to start a fight. Yes. Deputy Commander-in-Chief Chen, please rest assured that I will fully cooperate with you. If I can't get this clusterfuck sorted out within half an hour, I'll be expecting you to come in person."

The caller had obviously hung up the phone, as there was a long busy tone coming from the receiver. Wang Puchen took another puff but kept the phone stuck to his ear, pretending to listen and thinking about whether or not to call Zeng Keda again. But he didn't. Instead, he glanced at his watch and put down the phone.

Inside Liang Jinglun's separate room to the west side of He's house, He Xiaoyu silently lowered her head. Liang Jinglun also sat there with his head bowed.

"He didn't say anything while driving you back, did he?" After staying silent for about twenty seconds, Liang looked up at He Xiaoyu.

"He was silent all the way back. Nothing more." He Xiaoyu also raised her head. "Sorry, I didn't complete the task assigned to me by the Students' Union."

"You've done a very good job."

Astonished, He Xiaoyu looked at Liang Jinglun. Another voice rang in her ears at once!

It was Xie Peidong's voice in the bamboo grove of Fang's compound: "You've done a very good job."

Taking her astonishment as a natural response, Liang said softly: "Do you know who just called?"

"Wasn't it Professor Zeng of Tsinghua?"

"No, it wasn't. It was a comrade in charge of the Students'

Union." Liang Jinglun had to look He Xiaoyu in the eye when he said this. "He just called to find out about your meeting with Fang Meng'ao today." As he said that, he stood up.

He Xiaoyu stood up too.

"The comrade in charge of the Students' Union is still waiting for my answer. I can only briefly exchange views with you now. First, Fang Meng'ao acted quite normally today. If he agrees with you readily, it will be of little significance to engage with him. Second, you should not go and visit Xie Mulan today, nor let her come here. After returning to the living room, take her to your father's room and chat with him until I finish the call."

"I'll take her directly to your place in the Foreign Languages Bookstore." He Xiaoyu left the chair opposite Liang Jinglun and walked towards the door.

Liang Jinglun suddenly took her hand: "Xiaoyu, a few more words, let me finish, OK?"

He Xiaoyu's hand was in Liang's but her eyes were looking out of the door. She did not say yes or no.

Liang Jinglun gently recited in English:

> *The furthest distance in the world*
> *Is not being apart while being in love*
> *But when one plainly cannot resist the yearning*
> *Yet pretending you have never been in my heart.*

Liang Jinglun reluctantly loosened his hand.

"I'll go with her to Dad's room." He Xiaoyu walked away quickly, leaving behind a melancholy Liang Jinglun in that little room of his.

Sitting next to the telephone in the living room on the ground floor, Liang Jinglun heard a question in his right ear that upset him.

"What is *Fragment*? Who is Bian Zhilin?" asked Zeng Keda on the phone.

Liang Jinglun did not know how to answer, nevertheless, he had to say something.

"*Fragment* is a poem, Bian Zhilin is the poet."

There was a brief but apparently awkward silence on the caller's part.

Through his left ear, Liang Jinglun could hear the two girls singing from the first floor which made the old professor quite pleased.

> *The floating scattered clouds,*
> *The bright moon shines on the reunited people.*
> *Today is the happiest...*

"Professor Zeng, I don't have time to explain in detail." Liang Jinglun obviously hadn't been listening to Zeng Keda's boring inquiry for the past ten seconds. "And that's all they said when they met today... I can't make any judgment, still less draw conclusions..."

At the moment, Liang Jinglun appeared slightly shocked because the person at the other end had obviously hung up the phone. He slowly put down the phone and simply sat there, closing his eyes, listening to the song from the first floor:

> *This soft wind blows upon the beautiful flowers*
> *Blowing on the good flowers*
> *Full of warmth and affection between the people......*

He could not see them but he could imagine:

In He Qicang's room on the first floor, He Xiaoyu and Xie Mulan were standing, trying to please the old professor with their youthful singing as they repeatedly sang *Blooming Flowers, Full Moon*.

> *The floating, scattered clouds,*
> *The bright moon shines on the reunited people*
> *Today is the happiest...*

"Yes, Comrade Jianfeng, that's all Liang Jinglun just reported."

Zeng Keda's energy seemed to have been exhausted in his phone conversation with Liang Jinglun. He felt extremely tired when he was reporting to Comrade Jianfeng. Although he could hold the phone close to his ear, his body could no longer stand upright.

Making use of the silence that lasted for several seconds at the other end of the line, he supported himself with his other hand on the edge of the table.

"Repeat what Fang Meng'ao said about Cui Zhongshi." The silence at the other end of the line ended at the sound of Jianfeng's reverberating voice.

"Yes." Zeng Keda had to respond immediately but then he found himself at a loss. Which part of the conversation should he repeat? Then, as if he was able to see his bewilderment, Jianfeng reminded him on the phone: "The part about him and Cui Zhongshi being friends."

"Yes, Comrade Jianfeng." Zeng Keda immediately sensed the importance of why Comrade Jianfeng wanted to listen to that part of the conversation. Jianfeng must have detected some new meaning in it.

As he rapidly searched for the original words in his mind and tried to fathom the importance of it, he became even more cautious about his wording. "According to Comrade Liang Jinglun, Fang Meng'ao's original words to He Xiaoyu were: 'Cui Zhongshi and I are friends, he's like my big brother. No matter how and for whom he died, I'll find out who killed him, I will never let any of them go.'"

"What did he mean by those remarks?" said Jianfeng, questioning him closely. "Don't tell me how Liang Jinglun commented on this, I want to know your immediate thoughts now."

Zeng Keda was even more surprised.

Zeng Keda should have understood Comrade Jianfeng's mood today but he had not. He had just ignored a crucial point which was, when one's superior is in a bad mood, he is very prone to magnify his subordinate's weakness. It was really unwise of him to try to shirk his responsibility to Liang Jinglun. The sweat on his forehead and face dripped as he replied: "Yes, Comrade Jianfeng, I've thought about that too. First, this may be related to Fang Meng'ao's personal character: If you love someone, you want them to live; if you hate them, you want them to die. Second, it may also be the case that because he is unable to connect with the Communist Party, he uses such extreme means to force the underground Communist Party organisation to connect with him quickly."

"I want you to say what's on your mind." The voice on the phone was ice-cold, as if it carried a chill wind. "It's not the first possibility, nor the second. I don't want to hear any analysis now, I've had enough of your analysis! Tell me your intuition. Why is Fang Meng'ao so obsessed with Cui Zhongshi's killers?"

Zeng Keda was in such disarray that he dared not "analyse" it any more but replied with an analysis: "Yes, Comrade Jianfeng. I think this is because Fang Meng'ao has deep feelings for Cui Zhongshi."

Jianfeng's voice on the phone was even colder: "Are his personal feelings for Cui Zhongshi or for the Communist Party too deep?"

Flustered, Zeng Keda wiped away the sweat from his mouth. He had to choose an answer. "Based on my intuition, Fang Meng'ao must have had deep personal feelings for Cui Zhongshi."

"The Communist Party doesn't allow room for personal feelings. What does it tell us when Fang Meng'ao took it so personally? Think about it and find out the reason for yourself."

"Yes, Comrade Jianfeng." Zeng was unable to control his emotion and choked with sobs.

"Maybe it was wrong for me to suspect Fang Meng'ao at the beginning. I even suspected that Cui Zhongshi was a Communist because I was prejudiced."

"Why did you think so then?"

Zeng Keda tried to calm himself down.

"Fang Meng'ao's not a sophisticated man but he's intelligent. If Cui Zhongshi was a Communist, or if he knew that Cui Zhongshi was a Communist, he would never have risked his life by associating with Cui Zhongshi. At that time, you reminded me that both the members of the Communications Bureau of the Kuomintang Central Committee and the State Secrecy Bureau had thoroughly investigated his relationship with Cui Zhongshi, and there was no indication that he had been recruited by the Communist Party. And it's all because my stubbornness interfered with your judgment, which proves once again that I am prone to make mistakes if I don't believe you."

"Well, I'm glad you've raised the level of your awareness, which proves that I'm not wrong to believe in you." The tension in Jianfeng's voice on the phone finally eased. "Criticism and self-criticism are not the exclusive tag of the Communist Party. What do you plan to do next?"

Zeng Keda straightened up again.

"I will resolutely implement Comrade Jianfeng's instructions and unite all forces that can be united to suppress the rebellion and save the party-state. I assure you that by uniting with Fang Meng'ao and with Comrade Liang Jinglun, we'll be able to combat corruption in Peking, to secure the resumption of assistance from the US government, to make a concerted effort to facilitate the president's and your upcoming currency reform, and to defeat the Communist troops on various fronts. My resolve will never change until death."

"Let's work together to attain this goal."

There was a trace of sadness in Comrade Jianfeng's voice.

"Just now, the presidential chamberlain received a phone call from Chen Jicheng saying that he is on his way to the inspection brigade's barracks, threatening to arrest Fang Meng'ao. On behalf of the State Secrecy Bureau of the Ministry of Defence, you can call Wang Puchen of the Peking station and order him to stabilise the situation there. After that, go over there quickly and tell Chen Jicheng on my behalf that Fang Meng'ao is my man, he's not a Communist. If he dares to act like a bully again, warn him. I'll be here with the president all the time. I'll be informed of every move he makes. He has to call me first if he wants to make any arrests."

"Yes."

"When you're done with Wang Puchen, immediately open the dedicated transmitter-receiver," continued Comrade Jianfeng, lowering his voice on the phone. "I'll send you a top-secret telegram. You will understand once you've read it."

"Yes!" By then, Zeng Keda had come to realise that he had not fallen out of favour, rather, he was trusted all the more. He could not help but burst into tears.

Comrade Jianfeng hung up the phone gently.

Zeng Keda had dried his tear-filled eyes and managed to hold back the tidal surge of emotions. He immediately placed a call to the barracks' guard room.

"Is this the Inspection Brigade's guard room? I'm calling on behalf of the Ministry of Defence. Tell Station Master Wang Puchen to answer the phone right away!"

In the guard room of the barracks, Wang Puchen listened quietly to Zeng Keda's phone call.

"Yes, I understand. Deputy Commander-in-Chief Chen will arrive at the barracks in about half an hour. Well, I'll do my best to keep the situation under control before your arrival. I hope Inspector-General Zeng will arrive a little earlier."

Members of the executive group and Special Task Battalion of the National Revolutionary Army's Fourth Corps were all looking at him on the big open ground after he came out of the guard room. Secretary Sun, far outside the barracks' door, was also watching him. Wang Puchen, however, disappointed them as nobody could make out any information from the way he looked. He walked back to the original spot, took out another pack of cigarettes and distributed them among his subordinates with the Military Bureau of Investigation and Statisitcs. He glanced at his watch as he struck a match and walked over to the pilots who were still running. Secretary Sun, who was still standing outside the door of the barracks, followed him over to the pilots.

"Get some rest, everyone," said Wang Puchen, his voice louder than usual, as he stopped near the spot where the pilots were running in a circle.

While running, Chen Changwu exchanged looks with Guo Jinyang and Shao Yuangang.

"Attention! Halt!" Chen Changwu issued the command. All the pilots slowed down and eventually stopped.

"Maintain formation, rest where you are!" ordered Chen Changwu.

Still in a circle, the pilots stood facing out of the circle with their legs spread apart, their bare arms folded across their chests. Chen Changwu walked over to Wang Puchen, followed by Secretary Sun.

"Sir, what can I do for you?" Chen Changwu asked Wang Puchen.

"Deputy Commander-in-Chief Chen may come in person," said Wang Puchen in a gentle but deliberate tone. "Shall we open the door of the barrracks and let Captain Fang and Commissioner Xu come out?"

Secretary Sun's eyes brightened.

"Sir, allow me to report to you. According to Captain Fang's order, only when he asks us to open the door can we open it," answered Chen Changwu with the same look on his face as before.

"Then, can you please go in and report to your captain that Deputy Commander-in-Chief Chen is due to arrive?" Wang Puchen used the same manner as if he was consulting Chen.

"Sorry, sir, our captain's order is to do the running drill." With that, Chen Changwu turned and walked back to the circle.

"Listen up. Ready! Run!" The circle of pilots began to run again.

Wang gave a slight sigh, looked at his watch, exchanged a helpless look with Secretary Sun, took another puff of his cigarette, spun on his heel and went back.

"Station Chief Wang!" Secretary Sun finally spoke. Wang Puchen stopped and looked back at him.

"I believe our commissioner has been hijacked. Before Deputy Commander-in-Chief Chen arrives, you have the responsibility to go in to ensure the safety of our commissioner."

Wang Puchen looked listlessly into his face. "I forgot to ask. What's your name?"

Secretary Sun froze.

Wang Puchen dropped the question coldly. He didn't need an answer at all. He turned and walked toward the guard room.

Secretary Sun closed his eyes for a moment. When he opened them, he went back to the barracks door heroically and stood there motionless.

―――――

The door of Adjutant Wang's room in Gu Weijun's residential compound was closed and the curtains were drawn. Wang, wearing a headset with a transmitter-receiver, was translating the second page of the message while Zeng Keda was already anxiously reading the first page.

The difference in format between this message and the conventional ones was evident in that this message was marked 'Top

Secret' in red letters in the upper right-hand corner of the page. The message on this page was marked with only three code names. The first line contained nine Chinese characters representing the action code – code name 'The Peacock Flies Southeast'!

The personnel code in the second line astonished Zeng Keda: "Fang Meng'ao's code name is Jiao Zhongqing"!

The personnel code in the third line also surprised Zeng Keda: "Liang Jinglun's code name is Liu Lanzhi"!

"Have you finished translating?" he urged Adjutant Wang, sweating profusely.

"I'm almost done with the second page." Adjutant Wang stopped writing, turned his head and said: "There are still three pages to go."

"Be quick!"

"Yes!"

Zeng Keda leaned over and anxiously looked at the second page of the message that Wang was working on. The first line on the second page was clearly marked – "Operation plan".

The following two unfamiliar code names had appeared frequently: "Jiao Zhongqing" and "Liu Lanzhi!"

When Wang handed the second page of the decoded message to Zeng Keda, Zeng had already read it from behind him.

"Quick! Translate the next three pages as fast as you can."

"Yes."

While holding the same position, Zeng Keda's eyes were fixed on Adjutant Wang's pen. Several special nouns that had appeared on the third page of the message left Zeng Keda puzzled.

The Crescent School!

Song of the Sun!

Wen Yiduo!

Zhu Ziqing!

In his private room inside the brigade's barracks, Fang Meng'ao, who had been secretly given a code name, was clueless about what had happened. As always, he liked bright light. A twenty-square-metre room was illuminated as bright as day by a two hundred-watt lamp, just like the gargantuan terrace outside. Meanwhile,

Fang Meng'ao grabbed three cans of Coca-Cola in one big hand and held a bottle of French claret between his thumb and index finger. He put them on the table with a loud bang.

Ma Hanshan had returned to sit in his chair.

Although he had been 'released', Xu Tieying remained restrained as if he was under house arrest. He was forced to sit on a stool at the table opposite Ma Hanshan. Both of them, refusing to look at each other, were busy watching Fang Meng'ao as if he was playing a game.

Bang ! Fang Meng'ao uncorked the bottle of red wine with a small Swiss army knife. He then placed three army green enamel mugs side by side on the table. Red wine was pouring out of the mouth of the bottle across the three mugs. All the way over, all the way back. As the bottle was emptied, the wine was evenly divided among the three mugs.

With another bang, a can of Coke was opened and tipped into an enamel mug. Then two more cans were opened and poured into two more enamel mugs. Looking on, Ma Hanshan guessed that Fang Meng'ao must be mixing cocktails, which was quite a foreign thing. He became quite excited and opened his eyes wider than before. Xu Tieying only looked on with indifference. Although he didn't know the situation outside, he knew that his predicament here must have been reported to Chen Jicheng. All he could do now was wait. Meanwhile, he had to keep calm and avoid getting into conflict with Fang Meng'ao.

Fang Meng'ao, however, launched an intensive verbal offensive.

"Air forces all over the world are forbidden to drink when flying combat missions," he said. "But we broke this rule when we flew over the Hump because, as we all know, nine times out of ten, we would not be able to make it back after entering the cockpits, so we demanded that there would be no taking-off without drinking. How could you fly when you were drunk? The report was sent to Stilwell, who didn't know what to do about it. It was Chennault, the old man, who figured out this way, to mix Coca-Cola with red wine. A one-to-one ratio, one enamel mug per person. Drink first, then surrender the cup and take off. Let me ask both of you, what do I mean here?"

Fang Meng'ao looked at Ma Hanshan.

Ma Hanshan immediately took hold of the handle of the mug in front of him, held it up and recited the following lines:

> *The desolate gale freezes the River Yi,*
> *The doomed hero, once gone, will never return!*

"That's quite knowledgeable of you!" Fang Meng'ao looked at him with admiration.

In the face of such fulsome praise, Ma Hanshan was so excited that he raised his mug and was ready to drink.

"Slow down!" said Fang Meng'ao. "I only said you're knowledgeable, not that you gave the correct answer. Put the wine down."

Ma Hanshan felt depressed again. He reluctantly put the mug of wine back on the table and began to think attentively.

"Commissioner Xu, among the three of us, you're the best educated, so you must know what I mean by this. Now, do me the honour. If you do, we will drink up." Fang Meng'ao turned to Xu Tieying.

Xu Tieying, who had worked for the Kuomintang Central Party headquarters almost his whole life, had always been subtle and reserved. Now that he had fallen into the hands of two desperate men, although one was good, the other evil, he made the painful discovery that all the conventional methods he normally resorted to were useless. But he also wanted to safeguard his image as a veteran Kuomintang Party affairs official. "Captain Fang, the War of Resistance Against Japanese Aggression has been won and the party-state will always remember those martyred heroes. For them, you should also fly more missions, fulfill your obligations as a professional soldier, carry forward the glory of the past, suppress the Communist rebellion and make new contributions to saving the party-state."

Almost immediately, Fang Meng'ao's demeanour became callous. "I offer you a drink, you lecture me in return. Commissioner Xu, I'll walk out on you at once if you continue lecturing me. That way, you can drink this wine with Director Ma, though."

"I agree!" Ma Hanshan replied in a loud voice, and immediately stood up. At the same time, he exclaimed excitedly: "I raise my hand for it!"

With these words, he had already stepped onto the chair with one leg, and started rolling up his sleeves. He picked up an enamel mug in one hand and seized his gun with the other. That was by no means to entertain someone with a drink. Clearly, that was Ma Hanshan ready to fight tooth and nail with Xu Tieying at any time! Xu Tieying gritted his teeth and then closed his eyes.

"Commissioner Xu, I'll give you ten minutes. After that, I'll call my superior and report that you're interrogating Director Ma alone. When I hear shots fired, I'll come back with Chief Wang and his men. By that time, there should be a dead man lying on the floor. But I shouldn't be to blame."

"Nor am I to blame!" said Ma Hanshan. "I'll also report that someone has embezzled someone's money and when I found out about it, he had one of my arms broken a few days ago and threatened me not to say anything about it! Today, someone is trying to get rid of me as a witness through this interrogation. How can I not defend myself?"

Xu Tieying couldn't keep his eyes closed any more. When he opened them, he looked only at Fang Meng'ao.

"Captain Fang, if you have any idea, you can always tell me directly. I'm all ears. Although we belong to two different departments, we work in the same investigation group, after all."

"I have no idea whatsoever." Fang Meng'ao did not take the bait. "I just wanted to invite you to have a drink and answer my question."

"What is your question, anyway?" asked Xu Tieying, who had never felt so helpless.

"Why is Coke mixed with red wine in equal measures?"

Xu Tieying could only force himself to think.

At that instant, Ma Hanshan became rather impatient. He glared at Xu Tieying, hoping that he would not be able to answer the question.

"Don't bother, I'll tell you both the answer." Fang Meng'ao's cynical expression disappeared. By now he was looking rather stern, sad and dreary. "The red-wine half is to say goodbye to the pilots who may not return while the Coke-half is a blessing which represents the hope that they will make it back."

Ma Hanshan let out a long heavy sigh in response to Fang

Meng'ao's heroic utterance. But it was an eerie sign. Was it a sense of loss or just mixed feelings? He himself was not clear about it.

Xu Tieying, however, immediately felt something different. Fang Meng'ao was going to show his hand!

"So many planes, so many pilots, most of them didn't make it back." Fang Meng'ao ignored their response. "Instead, I came back every time. To this day, I still ask myself, if only I could have crashed this body and the plane on the Hump..."

Ma Hanshan dared not make any response either and the look on his face hardened. Xu Tieying was hiding his nervousness, waiting for Fang Meng'ao's imminent emotional outburst.

"In that case, I would surely have missed the chance to make friends with Cui Zhongshi!"

Fang Meng'ao's anger finally erupted. His flashing eyes glared first at Ma Hanshan, then straight at Xu Tieying.

"Such an honest and kind man, like a big brother, he had been visiting me at the aviation school every month for three consecutive years. I thought he was rich. When I arrived in Peking, I learned that he was being forced to make money for others every day but that he couldn't even afford to pay the tuition fees for his two children. I'm such a stupid fool! Why did I fail to anticipate his passing so suddenly? Why didn't I offer him a mug of Coke mixed with red wine before they took his life? Now, it's better that you drink on his behalf." He quickly picked up his mug then extended his other hand to Ma Hanshan.

Ma Hanshan was stunned at first, then understood and quickly handed the pistol to Fang Meng'ao who put the gun on the table in front of him, still holding the enamel mug in his hand. Ma Hanshan stretched out his hand towards the jar, then slowly lifted it up and looked at Fang Meng'ao. "I'll drink it! Anyway, I feel sorry for Cui Zhongshi. In the world of Chinese martial arts and outlaws, death is a cup of wine and living is also a cup of wine. Hey, you, Xu Tieying, do you know what's in store for us after drinking this wine?"

Xu Tieying did not touch the enamel mug. He managed to keep calm, looked down and thought for a moment. "Captain Fang..."

"Don't interrupt." Fang Meng'ao interjected. "Let Director Ma finish."

"He won't say anything honest."

"I want to hear it!" There was an even more stern look in Fang Meng'ao's eyes. "Do you hear me?"

"Then, go ahead." Xu Tieying could only close his eyes again.

Ma Hanshan stepped on the chair with one foot again and exclaimed: "There are only two results waiting for you and me. When you are drunk, you can still open your eyes after you close them, meaning you're still alive. If you can't open your eyes when you close them after you're drunk, you're dead! Drink!"

"Very interesting." Xu Tieying's eyes were wide open and sparkled. He laughed. He took hold of the handle of his mug and lifted it up. "It's amazing to hear Ma Hanshan say such a thing. I really must drink this wine."

Impressed, Fang Meng'ao looked at Xu Tieying, more relaxed now. The three men clinked their enamel mugs. Ma Hanshan drank first, making a gurgling sound and then showed the bottom of his mug. Fang Meng'ao nodded his head approvingly. At this moment, Ma Hanshan could not have cared less about Fang Meng'ao's praise. He was only concerned about Xu Tieying. Fang Meng'ao was also watching Xu Tieying while holding up his mug and waiting for him to drink.

"I'll drink," said Xu Tieying, looking at Fang Meng'ao. "I must explain myself to Captain Fang before I drink. Both your father and your uncle were in my office the night Cui Zhongshi died. Ask them whether or not I gave the order to execute him."

Then he slowly began to drink the mug of Coke mixed with wine.

Fang Meng'ao held the enamel mug in his hand and looked at Xu Tieying as he drank slowly. Fang Meng'ao's eyes, which had been burning with indignation up to that point, slowly became blank and empty, showing again the kind of bewilderment resulting from the fact that he couldn't spot any enemy aircraft in the sky.

Xu Tieying also drank to the last drop but without any flourish. Instead, he gently put the empty enamel mug back on the table.

Now, Fang Meng'.ao closed his eyes. With the mug of Coke mixed with red wine in his hand, he said bleakly: "Big Brother Zhongshi, this cup of wine is for you." He took a sip and then sprayed the wine on the ground.

Both Xu Tieying and Ma Hanshan seemed to be troubled by a sense of foreboding. Almost simultaneously, they cast their eyes on the pistol on the table. Sure enough, Fang Meng'ao opened his eyes and picked up the gun!

"Fall in!" Lieutenant Colonel Zheng suddenly gave a loud order.

The platoon of the Youth Army and the guards squad immediately ran out of the barracks gate and stood erect in two rows on the left and right sides of the road.

Wang Puchen, the Special Task Battalion and the executive group of the Military Council's Bureau of Investigation saw the motorcade coming along the bumpy road leading to the barracks. Four military motorcycles with sidecars led the way, followed by Chen Jicheng's American jeep, one of the latest models, followed by an American light truck, also of the latest model.

"Shall we line up, too?" Wang Puchen tossed his unfinished cigarette at his feet and stamped it out. Then he walked to the entrance and stopped on the left side of the barracks gate. The bureau's executive group followed closely behind him, standing in a row inside the gate on the left.

The special service battalion commander of the Fourth Corps quickly led his ten soldier agents to a spot opposite the executive group, standing in a row on the right inside the gate.

"Attention!" Chen Changwu also issued a command on the large terrace. The flyers, who had been running in circles, stopped where they were. Chen Changwu walked out of the queue and waved his hand. Shao Yuangang and Guo Jinyang immediately went up to him. All three looked towards the barracks gate and saw Chen Jicheng's motorcade bumping along the road. They were only a few hundred metres from the gate.

"Chen Jicheng's arriving but the captain is still inside. What shall we do?" Chen Changwu anxiously whispered to Shao Yuangang and Guo Jinyang. Shao Yuangang looked at Guo Jinyang.

"Go into the barracks, close the door and wait for the captain's command," said Guo Jinyang.

"Good. Bring the suspects in."

"And that Secretary Sun." Shao Yuangang was usually a man of few words but when he did speak, it was always to the point.

Chen Changwu and Guo Jinyang nodded simultaneously and the three returned to the line.

"Listen up! Take all these people into the barracks. Move!" ordered Chen Changwu.

"Yes sir!"

"Go!"

"Get up! Move!"

Chen Changwu walked in front with Shao Yuangang and Guo Jinyang following closely behind. With the pilots escorting the members of the Citizens' Food Distribution Committee, they soon arrived at the door of the large dormitories inside the barracks.

"Deputy Commander-in-Chief Chen is here, what are you up to?" Surprisingly, Secretary Sun stood up to block the doorway.

"Salute!" came the command of Lieutenant Colonel Zheng from a distance.

With a quick glance at the gate, Chen Changwu found that everyone was saluting. He winked at Shao Yuangang and Guo Jinyang, and they rushed forward to seize Secretary Sun, one on each side.

"What are you going to do? Guards!" Secretary Sun called out to the gendarmerie by the wall. However, with no orders from Xu Tieying or Wang Puchen, the gendarmes of the Peking Garrison Headquarters, who had been standing against the wall, remained stock-still.

Chen Changwu quickly unlocked the door of the barracks while Shao Yuangang and Guo Jinyang forcefully pushed Secretary Sun in through the door. Everyone in the Citizens' Food Distribution Committee being escorted by the pilots swarmed into the barracks.

The door of the barracks was closed from the inside at the precise moment when Chen Jicheng's motorcade rolled in through the main entrance. On entering the dormitory inside the barracks, Chen Changwu yelled at his captives: "Squat down! All of you, down!"

"Do you hear him? Get down, all of you!"

Section Chiefs Li and Wang and the other members of the Citizens' Food Distribution Committee crouched down between the beds. Guo Jinyang handcuffed Secretary Sun to an iron bar of a bunk bed with a loud click. Meanwhile, Chen Changwu, Shao Yuangang and Guo Jinyang exchanged glances as Chen Changwu alone walked to the door of their captain's private room in the rear.

The door to the captain's room was closed. Chen Changwu loudly reported: "Report to the captain that Deputy Commander-in-Chief Chen Jicheng of the garrison headquarters has just arrived."

"Surround the barracks!" Chen Jicheng personally gave the order, standing on the large ground inside the barracks. All at once, there was the sound of heavy boots running, and the gendarmes, who had been standing against the wall with their submachine guns, surrounded the barracks from all sides.

Inside the barracks, all the pilots picked up their pistols and looked at the captain's door. The door flew open and out came Fang Meng'ao with his gun. "Guard the doors and windows! Tell them this is the headquarters of the Investigation Brigade of the Ministry of Defence. We'll shoot to kill anyone who intrudes!"

"Yes sir!"

The door and the windows were immediately flanked by the pilots, with their guns all aimed at the possible intruders.

"Captain, do you want me to help you guard the window inside your room?" asked Chen Changwu gently, standing beside Fang Meng'ao.

"Go and pass my message on at the door! I'll take care of the situation inside." Fang Meng'ao went back in and the door was closed.

Chen Changwu walked to the door of the dormitory.

"Go!" Chen Jicheng ordered the battalion commander. "Give them my orders. Tell those inside to open the door right now!"

"Yes sir!" The Special Task Battalion commander waved his gun and charged menacingly to the door with his ten soldiers.

"Those of you inside, listen up!" roared the Special Task Battalion commander. "This is a direct order from Deputy Commander-in-Chief Chen. Open the door immediately!"

"Listen carefully!" Chen Changwu's voice came from the other side of the door. "This is the Inspection Brigade of the Ministry of Defence. If anyone dares to intrude, we will open fire!"

The Special Task Battalion commander looked back at Chen Jicheng. The ten soldiers also spun round to look back at him.

"Damn it!" he barked, mimicking President Chiang. His face turned menacingly pale as he barked: "Shoot! Shoot the door open!"

"Deputy Commander-in-Chief Chen!" It was a screech like an owl. Chen Jicheng looked back to where the sound came from. So did the battalion commander and his soldiers. No one could have imagined that this harsh cry had come from Wang Puchen's sick body. Never before had Wang Puchen moved so fast that only a few steps brought him to Chen Jicheng's side.

"Deputy Commander-in-Chief Chen, after all, they are from the Bureau of Reserve Cadres of the Ministry of Defence. If we fight them, there'll be casualties, and the consequences would be unthinkable."

"Goddamn it!" A sudden explosion of rage erupted behind Chen Jicheng's eyes. But he hesitated with a look of desperation as he pondered his next move.

All eyes were on him, waiting. Wang Puchen held out a cigarette to him with his eyes full of sincerity.

"Since when did you see me smoke?" snapped Chen Jicheng angrily. "Can you people with the Secrecy Bureau follow the president's call for the New Life Movement?!"

Seeing Chen's eyes sweeping over them, those in the Secrecy Bureau still with cigarettes in their hands had to drop them on the ground.

"Who the fuck do you think you are!" shouted Chen, turning his eyes to the barracks door. "At the Bureau of Reserve Cadres of the Ministry of Defence anyone who disobeys the ministry's military orders ceases to exist! Charge in through the door and windows..."

"Nobody move!" At that moment, Wang Puchen looked like a completely changed man, and his face actually took on the murderous look that used to be found on the former bureau head

Dai Li's face years ago. First, he stopped the Special Task Battalion soldiers and the gendarmerie, then with a sharp, authoritative bark, he told the bureau's executive group: "I have orders from the Ministry of Defence's State Secrecy Bureau. There must be no clashes of any kind today. All of you, go and stand at the windows and use your bodies to execute my order!"

While the whole team, including its group leader and the team members, hesitated, Wang Puchen pointed his gun at the group leader. "Move!"

"Five on one side, move!" The executive group team leader had to run in two directions to block the windows with his team members. Wang Puchen himself stood blocking the entrance to the barracks.

"Deputy Commander-in-Chief Chen, please, I beg you, let's wait ten more minutes."

"You son of a bitch! You're in charge of rules and regulations at the State Secrecy Bureau but I'm in charge here in Peking! How dare you disobey my order! Stand down!" Chen recovered from his astonishment, took out his gun and pointed it at Wang Puchen.

"Deputy Commander-in-Chief Chen, I am responsible to both the State Secrecy Bureau and to you! If you don't understand, just shoot me," replied Wang Puchen, putting his gun back into his trouser pocket.

"The party-state is being completely ruined by you fools! OK, I'll give you ten minutes. Keep an eye on the time. If they don't open the door in ten minutes, we'll shoot our way in! Anyone who dares to block it will be shot on the spot!" shouted Chen Jicheng, stomping his foot.

Fang Meng'ao's room had two windows, both of which were now wide open. At the left window, facing outwards, stood Xu Tianying; at the right window, facing outwards, stood Ma Hanshan. The windows were only about a metre high. As long as you could climb up to them, you could jump out of them easily. But the two men were still standing there, motionless. The reason was that they may have looked out of the window and seen the backs of the members of the executive group of the Bureau of Investigation and Statistics. Also visible were the gendarmes with their submachine guns pointing towards the room.

Another reason why they didn't make a move was that Fang Meng'ao, now sitting on the chair, had another gun in his hand, one pointing at Xu Tieying and the other at Ma Hanshan.

"You have all drunk the wine. The window is your Hump today. To jump out means you crash and die. If you stand firm, you may still live."

Outside the door of the dormitory, Chen Jicheng was checking his watch again. Out of the corner of his eye, he saw Wang Puchen's hand reaching into his pocket. Thinking that he was about to pull out his gun, Chen Jicheng abruptly raised his head and yelled: "What's up?"

Wang Puchen reached into his pocket and said: "Have a cigarette. After ten minutes, even if you don't shoot me, I'll be removed from this current post as station chief and it will be impossible for me to join the New Life Movement."

"It's good to know you understand the consequences," remarked a gloomy Chen Jicheng. "There are still four minutes left. Go ahead."

"Thank you, Deputy Commander-in-Chief Chen." Wang Puchen struck a long match, lit the cigarette and inhaled more than a third of it in one gulp. Amazingly, not a trace of smoke came back out. Chen Jicheng looked at him and frowned in disgust.

The jeep that Wang Puchen was expecting was now bouncing around like a cork in a storm on the road to the barracks. The road was in such poor condition that the vehicle was only in third gear. Still, Adjutant Wang had to keep flooring the accelerator all the time. In the back seat, Zeng Keda was still reading the last page of the telegram with his right hand holding a torch. With his left hand clutching the last page of the message, he kept his feet firmly on the lower frame of the front seat in an effort to brace himself. On the page marked 'five' was a poem entitled *Song of the Sun*. It was clear that Zeng Keda was not just reading the message but was trying to memorise the poem. His eyes were already fixed on the last stanza, which he was reciting to himself:

Ah, sun, the sun whose benevolent light shines on all!

The jeep suddenly sank into a pothole, followed by a violent jolt. In the back seat, Zeng Keda's head hit the roof. Adjutant Wang slammed on the brakes.

"Inspector-General..."

"Drive!"

"Yes sir!" The jeep scrambled out of the pothole.

"Don't slow down!" exclaimed Zeng Keda, turning his attention back to the message that he continued to read to himself:

Every time I see you in the future, I will see it as a homecoming. For my home now is not on Earth but in heaven...

Ten minutes had now passed and Chen Jicheng stopped to stare at Wang Puchen instead of looking at his watch. Wang Puchen eyed his watch nervously but his ears were listening. Chen Jicheng noticed something abnormal about the way he looked and quickly realised that a jeep was racing towards the barracks gate. Wang Puchen raised his head and looked towards the front entrance, to which Chen Jicheng also turned his head.

"Salute!"

Colonel Zheng's loud order came from the entrance of the compound. The Youth Army platoon and the guards squad saluted again. Zeng Keda's jeep raced straight into the compound without slowing down. Then, just a few metres away from Chen Jicheng and Wang Puchen, it skidded to a halt. Zeng Keda jumped out of the jeep while stuffing the message into the lower pocket of his jacket. Finally, Chen Jicheng realised that the State Secrecy Bureau of the Peking Station had chosen to side with the Ministry of Defence's Investigation Brigade. His face grew even darker and he turned around and glared at Wang Puchen, who had pharyngitis and had always wanted to cough, now he did not have to suppress it any more.

"Deputy Commander-in-Chief Chen!" Zeng Keda walked up to

Chen Jicheng and raised his hand in a standard salute. Only then did Chen Jicheng bother to look at him.

"Are there any new orders from the Ministry of Defence?"

"I haven't got any new orders from the ministry, but I'd like to invite Deputy Commander-in-Chief Chen to go to the guard house..."

"Shut up if you haven't got any!" barked Chen Jicheng, in an attempt to shut him up, knowing that he could not possibly have had any new orders.

"Wang Puchen!" he shouted. "Isn't this the ten minutes you wanted! From now on, you're no longer the Peking Station chief. Get the fuck out of here and cough wherever you damn well want!"

Defiantly, Wang Puchen still stood there coughing, coughing more and more seriously. Chen Jicheng raised his right hand, at which point the gendarmes behind him tightened the grip on their guns. They were waiting for his signal to storm the barracks. Just as Chen's hand was about to swing down, Zeng Keda clutched it tightly! Furiously, Chen Jicheng looked at Zeng Keda whose eyes flashed with commanding authority.

"You're wanted by special line number one. Please report to the guardhouse to answer the phone."

All of a sudden, Chen Jicheng froze in awe. Zeng Keda slowly put down the hand which he was gripping.

"With Nanking's special permission, the telephone here has been encrypted. Now it is directly connected to special line number one in Nanking."

Chen Jicheng secretly felt daunted but when he saw that Zeng Keda was waiting for him humbly, he slowly lowered the hand with which he might have waved his order to attack the barracks and walked towards the guardroom. Zeng Keda followed closely behind him.

"Yes, yes. Comrade Jianfeng, Deputy Commander-in-Chief Chen is here." Zeng Keda handed the phone to Chen Jicheng respectfully with both hands.

Who was Jianfeng? Of course, Chen Jicheng knew who Jianfeng was. At the moment, although the expression on his face changed, he still looked very serious. He took the phone and greeted Jianfeng with a term of endearment.

"Brother Jianfeng?"

On the phone, Chiang Chingkuo's voice echoed coldly.

"Deputy Commander-in-Chief Chen, don't be so polite, just call me by my first name, or call me comrade."

It was a calculated move to discourage familiarity, at which Chen Jicheng simply dropped the pretence.

"How is the commandant?" he asked straightforwardly.

"Which commandant are you refering to?"

Chen Jicheng was simply stunned.

"We've just ratified the Constitution, so please abide by it. Are you greeting the president?"

Chen Jicheng was left with no choice but to reply: "How is the president?"

"The president is fine. He keeps regular hours. It's a quarter past nine and I've just helped him go to bed. Is there a situation in the Peking-Tianjin area? Do you want me to report to the president? Do you want him to get up and answer your call?"

"No, absolutely not, Comrade Jianfeng," replied Chen Jicheng hurriedly, while changing his tone with Jianfeng. "Let's not disturb the president..."

"In that case, can you tell me first?"

"Comrade Jianfeng." Chen Jicheng knew that he could not go on to beat around the bush any more.

"You are in Nanking and I am in Peking, so I know the situation here better. There's a mole working for the Communist Party among the members of the Investigation Brigade of the Ministry of Defence. By taking advantage of your anti-corruption decisions, he is colluding with the Communists to incite student protests, aiming to create chaos throughout Peking..."

"I set up the inspection team," Chiang Ching-kuo interjected. "I put together the people. Who have you identified as the mole working for the Communist Party underground?"

"Fang Meng'ao! This man is a member secretly recruited by the Communist Party!"

"Evidence. Show me evidence that he is a secret member of the Communist Party."

"I can only say that there are indications and the indications are there," answered Chen Jicheng hesitantly. "There will be detailed follow-up reports drafted by the Party Communications Bureau and the State Secrecy Bureau to provide specific evidence."

"That's by no means evidence. That means that the indications are all your speculation."

"Comrade Jianfeng, I am entrusted by the president to protect Peking. I must be responsible to the president, and also to you," retorted Chen anxiously.

"You don't bother to inform me before arresting my men and without evidence you call them Communists. You are not obliged to answer to me, you're supposed to answer to the party-state!" said Chiang Ching-kuo, his voice turning harsh.

"Comrade Jianfeng!" Chen Jicheng flushed. "My operation today is being carried out under a direct order from the Ministry of Defence. It was approved by the president!"

"Did the president give you any clear instructions?" Chiang Ching-kuo's voice grew even harsher. "You colluded with others and made multiple phone calls to the president in the hope that he would agree to arrest my people, right?"

"God damn it!" Chen Jicheng almost blurted out the absurd national curse reserved solely for Chiang Kai-shek. Fortunately, he realised right away that the accent of the caller was pure Zhejiang Fenghua, and that it was pure Xikou intonation, so he didn't utter those three words, but they were stuck in his throat and silenced him. He began to sweat under his big-brimmed hat and couldn't help but look over at Zeng Keda who was standing beside him. Zeng Keda had his back to him, pretending to look away, but he had obviously heard every single word of Jianfeng's.

"Deputy Commander-in-Chief Chen, I want to hear your affirmative answer." The caller at the other end of the line, however, would not allow him to keep silent.

"Comrade Jianfeng," Chen Jicheng was still trying his best to save face, "I'd like to be instructed by the president in person."

"OK, then please listen to this and memorise it." Chiang Ching-kuo's voice on the phone became even louder.

"Of course!"

Chen Jicheng had to touch his heels and straighten up. Chiang Ching-kuo's voice assumed a very authoritative tone at this point.

"Chen Jicheng is my student and is still loyal to me. He might have his moments of weakness but that can be corrected. Tell him to take good care of Peking and work hard to prevent the Communist Party from instigating student protest and pro-democracy movements. In particular, it is necessary to thwart Communist subversion operations and cooperate with Fu Zuoyi in his fight against the Communist troops. There's no need to try to curry favour with the other factions and there's no need to wade into the murky waters of finance and the economy. If he gets too involved, no one can save him."

Chen Jicheng was still standing bolt upright even though Chiang Ching-kuo was done relaying Chiang Kai-shek's message.

"Deputy Commander-in-Chief Chen, can you hear me all right?" Although it was Jianfeng's voice, the accent remained that of Xikou, Fenghua.

"Yes, I do!"

"The commandant still has faith in you." Chiang Ching-kuo accepted his answer of compliance and offered to replace the title of president with commandant. "Let me give you a word of advice, don't carry out that military order of the Ministry of Defence for the time being. Turn over the responsibility of investigating the supplies of the Citizens' Food Distribution Committee and the accounts of the Peking branch to the Ministry of Defence's auditing team. I'm doing this for your own good."

"I understand, Comrade Jianfeng."

Chen Jicheng's motorcade drove off. Zeng Keda put down his saluting hand by the brim of his cap.

The gendarmes of the Special Task Battalion of the Fourth Army Corps and the Police Garrison Command stood upright, totally stupefied.

"You've done a good job, you can all leave now," said Zeng Keda. The battalion commander and the soldiers all boarded the jeep while the gendarmes regrouped and climbed onto the ten-wheeled truck. The three vehicles drove out of the gate, leaving only Zeng Keda, Wang Puchen and the dozen or so agents of the bureau's executive group. Quiet descended on the compound.

"Thanks a million, Mr Wang." Only then did Zeng Keda make himself officially available by extending his hand to Wang Puchen, who was back in a sickly state. "It's my job. It's what I should do."

"I've got another job for you, Station Chief Wang. Let's go in together." Zeng Keda let go of his hand. They walked towards the door of the barracks dormitory. The door was still closed and it was surprisingly quiet inside.

"I'm Inspector-General Zeng! Deputy Commander-in-Chief Chen and his troops have all gone. Please, open the door!" Zeng Keda called out.

In Fang Meng'ao's private room, Guo Jinyang brought in two more stools, placed them behind Zeng Keda and Wang Puchen and then left, closing the door behind him.

"No, thank you." Zeng Keda did not sit down. With Fang Meng'ao still sitting in his chair, the others could only stand.

"The nature of the Citizens' Food Distribution Committee case has changed." Zeng Keda glanced at Xu Tianying and then at Fang Meng'ao, as if he was consulting him. "Those who investigate the case and those who are investigated conspired with each other to compromise evidence of the crime, cover up the truth and falsely accuse the ministry's investigation team in front of the president. From now on, Ma Hanshan and several other criminals of the Citizens' Food Distribution Committee will be interrogated in isolation."

"I agree!" Xu Tianying knew that Chen Jicheng had gone and that now he had to fight alone as the Kuomintang Party Headquarters' co-investigator. "According to the military order issued by the Ministry of Defence, I'm here today to detain some important criminals, such as Ma Hanshan and his gang, for isolated interrogation at the Peking Police Bureau."

Zeng Keda watched with a slight sneer at the corner of his mouth. Chen Jicheng had been ordered to stand down in disgrace, so why was Xu Tieying trying to stubbornly resist while still in the name of the Kuomintang Party headquarters? It was evident how afraid they were of further investigating Ma Hanshan. He sat down, not even bothering to look at Xu Tieying. Instead, he turned to Fang Meng'ao. "I must share this with you both before I forget. According to the new instructions from Nanking, the military order of the Ministry of Defence will not be enforced for the time being and the felons, namely Ma Hanshan and all those involved, must be detained in a safer place. As to where, I'd like to hear Captain Fang's thoughts."

Fang Meng'ao appeared silent again, which gave everyone a bad headache. Because no one else could see that when he was caught up in silence, the sky would appear in his mind's eye and those in front of him would be imagined as bogeys. Zeng Keda was now imagined as his wingman, as if he were fighting alongside him, while Xu Tieying became the enemy aircraft pursued by himself as the captain and Zeng Keda as his wingman.

"Fire!" Fang Meng'ao gave the command to shoot down the enemy aircraft! But he quickly discovered that after he had pressed the trigger, the gun had failed to fire any shells.

Looking around, he found that Zeng Keda, his wingman, was turning a deaf ear to his instructions. Xu Tieying, the enemy aircraft, was still flying ahead of him! Fang Meng'ao's eyes flashed. As usual, he quickly returned from his wild flight of imagination. The sky disappeared and so did the bogey. In front of him, Zeng Keda was still Zeng Keda, Xu Tieying was still Xu Tieying, and he was still his lonely self.

"Deputy Director Ma, you've been very cooperative today, tell me who you are willing to go with?" Zeng Keda stopped looking at the two of them and turned to Ma Hanshan who sat facing out of the window.

He slowly turned around and asked: "Captain Fang, do you still remember the night when you and I were in the Houhai area?"

"Of course, I do."

Fang Meng'ao saw the loneliness in Ma Hanshan's eyes and it suddenly dawned on him what it meant for people to be sophisticated. Zeng Keda had to find the tacit understanding in him, and so did Ma Hanshan. Comparing the two, Ma Hanshan proved to be somewhat more congenial. Looking at this fragile man, he nodded his head and replied.

"While we were in the water, you asked me if I saw that person, you still remember that?" Fang Meng'ao looked heavily but nodded his head.

Xu Tieying, Zeng Keda and even Wang Puchen, who had been pretending to stay out of it, all pricked up their ears.

"I'll answer you now." Ma Hanshan suddenly became animated. "I saw the man and he spoke to me!"

"What did he tell you?" asked Fang Meng'ao.

"He told me that someone had him killed by framing him as a Communist in order to protect their fortunes, while others did the same for self-aggrandisement. It's my turn now."

Cui Zhongshi! This time, not only Xu Tieying, but also Zeng Keda understood who he was referring to. Both of them stared intensely at Ma Hanshan!

"Hear him out!" Fang Meng'ao looked encouragingly again at Ma Hanshan. "What else did he say?"

"As the old saying goes, there are no good people in Hongdong County government! He said that there had been lots of cheating in the gambling game! And it had been a con from the start. Those who cheated had earned the money, but he had lost his life."

At this point, Ma Hanshan's gaze turned to Xu Tieying and Zeng Keda. "Xu, that night at the police bureau, you said that Cui Zhongshi was a Communist agent and must be eliminated. After killing him, you said to Cui Zhongshi's body that he was not a Communist. Now, before Captain Fang, just tell us, was Cui Zhongshi a Communist or not? If he wasn't, why did you kill him? Who forced you to kill him?"

CHAPTER 12

Instead of being illuminated by the 200-watt lamp in Fang Meng'ao's barracks, Cui Zhongshi's courtyard house at No. 2 Dongzhong Hutong was humbly lit by a 15-watt lamp hanging under the eaves of the courtyard gate. As dim as the moonlight at twilight, it shone on the trees in the courtyard and on a solitary Fang Buting who was standing in the dappled shade. There were actually two other people standing by in the courtyard but out of the shade. One was Xie Peidong, the other was Cheng Xiaoyun who was carrying a gift bag in both hands, looking at the open door to the north house.

The light in the north room was then turned on and out came Ye Biyu who had rushed to greet the Fang cohort.

Ye Biyu was surprised to see Xie Peidong accompany the governor and his wife on their visit at such a late hour. Not knowing whether she should be flattered or apprehensive, she switched on the lights and returned but lost her usual sharpness commonly associated with a Shanghai woman. She almost spoke in awe.

"Governor, Madam and Assistant Governor Xie, please come in."

Xie Peidong and Cheng Xiaoyun both looked towards Fang Buting under the tree. But Fang Buting remained unmoved, his head slightly raised, as if staring at the tree or perhaps at the sky. It was a moonless night again and there was still a massive power outage in Peking, yet the sky was full of stars lying dormant above the tree canopy.

Ye Biyu was even more apprehensive and looked at Xie Peidong in a confused fashion.

"Governor, go and sit in the room."

"Oh."

Only then did Fang Buting slowly turn his head to look at the hostess and then at the lighted north room. A look of hesitation flashed in his eyes although it was not easily detectable by the others.

"It's nice and cool in the garden, so let's just sit here."

The quick flash of hesitation was seen by both Xie Peidong and Cheng Xiaoyun. Xie Peidong did not answer him, instead he looked at Cheng Xiaoyun. Apparently it had been agreed that it would be easier for the women to talk among themselves.

"Big Sister, the governor is afraid of the heat, so let's sit in the courtyard." Cheng Xiaoyun went up to greet her, appearing quite easy-going as she spoke.

"How can I let the governor and you sit in the courtyard?" Ye Biyu immediately felt apologetic. "There are birds' nests in the trees and there are insects, so it's not clean."

"Zhongshi is really blessed," exclaimed Fang Buting, after lifting the back of his tunic and sitting down on a stone bench beside the stone table under the tree. He looked at Cheng Xiaoyun.

"I've heard so much from her husband about her kindness and consideration. We've experienced it first-hand today. You should learn from her."

At this point, he turned to Xie Peidong and said: "There must be work for you to handle at the bank. Why don't you head back first and tell the driver to pick me up later."

"Yes sir."

"Deputy Director Cui has helped secure lots of US aid for the bank. Governor Fang's very happy about that. He felt obliged to pay you a visit to show his appreciation. Now, if you'll excuse me," replied Xie Peidong, turning to Ye Biyu.

"Thanks, Mr Xie, for everything."

Ye Biyu hurriedly followed Xie Peidong towards the gate which she opened for him respectfully.

Illuminated by the 200-Watt lamp, a man's figure could be seen flashing towards the door to Fang Meng'ao's private room in the rear of the barracks dormitory. With cat-like agility, Ma Hanshan lept at Secretary Sun who had just come in and stood in the doorway. He gave him a ringing slap on the face. The slap rang loud and clear. Secretary Sun raised his hand, in an apparent move to seize Ma Hanhan with a martial arts hold but abruptly stopped in the middle of it.

What kept him in check was what he saw: the black hole-like muzzle of a gun.

The hands of Fang Meng'ao, who was still sitting on the chair, were faster than Sun's and his gun was already aimed at Sun's head. Xu Tieying and Zeng Keda were stupefied. Even Wang Puchen, who had detached himself from the whole situation by standing at the window, also looked over at the commotion, startled.

"You dirty son of a bitch! I dare you to break this arm of mine today!" Not knowing whether seeing the gun behind him was meant to help him or not, Ma Hanshan grabbed Secretary Sun by the collar, the two of them face to face with each other, and yelled so loudly that his spittle sprayed on Secretary Sun's face.

"Stand down," ordered Fang Meng'ao.

Ma Hanshan slowly turned his head only to find the muzzle of Fang Meng'ao's gun pointing at Secretary Sun's head. Meanwhile, he also saw that Fang Meng'ao was looking at him. He felt reluctant to stand down because his blood was boiling at the sight of his rescuers.

"Stand down and let Commissioner Xu question him."

Ma Hanshan looked understandingly at Fang Meng'ao but he tugged forcefully on Sun's collar before letting go of him. He walked back again still seething with hatred.

"Go ahead!" said Fang Meng'ao to Xu Tianying, putting the pistol back on the table.

Having been a high-ranking figure in the party headquarters of the Kuomintang Central Committee throughout his career, Xu Tieying had never expected to be held hostage by anyone affiliated with the two departments under the Ministry of Defence that day. He felt ashamed to fight Ma Hanshan and didn't have the guts to fight Fang Meng'ao, so all he could do was look to Zeng Keda for help.

Zeng Keda also looked at him but did not answer.

Secretary Sun had been slapped and was angry but he had to stand upright. He would not confess a word of it if Xu Tieying did not question him. Xu Tieying slowly closed his eyes.

It had worked miraculously now, judging from the fact that Cui Zhongshi had given up on the rescue efforts made by the party and chose to die a not-so-heroic death. None of the intricate factions within the Kuomintang dared admit that he was a Communist agent and had to bear the consequences of killing him. Ma Hanshan's outburst completely exonerated Fang Meng'ao from being suspected of being a Communist agent, making it impossible for Xu Tieying to take advantage of the situation. The Iron and Blood Congress had also achieved its objective of rescuing Fang Meng'ao and could now carry out a war on two fronts against the Communist Party, one against the CPC, the other against corruption.

"Director! Please sit down." Secretary Sun broke the silence, looking at Xu Tieying. Instead of addressing him as Commissioner, he was using Director, his former title at the Kuomintang Party headquarters in Nanking.

Xu Tieying opened his eyes and everyone else looked at Secretary Sun.

"You represent the party headquarters of the Kuomintang, please sit down!"

Xu Tieying was quite awakened by this intrepid subordinate of his but felt confused at heart, so he nodded his head and sat down. Secretary Sun's gaze turned abruptly to Ma Hanshan.

"Tell him to stand up! You black sheep of the party-state."

Ma Hanshan stood up, hot and bothered, not because Secretary Sun had told him to stand up but because he wanted to slap Sun again.

"Ma Hanshan!" This time it was Zeng Keda who shouted. Ma Hanshan stood there, stunned, but still staring at Secretary Sun.

"Are you done putting on airs? If you are, answer Captain Fang's question," Zeng Keda ordered Secretary Sun.

"What question?"

"How did Cui Zhongshi die?"

"Can I name whoever is involved?"

"Captain Fang, is it possible to name your father if he is involved?" Sun's eyes looked towards Fang Meng'ao.

That big hand of Fang Meng'ao's suddenly reached over to the table again. All eyes stared over at the pistol on the table but Fang Meng'ao just picked a cigar from the pack.

"Catch!" He threw the cigar to Secretary Sun.

Secretary Sun caught the cigar, totally unprepared. Fang Meng'ao then picked up the lighter on the table again, stood up and walked over to Secretary Sun, handing him the lighter. "Calm down and speak slowly."

Meanwhile inside Cui Zhongshi's courtyard at No. 2, East Dongzhong Hutong, Fang Buting said, as if he was their kind grandfather: "There's no hurry, eat slowly."

Cui Zhongshi's daughter Pingyang was sitting on Fang's lap and his son Boqin was standing beside him, in Fang's arms. As the old saying goes, one would rather be motherless at the age of three than forced to leave the bed at five in the morning. The two children were sound asleep when their mother woke them. At first they were reluctant to stir but when they heard that Grandpa Fang had brought some chocolates that their father had bought from the US, they quickly got up. With each kid chewing a Cadbury's chocolate, their eyes kept looking at the open box of chocolates on the stone table. Fang Buting grabbed another handful from the box and stuffed them in Pingyang's hands.

"It's rude of you to eat like this," said Ye Biyu smilingly to Fang Buting. Pingyang withdrew her hand at her mother's words.

"Daddy will send you more from America. Don't listen to

Mummy today, just eat." Fang Buting put the chocolate in Pingyang's little palm.

Pingyang's little palms were spread upwards but she still did not dare accept the chocolates and looked pleadingly at her mother.

"Let her eat," said Cheng Xiaoyun. "Don't embarrass the governor."

"Well, then, just take it."

Ye Biyu stole a glance at Fang Buting but the latter only had eyes for the two children. Pingyang held the handful of chocolates that Fang Buting had stuffed into her hands. Boqin was ready for more.

"Count them, how many chocolates did Grandpa give you?" asked Fang Buting, instead of grabbing more chocolates from the box.

"Four," replied Pingyang after counting them.

"Your sister gets four, how many pieces do you want from Grandpa?" asked Fang Buting with a smile, turning his attention to Boqin.

"Three," replied Boqin.

"Why only three?" asked Fang Buting, looking at him in surprise.

"When I was small, my father often told me stories about Kong Rong giving up his pears..."

Fang Buting appeared rather slow as he reached out for the box on the stone table, trying hard to control his trembling hands.

"Big Sister, try one too."

Cheng Xiaoyun was well aware of Fang Buting's state of mind at that moment. She also felt equally saddened, yet she had to help him cover it up. So she grabbed a piece of chocolate and gave it to Ye Biyu.

"They are for the children, how could I take one?" she said, flustered. It turned out that Ye Biyu was quite distracted by Cheng's offer.

Fang Buting was quite aware of what Cheng Xiaoyun was doing, which helped him to regain his composure. He picked up three chocolates and stuffed them into Boqin's hand. Cheng Xiaoyun then took another one from the box.

"Deputy Director Cui said that Big Sister should eat some too. Why don't we eat together?"

Ye Biyu had to agree. Watching Cheng Xiaoyun putting a chocolate in her mouth, she did the same and took a small bite despite feeling a little shy. Cheng Xiaoyun forced a smile and looked at Fang Buting at the same time. Addressing the children, Fang Buting said: "Ask your mother if it's good."

Both children were watching their mother eating the chocolate, albeit discreetly. When Ye Biyu looked over at them, they quickly looked away again, to say nothing of asking their mother.

"Zhongshi's parenting is far better than mine," said Fang Buting, looking at Cheng Xiaoyun.

Back in Fang Meng'ao's private room in the barracks dorm, Secretary Sun, unaware of the consequences of what he had just said, refused to speak again, leaving behind a great deal of suspense. With a stubborn look on his face, he found that all the people in the room were silent. The air froze. Staring at Secretary Sun's hands, Fang Meng'ao found that Sun was holding his American-made lighter in one hand and the unlit cigar in the other.

"Commissioner Xu," said Fang Meng'ao, turning to Xu Tieying, who was also looking at him gloomily.

"Your secretary is too nervous. Do him a favour and tell him to light his cigar and have a few puffs."

"He... doesn't smoke," replied Xu Tieying coldly. "I never tell my subordinates to do something they don't want to do."

"What if you told him to kill Cui Zhongshi?" pressed Fang Meng'ao. "Did you also ask him whether or not he was willing to do that?"

"Good question!" Ma Hanshan's sudden response grabbed all the nervous onlookers' attention.

"Xu, as long as you have some sense of loyalty, you wouldn't put all the blame on such a loyal subordinate, would you!" Ma Hanshan did not care about the reactions of the others and was focused only on Fang Meng'ao.

"Inspector-General Zeng!" said Xu Tieying, unable to stand it any longer. "I'm also a member of the investigation team appointed by the Nanking authorities. I now propose that this corrupt criminal be escorted out immediately!"

Zeng Keda also despised Ma Hanshan but his purpose today was very clear: to win over Fang Meng'ao and to dig deeper into in the Peking corruption case in order to implement the important instructions of Comrade Jianfeng. With Xu Tieying's so-called proposal, he pretended to think about it and replied: "Of course Ma Hanshan should be imprisoned but now he is confronting Secretary Sun. Your subordinate's not cooperating, so perhaps you should tell your subordinate to cooperate first."

"Director!" Secretary Sun broke his silence and called out to Xu Tieying: "To protect the reputation of the Kuomintang Party headquarters, you don't have to cover up for others any more."

"Nonsense!" Xu Tieying's biggest worry at this point was that this loyal subordinate of his might commit another act of blind loyalty.

"Yes. Cui Zhongshi was taken to Xishan by Ma Hanshan and his stooges from the Peking Station and shot after Governor Fang left." Without looking at Xu Tieying, Secretary Sun turned to Fang Meng'ao.

"Go ahead, what did you say at that time when you pulled me aside!" Ma Hanshan was excited to see him speak.

"I communicated Director Xu's order."

"What order?"

"That Cui Zhongshi's case was too complicated and that he should be transferred to the Defence Ministry's investigation team."

Everyone understood that Secretary Sun was lying. But it was a reasonable lie and, besides, no one else could prove otherwise!

Everyone's attention then subconsciously focused on Ma Hanshan, waiting for him to pounce on Secretary Sun and fight him to the death! However, Ma Hanshan's reaction this time was a disappointment. He was neither angry, nor did he even stop looking at Secretary Sun, and slowly turned to Xu Tieying.

"Xu, you belonged to the Central Bureau of Investigation and Statistics, whereas I was with the Military Council's Bureau of Investigation. Even though we've been bickering since the day we were founded, there's still a bottom line: no one should plant evidence on anyone else. You're instigating your men to step over the line. You called to ask me to bring my men from the Peking Station to escort Cui Zhongshi to the Ministry of Defence's Investigation Group. What a stupid joke! You put all the cops to bed earlier, did you? Are you going to tell the truth or not? Are you forcing me to step over the line and expose all the things you've been doing behind the scenes with the Ministry of Defence's Investigation Group and the Peking branch?"

"Shame on you!" shouted Zeng Keda, slapping the table with the palm of his hand. "I am now giving instructions on behalf of the Ministry of Defence's Investigation Group in Nanking that Ma Hanshan and Sun Chaozhong be detained for questioning at the Peking station of the State Secrecy Bureau. Captain Fang and his Inspection Brigade will conduct a thorough independent investigation into the corruption case. If any department dares to interfere, I'll report it directly to Comrade Jianfeng! Captain Fang."

Fang Meng'ao stood up this time.

"Do you have any other questions?"

"Can I interrogate anyone who is detained at Peking station at any time?"

"The Peking station is also administered by the Ministry of Defence's Secrecy Bureau. Of course, you can interrogate them any time."

Fang Meng'ao sat down again.

"Does Commissioner Xu have any other comments? Hopefully, not."

Xu Tieying was totally defeated in this battle. He stood up abruptly and walked straight out of the door without answering or saying goodbye to anyone, leaving Secretary Sun all alone.

"Station Chief Wang," said Zeng Keda, also paying no attention to Xu Tieying and instead turning to look at Wang Puchen. "These two men will be in your custody. No one is allowed to interrogate them except the Ministry of Defence's Investigation Group."

"No problem," replied Wang Puchen, who immediately called out to those outside: "Members of the executive team!"

The executive group of the Military Council's Bureau of Investigation at the Peking station had been waiting just outside the door. On hearing the order, the team leader immediately came in with two men.

"Please escort Deputy Director Ma and Secretary Sun to Xishan."

"Yes sir." The executive team leader was originally waiting to capture Ma Hanshan but did not expect to seize Secretary Sun as well, so he looked at Secretary Sun with some surprise as he answered this call.

Secretary Sun, on the contrary, was very cooperative, and took the initiative to walk outside himself.

"Stop!" Fang Meng'ao called out to him. "Leave my lighter and cigar behind."

A man from the executive team took the lighter and cigar from Sun and put them back on the table. Only then did Fang Meng'ao say: "You can take him away."

The military officer escorted Secretary Sun out.

The only one left was Ma Hanshan. He was still sitting there, not looking like he was going to get up at all.

"Old Station Chief, it's impossible not to make some mistakes when working for the party-state. We'll get to the bottom of this. Shall we go now?" Wang Puchen was still polite to him.

"You're still young!" said Ma Hanshan, remaining seated, staring at Wang Puchen. "You'd better not take this case. You can't afford to take the responsibility if I die by your hand!"

"Shame on you!" Zeng Keda was furious and stood up abruptly. "I've got important issues to discuss with Captain Fang. Do you want to stay and join us?"

Of course, Ma Hanshan knew that he could not stay and participate, so he looked at Fang Meng'ao again, who in turn looked at Wang Puchen.

"You can take him with you. As I just said, I need to question him and to see Deputy Director Ma at some point. If anything happens to him, I'll hold you responsible."

Wang Puchen did not want to commit himself, so he turned to Zeng Keda.

"I'd appreciate it if you can cooperate in this matter," replied Zeng Keda.

"You have my word on that."

Ma Hanshan had to stand up. He actually extended his hand to Fang Meng'ao who leaned forward and reciprocated. Ma Hanshan clasped his hand tightly, a little excited. "Coke mixed with red wine, I'll remember that."

Zeng Keda frowned again.

"Death is a glass of wine but so is life. I'll remember that too," said Fang Meng'ao.

"I regret we didn't meet sooner." Ma Hanshan suddenly appeared heroic and, with these indescribable words, he went straight out, ignoring Zeng Keda and Wang Puchen.

The executive team leader and the other military officer went out with Ma Hanshan. Wang Puchen was in no hurry and shook hands with Zeng Keda and Fang Meng'ao.

"Inspector-General Zeng and Captain Fang, please rest assured he's in good hands."

With that, he strolled to the door. Only then did Zeng Keda get up and follow him. He did not mean to say goodbye but to close the door after Wang Puchen.

With all his silent discretion, Fang Meng'ao sat there waiting quietly.

Zeng Keda then turned around and walked back. He moved his chair to sit beside Fang Meng'ao with an earnest expression on his face. Suddenly he called out: "Comrade Meng'ao."

Fang Meng'ao gazed at Zeng Keda. He sized up Zeng Keda in an unfamiliar way while Zeng Keda waited patiently for him to respond. Having served in the Air Force for ten years, Fang Meng'ao had never had the chance to join the Kuomintang or the Three Youth League, so no one had ever called him comrade. Only that night when Cui Zhongshi secretly recommended that he join up did he call him comrade. No one else since had called him comrade.

It dawned on him that the moment he had been waiting for was finally approaching now that Zeng Keda was addressing him in this way. Fang Meng'ao slowly picked up the lighter and cigar from the table, then handed the cigar to Zeng Keda and said: "Smoke!"

Zeng Keda eyed the cigar being offered to him, the one that had just been offered to Secretary Sun. He was not offended in the least and took it without further ado. Fang Meng'ao then ignited the lighter and slowly stretched it out.

Zeng Keda awkwardly put the cigar in his mouth but the lighter that Fang Meng'ao was stretching out in front of him stopped in mid air.

"This is against the tenet of the New Life Movement, isn't it?"

"No big deal." Zeng Keda took the initiative to approach the cigar toward the lighter and sucked on it. "We've been working together for a month. I'd like to hear what you think of the organisation."

"Organisation? Which organisation?" said Fang Meng'ao as he closed the lighter.

"We, the Ministry's Investigation Team, and the Bureau of Reserve Cadres supervised by Comrade Jianfeng."

"I don't have any opinion. What opinion do you have of me? Be straightforward."

The Fang Meng'ao in front of Zeng Keda was not the same Fang Meng'ao as in the past and what was unfolding before him was the message sent to him by Jianfeng not long ago, which contained the three-character codename 'Jiao Zhongqing'!

"Good. Then I will first convey Comrade Jianfeng's evaluation of you." Zeng Keda appeared more generous and genial than ever, rather than adopting his previous patronising manner.

———

In the courtyard at No. 2, Mao'er Hutong, Old Liu opened the door by lifting the shutter upwards with both hands so that it didn't make any noise. Xie Peidong quickly stepped into the courtyard. Waiting for him inside the gate was Zhang Yueyin. Once again, Old Liu closed the door behind him.

Zhang Yueyin hurriedly shook hands with Xie Peidong without uttering a word and the two of them walked towards the north room followed by Old Liu.

———

"Fang Meng'ao is a rare talent, very healthy and dignified!" said Zeng Keda in Fang Meng'ao's private room in the barracks. However, to Fang's ears, the sound coming out of his mouth as he enunciated the words was no longer his voice but an echo from the sky behind him with a strong Zhejiang Fenghua accent.

The same thing proved to be true when Fang Meng'ao saw that the Zeng Keda sitting in front of him was no longer the original Zeng Keda. What he saw was a phantom! He tried hard to see the figure hidden behind it. But behind Zeng Keda was an open window beyond which was only an endless night sky.

"Very healthy, with dignified..." These words still echoed in the night sky outside the window, echoing in Fang Meng'ao's mind.

These six words were very familiar to Fang Meng'ao who recalled the evaluation of Mr Wen Yiduo's new poems by literary critics, the representative figure of the Crescent School of Poetry. Amazingly, the man behind Zeng Keda was capable of judging him with this review! Fang Meng'ao withdrew his gaze from the window and looked at Zeng Keda, trying to make sense of the source of the sound behind him from his eyes. Zeng Keda's eyes indicated that he was trying to remember, so his mouth opened and closed mechanically. The origin of the voice was hard to identify and the echoes of the Zhejiang Fenghua accent were always drifting in the distance:

"...Those who don't know him can't accept the way he expresses himself. Only those who know him can appreciate his spirit that transcends utilitarianism, which was 'the Spirit of the Universe', a notion used by Mr Wen Yiduo when reviewing Tang dynasty poetry. Our past mistakes have been our inability to accept such a talent and such a spirit..."

A boundless sky appeared before Fang Meng'ao's eyes where there was a backlight which was quite a taboo when flying his aircraft.

"Please share a poem with him on my behalf. It is his favourite but I like it too."

Zeng Keda's figure had completely dissolved, silhouetted against the backlight, and the distant one with a thick Zhejiang Fenghua accent began to read aloud in cadence:

> *Ah, sun, the sun that pierces my heart with pain!*
> *Again you drive away the wanderer's homecoming dream*
> *And add to his suffering, wrenching pangs of day and night.*

Ah, sun, the sun that burns hot like fire.
You evaporate the dew on the tiny blades of grass,
But can you evaporate the cold tears that fill the wanderer's eyes?

The poem that Comrade Jianfeng told Zeng Keda to read to Fang Meng'ao was actually Wen Yiduo's *Song of the Sun*.

The backlight was gradually receding and a bright sun appeared before Fang Meng'ao's eyes over the distant mountains. Travelling back in time to 1943 in Yunnan Province where there was an empty airport, wide and open in the distant suburbs of Kunming…

On the makeshift lectern with its back to the sun stood the unyielding Mr Wen Yiduo in his tunic representing the eternal Chinese nation!

The unruly hair that vigorously aspired to the firmament like a flying cloud, the whiskers as hard as pine needles that were deeply rooted in the earth, the eyes that were deep and sorrowful behind the lens, and the huge pipe in his hand with which he drew an arc!

In front of the podium, rows and rows of young Flying Tigers pilots were standing tall and strong. With youthful faces, these young men were ready to die for their country. Of all the young faces, Fang Meng'ao's stood out most prominently. He watched in awe while Mr Wen Yiduo made his impassioned speech laden with sorrow.

In reality, Zeng Keda's lips were still mechanically opening and closing, conveying the message of the man behind the scenes. However, what Fang Meng'ao actually saw and heard was Mr Wen on the podium who spoke like the howling wind and tidal waves of the sea that day.

A voice from a distant space overlapped with a voice from a distant time. With two radically different accents, one identified as Zhejiang Fenghua, the other as a Hubei Qishui, one could hear two extremely disharmonious recitations of the rest of the *Song of the Sun*.

Ah, sun, the sun that newly rises from the roof's corner!
Didn't you just come from our east?
Is everything still fine in my hometown?

Ah, sun, the sun that comes from my hometown!
Have the willows inside Peking City wrapped themselves in autumn?
Alas, I am as withered as the deep autumn!

Unlike Fang Meng'ao's private room inside the barracks, which was illuminated by two 200-watt lamps which looked like the sun over Kunming Airport to Fang Meng'ao's eyes, the north room at No. 2, Mao'er Hutong was lit up by a dim kerosene lamp. Zhang Yueyin sat at the top of the quadrangular table, while Xie Peidong sat on the east side, with Old Liu sitting on the west side. This was a formal meeting of the upper echelons of the Peking Urban Works Department, presided over by Zhang Yueyin.

Both Zhang Yueyin and Old Liu said something before, which seemed unimportant now, as both of them were looking at Xie Peidong who was going to make the following remarks that obviously proved to be more important.

"The internal strife within the Kuomintang has fully intensified due to the sudden suspension of US economic aid," said Xie Peidong with a gloomy look on his face. "The Iron and Blood Congress went so far as to also crack down on Chen Jicheng, the one they promote as the vanguard is Comrade Fang Meng'ao. Based on our intelligence analysis on the economic front, once the US resumes its aid, the Kuomintang will immediately implement its currency reform. The main focus of the currency reform in the Peking-Tianjin region was the Peking branch of the Central Bank." At this point, Xie Peidong paused and struggled with the name which he had a hard time saying.

"Chiang Ching-kuo will use Fang Meng'ao against Fang Buting at any cost with the purpose of removing all obstacles... At this point, I would like to ask the organisation to carefully consider whether or not we should engage Comrade Fang Meng'ao."

Old Liu looked towards Zhang Yueyin. But Zhang Yueyin did not look back at him in return, instead, he eyed Xie Peidong calmly. "I guess Mr Xie's concern has two implications. First, the person you mentioned has already deployed all-round surveillance and any attempt we make will be discovered by the Iron and Blood

Congress. Second, shall we continue to use Liang Jinglun to get Comrade He Xiaoyu to meet with him? The reason for the concern is that we are worried that Comrade He Xiaoyu has neither the experience nor capacity to deal with Liang Jinglun, much less to deal with such an intricate conflict of interests."

Xie Peidong and Old Liu nodded their heads. This time it was Zhang Yueyin who fell silent.

Back in his private bedroom in the barracks, Fang Meng'ao had closed his eyes and the sun was gone from his eyes. All that was left were the 200-watt lamps shining on a sweating Zeng Keda, who had apparently forgotten the last lines of the poem and had to reach into his lower jacket pocket for the teletype paper.

Fang Meng'ao, however, recited those last lines by heart:

> Ah, sun, the sun whose benevolent light shines on all!
> Every time I see you in the future, I will feel I have also come home.
> For my home now is not on Earth but in heaven!

"No need to read it." Fang Meng'ao opened his eyes and interrupted Zeng Keda who was holding the teletext paper.

"Why do you want to read this poem to me?"

"Comrade Jianfeng wants to know how you felt after I shared it with you," said Zeng Keda, after putting the teletext paper back in his pocket again.

"It didn't make me feel anything."

Fang Meng'ao slowly turned his gaze to Zeng Keda. "I just remember that the person who wrote this poem is dead."

"Yes." Zeng Keda's tone was remarkably heavy. "That's the next topic Comrade Jianfeng asked me to talk to you about."

"What is it anyway? We've just finished talking about a dead person all night long, now we have to talk about another dead man?"

Zeng Keda could tell from Fang Meng'ao's eyes that it was only a rhetorical question.

In the north room of the courtyard at No. 2, Mao'er Hutong, Zhang Yueyin still hadn't answered Xie Peidong and Old Liu after several minutes' silence but he suddenly called out to someone in the next room from which Wang immediately emerged.

"Do we have any message from the North China Urban Works Department?"

Wang had seldom heard such questions from Comrade Zhang Yueyin because he would normally submit such telegrams as soon as he received them. So why bother to ask? He had no answer, all he could do was to shake his head.

"Send a telegram to the North China Urban Works Department immediately, six words: 'Time is limited for number three'. Quick, Go! Go!"

"Yes sir." Wang quickly walked back into the next room.

"Mr Xie, you're requested to come here tonight because our superiors have important instructions for you, me and Comrade Liu."

"Instructions on the currency reform, or on Comrade Fang Meng'ao?" asked Xie Peidong.

"Perhaps both." Only then did Zhang Yueyin answer the question that he could not answer just a few minutes ago, deliberately trying to theorise about the current situation: "The analysis you have just made on the complexity of the struggle brought about by the need to face it promptly has happened against our will. Things tend not to be shifted by human will. Comrade Fang Meng'ao should have been used to lead his aviation brigade to revolt against the Kuomintang at the critical moment. The sum of all social relations has changed the course of action in another direction. Comrade Fang Meng'ao is not prepared for this, nor are we. Mr Xie, let's wait for further instructions from the higher-ups."

Zeng Keda was genuinely excited, thanks to Comrade Jianfeng's regular tutoring, and most recently his instruction to learn Wen Yiduo's poems by heart. Now he fully understood that sincerity was the only way to treat sincerity! He stood up, fully aware of the situation. "According to Comrade Jianfeng, we have been making the same fatal mistake for thousands of years, namely, that we tend to alienate the best and the brightest among our children."

"Who is this 'we'?"

"There are too many of them. For example, those who killed Mr Wen Yiduo and those who wanted to arrest you today, all of them."

"And who are those people working for?"

"They work for nobody. They claim to be working for the party-state, but in fact they are the ones who harm the party-state."

"What does this have to do with thousands of years?"

"Inertia! The powerful inertia resulting from thousands of years of history! This is the exact significance of what Comrade Jianfeng wants me to share with you today."

"It's too sophisticated, isn't it? I just don't understand." Fang Meng'ao took another cigar from the pack on the table and instead of handing it to Zeng Keda, he ignited the lighter and started smoking himself.

"Comrade Jianfeng said you'll understand." Zeng Keda was very patient and tried his best to speak like Comrade Jianfeng. "The history of thousands of years of feudal dictatorship is a history of defending vested interests. As for who will defend these vested interests, they can only rely on villains. The inevitable consequence of this is the exclusion of the best talent. The banishment of Qu Yuan from the State of Chu and the killing of Ji Kang by Sima's clique are classic examples. The result is either a swift demise or the creation of a bad culture of silence. On the contrary, there are two typical good examples. Emperor Su Zong of the Tang Dynasty did not kill Li Bai, and Emperor Shenzong of the Song Dynasty did not kill Su Dongpo, because they had learnt lessons from their predecessors, namely, that 'It's ominous to kill a man of noble character!' Thus, a benevolent thought that protected Li Bai and Su Shi has left an irreplaceable heritage for our nation which has contributed immensely to the longevity of the two dynasties. Comrade Jianfeng often reflected on this history from which he wishes to draw useful lesssons. He has repeatedly emphasised that we, as a people, must learn to love our best sons."

"I seem to have understood a little bit," said Fang Meng'ao, interrupting him. "Are you telling me that no one should be held responsible for the murder of Mr Wen Yiduo?"

"It's not a question of who did it," said Zeng Keda, becoming agitated again. "I've told you Comrade Jianfeng admitted it was a mistake that should never have happened. After the assassination of Mr Wen, the leader was so angry that he ordered the villains to be punished. Comrade Jianfeng was so distressed by Mr Wen's death that he talked to us about the lesson drawn from that period of history. For example, today, isn't it a testament to Comrade Jianfeng's attitude that you survived being held at gunpoint by Chen Jicheng?"

"Inspector-General Zeng, I don't understand your analogy."

"What don't you understand?"

"According to you, Qu Yuan, Ji Kang, Li Bai, Su Dongpo and Mr Wen Yiduo, they are all men of noble character. I am just a soldier."

"You are a soldier who can protect a man of noble character! Why does Comrade Jianfeng offer to share Mr Wen's *Song of the Sun* with you? Because he knows you admire Mr Wen Yiduo, and like Mr Wen, you love our nation, our excellent culture and all our compatriots!"

Fang Meng'ao started to fall silent, then laughed.

"It's too big a deal, isn't it? Am I such a benevolent person?"

"Responsibility! It's the sense of responsibility that counts! Why do we come to Peking? Because there are noble characters here like Mr Wen, Mr Zhu Ziqing and Master Chen Yanque who've been suffering from food deprivation! And the two million residents in Peking included. You and I, we both have the responsibility to protect them."

"What do you want me to do? Just say it." Fang Meng'ao slowly extinguished his cigar in the ashtray.

Zeng Keda's eyes brightened. He felt that Comrade Jianfeng's instructions were working. He took out a pen from the upper pocket of his jacket and a piece of letter-headed paper from the lower one.

Fang Meng'ao saw him slowly write down four words on the piece of paper: "The Peacock Flies Southeast".

And slowly Zeng Keda wrote three more characters: "Jiao Zhongqing"!

Inside the cable room of the North China Communist Party Urban Works Department, Fuping County, Hebei Province, one could hear the ticking sound of the transceiver. The hurricane lamps, one, two, three of them in all. All the windows were covered with military blankets, even at night, and as a result it was as hot as a sauna in the cable room. In front of the radio station, several PLA messengers were busy receiving and sending telegrams while others, who were sweating, were busy translating the telegrams in front of a long table.

Standing next to a decoder, Liu Yun took hold of a telegram just sent from Peking while agitating his palm-leaf fan.

"Minister, it's not signed, it's from the Ministry of the Urban Works Department in Peking," said the decoder in a soft voice.

"Number Three has limited time." Liu Yun's eyes were fixed on the message.

What's the rush! Liu Yun said to himself, his brow furrowed. Then he looked at the radio furthest away in the corner.

"Zhang Yueyin certainly doesn't make a good general." With that, he threw the telegram on the table, stalked past a couple of radios to the innermost one and asked the radio operator: "Nothing yet from the Central Committee?"

"As soon as the instructions from the Central Committee arrive, operators submit them. Why do you need to ask?" The radio operator regarded the minister with a puzzled expression like Xiao Wang working for Zhang Yueyin. Liu Yun immediately understood that he had not asked the question in a professional manner, in the same mood as Zhang Yueyin's. So he waved the palm-leaf fan in his hand and spat out a sentence that puzzled the telegram operator even more: "I've not been made a general either." He went back to the decoders' table, fanning himself with his palm-leaf fan.

Suddenly there was a knock on the door: three knocks, three more knocks, then another three! All eyes turned to the invisible night sky, listening intently for what was to come! Liu Yun stopped fanning himself and also listened carefully.

The sound of an aircraft engine could be faintly heard in the silent night sky. The door was gently pushed open and in came the guard platoon commander with a pistol at his waist, announcing somewhat nervously: "Kuomintang bombers, two of them! Please, sir, all of you, go straight to the air-raid shelter!"

Liu Yun's eyes turned to Zhang Yueyin's telegram he had placed on the table, then to the radio designated to receiving the instructions from the central authorities. He waved his fan again, as if to fan away the roaring of the plane engines from time to time. "It's just a random surveillance mission. Don't pay any attention to it. All units, continue to work."

Several transceivers continued to receive and send messages which the decoders continued to decode.

"Sir, please seek shelter before it's too late!" insisted the platoon commander. He saluted and pressed on.

Liu Yun's eyes were now keenly focused on the radio in the corner where the operator was receiving a telegram. At long last, the instructions from the Central Committee had come!

"Listen up! Keep watching and be on full alert!" said Liu Yun to the guard platoon leader blocking his way.

The guard platoon leader had no choice but to stand to attention and salute. "Yes!" He then walked back to the door, opened it and departed.

"Minister, it's signed by Vice-Chairman Zhou!" said the radio operator who stood up and handed over the coded telegram with both hands.

"Please decode this immediately!" demanded Liu Yun, snatching the coded telegram and directing his order to the senior decoder back at the decoders' desk.

The decoder was quite skilful and penned the words Liu Yun was eager to see with a pencil as fast as possible:

> Pits of ash were not yet cold, disorder reigned east of the Xiao Mountains.
> As it turned out, Liu Bang and Xiang Yu could not read.
> Find a copy of *New Songs from the Jade Terrace* to read and report to Peking Number Two.

Liu was confused because all he had to do now was to locate a book to read based on the content of a telegram signed personally by Vice-Chairman Zhou after waiting so long for the Central Committee's instructions. Confused and amazed, Liu Yun stared at the telegram, the content of which was as complicated as the matrix design of the stone-paved street. His eyes subconsciously turned to the portrait of Chairman Mao on the right side of Commander-in-Chief Zhu De in the middle of the wall. Then he whispered as if for help: "Chairman!" Anxiously, he began to sweat.

"Section Chief Ye!" he called out.

"Yes sir." Ye hurried over.

Having already put down the fan, Liu Yun picked up a pencil from the table and wrote down the words *New Songs from the Jade Terrace, Volume One* on a blank piece of paper and handed it to Chief Ye.

"Take a squad, go and find Principal Shi at the county high school. Borrow this book immediately, no matter what it takes. Tell him I want to read it."

"Yes sir," said Section Chief Ye, taking the note with both hands, before walking out.

Liu Yun strode right away to a transmitter in the interior against the wall and handed over the message from the Central Committee he had just received. "Send a message to Peking Number Two word for word the same as the original text."

"Wait!" Liu Yun took it back as soon as the operator reached out to take the message and put the paper the message was written on back on the table in front of the radio transmitter. He picked up a pencil and circled the character "first" in "first reading" on the message. He then drew a line that went to the margin, where he wrote the character "prepared".

The phrase "first reading" was replaced by "preparatory reading". When the operator came to pick it up, Liu Yun stopped again and crossed out the character "preparatory" that he had written.

"Let's go with the original."

He handed it to the operator with just two words: "Send it!"

With a click-clack sound, the message was sent back to Peking and received by the codebreaker in the courtyard house in Mao'er Hutong. It was still dark there and people's livelihoods had long been unable to be guaranteed in Peking, where there were still massive power outages in residential areas.

In the north house of the quadrangle at No. 2, Mao'er Hutong, Zhang Yueyin, Xie Peidong and Lao Liu were standing at a table in front of a kerosene lamp, reading the message they had just received:

> Pits of ash were not yet cold, disorder reigned east of the Xiao Mountains. As it turned out, Liu Bang and Xiang Yu could not read. Find a copy of *New Songs from the Jade Terrace, Volume One* to read without delay.

After reading the message, Old Liu looked at Zhang Yueyin, full of doubt, while Zhang Yueyin was still trying to digest the contents without asking any questions but he appeared even more anxious and gravely concerned. He looked up at Old Liu and then at Xie Peidong.

"This is not a formal instruction, it's an urgent notice forwarded by the Urban Works Department in North China because the official message code from the Central Committee will have changed. It is imperative to find a copy of *New Songs from the Jade Terrace, Volume One*."

"What book is it? Do you think we can we borrow one from our comrades?"

"It's a collection of ancient poems. You won't find them at their places," said Zhang Yueyin, shaking his head.

"Then we'll have to go to Liulichang." Old Liu immediately understood the importance of this book. "Let me go and find it."

"The entire city is under martial law, you can't go to Liulichang right now," warned Zhang Yueyin, dismissing his suggestion out of hand. With that he turned to Xie Peidong.

"Sir, you cannot stay here long. We'll contact you when we receive official instructions. Can we call you at the Fang residence before or after dawn?"

"I can be reached by phone any time. Fang Buting is visiting

Comrade Cui Zhongshi tonight and will go to see He Qicang after dawn, partly to avoid Fang Meng'ao and partly to find out from He Qicang what the US intends to do about the currency reform."

"Sir, your information is also important," said Zhang Yueyin, looking at Old Liu. "I'll send it along to the Urban Works Department as well. Comrade Liu, take Mr Xie to the gate and tell the guard escorts to ensure his safety."

"Sir, permit me to walk you out." Instead of replying to Zhang Yueyin, Old Liu accompanied Xie Peidong out of the room. Obviously, Zhang's warning had caused a trace of unhappiness that could be detected in his eyes. Xie Peidong stood up and shook the hand that Zhang Yueyin was extending to him. Meanwhile, Old Liu opened the door for Xie Peidong.

The door opened. It turned out that the cell was where Liang Jinglun had been detained not long before in the military's secret prison in the northwestern suburbs of Peking.

"Secretary Sun," said the Military Council's escort agent politely. "You'll have to make do with this tonight. Anything you need I'll bring you tomorrow."

"They are all taking a shower, can I do so too?" asked Secretary Sun.

"I'm afraid not." The agent didn't even bother to explain why. "We've been thrashing about for half the night. Go to bed now."

Secretary Sun didn't persist with his question, tugged at the hem of his jacket out of habit and walked straight into his cell. The door closed with a bang behind him.

"How far away is Comrade Yan Chunming's hiding place?" Zhang Yueyin looked at Old Liu who had just got back to the north room inside the courtyard house at No. 2, Mao'er Hutong.

"It's not far, in the next alley."

"Can you get him here right away?" asked Zhang Yueyin.

"Yan Chunming has appeared quite suspicious lately," remarked

Old Liu, before falling silent, but a short while later he continued: "It's not appropriate to let him know such an important instruction. At the same time we cannot afford to let him know that you are here. I'll think of some other way to locate the book."

"There aren't any other ways, so bring in Comrade Yan Chunming immediately." Zhang Yueyin turned his attention back to the telegram.

Old Liu eyed Zhang Yueyin suspiciously. To him, Zhang Yueyin's demeanour indicated that he regarded the cadres with workers' and peasants' backgrounds as somewhat lacking in political consciousness. Old Liu continued to be silent, as if in protest.

Zhang Yueyin raised his head, assessing Old Liu's reaction. He became even more serious.

"According to the organisational principle, if you and I disagree on the instructions of the Urban Works Department of North China, we can appeal to Comrade Liu Yun for a ruling. But today's message is a most significant one."

"Didn't you forward the instructions of the Urban Works Department of the Central Committee?"

"Whose instructions from the Urban Works Department of the Central Committee?" retorted Zhang Yueyin.

"Direct instructions from Vice-Chairman Zhou?" Again, Old Liu became solemn.

"No doubt the instruction must have been given by Vice-Chairman Zhou but the content of the message seems to be written in Chairman Mao's style!"

Old Liu was shocked. Although he was in civilian clothes, he stood upright as if in military uniform. He straightened up and looked nervously at Zhang Yueyin.

"Chairman Mao is very erudite. With some of his instructions, even the central leadership have to go through many books to understand them. The book we've been told to look for, according to the cable, was full of classical literary allusions which are key to understanding the message that follows. Neither you nor I have reached that level of literacy, so it's imperative that we find Comrade Yan Chunming immediately."

"I arranged for his transfer to this safe place. He didn't have this book with him for sure." Old Liu was still adamant.

"Bring him here now with or without this book."

This was by no means discussing the job they were focusing on, so Old Liu became silent again. Zhang Yueyin had no choice but to wait patiently for his attitude to change.

Old Liu's half a lifetime of involvement in brutal revolutionary struggle led him to believe that intellectuals always lost out by relying on their own book knowledge. However, he deeply admired Chairman Mao and Vice-Chairman Zhou for their erudition and firmly believed that it was the true skill of combining literary knowledge with Chinese revolutionary practice. Now when it came to understanding Chairman Mao's and Vice-Chairman Zhou's great learning, he really had not reached that level of literacy. Suddenly, it dawned on him that after the victory of the revolution, China might still rely on party intellectuals like Zhang Yueyin and Yan Chunming.

"All right." He could no longer dismiss Zhang Yueyin's suggestion. "I'll bring him in."

"Be safe," said Zhang Yueyin as he walked him towards the door without opening it immediately. "Comrade Liu, the party has entrusted us with the important responsibility of running the Peking Urban Works Department. To do our job better, may I give you a piece of advice?"

Old Liu looked at him, his eyes clearly conveying that he was apprehensive about what Zhang Yueyin was going to say.

"You said just now that you would *bring* Comrade Yan Chunming in," admonished Zhang Yueyin who seemed deliberately critical of Old Liu today. "On behalf of the organisation, I would like to suggest that you rephrase it. You're not to *bring* Comrade Yan Chunming here, you're to *invite* him here."

"Can I not accept this advice of yours?" Old Liu replied begrudgingly, no longer disguising his worker-peasant background.

"As long as you can give me a reason why."

"If he is a democratic personage without party affiliation, of course, I'll go and invite him. Since he is one of my peers, a fellow comrade of the party, there doesn't seem to be any such rule guiding what I should do."

"Subordinates, of course, obey superiors. But that's two different things." Zhang Yueyin became even more gravely concerned. "Comrade Yan Chunming used to be a professor in the Department of Chinese at Nankai University but because of the importance of the Peking student movement, he transferred to Yenching University as the chief librarian. Vice-Chairman Zhou has had specific instructions that we must show proper respect to such a great intellectual like him in the party."

Again, it was Vice-Chairman Zhou's instruction!

"I accept the criticism. I'll go and ask him to come here." Old Liu was no longer defiant.

"Xiao Wang ..." Zhang Yueyin whispered to the side door as he watched Old Liu walk out of the room. Wang walked out of the side door.

"Stick to the radio. If you receive a new message and if the code doesn't match, just give it to me," instructed Zhang Yueyin.

"Yes sir." Wang went back into the next room.

Contrary to what happened to Secretary Sun, Ma Hanshan was treated very differently. First, he took a bath in the company of his former subordinates, then stood at the door of the lounge in the secret prison of the Military Bureau. The face that used to make him look like someone from the underworld mafia was evidently less sinister and calmer than usual. He surveyed the room which appeared quite strange to him. Wang Puchen was present together with three agents who had also taken a bath. They stood behind him, waiting for Ma Hanshan to enter the lounge.

"Is this the room where I used to sleep?" Ma Hanshan was still standing in the doorway.

"Yes, Station Chief. Please, this is all yours now," replied Wang Puchen.

"Where's that bed made of yellow rosewood and the table made of the small-leafed red sandalwood? Have you sold them already?"

"No, they're all locked in the warehouse." Wang Puchen chuckled. "If you find it uncomfortable to sleep in a single bed, I can ask them to scrub the double bed and move it in."

Ma Hanshan was taken aback at first, then shook his head and walked towards the bed against the wall and sat down on the edge of it. Wang Puchen followed him into the room. He removed a few books and a large ashtray placed on the wooden chair beside the bed, and sat down on it.

"Of all the station masters in the country, very few are as self-disciplined and frugal as you." Ma Hanshan took another glance at the two bookcases and a wooden desk next to the wall, turned to Wang Puchen and sighed with emotion.

"Come on in, all of you." At this point, Ma Hanshan looked at the three bureau agents who were still standing at the door.

With his permission, the three military agents walked in.

"That bed is not for sleeping on. Ask them if I slept on it when I moved it in here two years ago," Ma Hanshan said to Wang Puchen again.

The three agents really didn't know how to respond to Ma's question and they just shook their heads.

"Do you know why I don't sleep on the bed?"

When Wang Puchen looked at Ma Hanshan again, his eyes inadvertently swept over the small alarm clock on the desk, patiently listening to what else he had to say about the history of the bed.

"Zhang Boju saw it, more than three hundred years ago," Ma Hanshan said. "When Li Zicheng and his peasant rebels occupied Kaifeng, it was from this bed that he caught the King of Fortune, Zhu Changxun, something truly royal. It's unlucky but it's worth a lot of money. I understand the operational cost of Peking Station was high, so I left this for you when I departed. If you had sold it at that time, it would have been worth a hundred thousand silver dollars but I didn't expect you'd keep it in the warehouse. Don't leave it unused, I'll hook you up with a buyer tomorrow, it's worth twenty thousand even if you sell it now."

"Well, let's talk about it tomorrow." Wang Puchen stood up, went to the desk, opened a drawer and took out a whole pack of cigarettes, then picked up a book and the alarm clock from the desk. He said to the three bureau agents: "The old station chief is also tired, get some rest once he goes to bed."

"It's still early," remarked Ma Hanshan, also standing up. "Why, Puchen?"

Wang Puchen had to stop and turn around, and look at him again.

"I appreciate it so much you letting me use this room. But I don't read, so can you tell them to move that table closer to me?"

All four pairs of eyes looked at him.

"Why don't you tell them to play mahjong with me in the room instead of standing guard outside the door?"

Wang Puchen tried to avoid Ma Hanshan's gaze. Instead, he looked at his three subordinates, only to find that they were quite expressionless.

"The old station chief didn't have any money on him today, so go to the general affairs office and make an advance payment of five hundred dollars to the operation fund account which I'll sign afterwards."

"Yes sir," answered the three men loudly before walking out, leaving only two people in the room, Ma Hanshan and Wang Puchen.

"Station Chief, this used to be your home and still is." Only then could Wang Puchen offer Ma Hanshan some comfort. "I'm kind of fading, so I'll go to bed. If you need anything, you can always call me. I'll be at your beck and call."

As Ma Hanshan stood there, his eyes suddenly moistened. "Go to my place when you're free tomorrow. There's quite a lot of good stuff left behind. Take whatever you like. Don't let those ungrateful villains benefit."

Wang Puchen listened quietly.

"They aren't merely worldly possessions. In our line of work, our lives are not our own but our bodies are. There is a box engraved with Tibetan scriptures in which you'll find two catties of superior Chinese caterpillar fungus. You must take it. At night before going to bed, soak five roots in boiling water, drink it and eat the fungus in the morning. It's good for your health."

"Thank you, Chief," replied Wang Puchen. With that he walked out.

Ma Hanshan sat down on the edge of the bed and became lost in deep thought. What he was thinking? It's possible he didn't know himself.

In the radio room of the Urban Works Department of the CPC's North China Bureau in Fuping County, Hebei Province, this time it was the radio operator who walked up to the codebreakers' desk with the newly received telegram. "Minister, a new telegram from the Central Committee, signed again by Vice-Chairman Zhou himself."

"Translate it right now." Liu Yun, apparently moderating his eagerness, received the telegram calmly and turned it over to the senior decipherer at the table.

The decipherer took the telegram and began to decode the message from the table based on the codebook.

Exactly at this time, Section Chief Ye, who was sent to look for the book, pushed open the door and walked in.

"I got it, Minister, please take a look at it."

Liu Yun took the thin threadbound book made of rice paper from Section Chief Ye. On the cover of the book, in the long line frame on the left, four big characters were vertically printed on the top, *"New Songs from the Jade Terrace"*, while at the bottom in small characters, it read: "Book I".

Liu Yun flipped open the cover and, sure enough, in the first line on the first page he saw "Volume 1", two photocopied Song-style characters! Only then did Liu Yun smile.

"Not bad. Principal Shi really has all sorts of books. You name it, he has it."

"Excuse me, Minister!" The decipherer was frustrated. "Most of the codes in this message cannot be deciphered."

"Decode the ones that can be deciphered first, and keep those you can't decode in their original form."

"Yes sir!" The codebreaker was relieved and the message was quickly translated. Liu Yun took the telegram.

Its content was as follows:

Please be informed that the exam questions will be written by Number One and supervised by Number Two, and the question items will be 0040, 0004, 0001, 0002, 0003, 0004, 0005. Candidate A is 0040, 0002, 0011, 0012, 0013. Candidate B is 0040, 0002, 0014, 0040, 0086, 0001, 0002. Quickly identify the specific answers to the exam items and confirm their true identities based on the candidates' code numbers.

Liu Yun turned to the book he held in his other hand, *New Songs from the Jade Terrace, Volume One*, then walked to his own room next door. On the square table in Liu Yun's office, the telegram with numbers in it was on the left side, while on the right side was the copy of *New Songs from the Jade Terrace, Volume One*.

Liu Yun picked up a pencil, circled "Number One" on the message, then drew an arrow towards the blank space above and wrote the word "Chiang Kai-shek". He went on to circle 'Number Two', drew another arrow, and wrote "Chiang Ching-kuo" next to "Chiang Kai-shek".

Immediately afterwards, with his left index finger he pointed to the first code number 0040 in the message and his right hand began flipping through the pages of *New Songs from the Jade Terrace, Volume One*, reaching page 40. His left index finger moved to the second code number 0004, and his right hand moved to the fourth line on page 40 of the book. He looked at it carefully, with a puzzled look on his face. He rejected the number and pondered. He had a new idea which made him flip through the book again. He turned to the first page of text.

The four characters "Eight Ancient Poems" in the first line stood out clearly. Liu Yun seemed to have an idea, took a pencil and wrote down the Arabic number 8. Then he flipped through a few pages and his eyes fixed on the line: "Six Ancient Poems of the Music Administration"!

Liu Yun quickly wrote a plus sign after the character "8" and then wrote "6". He then turned to the next page, which read "Nine Poems of Mei Cheng".

The pencil continued writing "plus" and "9"! He continued to flip through the book and the pencil was writing the plus sign. When he reached the last two pages of the book, his eyes were fixed on it. This poem did not have characters such as "first poem" in the previous poems but there was simply printed: "Ancient poem written by an unknown person for Jiao Zhongqing's wife (with preface)"!

Liu Yun flipped through the last two pages and found that these were already the last ones. He then mentally calculated the number he had written down earlier and the pen came up with a number equal to "39"!

On second thoughts, his brow widened and he wrote a plus after the number 39, then pencilled in an arrow pointing directly to the last part: "Ancient poem written by an unknown person for Jiao Zhongqing's wife (with parallel preface)". In the margin above the poem, he emphatically wrote the number "0040"!

The code was hidden in the poem! Realising this, Liu Yun continued to pin down the poem by comparing the second code number, 0004, and counted to the fourth line. His eyes lit up: the first five characters of this line impressively read: *The Peacock Flies Southeast*!

Liu Yun's eyes stared at the five sets of ciphers: 0001, 0002, 0003, 0004 and 0005, after 0004. There was no more doubt about the fact that the test question was based on the four words. In fact, Number One gave the question and Number Two supervised it. After "The question is", the pencil wrote the standard answer against the five codes: "The Peacock Flies Southeast"!

The pencil wrote the answer: "Jiao Zhongqing" above the code after Candidate A! Next, the pencil wrote the answer: "Liu Lanzhi" above the code after Candidate B! Liu Yun let out a sigh of relief and put down his pencil. The text of the message had now been completely decoded.

I've been informed that the exam paper will be given by Number One and supervised by Number Two. The exam question is: The Peacock Flies Southeast; candidate A is Jiao Zhongqing; candidate B is Liu Lanzhi. Find out the answer to the exam question and confirm their identity based on the examinees' codes.

Liu Yun picked up the message, which he had deciphered himself, and compared it with the one received a short time ago:

> Pits of ash were not yet cold, disorder reigned east of the Xiao Mountains. As it turned out, Liu Bang and Xiang Yu could not read. Please refer to *New Songs from the Jade Terrace, Volume One* and report to Number Two in Peking.

He immediately understood that he could not send the deciphered message directly to Peking Number Two and that the deciphering work there could only be done by Zhang Yueyin himself. With this in mind, he picked up a rubber and erased all the words he had written in pencil on the telegram. Then he put the untranslated manuscript into his pocket and walked quickly to the radio room outside. Liu Yun went straight to the radio in the corner and said to the operator who had just received the report:

"Send two telegrams!"

The operator turned to look at Liu Yun. When he found that he had no telegram in his hand, he stared at him in confusion.

"Send the first one to the Central Urban Works Department. I'll dictate."

"Yes sir." The radio operator turned around and touched the transmit button.

"Instructions received, mission understood, please rest assured. Liu Yun," dictated Liu Yun.

"Repeat it," ordered Liu Yun in a low voice.

"Yes." The announcer replied. "Instructions received, mission understood, please rest assured. Liu Yun."

"Send the second copy to Peking Number Two."

"Understood." The operator was ready to send the message again.

"Send the original Central Committee message!" Liu Yun pulled out of his pocket the message from which he had erased the pencilled handwriting.

"Yes sir." This time, the operator hit the keys very fast.

In the radio room in the secret prison of the Military Bureau of Investigation and Statistics, the alarm clock in Wang Puchen's hand began to ring when he closed the heavy iron door and walked to the desk.

Placing the alarm clock on the desk, he took his customary glance – the alarm had stopped, with the short hand pointing at two, the long hand at twelve! Wang Puchen immediately turned on the transceiver, put on the headphones and picked up a pen. The code click was soon audible through the earphones. Wang Puchen made a quick record of it.

The message paper was quickly filled with a set of ciphers. Then Wang Puchen began to decipher the coded message. What was written in pencil was also the same five characters: The Peacock Flies Southeast!

Wang Puchen wrote swiftly. The mission: to investigate the corruption of the Peking Citizens' Food Distribution Committee... to prepare for currency reform... and to establish Fang Meng'ao's Aviation Brigade... for airlift operations!

Wang Puchen was still writing and translating:

Core members include Fang Meng'ao, codename Jiao Zhongqing, and Liang Jinglun, codename Liu Lanzhi!

Wang Puchen continued.

State Secrecy Bureau, Peking Station: Closely monitor all contacts with Jiao Zhongqing and Liu Lanzhi, and arrest them if they are found to be Communists!

After finishing the translation, Wang Puchen's pen paused for a moment before solemnly writing down the last two characters: Jianfeng.

Putting down the pen, Wang's face was now covered with beads of sweat. Then he turned on the transmitter button, expertly struck the keys and sent a telegram back to Nanking.

CHAPTER 13

In the north room of the quadrangle courtyard at No. 2, Mao'er Hutong, Yan Chunming sat alone in front of a kerosene lamp. Zhang Yueyin and Old Liu stood behind him, one on the right, the other on the left. The exact same copy of the message with text and numbers that Liu Yun saw was placed on the table.

Please be informed that the exam questions will be written by Number One and supervised by Number Two, and the question items will be 0040, 0004, 0001, 0002, 0003, 0004, 0005. Candidate A is 0040, 0002, 0011, 0012, 0013. Candidate B is 0040, 0002, 0014, 0040, 0086, 0001, 0002. Quickly identify the specific answers to the exam items and confirm the true identities based on the candidates' code numbers.

Yan Chunming was concentrating on the message, the pen in front of him hadn't moved and the piece of paper was still blank. Old Li already looked agitated. He looked at Zhang Yueyin who was calmly waiting for Yan Chunming.

Yan Chunming finally raised his hand. Zhang Yueyin and Old Liu's eyes lit up. Yan Chunming's hand, however, wasn't going for a pen. Instead he pulled out a handkerchief from his pocket to wipe the sweat from his face.

"This is not fortune telling!" said Old Liu, finally losing his patience. "Stop speculating! It won't be accurate to come up with it like that either. I'll go and find that book."

"I think I've figured it out." Yan Chunming didn't dare to look at Old Liu. Instead, he looked at Zhang Yueyin.

Old Liu stopped to look at Yan Chunming with suspicion still evident in his eyes.

Zhang Yueyin winked at Old Liu then whispered to Yan Chunming: "What's it all about? Could you write it down first so we can take a look?"

"I'm quite sure about those characters but it's the content that I don't understand," said Yan Chunming, still hesitant.

"Write it down and let's try it together."

Only then did Yan Chunming pick up his pen and nervously look at Old Liu. Old Liu seemed to sense that his subordinates were afraid of him, so he toned it down a bit.

"Go ahead, it doesn't matter if it's wrong, I'll go and find the book anyway."

Yan Chunming quickly wrote five characters on the paper:

The Peacock Flies Southeast!

Old Liu looked at Zhang Yueyin, whose eyes shone brightly, and nodded his head affirmatively but was not totally convinced.

"What are the other two questions?"

Yan Chunming wrote out the answers to two more questions: "Jiao Zhongqing and Liu Lanzhi!"

By then Zhang Yueyin was convinced that Yan Chunming had deciphered the exam title and the two coded question items, Question 1 and Question 2! But in order to put Old Liu at ease and for Yan Chunming not to feel pressurised, he intentionally asked: "Why these answers? Could you explain to us?"

"OK," answered Yan Chunming, somewhat like a university professor. He pointed at the numbers in the message and explained: "I thought the number '0040' referred to page forty, but when I thought about the content of page forty, I couldn't make sense of it! Later on, it dawned on me that there are forty poems of *New Songs from the Jade Terrace, Volume One*, and when I thought about the fortieth poem carefully, I got it: 0040 refers to the fortieth poem."

Old Liu looked at Zhang Yueyin again but this time Zhang Yueyin didn't nod.

"The title of the fortieth poem? Although many people used to call it *The Peacock Flies Southeast*, I remember it being printed on

New Songs from the Jade Terrace, Volume One as *An Ancient Poem Anonymously Written for Jiao Zhongqing's Wife.*"

"How knowledgeable Comrade Yueyin is!" Yan Chunming looked at Zhang Yueyin in astonishment and praised him heartily. In fact, he became more enthusiastic when he pointed his finger at the telegram. "I understood it from the next 0004 code and then from the following five codes: 0001, 0002, 0003, 0004 and 0005. The first line of the fortieth poem in *New Songs from the Jade Terrace, Volume One,* is the title of the poem, which is the same as the line *An Ancient Poem Anonymously Written for Jiao Zhongqing's Wife,* as just mentioned by Comrade Yueyin. The second and third lines are the preface to the poem, 0004 would be the fourth line and 0001 through 0005 would be the first to fifth words of the fourth line, the first line of the poem: *The Peacock Flies Southeast*!

"There's no mistaking it," said Zhang Yueyin. "The title of Exam Paper Number One is *The Peacock Flies Southeast*!"

"As for the answers to the next two questions..." Yan Chunming also saw that Zhang Yueyin had meant to ask him to explain in order to reassure Old Liu, and he was ready to do so.

"I believe you, no need to explain." Old Liu confirmed voluntarily to Yan Chunming this time. "It's Jiao Zhongqing and Liu Lanzhi!"

"Comrade Liu knows this poem too?"

"No, I don't."

A self-mocking smile flashed across Old Liu's face. What he said next was noteworthy. "I have seen the Peking Opera performed by Jiang Miaoxiang and Cheng Yanqiu, in which the male character is called Jiao Zhongqing and the female character is called Liu Lanzhi. It is anti-feudal. The poem is great and the play is fantastic opera."

Zhang Yueyin laughed cheerfully but with a hint of secrecy while looking at Yan Chunming and Old Liu.

Yan Chunming, however, did not dare to laugh yet and noticed that Old Liu's smile had faded and his attitude had turned serious again.

"Comrade Liu was right just now, the Communists are not fortune tellers." Zhang Yueyin looked at Old Liu. "I insisted on asking Comrade Yan Chunming to come and help because I was sure he would be able to crack the code. The year before last,

Comrade Chunming gave a series of lectures on 'Ancient Yue Fu Poetry' at Nankai University, and one of his lectures was on *New Songs from the Jade Terrace*. I sat in on one of his lectures and found that he had no textbooks with him, yet he could recite every single one of them."

Old Liu's eyes widened.

Yan Chunming appeared very excited all of a sudden. "Comrade Yueyin, did you attend my class at Nankai?"

"Half for work, half for study, but only as an auditor. Your class is very popular. There were people standing outside the window and one of them was me," said Zhang Yueyin, laughing.

Of course, the astute Old Liu fully understood that Zhang Yueyin was not only implementing Vice-Chairman Zhou's instruction to respect intellectuals but also trying to persuade him to follow the practice. The facts were being laid bare in front of him, so he accepted the facts and looked at Yan Chunming.

"Comrade Chunming, what I said about you in the library is null and void. After the victory of the War of Liberation, I will be the first to sit in on your class."

Yan Chunming was so amazed that he didn't know how to answer. But what happened next was even more flattering. Old Liu, whose attitude changed dramatically, turned to Zhang Yueyin.

"Comrade Yueyin, I suggest that Comrade Chunming rest here in the east wing room. He is indispensable to understanding the instructions of our superiors. What a great intellectual he is!"

"I agree."

"I concur with the organisation," said Yan Chunming gratefully.

"I'll walk you out." Old Liu went to open the door.

Zhang Yueyin looked respectfully as Yan Chunming and walked towards the door that Old Liu had opened for him. Turning his head, Zhang Yueyin whispered urgently to the next door.

"Xiao Wang!"

"Here I am!" Xiao Wang always appeared from the side door on cue, and this time he even took a folder and a pencil.

"Send a telegram back to the Urban Works Department of North China immediately. I'll dictate."

Xiao Wang was ready with the pen.

"Instructions received, mission understood. Will immediately implement it. Rest assured of its completion."

After he had finished taking notes, Xiao Wang handed the folder and pen to Zhang Yueyin who made sure that the record was correct. He then signed the telegram with which Xiao Wang returned to the next room. There was soon the faint sound of a transmitter clicking away. Zhang Yueyin's eyes went back to the message on the table that had been translated by Yan Chunming. His expression was as dignified as that in *New Songs from the Jade Terrace, Volume One*.

What was *The Peacock Flies Southeast*? Who was Jiao Zhongqing? Who was Liu Lanzhi? He had promised to complete the task, but how?

The kerosene lamp on the table was still lit and outside the window behind Zhang Yueyin the rising sun was lighting up the sky.

The shadows of houses, trees and people all looked like silhouettes before dawn during summertime in Peking. It was not as hazy as in the south at dawn. In the front courtyard of the Fang mansion, Fang Meng'ao led Shao Yuangang and Guo Jinyang into the courtyard with the gate wide open. The entire courtyard was empty, except for a man who was slowly sweeping the fallen leaves with a large bamboo broom.

It was Xie Peidong! Fang Meng'ao stood still. Shao Yuangang and Guo Jinyang were standing behind him. Fang Meng'ao was also standing there, his eyes closed. They could all see the pain in their captain's heart.

"You guys can stand guard here for now."

Fang Meng'ao said this softly and walked alone towards Xie Peidong who kept on sweeping the leaves in the courtyard.

"I'll be done here in a few minutes..."

"I've given you time and I've given you the opportunity." Fang Meng'ao walked over to the broom, his boots stepping on the fallen leaves.

"Then I'll stop sweeping." Xie Peidong leaned his broom against a tree and clapped his hands as if to dust off something. "The governor went out last night but I have all the accounts with me. I'll cooperate and represent the Peking branch."

With this, Xie Peidong took out his keys and walked towards the front door of the house. He unlocked the door and entered the living room. Only then did Fang Meng'ao's pair of military boots begin to move, heading towards the house. Walking into the living room on the ground floor, Fang Meng'ao stopped at the bottom of the straight staircase as if his boots were again nailed to the floor like cast iron.

The stairs were empty, there were no footsteps but the boots of a soldier climbing the stairs were faintly audible, echoing in the emptiness of the large living room, where the financial power of Peking resided.

Just after he opened the door of Fang Buting's office on the first floor, Xie Peidong heard the approaching sound of someone climbing the stairs. He turned around quickly, only to find that Fang Meng'ao was still standing at the bottom of the stairs. Xie Peidong realised that he was hearing voices. There were no more than twenty steps on the staircase but it seemed so far away now! In Fang Meng'ao's eyes, Xie Peidong seemed to be a speck on the distant horizon.

"Here are all the accounts." Xie Peidong's voice sounded as if it was coming out of an aircraft headset.

"On behalf of the Defence Ministry's investigation group, I need to investigate Fang Buting, governor of the Peking branch of the Central Bank." Fang Meng'ao closed his eyes for a moment to drive away the image of the sky that always haunted him.

"On behalf of the Peking branch of the Central Bank, I accept all investigations by the ministry's investigators."

"You can't represent the Peking branch." Fang Meng'ao looked at the only elder he respected in his family. His Adam's apple moved, as if he was swallowing the unspeakable pain.

"You don't need to represent the Peking branch either. Call and ask your governor to come back."

Xie Peidong looked at Fang Meng'ao with melancholy eyes for several seconds and then replied: "I don't know where the governor is now, either."

"He left the accounts to you but hid himself?"

"There's nothing to hide," replied Xie Peidong grudgingly. "Last night, he and his wife went to visit Deputy Director Cui's family with gifts."

Fang Meng'ao's chest felt as if it had been dealt a heavy blow, then the military boots moved. This time the stairs really thundered.

"Let's go and check the accounts!" Fang Meng'ao went upstairs.

Maybe he really was hiding from his eldest son or maybe not but Fang Buting did not head home after his visit to Cui Zhongshi's family the previous night. Instead, he told the driver to park the car outside the main gate of Yannan Garden in the middle of the night and slept in the car until dawn.

It was dawn but still quite dark inside the car. The driver was sleeping soundly, propped against the steering wheel. Cheng Xiaoyun, who was in one of the rear seats, stayed awake because she couldn't sleep with Fang Buting's head resting on her shoulder. Looking out of the window, she saw the gate of Yannan Garden a few dozen metres away being opened by the janitor. Only then did she gently turn her head.

"Governor, the gate is open now," said Cheng Xiaoyun, addressing him softly. Fang Buting was still sleeping like a child.

The driver woke up with a start. He sat up and didn't dare to turn around but instead looked in the rearview mirror to see Fang Buting leaning on his wife's shoulder. He was still asleep with his eyes closed. But the driver was too embarrassed to look in the mirror any more, so he turned to looked at the gate.

"Go and get some water." It was the voice of the governor.

"Of course," answered the driver. He opened the door, picked up a small iron bucket on the front seat and got out of the car.

From He Qicang's room on the first floor of the house came the rhythmical tapping of the keyboard of the English typewriter. As Liang Jinglun's skilful fingers tapped, the paper at the top of the typewriter was rising, lines of English words stacked on the paper, roughly to the following effect:

It is therefore imperative to issue a new currency to replace the old *fabi* currency that is no longer in circulation, although intervening in the issuance of currency by means of military control goes against the laws of economics!

At this point, he had finished typing *On the Feasibility of Immediate Abolition of the Old Currency and Implementing the New Currency System*, the thesis to be submitted to the Nanking authorities.

Liang Jinglun's eyes turned to He Qicang, who was sleeping on the couch, covered with a thin blanket. For countless nights, he had grown accustomed to falling asleep to the rhythmic tapping of his student's typewriter keys. Therefore, Liang Jinglun's hands could not stop and his fingers continued mechanically to tap the keys of the typewriter.

The typewriter spat out another page of blank spool paper on which the English appeared as a repetitive phrase that had nothing to do with the text...

Economic Laws, Economic Laws, Economic Laws... with those, He Qicang was then able to continue to sleep in peace and quiet. The lamp on the table was still on but it was getting brighter and brighter outside the window.

The driver returned with a bucket of water which turned out to be for Fang Buting and Cheng Xiaoyun to wash in the car. Fang Buting used a towel but Cheng Xiaoyun used a handkerchief and the two of them awkwardly washed their faces in the back seat of the car.

The driver in the front seat was in a bit of a bind today as there was only one toothbrush mug and one toothbrush. He turned sideways, held the mug steady with one hand, watched the governor and his wife wash their faces and handed the jar and toothbrush to them.

"Sir, would you like to brush your teeth first? I'll fetch more water for your wife once you've finished."

"That's not necessary." Fang Buting took the mug and toothbrush and handed them to Cheng Xiaoyun. "You go first, just leave me half a mug of water." That was what made Fang Buting so gentle and considerate. Cheng Xiaoyun took the mug and toothbrush, and began to brush her teeth extremely carefully over the small bucket below. She could not stretch her arms in the cramped space, which reminded her of how many times Fang Buting had washed in the car like this, and her eyes filled with tears.

He Xiaoyu woke up in her bedroom all by herself despite not having set the alarm clock the previous night. Looking at the clock on the table, she found that it was already five in the morning. She looked at Xie Mulan, who was still sleeping beside her, got out of bed very gently, got dressed and went to open the door. Meanwhile, she could hear the faint sound of typewriter keys being tapped from her father's room across the hallway. She stepped lightly out and pulled the door shut.

Xie Mulan, who had been pretending to be asleep, opened her eyes. She looked at the wall in front of her, only to find that the sound of the typewriter keystrokes she could hear a moment ago had stopped. Yet the keystrokes were still ringing in her heart, getting louder and louder. She imagined that He Xiaoyu was asleep in bed and she herself was the one who had got up, gone downstairs and cooked Professor Liang his favourite breakfast.

As usual, the dough had been prepared the night before and the pot containing the buns had been placed on the honeycomb coal stove in the living room on the ground floor. He Xiaoyu heard a soft knock on the door. Startled, she subconsciously glanced up at the first floor, then hurried to the door and asked softly: "Who is it?"

He Qicang opened his eyes while Liang Jinglun stopped typing. Both of them knew there were visitors downstairs. Liang Jinglun stood up and came over to help his professor get up off the couch.

"Are you done with typing the report?" asked He Qicang without mentioning the visitors downstairs.

"It's all done, sir. Take a look. If you need to have it delivered quickly to Minister of Finance Wang Yunwu, there is a flight to Nanking at ten in the morning."

"I'm afraid we won't be able to catch the ten o'clock flight," said He Qicang, who managed to stand up with the help of Liang Jinglun. He took a glance at the long paper trail of reports already stacked on the floor.

"Any idea who is visiting?"

"Is it Fang Meng'ao?"

"The Central Bank is most interested in this report. It must be Fang Buting." He Qicang shook his head.

"Do you want to meet him, sir? If you don't, I'll go and explain to him."

"Fang Buting is here on behalf of the Central Bank to find out what's going on. The Central Bank is supposed to print and issue banknotes. Without the green light from the Central Bank, any attempt by the treasury to introduce a new currency system is nothing more than a piece of paper. You haven't slept for two days and nights, go and get some sleep. By the way, tell Governor Fang to wait for me downstairs until I'm done with the proposal."

"OK." Liang Jinglun went back to the typewriter and pulled off the paper that was still attached to it. He then picked up the paper cutter on the table, ready to cut down one page at a time.

"Don't cut it," said He Qicang. "I'll just read it like this."

Liang Jinglun, still holding the paper cutter, stood at the edge of the table and said: "It concerns the livelihood of two million people in Peking and countless more in so many other cities. This proposal had better be submitted to Nanking in time on that flight before ten o'clock. If the Central Bank makes things difficult, we may want to ask the Treasury Department to make a copy for Ambassador Leighton Stuart."

"I know what to do. Go and eat something and get some rest."

"OK." Liang Jinglun had to put down the paper cutter. "If you need to make an urgent delivery, call me anytime, sir."

As he said so, Liang Jinglun helped He Qicang sit down at the table, then he picked up the paper report on the floor, rolled it up and placed it in front of He Qicang before walking out of the room.

Wearing He Xiaoyu's nightgown, Xie Mulan was already standing behind the closed door in He Xiaoyu's bedroom on the first floor. The door across from the room opened very softly but her heart thumped with a sudden jump. She pulled the door open. Across the corridor, Liang Jinglian had just closed the door and turned round. Unable to control herself, Xie Mulan looked straight into Liang Jinglun's eyes. Liang Jinglun was startled at first, then a rare smile crossed his lips. Xie Mulan was about to come out in her nightgown. But Liang Jinglun's glare forced her to stop, as his two fingers slowly pressed the corners of his eyes towards his forehead, which was a typical posture of a great scholar deep in thought! But make no mistake, Liang Jinglun was ordering her to go back to sleep, even though Xie Mulan was growing more passionate. However, Liang Jinglun's long gown had gone "far" towards the stairs, even though Xie Mulan was still standing there, quite eager to listen to whatever words he might possibly utter.

"Good morning, Governor Fang."

The greeting by Liang Jinglun scared her so much that she closed the door quickly. The people she was most reluctant and afraid to contact were now members of her family who had supported and cared for her for so many years. That included her father who loved her deeply, her uncle who doted on her and her younger cousin who had always taken care of her. Leaning against the door, Xie Mulan was in a panic and stood staring emptily into space.

Inside the governor's office on the first floor of the Fang mansion, Xie Peidong was busy taking out another stack of ledgers from a large metal cabinet against the wall when Fang Meng'ao popped the question: "Sir, isn't Mulan home either?"

He was quite taken aback so he turned his head. Fang Meng'ao was still standing by the large desk looking over the ledgers.

"He argued with me and moved out to Xiaoyu's two days ago." Xie Peidong walked towards his desk with his ledgers. "Times have changed, none of us make good fathers any more."

Fang Meng'ao raised his head and looked at Xie Peidong, the assistant manager of the Peking branch, as well as the only elderly person who made him feel connected to the family. Xie Peidong stood still without putting down the account books.

"Indeed, none of us will." Fang Meng'ao looked down at the ledger again. "The man worthy of being a father has died. You mentioned you went to visit Deputy Director Cui's children last night. Did Boqin and Pingyang ask about their father?"

Xie Peidong didn't answer. He just put down the ledger and got ready to move the other ones.

"What did you tell the children?" Fang Meng'ao's tone was a little harsh.

Xie Peidong replied: "I told them that Deputy Director Cui has gone to the US to help the government get more American aid."

"Shame on you!" With a loud bang, Fang Meng'ao slammed a ledger down on the table. Xie Peidong turned round sharply and looked at Fang Meng'ao.

"He signed his name on every account but you burned him to ashes!" Fang Meng'ao's fingers drummed on the books. "And continued to cheat the poor orphans and his widow. Don't you think you're way too shameless?"

"I can't answer that question but I can answer any question related to every account book left behind by Deputy Director Cui," replied Xie Peidong, while managing to swallow the acidic liquid welling up in his throat from his stomach.

The two focal points of light in Fang Meng'ao's eyes turned to the vast sky again and Xie Peidong, whom he was aiming at intently, disappeared. He was trying to concentrate on the enemy aircraft he was meant to shoot down but there wasn't one in sight – Xie Peidong didn't look like a potential target of attack at all.

Seeing Fang Meng'ao's expression, Xie Peidong felt a sense of urgency looming over him and couldn't help but glance at the phone on his desk.

"I don't mind if you can't," said Fang Meng'ao, "but call your governor and tell him to come back to answer the questions."

"Meng'ao," said Xie Peidong, no longer addressing him as Captain Fang. "No matter what, he is your father after all, not to mention that you've been kept in the dark about many things. In this regard, they really shouldn't make his son persecute his father."

"On behalf of the Defence Ministry's investigation group," said Fang Meng'ao, remaining unswayed, "I'm asking you to make a call and tell Governor Fang Buting to come back immediately to be investigated."

"Give me half an hour. Let me brief you on the general situation first so that you'll know what to ask him when the governor returns." Xie Peidong looked at the clock on the wall and then at Fang Meng'ao.

"OK, I'll give you half an hour." Fang Meng'ao was silent for a few seconds, looking down at the ledger on the table.

In the living room on the ground floor of the He residence, Cheng Xiaoyun was helping He Xiaoyu with breakfast at the open kitchen table when she noticed He Qicang standing at the stairway on the first floor.

"Hi, Xiaoyun, great to see you!"

"Good morning, Mr He!"

"Father."

"Uncle He!"

Both He Xiaoyu and Xie Mulan looked up at He Qicang and saw him standing there without his walking stick. He Xiaoyu turned on the tap to wash her hands, ready to help her father downstairs.

"I'm not coming down. But where is Governor Fang?"

There was no sign of Fang Buting or Liang Jinglun in the living room, so He Xiaoyu responded: "He thought you were busy reading the report, so Uncle Fang went to have a chat with Mr Liang in his room. Shall I go and ask him to come?"

"No. Go ahead and prepare breakfast. But ask him once you're done." He Qicang was silent for a while. With that, he turned and walked slowly back to his room.

Actually, Fang Buting was sitting in Liang Jinglun's small study, looking at the English tomes on the desk.

"May I take a look at them?"

"Sure, please, Governor Fang," remarked Liang Jinglun, standing beside him.

"A collection of the latest papers on economics published by Harvard?" Fang Buting took the hardcover book on the top.

"That's right."

"Technically, you and I are alumni, schoolmates per se." Fang Buting opened the book.

"Yes."

363

"Since the Boxer Indemnities, many students have gone to the US to study but there aren't many talented returnees. But Professor Liang is a rare talent." Fang Buting looked up at Liang Jinglun.

"Compared with my mentor and Governor Fang, I still have a lot to learn."

"Don't be too modest. Mulan has told me on many occasions that Professor Liang is much better at economics than me. Mulan and other students are lucky to be your students," noted Fang Buting with a chuckle.

Liang couldn't very well respond but managed to reply with an extremely measured smile. Whether it was because he didn't dare or didn't want to talk about the subject remained unknown.

Fang's instincts were so strong that in a round or two of conversation he found out about the man with whom he had always wanted to touch base. He looked again at the book in front of him. "We've overthrown the monarchy with thousands of years of history but it's hard to do away with backward feudal thinking. Especially our generation born during the reign of Emperor Guangxu, which migrated from the countryside to the city with our pigtails in tow when we were young. Later, I went abroad to study with my pigtail cut off and witnessed how developed their industries were. But after I came back, I still wanted to live in the old way. China had to develop its industry, grow its economy and move towards democracy. We can't accomplish that in our lifetime. We can only place our hope in those who come after us. You belong to a different generation and it'll be even better when it reaches the generation of Xiaoyu and Mulan, both of whom are progressive youths. Professor Liang, don't you think these girls are lovely?"

"Indeed, they are."

"On a personal note, Professor Liang, if you were all for free love, would you prefer Xiaoyu or Mulan?" Fang Buting threw the card out there aggressively.

Finally! Liang Jinglun had come to realise that he was dealing with a man with a bit of fight, the infamous Peking branch governor who had walked tall in the Peking-Tianjin region. He was left there, totally stunned.

"Am I being rude?" Fang Buting slowly raised his head again.

"I don't understand why Governor Fang would ask such a question." Liang Jinglun couldn't avoid his gaze any more.

"Because I'll talk about this issue with Chancellor He today. No matter how chaotic the times are, our children's marriage is still a major concern. It's not been for just a day or two that Mulan has adored you. I think it's high time for you, Mr Liang, to give her a definite answer. I'll also need to discuss this with Chancellor He. What do you think?"

When answering an elder's question, etiquette demands that one cannot look directly in the elder's eye. Just now, Liang Jinglun did what he had been taught since he was a child, making no attempt to make eye contact with Fang Buting. Faced with such a direct challenge, Liang Jinglun just dropped the etiquette. He looked into Fang Buting's eyes in a disturbed manner while revealing his own sharp eyes.

Fang Buting's eyes were not as sharp at the moment but feebly showed only a few signs of expectation. Liang Jinglun found himself engulfed in his gaze. The depth of Liang Jinglun's eyes was absorbed little by little by the illusory eyes of Fang Buting. Time seemed to freeze at this moment. Liang Jinglun didn't know how much longer he could hold on to this stare.

"Uncle! Professor Liang!" Xie Mulan called out from outside. "Uncle He is expecting you for breakfast!"

Liang Jinglun's eyes were finally able to turn to the door.

"The topic we discussed just now is quite personal in nature," said Fang Buting, standing up slowly. "However, there's another more important topic. Chancellor He is demonstrating the reform of the government's currency system. You should have a better understanding of Western economic theories and it's your duty to remind Chancellor He to analyse the feasibility of currency reform according to economic laws."

Liang Jinglun had to give a response. "With all due respect, Governor Fang, you and I talked about two topics early in the morning but I still don't understand which one of the two topics concerns me."

"Actually, they are one and the same topic, namely, that it's young people like you who can really save China. Now, we're expected for breakfast, let's go."

Seeing Liang Jinglun still standing there, Fang Buting walked out first without sticking to protocol. Liang Jinglun waited until he had reached the courtyard before walking out of the door.

———

Two young men in student uniforms, the two from the same group of young men who would escort Zeng Keda to meet Liang Jinglun on his bicycle, stood waiting patiently in the corridor outside Zeng Keda's room. From the path in the back garden, Adjutant Wang arrived with a glass-covered tray of food for breakfast. The two young men looked at him.

"Comrade Keda has just come back, too. Just wait." The adjutant went to tap on the door twice.

"Come in." It was the voice of Zeng Keda.

Zeng Keda had walked into the living room after taking a shower. He felt refreshed and excited as he fastened the buttons of his short-sleeved uniform. He was ready for action.

"General, please eat first." Wang placed the tray on the coffee table and lifted the glass cover.

On the tray were just a big bowl of porridge, a plate of Liu Biju's pickles and four large steamed buns.

"Are they here yet?" asked Zeng Keda.

"They're waiting outside. Please, have your breakfast first," replied Adjutant Wang, as he pulled out two thin volumes from a large pocket in his uniform and handed them to Zeng Keda.

"Here's the *Poetry Collection of the Crescent School* with a copy of *The Peacock Flies Southeast* attached to it."

Zeng Keda took the book, stared at the cover and flipped straight to the stapled, hand-copied *The Peacock Flies Southeast* at the end.

A line of charcaters with both short and long-form strokes looked the same in Zeng Keda's eyes.

"Jiao Zhongqing!" It was as if he heard the name being called again in the familiar Fenghua accent. He turned another page and again there were lines of characters with short and long-form strokes.

"Liu Lanzhi!" Once again, he thought he was hearing voices

because someone had called the name with a Fenghua accent. He then snapped the book shut and placed it on the table.

"Tell them to come in."

"Perhaps you should eat first."

"Call them in," insisted Zeng Koda.

"Yes sir." Adjutant Wang didn't dare to ask again and opened the door.

"Come in."

The two young student spies came in quietly. Dressed in their student uniforms, they saluted Zeng Keda.

"General!"

With a steamed bun in each hand, Zeng Keda handed them over to the two students. "Eat something first."

"Yes sir." The two young men brought their legs back to attention and took the steamed buns. Zeng Keda sat down and picked up a steamed bun too. As he chewed the bun, he began to drink the congee from the bowl.

"Eat."

"Yes." The two men started chewing their steamed buns.

"Where is Professor Liang now?" asked Zeng Keda as he ate.

The two men exchanged a look and decided that the one on the left would answer.

"We can report to the general that Professor Liang stayed at Vice-Chancellor He's house last night and is still there. Also, Fang Buting went to visit Vice-Chancellor He just before dawn. Now they are all at the vice-chancellor's house," replied the one on the left.

Zeng Keda stopped drinking from the bowl and stopped eating his bun as well. The two young student spies did not dare chew the remaining steamed buns in their hands and looked quietly at Zeng Keda.

"Finish what you're eating." Zeng Keda stood up and moved towards the door alone. The two students resumed chewing their steamed buns.

"Did Professor Liang say when he could come out?" asked Zeng Keda, turning back round again.

"General, as you instructed, we are not allowed to contact Professor Liang," replied the one on the right.

"Go back and tell the people there to keep monitoring the situation," said Zeng Keda with a wave of his hand.

"Yes." With steamed buns in their mouths, the two men turned around and walked out.

Zeng Keda went to the phone on the desk.

"The only alternative is to call him, right?"

"I suppose so," replied Wang vaguely.

The telephone in the governor's office on the first floor of the Fang residence was ringing so quietly that it looked as if it was also afraid of Fang Meng'ao standing in front of it.

"May I?" asked Xie Peidong, looking towards Fang Meng'ao.

"Of course." Fang Meng'ao was still auditing the books with his head hanging low.

Xie Peidong held the phone in one hand and pulled up the cord with the other, apparently wanting to walk away from Fang Meng'ao before answering it.

"Answer the phone right here." Fang Meng'ao still had his head down.

Xie Peidong had to stand where he was. Holding the telephone in his left hand, he picked up the receiver.

"Peking branch of the Central Bank, who's speaking, please?" Fang Meng'ao's eyes glanced at him.

"Sorry to bother you so early." Zhang Yueyin was immediately alerted by the voice at the other end of the line in a room in an unknown location. His eyes flickered and he replied in a low voice: "This is the Peking branch of the Bank of China and we'd like to consult the Central Bank about an account. May I speak to Governor Fang or Assistant Manager Xie? Is it convenient to speak now?"

"Yes."

The voice was low but, surprisingly, it was Fang Meng'ao who answered. Although both of them were at the same desk, one was standing at the east end and the other at the west. It was amazing that Fang Meng'ao could actually hear so clearly what was being said down the line, given that Fang Meng'ao was about two metres away from him.

"Yes, please," replied Xie Peidong reluctantly. The caller, however, did not answer immediately. Fang Meng'ao gazed at the receiver which Xie Peidong held it close to his ear.

"Please, speak."

Fang Meng'ao shifted his gaze to the account books again. Zhang Yueyin pressed the receiver close to his face, deliberating over the words and tried to convey the instructions accurately to Xie Peidong.

"Our board of directors was informed last night that Nanking is investigating a bad debt, a bad debt coded with an ancient poem. We must understand what kind of bad debt it is very soon and report it to the head office. Please ask Manager Xie to contact the person sent by Nanking immediately and ask him if he knows how Nanking is handling this bad debt and who is handling it. I would also like to ask you to explain to him clearly and thoroughly the circumstances surrounding his personal previous accounts, without any further concealment. Make sure that he believes that we acknowledge all his debts. Let him understand that the debt has to be paid, all the debts have to be paid, and that it is time to settle the general account with those people. Assistant Manager Xie, I wonder if I've communicated the board's views accurately."

"Very accurately," replied Xie Peidong.

Fang Meng'ao stopped examining the ledger and sat in that office chair of Fang Buting's, looking back at Xie Peidong who continued to speak clearly into the phone.

"The man from Nanking is right next to me and there are only two of us in the office and the whole house. I know what to tell him and I would like to know if there is anything else that I should ask him."

"Very well. Convince him to trust you and to trust us." Zhang Yucyin looked even more solemn. "And ask him to tell us in detail the latest mission entrusted to him by Nanking. We must report to the head office this morning."

Fang Meng'ao watched as Xie Peidong put down the phone and moved to the south-facing balcony. He watched Xie Peidong stand on the balcony for a full minute. When he turned and came back towards the desk, Fang Meng'ao found that the pair of eyes looking at him were both familiar and unfamiliar at the same time.

Xie Peidong walked to the desk and continued looking at Fang Meng'ao like that. Fang Meng'ao slowly stood up.

"Captain Fang, the accounts you want to audit are not available in this office. I will take you to the place where all the account books are located. And I will explain everything to you clearly."

"Where are we going, then?"

"The bamboo grove in the courtyard."

Fang Meng'ao's gaze was abruptly directed towards the balcony where Xie Peidong had just been standing, only to find that the sun was shining fiercely and stingingly up in the sky.

"Good, let's go!"

He Qicang was absent from the dining table in the living room on the ground floor of the He household. Except for a steamed bun on a small plate in front of Fang Buting, who was sitting at the top of the table, there was also a glass of half-drunk milk. The plates in front of Cheng Xiaoyun, He Xiaoyu, Xie Mulan and Liang Jinglun were all empty, as they had all eaten the last bits of their steamed buns.

No one spoke and everyone was avoiding eye contact.

"Uncle Fang, you haven't eaten your steamed bun yet," said He Xiaoyu, eliciting a smile from Fang Buting.

"Eat up. Chancellor He is still waiting for you upstairs," continued Cheng Xiaoyun.

"Professor Liang is one of our country's rare talents but if he can't even get a full meal, we aren't doing our job well. Mulan, give my bun to Professor Liang." Fang Buting smiled at Liang Jinglun.

Without thinking, Xie Mulan took the steamed bun in front of Fang Buting. But as she was about to place the plate in front of Liang Jinglun, she froze with shock.

Liang Jinglun's eyes were gazing straight ahead into the void. While everyone was looking at the plate in Xie Mulan's hands, she dared not hand it to Liang Jinglun, nor could she put it back in front of Fang Buting. Cheng Xiaoyun eyed He Xiaoyu with a view to taking the plate from Xie Mulan.

"Professor Liang, perhaps you should take it first, whether you eat or not." She then put the plate in front of Liang Jinglun.

"Oh." Only then did Liang Jinglun focus his gaze on what was in front of him. "Sorry, I got distracted and was thinking about a problem. What did Governor Fang just say?"

Again, Fang Buting smiled back in return, picked up the glass of milk in front of him and drank it slowly. He put down the glass, put the napkin on his lap back on the table and slowly stood up.

"Please clean up the table, I should go upstairs."

Everyone at the table watched as Fang Buting moved towards the stairs when the telephone rang on the coffee table near the sofa. But Fang Buting's steps were not affected by the phone ringing. He continued to ascend the stairs.

Just as He Xiaoyu was about to answer the phone. Liang Jinglun stood up.

"I'll go and answer it."

Only then did Xie Mulan manage to raise her head, realising that Liang Jinglun hadn't been looking at He Xiaoyu when he said this. Her eyes lit up but she quickly turned back to look at the table.

"Aunt Cheng, Mulan, let's go to the courtyard and get some fresh air," He Xiaoyu said to her guests as Liang Jinglun went to answer the phone. Cheng Xiaoyun also got to her feet.

"Again, it's about the feasibility of that report of ours." In the living room of his apartment, Zeng Keda tried his best to sound decisive and calm on the phone. "Last night at midnight, our chancellor decided on a new theme and defined specific requirements. I can't tell you more over the phone but it's urgent that you come and read the report in person. To be precise, I will send a student to pick you up."

"Perhaps you'll have to wait till after ten o'clock because Chancellor He has an important proposal to be delivered by air to Nanking. This project is very important and I have to make sure it gets picked up at nine." Liang Jinglun also tried to speak in a calm tone.

"OK. Please make sure you're there by eleven o'clock!" Zeng Keda looked at his watch.

The caller had already hung up the phone, as Liang Jinglun looked up to the first floor. Suddenly, he saw an object swinging out of the corner of his eye. Liang Jinglun turned to look at it.

It was the pendulum of the clock, which had been rendered silent, that was swinging. It was eight o'clock in the morning! He stood up, headed for the stairs, walked a few steps, and then stopped there, looking at the first-floor hallway and then back out of the window.

Outside the big glass window, in the courtyard, He Xiaoyu accompanied the others, including Cheng Xiaoyun, and slowly walked by. Xie Mulan followed them awkwardly. Liang Jinglun closed his eyes. What a dilemma!

The bamboo grove in the courtyard of the Fang residence was the place where the bamboo grove was at its thickest. To be exact, it happened to be where the courtyard gate could be seen with a sideways glance. Not long ago, Xie Peidong had sat on the stone bench in front of them where he assigned He Xiaoyu the task of contacting Fang Meng'ao.

"It's such a long and complicated story, I hardly know where to start." Xie Peidong came to a stone bench on the path in the bamboo grove and stopped.

Fang Meng'ao kept a distance of about two metres behind him. He also stopped. Xie's remarks made his brow furrow and his eyes sharp again. Last night, Zeng Keda told him about many of the stories in the *Twenty-Four Histories*, some of which he could accept, but most of which he resented.

"You didn't bring me here to talk about history, did you?"

"Who else told you about history?" said Xie Peidong turning abruptly.

Fang Meng'ao was so sharp that he could extract more from any given message than anyone else. Moreover, the tone and demeanour of his uncle, Cui Zhongshi's immediate supervisor at the Peking branch, was so obvious and so abnormal that he didn't resemble the person under investigation at all. He foresaw that the mystery that had confused him for years and caused him to suffer day and night, was being solved.

"I am auditing the accounts of the Peking branch on behalf of the Ministry of Defence Investigation Group." Fang Meng'ao knew that he had to keep calm, especially at that moment. "I'm not here to be lectured on the *Twenty-Four Histories*."

"Everything has its cause and effect, and a history."

"OK. Please sit down. I'm all ears."

Several seconds passed, then Xie Peidong sat down and looked at Fang Meng'ao, who was standing tall and strong in front of him like a mountain. At the same time, he felt that the interwoven bamboo groves behind him were like scenes of past events reappearing in his mind.

"What do you most want to know about now?" Xie Peidong looked Fang Meng'ao in the eye again.

"The accounts of both the Peking branch and the Peking Citizens' Food Distribution Committee. And Cui Zhongshi's death as well."

Xie Peidong shook his head gently. "No, these two issues are not what you're most keen to know about."

Fang Meng'ao stared at him intensely.

"What you're most keen to know is whether Cui Zhongshi was a Communist or not."

Fang Meng'ao was silent for a few moments.

"Go on."

"The most important thing to know is whether you yourself are a member of the Communist Party!"

"Please stand up," said Fang Meng'ao.

Xie Peidong did not stand up but looked up at him.

"Stand up!" Fang Meng'ao's tone was low and harsh.

Xie Peidong had to stand up slowly.

"Stand over here next to me."

Xie Peidong had to stand back on the stone path while Fang Meng'ao walked over and sat where Xie Peidong had been sitting. The host and guest changed positions, with Fang Meng'ao sitting, asking the questions, while Xie Peidong stood being questioned.

"Go on."

"OK." There was no change in Xie Peidong's demeanour

whether he stood or sat. He had become accustomed to this kind of conversation when confronted by Fang Buting for more than ten years.

"I am telling you clearly that Cui Zhongshi was a member of the CPC."

"Go on."

"Fang Meng'ao is also a member of the CPC."

What followed was, of course, silence; silence as a result of Fang Meng'ao's forceful stare.

"Why the silence? Go on." Obviously, he was the one who had initiated the silence but Fang Meng'ao persisted with the question.

Xie Peidong raised his eyes to the top of the bamboo groves and spoke slowly. "Cui Zhongshi was a member of the CPC. I recruited him in Shanghai in 1938."

Fang Meng'ao slowly stood up and looked directly at Xie Peidong. Still avoiding his gaze, Xie Peidong continued: "I joined the CPC in 1927 when the Great Revolution failed."

In Fang Meng'ao's eyes, Xie Peidong's voice was like a bamboo whistle blowing against the wind over the tops of the bamboo trees.

"Also, your aunt joined the CPC that same year."

Back in the living room of the He residence, Xie Mulan seemed distraught. Only Cheng Xiaoyun was watching her silently on the sofa. She tried to hide it, pretending to be relaxed as she paced back and forth in the living room, looking up at the hallway upstairs. She deliberately stepped on the stairs, and pretended to go up the stairs very slowly and gently.

"Don't interfere with your uncle and Chancellor He," said Cheng Xiaoyun softly from behind her.

Xie Mulan stood still, turned to Cheng Xiaoyun with an unnatural smile and walked gently down the stairs. She then trod softly to the window by the front door. She was very still, her eyes glassy. Liang Jinglun's small house outside was the place her heart yearned for!

"Professor Liang and Xiaoyu are also talking about business. Why don't you sit down and talk with me?"

"OK." Xie Mulan, still concealing her yearning, walked back over to the couch and sat down on the single sofa.

"Auntie Cheng, go ahead."

Cheng Xiaoyun looked at her and was deliberating how to speak to her but Xie Mulan's eyes were already looking out of the window to the courtyard.

"Secure the perimeter and don't allow anyone to enter the bamboo groves," ordered Fang Meng'ao, addressing Shao Yuangang and Guo Jinyang who were listening attentively at the juncture of the stone path in the bamboo groves and the courtyard.

"Understood." Fang Meng'ao turned around and strode along the stone path towards the depths of the groves.

After walking past the location where the conversation had taken place, he made another small turn and saw Xie Peidong standing about five metres away from the stone path. He went in. Xie Peidong handed him a bamboo knife.

"It's usually used for repairing bamboo branches. Take it and help me."

Fang Meng'ao took the knife from him while continuing to look at him. Xie Peidong raised his hand to touch a thick length of bamboo eight or nine metres tall beside him. He wanted to feel a bamboo joint on it, then he said: "It's only been two years and it's growing so fast that I can't reach it. Meng'ao, do you see the mark on it?"

When Fang Meng'ao looked up, he saw that there was a long scar on the bamboo joint that had healed but was still visible.

"You're tall. Help me cut down the bamboo knot below the scar."

Fang Meng'ao no longer hesitated, made one cut, two cuts, and then reached out his hand to pull at it. The top half of the bamboo with its luxuriant leaves broke off with a crashing sound but it was still attached to several nearby bamboos.

Xie Peidong went to tug on the bamboo pole but it wouldn't budge. "Let me do it." With just one hand, Fang Meng'ao dragged down the bamboo pole that was resting on the other bamboos. He then spread it on the ground. Xie Peidong squatted down and tightened his fingers, reaching into the severed empty bamboo tube, obviously trying to grip onto something. Fang Meng'ao tried his best to look calmly at Xie's hand, which seemed to be pulling something out and slowly withdrawing it. A long oil-cloth bundle, tightly bound, was pulled out.

Xie Peidong struggled to untie the wire tied around a long tarpaulin wrap but the wire wouldn't budge. Xie Peidong looked up at Fang Meng'ao, who squatted down, pinched the knot of wire with his two fingers, and quickly took the wire off in an anti-clockwise direction. Then the other wire on the upper side was untied in the same way. Xie Peidong reached over with both hands and slowly unfolded the wrapping, in which was a large brown paper envelope still slightly rolled up.

Xie Peidong and Fang Meng'ao looked at each other as they crouched there in a squatting position.

"Have you secured the area?"

"Yes, absolutely."

Only then did Xie Peidong open the seal on the bag and pull out a thin magazine. He looked at it for a moment, then settled down and handed it to Fang Meng'ao.

"It's all in here, you can read it."

Fang Meng'ao took the magazine with both hands and looked at Xie Peidong first before flipping through the pages. There was something in the middle and he went to that page. Fang Meng'ao was stunned.

It was a picture. The man in the middle was often seen in the newspapers; it was Zhou Enlai! The man on the right, who looked younger and more radiant than he did now, was his uncle who was now squatting in front of him! The person on the left made Fang Meng'ao's eyes wet. He whispered.

"Is this my aunt?"

Xie Peidong's eyes also teared up and he nodded his head.

Fang Meng'ao wiped his left eye with his palm, then his right eye with his finger.

"After Auntie died, did you bring Mulan to my father?" he asked in a soft voice.

Xie Peidong blinked his eyes. His tears had dried up, so he did not reply. He tried to stand up. Fang Meng'ao stretched out his hand to help him up.

"I remember you saying that my aunt died of an illness while on the run, which is not true, but your superiors sent you to work for my father, right?"

Xie Peidong shook his head.

"Not at that time. Most of our underground committee members were killed and the rest were scattered. I lost contact with the organisation, so I brought Mulan to stay with your family. A year later, the organisation sent someone to convey the instructions of the higher-ups, which stipulated that I work for your father to gather information internally on the economic policy of the Kuomintang."

"Does my father know your identity?" A kind of wishful thinking suddenly sprang up in Meng'ao's heart.

Xie Peidong's response disappointed him as he slowly shook his head.

"My dad is so cunning, yet he failed to identify you as an undercover agent for a decade?" Fang Meng'ao was still reluctant to acknowledge the fact.

Xie Peidong, of course, understood his feelings at that moment and replied: "The people at the Central Bank are economics experts, they're different from those involved in politics in other departments within the Kuomintang. No one, including your father, wanted to get too involved in the Kuomintang's party politics but economics and politics have always been inseparable. Fortunately, during the eight years of the War of Resistance Against Japanese Aggression and the cooperation between the Kuomintang and the Communist Party, my job was to work more with your father to raise funds for the war. It was only when the Kuomintang started the civil war that Comrade Cui Zhongshi and I really began to work in secret, gathering information about their politics and military through their economic policies. During that period, Comrade Cui Zhongshi did most of the work. He was fighting on the front and I was covering his back. Alas, in the end, suspicion fell on him alone."

"Uncle Cui was instructed by you to come to the flight school to recruit me, wasn't he?"

"Yes."

"To take advantage of Mengwei's feelings for me, you two

colluded and asked Mengwei to tell Uncle Cui to visit me at the flight school every time, didn't you?"

"Yes."

"I understand, so my father wouldn't suspect you."

"That's right."

"In order to keep you from being exposed, or let me put it this way, to keep the organisation from being exposed, you ended up deciding to sacrifice Uncle Cui again!" Fang Meng'ao's tone suddenly became harsh.

Xie Peidong shook his head gently. "No."

Fang Meng'ao was no longer looking at Xie Peidong but only at the ground, at the severed bamboo stick. "But you watched Uncle Cui die! From the moment he was arrested until he was murdered. You and my father knew about it and you both went to the police station. As soon as you left, Uncle Cui was murdered. I want to know the truth. Is it that you couldn't save him, or that you had made a decision to let him die?"

"Neither."

Fang Meng'ao raised his head again and looked at Xie Peidong.

"The organisation made a detailed rescue plan, the most important part of which was to persuade your father, through me, to come forward to save Cui Zhongshi. You were at home that day, so you should understand that your father went to the police station because, in all honesty, he wanted to save Cui Zhongshi for the sake of your and Mengwei's feelings. Trust me, he wanted to save Cui Zhongshi. Your father negotiated with Xu Tieying with the money and the leverage he had against Xu Tieying. The result was Xu promised your father that he would not kill Comrade Cui Zhongshi for the time being. But Comrade Zhongshi was killed by them anyway. You should know better than I do what the problem is because you've been pursuing it for the last few days. This is also what the organisation wants to know."

Fang Meng'ao closed his eyes. The breeze was picking up again, rustling through the bamboo leaves. The sky did not appear in his eyes but he could faintly make out the sound of the piano playing, coming from Fang's house.

It was Bach/Gounod's *Ave Maria*. It was the prelude in C major that seemed to flow like a spring breeze at dawn. It was his father who had come back from the police bureau that day, exhausted and reluctantly playing the piece.

His eyes snapped open, with only the rustle of the bamboo leaves over his head.

"Where is he now?" asked Fang Meng'ao.

"At Vice-Chancellor He's house."

"Let's be clear," said He Qicang, now sitting in the reclining chair in his bedroom on the first floor of his residence, looking at Fang Buting, who was sitting in front of the desk with the typewriter.

"Does the Central Bank want my proposal to favour the abolition of the old *fabi* currency and the introduction of gold bullion, or to argue that the monetary reform cannot be implemented?"

"The Central Bank is not ours, and we don't have anyone who can influence Central Bank policy." Fang Buting laughed bitterly. "Brother Qicang, you and I both studied finance and economics, not Wang Yunwu, who was known for running his Commercial Press. And you know as I do, the entire government is already running a deficit of forty trillion dollars. Without reserves and supplies, how can printing new paper money save an already collapsed economy?"

"Up to now, what is there to talk about whether one knows the economy or not? More than ninety per cent of the economy is primitive subsistence farming and less than ten per cent of the urban economy is in the hands of a small number of bureaucratic capitalists. With such a large government, such a large army and a civil war to fight, who among those bureaucratic capitalists are willing to pay a penny to support them? Without money, they tried to print money and the currency has depreciated by four hundred and seventy thousand times. Neither of us studied this kind of economic situation in the US. What kind of currency reform plan do you think I am willing to write? You are in charge of finance in the Peking-Tianjin region, I'm sure you know that even college professors earning hundreds of thousands of dollars a month are starving every day, not to mention the common citizens? Yesterday, I consulted the Social Welfare Bureau, they told me that more than six hundred people are starving to death every day in Peking. I'm an economic adviser to the Nationalist government which is why I had to write all that crap."

"This is exactly why I came to meet with you." Fang Buting stood up. "The so-called currency reform, to be frank, is military control of the economy and no one can stop it. But Nanking's top concern is Shanghai. Brother Qicang, can you help us to get more American aid and supplies for Peking and Tianjin? After all, most of the country's cultural elites are in Peking, and Peking has become the worst victim of the student riots. As you know, the Fifth of July Incident has brought Nanking down a peg. The new faction will crack down on the old one but when it doesn't work, they use my son to attack me. What would that add up to? I am nothing but a manager of a first-class branch. It would be more chaotic if I step down and someone comes to replace me at the Peking branch. It is the people of Peking and Tianjin who are suffering the losses, including the high-profile intellectuals and students."

He Qicang was silent, then he propped up a chair to stand up. Fang Buting came over to help him.

"There is a flight to Nanking at ten this morning. I planned to send this proposal to the Ministry of Finance today but I've changed my mind. Why don't you just stay with me for a day and help me revise the proposal?"

Fang Buting was no longer the proud governor of the Peking branch. Like an old brother, he patted He Qicang on the arm, his eyes wet with tears. He Qicang was also emotional.

"I've met Meng'ao several times and even had a lengthy conversation with him once. He fell into misfortune as a child and the stories of his near misses in many battles are even more amazing. I know it's difficult for you to be his father. I'll try to straighten him out when I have a chance."

"Let's not talk about him today, let's focus on your proposal." Fang Buting clasped He Qicang's arm tightly.

"Good, good," said He Qicang, raising his voice and calling out: "Xiaoyu! Xiaoyu!"

"Governor, is the chancellor calling Xiaoyu?" It was Cheng Xiaoyun's voice coming from downstairs.

"Yes. Tell Xiaoyu to come upstairs." Fang Buting went to open the door.

"Then don't call Xiaoyu." He Qicang looked at Fang Buting at the door. "Call Liang Jinglun to come up here and I'll tell him not to have the proposal delivered today."

Fang Buting nodded and called out. "No, not Xiaoyu. Please ask Professor Liang to come up!"

"Auntie, I'll go and get him!" This time it was Xie Mulan's voice.

When Fang Buting turned back, He Qicang's eyes met his.

The two old men simultaneously avoided each other's glances.

In the minds of both of them, the issue of their children's love life was best summarised in a quote from a poem by Mao dedicated to his former wife Yang Kaihui: "Does heaven know man's weal and woe?"

CHAPTER 14

Walking into the Foreign Languages Bookstore outside the east gate of Yenching University, Liang Jinglun noticed that among the few students reading books in front of the shelves, two from the Chiang Kai-Shek Student Society were secretly eyeing him.

"Morning!" said Liang Jinglun in English, walking towards Miss Sophia in front of the bookcases.

"Morning !" replied Miss Sophia, also in English, always happy to see Liang Jinglun. "Professor Zeng from Tsinghua is expecting you," she said, switched to her fluent Chinese. "He said he had an appointment with you and is waiting for you upstairs."

"Thank you!" Liang Jinglun smiled and nodded, heading inside.

The two Chiang Kai-Shek Student Society members continued to pretend to read their books, although their eyes were secretly scanning the other students who were reading. Those students were indeed reading with their heads down. Peking University students who did not participate in the student movement were very rare.

In the room reserved for Liang Jinglun's use on the first floor of the Foreign Languages Bookstore, Zeng Keda was feeling particularly uneasy for he was accustomed to the uniform of the Youth Army and the change into civilian clothes made him uncomfortable. He sat there, having already removed his hat and glasses, and put them on the table.

"Sorry to have kept you waiting, Professor Zeng." Liang Jinglun closed the door behind him gently.

"Professor Liang, thanks for coming. Please sit down."

Zeng Keda stood up in front of the table with a rare smile, still looking concerned. They sat down across the table facing each other.

"Here are the operational instructions Comrade Jianfeng sent last night."

Zeng Keda handed over the telegram which Liang Jinglun took with both hands. He read it quickly. The key words were all so striking: "The Peacock Flies Southeast!"

"Comrade Fang Meng'ao, code name Jiao Zhongqing! Comrade Liang Jinglun, code name Liu Lanzhi!"

Liang Jinglun looked up enquiringly at Zeng Keda.

"It was the organisation's decision," said Xie Peidong in the bamboo grove in the courtyard of the Fang residence. He was trying his best to explain to Fang Meng'ao in the most concise language possible.

"You've not been given any assignments, nor will you be given a deeper understanding of what Communism is, for only one reason – which is, they don't suspect you."

"Then how did you know I would agree to join up?"

"Because you love China."

"Isn't there anyone else in the Kuomintang who loves China?"

"Yes, but they are more interested in working for personal gain. You know, the Kuomintang can't save China."

"So you sent a frugal and loyal man like Uncle Cui to recruit me?"

"All members of the Communist Party live frugally."

After saying this, Xie Peidong looked at the sky in the gap between the bamboo canes. A short while later, he added: "You're not wrong in saying that he was loyal and generous. But it is more accurate perhaps, to say that in our party, Comrade Zhongshi belonged to the category of honest and noble people that Chairman Mao refers to with high praise."

"What did my father say during his visit to Uncle Cui's last night?" asked Fang Meng'ao, his eyes looking at the chequered shadows of the sunlight on the ground.

"He said the same thing as you did, faithful and honest not only last night, but also on that same day when he heard about his death. He said he was sorry on separate occasions."

"Sorry that he was a Communist?"

"It doesn't matter what your father's regret was. Do you want to know about Uncle Cui's regrets?" Xie Peidong's eyes narrowed.

At this point, Xie Peidong slowly opened the rolled-up photo in his hand to reveal the image of Zhou Enlai in the middle. Fang Meng'ao seemed to understand something and looked at Xie Peidong closely.

"He never met Vice-Chairman Zhou, and the only people who have met him are your aunt and me."

Pulling out a box of matches from his pocket and handing it to Fang Meng'ao, he said: "Light it and dedicate it to Uncle Cui."

Fang Meng'ao did not pick up the match. He was now deep into the bamboo grove. Xie Peidong had to strike a match himself to illuminate the photo. At that moment, another gust of wind blew through the spiky bamboo branches.

Yet, the image conjured up in Fang Meng'ao's mind's eye was of his jeep speeding by that night while the voice of Cui Zhongshi floated in the wind: "If I were to lie to you, it would be necessary, because I was never a member of the underground CPC in the first place. Therefore, you were never a member of the CPC underground, either."

The photo in Xie Peidong's hand was almost burnt out, its embers, white as a sheet, suspended by a gust of wind, rose straight up into the sky, floating over the top of the bamboo.

"I knew then why Uncle Cui said he wasn't a Communist..." Fang Meng'ao watched the rising plume of white ashes disappear over the bamboo grove.

"He knew after his death you'd demand an explanation from those people. By totally disassociating yourself from the CPC organisation, what was left in your heart was a purely personal relationship with him, and that made you behave more like yourself by being unforgiving to those people. Comrade Zhongshi was protecting you dutifully from the moment he recruited you until the day he died."

Only then did Fang Meng'ao slowly turn to Xie Peidong again.

"If Uncle Cui was so willing to give his life to protect me, why did the organisation send Xiaoyu to meet with me. She's just a girl who doesn't know anything, does she? Why are the Peking Students' Union and Urban Works Department behind her? Who is she? And who is Liang Jinglun anyway?"

"Clearly, my understanding of how Comrade Jianfeng uses talented people is too shallow," said Zeng Keda in Liang Jinglun's room on the first floor of the Foreign Languages Bookstore, while placing his hands on the table and looking into Liang Jinglun's eyes more transparently and more sincerely than before.

"He chose to be as sincere as possible, much like Duke Zeng Guofan. Only in this way could he compete with the CPC in the struggle to win the hearts and minds of the people. Last night I conveyed Comrade Jianfeng's message to Fang Meng'ao, which was well received. So it doesn't matter whether Fang Meng'ao was once a Communist or not, he is 'Jiao Zhongqing' now!"

"What is the relationship between 'Liu Lanzhi' and 'Jiao Zhongqing'? How do they work together? I would like to hear more instructions from Comrade Jianfeng."

"Of course, Comrade Jianfeng has clear instructions. When we spoke last night, Comrade Jianfeng told me to convey his assessment of you first. Do you want to hear it?"

Liang Jinglun stood up.

"Sit down, we are all comrades, we'll just keep that respect in our hearts." Zeng Keda seemed to have mastered Comrade Jianfeng's knack of doing ideological work.

"Please sit."

Liang Jinglun sat down again, in anticipation of Comrade Jianfeng's comments about him.

"It is important to fully understand the enormity and importance of Comrade Liang Jinglun's work. His contribution to 'One Revolution, Fighting on Two Fronts' is irreplaceable. My evaluation of him can best be expressed in eight characters: 'Great talent, extremely good and utter sincerity.'"

Liang Jinglun stood up again. The first time he stood up was out of military discipline but this time he was truly moved. Trapped for a long time between being a member of Comrade Jianfeng's secret organisation and an underground member of the CPC's Peking Student Committee, his faith and ideals were already misty and the biggest obstacle was that both sides were ultimately suspicious of him, the end result being that no one trusted him. Now hearing these eight characters, Liang Jinglun was truly moved. While most people were aware that he specialised in economics, Comrade Jianfeng also knew that he was well versed in ancient texts and understood the origin of these eight characters. Looking at Zeng Keda, who served as the communicator and perhaps barrier between himself and Comrade Jianfeng, he wondered aloud whether he could understand Comrade Jianfeng's evaluation.

Before his eyes, Zeng Keda was the one who arrived in Peking on 6 July. "Comrade Jianfeng asked me to convey his evaluation of you, to the effect that if the party-state had a hundred talents like Comrade Liang Jinglun, there would be hope for success in crushing the Communist insurgents and saving the state."

Before his eyes, Zeng Keda came to himself and said: "To explain this eight-character evaluation, I consulted Comrade Jianfeng. He said: 'You are not only an excellent economist but you are also proficient in Chinese language, well versed in classical Chinese and would understand the origin of these eight characters. The first four characters are Zeng Guofan's comments when recommending Li Hongzhang to the Imperial Court and the last four characters are Zhu Xi's highest evaluation of the Confucian notion of cultivation of character. Comrade Jinglun, please sit down."

To his great surprise, Liang Jinglun found that Zeng Keda was no longer as he was more than a month ago. Comrade Jianfeng's cultivation of his subordinates was worthy of catching up with Duke Zeng Wenzheng! When he looked at Zeng Keda again, there was more affection in his eyes and also more trust in him. He did not sit down.

"I'd like to ask Comrade Keda to report to Comrade Jianfeng that I'm very grateful for his trust but that since this mission is code-named *The Peacock Flies Southeast*, it will, of course, end with Liu Lanzhi 'throwing herself into the cold and chilly pond' and Jiao Zhongqing 'hanging himself on the courtyard tree facing the southeast'. As long as it is useful for the cause of crushing the Communist insurgents and saving the state, I'm willing to die afterwards."

Seeing Liang Jinglun still standing, Zeng Koda stood up himself and, with a wave of his hand, replied firmly with the phrase: "On the contrary." He then began to pace up and down, deliberating over the following words.

In order to assign special tasks to these two characters with special status, poor Zeng Keda had stayed up the previous night to make up for his lack of knowledge of Wen Yiduo's *The Song of the Sun*, which seemed to have moved Fang Meng'ao and indeed moved himself. Early that morning, he had ordered someone to get a copy of *A Poetry Collection of the Crescent School* and of a poem called *The Peacock Flies Southeast*. On his way to see Liang Jinglun, he had put aside the poetry book but had tried to memorise *The Peacock Flies Southeast* and had acquired some understanding of the poem's main theme. Now that he saw Liang Jinglun was so deeply moved, he further understood the greatness of Comrade Jianfeng's spiritual power and could not help but feel impassioned.

"Comrade Jianfeng uses this poem as the code of operation because he's determined not to repeat the tragedy of history. Appointed in a time of crisis, the president was going to battle the Communists on the front lines across the country and entrusted Comrade Jianfeng with the important task of reorganising the economy at the rear. *The Peacock Flies Southeast* is a key move in a major two-front war. By starting with the fight against corruption and cleaning up the economic sector in the Peking-Tianjin municipalities, we hope to deter the corrupt upper echelons in Shanghai and Nanking, and clear the way for monetary reform in Shanghai and five other major cities. This time, it is not us who will have to throw ourselves into the 'cool and chilly pond' or hang ourselves on 'the courtyard tree facing the southeast', but them! Therefore, it is especially important that you and Fang Meng'ao join forces. The way to reach him remains the same, through He Xiaoyu. The nature of the mission has been adjusted. Do not mention your background in the Communist Party-controlled student committee any more and do not try to recruit Fang Meng'ao to join the Communist Party. Of course, don't reveal your true identity in our organisation."

At this point, Zeng Keda looked at the clock on the wall, then went to open the door. "You can't stay long. I have a few more words to say, so let's talk as we walk."

Back in the bamboo groves in the courtyard of the He residence, the two men had returned to the stone path and were sitting on the same stone bench where Xie Peidong was talking to He Xiaoyu. Apparently, Xie Peidong had already explained to Fang Meng'ao why he had sent He Xiaoyu to meet him. When the wind stopped, the two of them were silent for a while and it became very quiet in the bamboo grove.

"You still haven't talked about the last issue," remarked Fang Meng'ao, breaking the silence.

Xie Peidong had obviously left this topic undiscussed on purpose, as he was expecting Fang Meng'ao to ask about it. At this moment his demeanour was extremely serious. He whispered: "That's the most important thing I've told you about today. And I hope you are prepared."

Fang Meng'ao looked at the courtyard at the far end of the stone path. It was empty. Apparently, Shao Yuangang and Guo Jinyang had a done a good job of securing the entrance to the courtyard. Fang Meng'ao was still looking at the courtyard over the stone path.

"Go ahead."

"As for Liang Jinglun, first off, he's identified as a professor at Yenching University. Second, he has been identified as an underground member of the Peking CPC's Urban Works Department's Students Committee. But that's not who he really is."

At this point, he stopped. Fang Meng'ao actually did not look back, his eyes were still focused on the courtyard over the stone path.

"I am listening."

"He was a core member of the Kuomintang's Iron and Blood Congress." Xie Peidong intentionally lightened his tone.

Xie Peidong was taken aback that Fang Meng'ao was still sitting there quietly, without any response.

"Does He Xiaoyu know who he really is?" asked Fang Meng'ao after a short delay.

"So far, Xiaoyu does not know his real identity," replied Xie Peidong.

"Was it so that He Xiaoyu would be emotionally unburdened, or so that Liang Jinglun would not suspect He Xiaoyu?" Fang Meng'ao remained so calm that Xie Peidong was secretly surprised.

Having worked as an underground agent for decades, Xie Peidong, who used to receive instructions and guidance from Vice-Chairman Zhou, had to deal with people from various departments of the Kuomintang authorities but he had never had such a hard time communicating with Fang Meng'ao as he did today. The images of quite a few people popped up in his head – including Xu Tieying, Zeng Keda and Ma Hanshan. Then Fang Buting and Cui Zhongshi.

He came to realise how tough it must have been for those who dealt with Fang Meng'ao who had proved to be such a huge headache. At the same time, he felt hugely grateful that Cui Zhongshi had been working so hard to recruit Fang Meng'ao over the past few years. However, on a deeper level, he was alarmed at the fact that the head of the Iron and Blood Congress could be so reckless as to promote Fang Meng'ao, and that this organisation and the person who controlled it, were even more resourceful than the CPC had originally thought. This rich and essential information had to be reported to the higher authorities clearly and promptly.

Those were all the distracting thoughts, although the important thing for the moment was to extract from Fang Meng'ao what Zhang Yueyin needed so that he could report to his superiors. What was even more important was to relieve Fang Meng'ao of the baggage, face up to reality and be firm in his beliefs before asking him for the information.

"In our job, the hardest thing to do is to bury our personal feelings deep in our heart. For inexperienced comrades, the best way to protect them is to limit their knowledge about the real situation. Just as you are not allowed to know more, the organisation cannot allow Comrade He Xiaoyu to know the true identity of Liang Jinglun."

"Uncle Cui died for me," bemoaned Fang Meng'ao, no longer able to hide his emotion, "and it's you who sent him to recruit me. At this point, you sent another inexperienced person, He Xiaoyu, to contact me while you yourself were hiding behind a curtain!"

Xie Peidong looked at Fang Meng'ao but Fang refused to look back at him. The breeze blowing through the bamboo groves swept across Xie Peidong's face and drowned out his soft sigh.

"My role in the Party is not that important. It's just that the person in the Kuomintang who uses you is too important."

"I'm listening."

"He was no more than thirty-eight years old this year but everyone from the senior members of the Tung Meng Hui [the Chinese Revolutionary League] to the first batch of graduates from the Whampoa Military Academy, they all call him Mr Ching-kuo, while all his subordinates call him Comrade Jianfeng. He's also held in very high regard by some in our party, not least because he was the eldest son of Chiang Kai-shek, but also because of something more than that."

"Someone so important is using you so much at this time. Now, your role in the party is more important than mine," he said with added emphasis.

Finally, Fang Meng'ao looked at Xie Peidong, face to face.

"You joined the Air Force at the age of seventeen and fought in the War of Resistance Against Japanese Aggression, and joined the party at the age of twenty-six when Comrade Cui Zhongshi came to recruit you. However, the person in the Kuomintang who uses you as a valuable asset was sent to study in the Soviet Union at the age of fifteen by one of the founders of our party, Mr Li Ta-chao. There, he spent twelve years surviving the complicated struggle of the Communist International. He returned to China in 1937 and experienced another eleven years of cooperation between the Kuomintang and the CPC, and the Civil War that ensued. This man understood the nature and goals of our party, its policies and strategies, which might have been beyond your imagination and that of many of our party leaders and comrades! In April this year, he founded the Iron and Blood Congress because he realised that the Kuomintang regime was at the tipping point of total collapse. He proposed that 'one hand should be resolutely anti-Communist, the other anti-corruption; one revolution and fighting on two fronts'. The organisation he established and the actions he took have caused shocking consequences within the Kuomintang, and our party is paying close attention to it. But we never expected that he would suddenly intervene and boldly employ you to his advantage, a special member of our party to fight against the corruption of the Kuomintang. The fact that you and your flying brigade ended up in Peking was not only unforeseen by Comrade Zhongshi and me but also unpredicted by our superiors. His notion of 'fighting on two fronts' presented us with a big problem."

"So even Uncle Cui had to deny that he was a Communist and affirm that I wasn't one either, didn't he?"

"Alas!" Xie Peidong sighed again, "I'm telling you the truth. You have to be calm."

"I am calm, aren't I?"

"It's good to be calm. Let me tell you that, actually, it was your father who first discovered that Comrade Zhongshi was a Communist, not the Iron and Blood Congress."

"It was he who reported Uncle Cui to Zeng Keda!" said Fang Meng'ao, standing up abruptly.

"No," Xie Peidong replied unequivocally.

"That day when you went to rescue Uncle Cui at the police station, my father already knew he was a Communist?"

"Yes."

"For me?"

"At least, it was for you then, for you and for Mengwei's feelings for Uncle Cui. You tuned the piano and asked your father to play *Hymn to the Virgin Mary*. You understand music, so you should have heard from his performance that your father was really playing with huge sadness. People can tell lies but music can't."

"But Uncle Cui is dead anyway."

Xie Peidong looked to the sky between the tops of the bamboo canes and said: "It's too complicated for me to explain it all to you now. But there is one reason why Comrade Zhongshi had to die, and that is, the Iron and Blood Congress had to cut off the single line of communication between you and Comrade Zhongshi so that they could use Liang Jinglun's position in our party-controlled Student Committee to send He Xiaoyu to test you and spy on you. In response, we had to risk sending Comrade Xiaoyu to take a meeting with you."

"And then the organisation will tell He Xiaoyu to meet with me again?"

"Now it's my turn to connect with you."

"What about Liang Jinglun, what about the Student Committee? Will they continue to dispatch He Xiaoyu to recruit me?"

"I will send Xiaoyu to continue to contact you. It's good that Xiaoyu doesn't know the true identity of Liang Jinglun while Liang Jinglun doesn't know the identity of Xiaoyu's special party membership, only that she belongs to the Committee's Peripheral Progressive Youth. Peripheral youth are not eligible to recruit you. At the moment, Liang Jinglun is arranging for He Xiaoyu to contact you as a test for surveillance. If they really want to recruit you, Liang Jinglun must first seek permission from the Student Committee and get its approval before contacting you directly. According to our analysis, the Iron and Blood Congress hired you specifically because of your abhorrence of corruption in the Kuomintang, and used the conflict between you and your father to start with the Peking branch in order to force the Central Bank's opponents of the currency reform to give in, allowing you to serve as a tool for their upcoming currency reform. To that end, all they have to do is sever your ties with the party, and they should no longer allow Liang Jinglun to recruit you, but they will continue to send Comrade He Xiaoyu or even Liang Jinglun to contact you personally, to test your political attitude, and to monitor whether our organisation is secretly engaging you. From now on, the organisation will not allow Comrade Xiaoyu to meet you again. More importantly, when you come into contact with Comrade Xiaoyu again, you must not reveal Liang Jinglun's true identity, otherwise

Comrade Xiaoyu will be in danger of being exposed. Your safety is guaranteed by the organisation. Her safety is guaranteed more by you."

This time, Fang Meng'ao remained silent. In the past, he might have been as active as a rabbit, or as quiet as a virgin, to use an old Chinese proverb, but no matter what he said or did, everything was true and from the heart. His silence now meant that he might have to behave differently from what he had done previously, and that he could no longer live honestly. He had a lifelong aversion to politics, for that sole reason he could live honestly. Just because he pursued his ideals, he accepted Cui Zhongshi and chose to side with the CPC. But since its inception, he only promised to instigate and fly his mutinous brigade to the Communist-controlled areas when the critical moment arrived. The agreement he reached with Cui Zhongshi was not to get involved in complicated politics. However, he found himself entangled in the complicated politics now. And to make things worse, He Xiaoyu was being dragged into this kind of complexity!

"Good. What should I do now?" A desire to protect He Xiaoyu crept into his mind.

"Check the accounts. Check the accounts on behalf of the Ministry of Defence's investigation team."

"For real or for fake?"

"That's their business. Sometimes they'd tell you to do a real check, sometimes they'd tell you to do a fake check."

"They should know that I never cheat."

"They also know you don't specialise in economics. You can't detect the falsehoods in the books and you can't detect the falsehoods behind the books."

"But you know what is cheating and what is not." Fang Meng'ao really meant business this time. "What about the attitude of the organisation? Shall I investigate for real, or shall I fake it?"

"The party organisation certainly has an attitude and I will cooperate with you when the time comes." After this, Xie Peidong switched to the subject of the day. "Which is also the reason why the organisation sent me to contact you. According to our intelligence from Nanking, they've developed a plan of action. It should be related to your current investigation. The organisation wants to get information from you to further analyse their next move and purpose."

Fang Meng'ao was listening very attentively.

But Xie Peidong stopped again and remained silent for a while. Then he said in a more calculated manner: "It's been quite some years, please consider this the first task assigned to you by the organisation."

Fang Meng'ao ended up losing his cordiality, so unaccustomed was he to the kind of insincerity and pretence that he felt in the presence of his uncle, a party higher-up, who he felt was not as approachable and friendly as Cui Zhongshi, so he replied indifferently.

"If I come to know anything, I'll tell you. Please don't make it a task."

"As you wish." Xie Peidong immediately realised that he had made a mistake by making an easy matter much too complicated. Without further ado, he asked: "Do you happen to know that the operation they've planned is code-named after an ancient poem?"

"I do, it's called *The Peacock Flies Southeast*."

"Do you know the code name of the executor and the specific executor?" Xie Peidong asked after a short while, gently nodding his head.

"The code names are Jiao Zhongqing and Liu Lanzhi. Zeng Keda told me last night that Jiao Zhongqing is me."

"How about Liu Lanzhi?"

"He didn't say."

"Then you should never ask Zeng Keda about it. What is Jiao Zhongqing's task?" asked Xie Peidong casually, after pondering for a moment.

"Restore the flight schedule of the Peking Youth Aviation Brigade and form a special flight squadron to transport emergency supplies to Peking in accordance with the newly issued currency."

Xie Peidong nodded gently, then pondered.

"Can you tell me if I have permission to transport supplies to assist in their currency reform?" Fang Meng'ao, however, did not allow him time to contemplate.

"Give me a day, I'll consult my superiors and tell you clearly."

"Who is this superior?" Xie Peidong was stunned but he could only look at Fang Meng'ao.

"I hope this superior is Vice-Chairman Zhou." With that, Fang Meng'ao strode out of the bamboo grove, not bothering to wait for Xie's answer.

"Meng'ao!" Xie Peidong called out in an attempt to stop him.

"Without Zhou's instructions, I don't want to hear anything else." Fang Meng'ao quickly exited the bamboo grove.

Xie Peidong was left confused.

In the courtyard outside the bamboo grove, Shao Yuangang and Guo Jinyang approached Fang Meng'ao. They nodded their acknowledgment at Fang Meng'ao's orders. The two of them stayed where they were while Fang Meng'ao walked out of the gate alone. Xie Peidong was quite startled to see Shao Yuangang and Guo Jinyang looking his way, obviously waiting for him. It took him a while to compose himself before he walked over to join them.

"Let's continue to check the accounts," said Guo Jinyang.

The two headed to the Western-style house.

"Where did your captain go? He's supposed to audit the accounts, isn't he?" Xie Peidong remained where he was standing.

"He's on his way to Vice-Chancellor He's."

"To check up on our governor?"

"Why would he bother to check out your governor?" Guo Jinyang smiled ambiguously as he looked back at Xie Peidong. "He's gone to see Miss He. He didn't tell you, did he?"

"Oh," Xie Peidong responded casually, concealing his surprise.

In his room on the first floor, He Qicang found himself glued to the person who was typing while he sat in his recliner day in and day out because of his back and leg problems. This was the only person he had ever known, apart from Liang Jinglun, who could type so quickly on an old English typewriter. Clearly this pair of hands was more rhythmic than those of Liang Jinglun.

"Do you still play the piano?" He Qicang asked Fang Buting.

"I haven't played for years," replied Fang Buting as he continued to type.

"A few days ago, Meng'ao and Mengwei moved my piano out into the drawing room and I played it again."

"After neglecting it for so long perhaps it could be out of tune. Can you still play it?"

"Meng'ao tuned the piano." Fang Buting was still typing rapidly. "I haven't seen him for more than ten years and I don't know where he learned how to do it."

"Does Meng'ao play too?"

"He should be able to. But I played last time and he sang to accompany me. He sang really well. This boy, I'm the one who's been holding him back."

"When the country is in chaos and loved ones are lost, you're not entirely to blame." He Qicang sighed mournfully. "Do you still play the song *Blooming Flowers, Full Moon*?"

Fang Buting's hand stopped for an instant, then he continued: "It's *Ave Maria*."

He Qicang fell silent.

Fang Buting's hands typing on the keyboard seemed to be playing the melody of *Ode to the Virgin Mary*.

"He's thinking of his mother, I guess."

"I guess so, too."

"Meng'ao and Mengwei's mother and Xiaoyu's mother are both good women."

"Like her mother, Xiaoyu is an incredibly good woman." After saying this, Fang Buting's hands slowly stopped and he looked at He Qicang.

"You've been typing for hours but your energy level is still the same as when you were at Harvard. Take a break, my friend," said He Qicang, as he looked out of the window at the sycamore tree.

"OK," replied Fang Buting. "Just a quick test on the source of some classical Chinese poems in English translations. See if you still remember them."

"Hooray." It was as if the two old men had hit it off and were back in the days when they were schoolmates again.

Fang Buting quickly typed a few words.

"Finished?"

"Just a few sentences."

"Read out loud."

Fang Buting read it in English:

We rode horses in pursuit of the days of our youth, only to find today that we are not the same. The spring breeze blew green in the fields and white in our beards. What else can we do? Give the lord of the manor that 10,000-words worth of my ideal, and let him plant his own tree.

"Let me think... it's Xin Qiji's *Partridge Sky*, right?" He Qicang's eyes were glittering.

"That's right! How about the original poem?" He Qicang closed his eyes, thought for a while, then opened them abruptly, as if he had seen through his tricks.

"Didn't you switch the concept?"

Fang Buting laughed and waited for him to recite the poem.

"'A guest talked about fame and glory with emotion, reminiscing about his youth. For Drama'," recited He Qicang slowly. "That's the preface to the poem. Do I still have to read the lines you translated?"

"Of course."

"Listen carefully," said He Qicang, raising his voice.

Now thinking of the past,
How one sighs to be neglected.
Spring won't bring back the black to my head.
You can't imagine the tracts I wrote on tactics for this country.
In return I'm given this poor bent field mattock
And a somewhat weather-worn tree-planting manual.

Upon finishing the poem, he stared at Fang Buting.

"The last sentence clearly says that the poet wants to make an exchange for a book on tree planting but why is it that in your version you make the author plant trees himself?"

"I'm glad you know it." Fang Buting laughed out loud.

Fang Buting's laughter was infectious, causing He Qicang to burst out laughing as well, to the point where both men were almost in tears of laughter.

When was there ever such laughter in He's house! Moreover, it was the dignified scholar Vice-Chancellor He and the reserved and stately Governor Fang laughing like this! Both Cheng Xiaoyun and Xie Mulan looked at He Xiaoyu. When He Xiaoyu looked up at the first floor, she could also hardly believe it.

"I'll go and check," said Xie Mulan, jumping to her feet as she was about to go upstairs.

"Don't go!" whispered Cheng Xiaoyun, in an attempt to stop her.

The laughter stopped abruptly. All three of them held their breath. Strangely enough, they heard another sound coming from outside. Who would dare to drive a car so fast and make such a din in Yannan Garden, which was always quiet and peaceful?

With tears of laughter still in his eyes, Fang Buting looked out of the window, only to find a jeep that had come to a sudden stop. He saw his oldest son jumping out of the jeep.

"It's Meng'ao, isn't it?" He Qicang had guessed right.

"He's coming for me. I'll go and meet him downstairs." Fang Buting stood up. "As you sow, so shall you reap," he said, and walked towards the door.

"Let him come up," He Qicang called out to him.

"Your report is important. I can't afford to let him bother you."

"What does the report matter?" He Qicang blurted out as if he was still the head of the fellow students in the past. "I'd enjoy his annoying company. Sit down and wait for him to come up."

Nodding his head, Fang Buting retreated to the table and obediently sat down again. He Qicang, who had been sitting, decided to lie down.

"Put your legs up and act like a father."

Only then did Fang Buting realise that he was sitting so stiff and upright on his back, so he smiled awkwardly, relaxed and moved his chair toward the door. When he sat down again, he lifted the hem of his long *tunic* and put his right leg over his left one.

"Hi, Stepmother. Is my father here, too?" The living room door on the ground floor of the He household was open. Fang Meng'ao was standing in the doorway, gazing at Cheng Xiaoyun.

Cheng Xiaoyun's heart gripped even tighter, looking at He Xiaoyu and Xie Mulan, and then at Fang Meng'ao.

"Your father's car is parked just outside the gate, you should have seen it."

"I saw it." Fang Meng'ao turned his gaze to He Xiaoyu. "Can I come in?"

"If it's on behalf of the Department of Defence investigation team, can you come back another time? I have guests at home."

"I'll just represent myself."

"Why are you making him so nervous?" asked Xie Mulan to relax him. "Brother, come on in."

Fang Meng'ao was still waiting for He Xiaoyu's reply. He Xiaoyu no longer avoided his gaze.

"Don't go upstairs because you'll disturb my father, he is sick and he doesn't like you."

Fang Meng'ao stepped inside the living room.

The door to He Qicang's room on the first floor had just been opened by Fang Buting and part of the conversation on the ground floor could be heard while some could be imagined. The two old men, one lying in a chair, the other sitting at a table, no longer under any pretences, were listening intently to what was going on down below.

Fang Meng'ao had stepped inside the house.

> *While young, beneath my flag I had ten thousand knights:*
> *With these outfitted cavaliers I crossed the river.*

He Qicang suddenly began to recite the poem in a sonorous tone that startled Fang Buting.

"You were the one who tested me just now, now it's my turn to test you. Here are the first two lines of the poem, what are the next two?" asked a smiling He Qicang.

Fang Buting shook his head and smiled awkwardly. He was not able to answer the question.

"If you can't, I'll answer it for you."

> *The foe prepared their silver shafts at night;*

During the day we shot arrows from golden quivers.

After reciting these two lines, He Qicang looked out of the door, then stretched out a finger to point at Fang Buting, saying: "The present-day Xin Qiji is coming to arrest Zhang Anguo."

"Well, I'll rely on you to block the arrows." Fang Buting could only smile bitterly.

"Serious, enough." He Qicang waved his hand. "You aren't Zhang Anguo and I am not a Jin Dynasty soldier. Wait until he comes up."

Behind He Xiaoyu was the stairway, and in front of him stood Fang Meng'ao, unmoving, but his eyes looked over He Xiaoyu's head to the hallway on the first floor, to the door of He Qicang's bedroom.

Both Cheng Xiaoyun, standing on one side, and Xie Mulan standing on the other, were growing ever more nervous. They knew that if Fang Meng'ao wanted to go upstairs he would do so at any time.

But Fang Meng'ao suddenly laughed and asked: "Did you hear that?"

Cheng Xiaoyun and the two girls exchanged glances and both looked at Fang Meng'ao, but no one replied.

"I heard it, Uncle He seemed to be reading a poem by Xin Qiji. Stepmother, you're well versed in classical Chinese literature, tell us which poem Uncle He is reading!"

"I didn't hear it," Cheng Xiaoyun had to reply, "I really didn't."

"When I was young, my parents forced me to memorise Xin Qiji but later I forgot all about it and could only remember a few lines."

At this point, he looked at He Xiaoyu as if expecting her to answer.

He Xiaoyu just would not.

"Brother, which lines?" Xie Mulan was finally able to join in, even though she knew she was not able to do much to help today.

"Recite it to us."

Fang Meng'ao looked straight at the stairs behind He Xiaoyu and recited:

The youth knows not the taste of sorrow, but loves to go upstairs, loves to go upstairs.

Then he stopped abruptly.

It was a deliberate attempt to create tension, aimed at the woman and the two girls. He Xiaoyu had no time to react to his ill intention, only to find that Fang Meng'ao's eyes were looking straight at her. Only then did He Xiaoyu realise that he might not be looking for his father this time but for herself, so she looked straight at him and met his eyes. It turned out that Fang Meng'ao did intend to strike up a conversation.

"I can't remember the next line but I only remember what it was about: 'To dedicate this new poem for...' Xiaoyu, you should remember it."

He Xiaoyu's heart almost missed a beat.

The foot of the Great Wall.

The Crescent School.

New Poetry! Wasn't it the case that Fang Meng'ao had taken the initiative to come and meet her?

But why did it have to be this way? He Xiaoyu didn't know what to say.

"It's *'For a New Poem...'*" Xie Mulan, not knowing the truth, snatched up the conversation to take the pressure off He Xiaoyu.

"I didn't ask you," snapped Fang Meng'ao, interrupting Xie Mulan, still staring intently at He Xiaoyu.

"It's 'To compose a new poem to express his sorrow!'" He Xiaoyu could only speak up and said: "Everyone else is wrong but you, satisfied?"

Both Cheng Xiaoyun and Xie Mulan felt that He Xiaoyu and Fang Meng'ao were saying things that only they could understand. Fang Meng'ao's subsequent demeanour was even more intriguing. He narrowed his eyes, smiling rather than laughing, and flashed the kind of charming manly tease that most girls found alluring.

Cheng Xiaoyun's heart skipped a beat, as she suddenly saw a familiar look in Fang Meng'ao's eyes, the same look Fang Buting had when he looked at her many years ago!

Standing on the other side of the room, Xie Mulan's heart was also pounding inexplicably. She was reminded of Rhett Butler from *Gone With the Wind*! Of course, He Xiaoyu was Scarlett O'Hara!

He Xiaoyu couldn't stand the anxiety any longer and looked away abruptly. "If you are satisfied, please leave. If you want to investigate anything in the future, please don't come to our house."

"Good, I'm leaving."

Fang Meng'ao stood straight with his two legs so close that he could actually make a loud sound when he clicked his heels.

Was he just going to walk away like this? Three pairs of eyes followed Fang Meng'ao's footsteps as he exited. But Fang Meng'ao's steps came to a halt outside the living room door. He slowly turned back to look at He Xiaoyu.

"Is it OK for you to walk me out?"

Cheng Xiaoyun and Xie Mulan came to their senses and looked at He Xiaoyu. Cheng Xiaoyun glanced across at her while Xie Mulan, on the other hand, tilted her chin directly toward her big brother, indicating that He Xiaoyu should hurry to walk him out.

He Xiaoyu was sure that he was looking for a meeting, so she walked over in front of Cheng Xiaoyun and Xie Mulan to Fang Meng'ao, feigning reluctance.

"What on earth are you up to?" asked He Xiaoyu gently with a sidelong glance, walking up to Fang Meng'ao.

"Come out with me, I've got something to ask you," said Fang Meng'ao in a low voice.

He Xiaoyu could only look at him.

"Pretend you don't want to, just follow me," muttered Fang Meng'ao in an even lower voice. With that, he grabbed He Xiaoyu's hand and walked towards the courtyard gate. Cheng Xiaoyun was confused at first and then her eyes glistened. Xie Mulan's eyes were already sparkling and the sunlight outside the door was as bright as a silver screen: Rhett Butler was carrying Scarlet O'Hara on his shoulder!

The jeep could be heard roaring away outside the window.

"What an unfilial son!" scoffed Fang Buting, withdrawing his gaze. He slapped the table, stood up abruptly and walked towards the door of the room.

"What are you doing?" asked He Qicang, sitting up.

"If you want to find me, find me, and if you want to check the accounts, just check the accounts, but don't let him get Xiaoyu involved!"

"Why! You can't catch up with his jeep, can you?"

"You don't understand. He's been hanging out with those US GIs. If he really did something to Xiaoyu, how could I live with myself?" Fang Buting, standing in front of the door, appeared distraught.

"What do you mean by 'couldn't live with yourself?' Huh? Can't you explain yourself?"

"Yuck!" Fang Buting turned his head. "You don't know..."

"You don't know your son but I still know my daughter. Fang Buting, you've made the mistake of being too smart all your life. I don't understand why you smart people always have to make things so complicated when they are in fact so simple. You've been my classmate for decades. Since you've come to me today, let me just tell you one thing: don't make things any more complicated. Finish the currency reform, then quit your job at the Central Bank. Don't interfere in the affairs of the younger generation."

Fang Buting was stupefied at He Qicang's admonition when suddenly the phone on the ground floor rang.

"Governor! It's Uncle Xie calling from home!" said Cheng Xiaoyun.

Fang Buting looked at He Qicang.

"Go and get it. Why are you looking at me?"

Xie Peidong was holding a phone in front of his desk in the governor's office on the first floor of the Fang residence. Guo Jinyang and Shao Yuangang were next to him, flipping through the books. Even though they were not monitoring him by staring at him, they were listening to what he had to say, judging from the look on their faces.

"Yes sir," replied Xie Peidong, "the two officers of the inspection group are auditing the accounts," replied Xie Peidong. "Now the two officers of the audit team are investigating the accounts, there are many things I can't explain to them clearly. If Meng'ao is with you, ask him to come over immediately..."

Obviously, Fang Buting's voice on the phone was kept very low. Xie Peidong listened and suddenly became silent. Guo Jinyang and Shao Yuangang couldn't help but look over.

They found an apparently startled Xie Peidong.

"Governor, this won't work," said Xie Peidong, coming to his senses. "How could Meng'ao get Xiaoyu involved in this? You know that Xiaoyu is a member of the Peking Students' Union and it would be unmanageable if a new round of student protests occur. Governor, hurry up and take Vice-Chancellor He in your car and find her. We have to find Xiaoyu, no matter what."

Both Guo Jinyang and Shao Yuangang stopped flipping through the books to look at Xie Peidong. Both pilots had excellent hearing and could hear the phone clanging on the other end, but Xie Peidong still held the phone in his hand and was reluctant to put it down.

Guo Jinyang and Shao Yuangang looked at each other, smiled and began to look through the books again.

It was a hot August afternoon and the sun was spitting fire.

At a checkpoint in the southwestern suburbs outside Peking, Fang Meng'ao's jeep was parked behind a barrier where a major battalion commander was checking his papers. On both sides of the checkpoint there were two circles of sack fortifications stacked one-person high, with soldiers wearing helmets ready for combat. There were endless lines of trenches and barbed wire on both sides of the highway. Numerous Kuomintang soldiers were digging trenches.

"Sir!" The battalion commander saluted, then handed back his papers to Fang Meng'ao in the driver's seat. "A few dozen kilometres from here, there are Communist troops, it can be very dangerous. Sir, please return the way you came."

Having said that, he couldn't help but look at He Xiaoyu in the passenger seat.

"I'm just going over to inspect the forward position," said Fang Meng'ao politely to him. "Open the barrier."

"Excuse me sir, this lady…"

"The *Central Daily News* is going to report on the battle ahead."

"Sir, could you wait five minutes? I'll have to report it to my superior." One with the Ministry of Defence, the other with the *Central Daily News*, the battalion commander was faced with a dilemma.

"Yes. But in five minutes, I'm going over there with or without the approval of your superiors."

"Yes." The battalion commander answered a little reluctantly and walked to the guardhouse beside him.

Fang Meng'ao picked up the military water bottle in the car and handed it to He Xiaoyu. "It's clean. You can drink from it, you can also wipe your face with it."

He Xiaoyu's hair was all sweaty and her summer cloth singlet was so soaked through that it clung to her body, making her bosom faintly visible. She did not pick up the bottle but looked sideways out of the window, as if preoccupied by something else.

Fang Meng'ao lifted the rope attached to the bottle and hoisted it over. With the bottle dangling in front of her eyes, He Xiaoyu had to take it.

"I'm getting out for a smoke."

Fang Meng'ao left his military cap on the seat and got out of the jeep. He Xiaoyu couldn't help but look at the Air Force cap on the driver's seat and found that the brim was also damp with sweat.

Looking into the rearview mirror outside the driver's window, her heart stirred as she suddenly remembered the song *Fragment* – Fang Meng'ao was lighting a cigar, basking in the sun, watching soldiers digging trenches under the sun in the distance – while He Xiaoyu was eyeing Fang Meng'ao in the rearview mirror.

The phone in Xu Tieying's office in the Peking Police Bureau was ringing right beside him. He was leaning on the back of the chair with no one knowing if he was asleep or not, although the bags under his eyes appeared smaller than usual. Strangely, he left the phone ringing. The phone continued to ring. Xu Tieying's eyes were still closed but he suddenly reached over, lifted the phone, pressed the key and tossed the phone aside. Then he leaned back in the chair again.

Xu Tieying had gone to arrest Ma Hanshan the previous night, only to have his secretary arrested. He returned having been humiliatingly defeated, so he had complained to Director Guo of the Nanking Kuomintang Communications Bureau but was scolded instead. Then he scolded and dismissed all those who had come to report public affairs or to curry favour. He turned on the bathroom tap and kept it running until dawn. As of now he was still asleep in a chair; perhaps he would not get up until the fall of the Party-State.

"Commissioner, Commissioner!" Outside the door, someone called him very gently, obviously afraid of being scolded.

When he heard that it was Shan Fuming, Xu Tieying didn't bother to get angry, he just ignored him. Surprisingly, Shan knocked on the door again. But Xu Tieying continued to ignore him while he gently knocked on the door.

"Commissioner, Commissioner..." The deputy director was calling at the door which he pushed open from the outside.

"Get out," barked Xu Tieying, keeping his eyes closed.

"Commiss..."

"Get out!" Xu Tieying picked up the pistol on the table and pointed it in the direction of the speaker.

Shan Fuming dashed to the door in fear. Hiding outside the door, he said: "It's Deputy Commander-in-Chief Chen. He's threatening to reorganise the Peking Police Bureau if you don't take his call."

"Tell him on the phone, the Peking Police Bureau was disbanded a long time ago." Xu Tieying lowered his pistol but still leaned back with his eyes closed.

"Commissioner, if Deputy Commander Chen scolds me, what should I say to him."

It was so serious that Xu Tieying couldn't get angry even if he had wanted to, so he had to coach him.

"Tell him it's what I said. Peking has been taken over by the Ministry of Defence's Bureau of Reserve Cadres. If there's anything he wants, Deputy Commander-in-Chief Chen should call Zeng Keda, or simply appoint Fang Meng'ao to be the commissioner."

"Deputy Commander-in-Chief Chen said that Fang Meng'ao drove out of the southwestern defence line in a jeep headed for the Communist troops. He called to discuss with you how to capture him," said Shan Fuming, his voice outside the door growing louder.

Xu Tieying's eyes popped wide open, and he looked at the phone he had just tossed aside on the table. He then picked up the phone but remembered that Shan Fuming was still standing outside the door.

"Go and tell him I took sleeping pills last night and that you woke me up. I'm rinsing my hair with cold water and asking him to call me back."

"Yes!" The answer was loud and clear.

Wang Puchen was also on an urgent call, using a large headset microphone from the secret prison of the Military Council's Bureau of Investigation in the northwestern suburbs of Peking. With the thick metal door closed and the fan on, he stood in front of the desk, surveying the 'Military Fortress Map of the Peking Theatre'. Sweat was running down his face.

Sliding his long, thin finger along a road line on the map, he reported into the phone: "It's southwest, Comrade Jianfeng. Now we've crossed the outer city line and beyond the Lugou Bridge is the Zhuozhou line... Yes, the stalemate zone with the Communist troops... Yes, it's still a long way off... No, I don't think Fang Meng'ao could have gone there to contact the Communists, either. What I'm worried about is that girl in the jeep, He Xiaoyu, and whether or not she has a Communist Party Urban Works Department background. Do you want me to tell our troops to block them immediately at the Zhuozhou defence lin and then investigate secretly?"

Comrade Jianfeng interrupted him and gave very clear instructions. "Yes. I won't get involved in the investigation of this matter."

Wang Puchen replied: "I'll call Comrade Keda right now... Yes, I'll call Chief Inspector Zeng and tell him that Chen Jicheng is handling the matter... Yes, I'll let him handle it and report back to you at a later date."

———

Fang Meng'ao's jeep whizzed along the Peking-Shijiazhuang Highway and the Lugou Bridge was soon in sight.

Just one month and four days after the third anniversary of the Seventh of July Incident, and five days to the third anniversary of the Victory Over Japan Day, the sacred Lugou Bridge lay silent ahead!

Even though the war was raging intensely, the Nationalist army didn't build any fortifications at the bridgehead but set up sandbags, bunkers and guard rails about five hundred metres from Lugou Bridge on each side. Fang Meng'ao's jeep was fast approaching the bridge. Obviously, the garrison troops had been informed, so the barrier for the northeast direction of the Lugou Bridge was lifted. Upon reaching the bridgehead, the jeep came to a screeching halt.

Fang Meng'ao remained behind the wheel for a moment before opening the door and getting out. He Xiaoyu looked out from inside the jeep at Fang Meng'ao.

Fang Meng'ao walked to the front of the vehicle and swiftly offered a solemn military salute to Luguo Bridge! He got back into the jeep and closed the door behind him. He drove across the bridge at the slowest possible speed, as if he were a baby crawling over his mother's body.

He Xiaoyu had been to Lugou Bridge many times but never before had she felt quite like this, especially when she found that the lions topping the balustrades were gazing at her in fascination. She surreptitiously glanced at Fang Meng'ao but he kept staring straight ahead. When she looked closely, she found that he had tears in his eyes. He Xiaoyu's heart ached.

Finally, the jeep slowly crossed the bridge and began to pick up speed again.

Apparently, the soldiers were instructed to pull up the railings to the northwest of the Lugou Bridge long before the jeep arrived, allowing Fang Meng'ao's jeep to whiz by. The Lugou

Bridge was left far behind the jeep, along with the Yongding River.

"Is that Lugou Bridge?" Zeng Keda's call from his room was traced to the guard house at Lugou Bridge.

"Yes," answered the guard.

"Have you seen a Ministry of Defence jeep pass by?" asked Zeng Keda sharply, before turning pale. "Who told you to let the jeep go?"

"The Garrison headquarters!" responded the person at the other end clearly.

"Damn it!" cursed Zeng Keda, pressing the key violently.

After some quick thinking, he dialled another number.

"Peking Police Bureau? This is the Ministry of Defence's Investigation Group. Please put your Deputy Commissioner Fang Mengwei on the phone."

The person at the other end replied that Deputy Director Fang was not available.

"Contact him immediately and tell me exactly where he is right away. Forget it, I'll call you in ten minutes."

"Is that Deputy Commissioner Fang? Please wait a second." Guo Jinyang was also looking for Fang Mengwei from the governor's office in Fang Buting's house. Much to his surprise and delight, he found him. Covering the phone, he looked at Xie Peidong beside him.

"I've found him for you, so talk to him yourself."

"Thank you!" Xie Peidong immediately picked up the phone. "Mengwei? Yes, it's me. Yes, just now, it was your big brother's fellow inspector on the phone. Yes, they are checking the accounts. Listen, let me tell you what..."

As Xie Peidong was still speaking, Fang Mengwei interrupted him loudly: "Tell them to wait, I'll be there right away!"

"Don't come, don't hang up the phone," said Xie Peidong

hurriedly. Both Guo Jinyang and Shao Yuangang heard a long, buzzing tone from the phone in Xie Peidong's hand!

In the duty room at the Peking Police Bureau, all the officers on duty stood up to greet Shan Fuming, who demanded: "You shall report to the commissioner yourselves!"

"Yes!" said the policeman answering the phone.

"Don't be nervous, speak slowly." Xu Tieying put on a gentle smile.

"Yes sir," said the same policeman. "At first it was the Ministry of Defence's Investigation Group that enquired about Deputy Commissioner Fang, then the Peking branch asked for him. We managed to get in touch with him where he is now working on the burial of those starved to death outside the city. He has probably spoken to the Peking branch already."

"Then, how about the Ministry of Defence's Investigation Group?"

The policeman looked at his watch and replied: "They said they would call in ten minutes; that leaves two minutes to go."

"Shan, how do you think we should reply to them?" asked Xu Tieying, looking at Shan Fuming.

Shan Fuming was pretty sober-minded at this point. "What do they mean by the Ministry of Defence's Investigation Group? Our commissioner represents the investigation group of the Ministry of Defence. Why is it that they didn't call you but our duty room? This is an overreach of authority."

Xu Tieying nodded in agreement.

Shan Fuming gave an order to the policeman who answered the phone: "If they call again, tell them we can't find him. Do you hear?" Although his order was directed at the policeman on duty, his eyes were on Xu Tieying.

"It'd be better for you to personally take command here, because you know the shit. I'll feel reassured with you behind the wheel." Xu Tieying smiled and nodded at him.

"Don't worry. Go and get some sleep, Chief."

Xu Tieying nodded to the other policemen and finally looked at the policeman who answered the phone. "That's a nice watch you have. Pay attention to the time."

"Yes sir." The policeman just lifted his hand and suddenly realised that it was an expensive watch, and instantly became disturbed.

"Get ready to answer the phone." Xu Tieying had already turned and walked toward the door.

"Are you here to visit a brothel? Damn, you're wearing an expensive watch on duty, aren't you? Put away your watches and pocket watches from now on!" Looking at Xu Tieying's back disappearing outside the door, Shan Fuming reprimanded him in a low voice.

"Yes, Chief Shan," replied more than half of the police officers.

And then the phone rang.

The policeman who had answered the phone previously picked up the phone again.

"Who is it? The Ministry of Defence? This is not the Ministry of Defence, wrong number!" He put down the phone and looked at Shan Fuming.

"You son of a gun, you're such a badass!" cursed Shan Fuming, laughing as he spoke.

"Really? I've seen much of the world already. Deputy Commissioner Shan, you should also go and get some sleep," replied the policeman, also laughing.

"Yeah, go and get some sleep too," echoed all the police officers present in the room, as if in a chorus.

"Want to play cards again?" asked Shan Fuming.

At this point, the phone rang once more. This time, no one answered it.

"Do whatever you want, I don't give a damn." Shan Fuming walked out even though he could hear the phone ringing.

Two decks of cards were immediately brought out and the people around the two tables began to play. Zeng Keda could no longer find out where Fang Mengwei was from this source.

The door of Fang Buting's office on the first floor was slammed open from the outside and Fang Mengwei came striding in. He stopped in the middle of the room and looked at Shao Yuangang and Guo Jinyang, each holding an account book in front of the desk. Shao Yuangang and Guo Jinyang looked back at him in confusion. Fang Mengwei's eyes slowly sought out his uncle who was sitting alone on a chair by the balcony. He found that his uncle had never been so helpless as he was now.

Fang Mengwei took a few steps over to the desk, grabbed the books from Shao Yuangang, slammed them on the desk, then grabbed the books from Guo Jinyang and did the same. Without the account books in their hands, they looked at Fang Mengwei in total confusion.

"Who gave you the authority to raid my house!"

"Mengwei." Xie Peidong stood up.

"Please, don't interrupt."

"Where's your captain?" Fang Mengwei continued to stare at Shao Yuangang and Guo Jinyang, yet his eyes were no longer as fierce.

They looked at each other but didn't answer and didn't know how to answer.

"Mengwei, it's the governor's order to cooperate with them in auditing the accounts. You should go and find your big brother now." Xie Peidong came over.

Fang Mengwei slowly turned to look at Xie Peidong again in astonishment when the phone on the desk began to ring.

"It should be the call from our governor." Xie Peidong looked to Shao Yuangang and Guo Jinyang as if to ask for their permission, then looked at Fang Mengwei, gesturing for him to pick up the phone.

The phone was still ringing but Fang Mengwei didn't even look at the phone, as he had left home angrily several days ago. Xie Peidong became even more anxious.

"Can I ask the investigation team if we can answer the phone?"

No one stopped them from answering it. Shao Yuangang and Guo Jinyang looked at each other, quite bewildered. This provocation did the trick; Fang Mengwei suddenly picked up the phone, apparently not wanting to hear his father's voice.

"Peking branch, please speak to Assistant Manager Xie!"

He was just about to hand the phone over to Xie Peidong when the caller spoke up: "Deputy Commissioner Fang? This is Zeng Keda."

It wasn't his father on the other end of the line. It turned out to be the person he hated the most.

"Zeng Keda!" The voice provoked a new bout of spontaneous anger and what he said next was even more incomprehensible. "Do you have a father?"

Xie Peidong, as well as Shao Yuangang and Guo Jinyang, were all taken aback. Clearly, Zeng Keda, on the other end of the phone, was shocked and silenced by his question.

"Do you have a mother? Do you have brothers and sisters? Answer me, first answer these questions, then say what you want to say!" Fang Mengwei didn't let his opponent breathe.

"Good. I'll answer you." Zeng Keda, who managed to project a more dignified image of a man who would not be startled by such an outburst, took the phone and replied: "I have a father and a mother, both of whom are now in southern Jiangxi Province. They don't have any positions in the government. They're illiterate, they're farmers and they farm the family's ten *mu* of land. One of my older brothers, who lives independently from my parents also farms about ten *mu* of land. I send half of my salary to them every month to supplement the family income."

At this point, Zeng Keda found Fang Mengwei silent on the other end of the line and knew that his honesty had once again given him spiritual strength! "Deputy Commissioner Fang, shall we proceed?"

The hostility in Fang Mengwei's eyes dissipated, to be replaced by a dazed expression. Although he could not hear what the other man was saying, Xie Peidong had noticed that Zeng Keda's reply had calmed him down, judging from the change in Fang Mengwei's expression. He wouldn't allow Mengwei to continue to be capricious. He coughed, indicating that Mengwei should talk to him properly.

"We can talk now, go ahead," replied Fang Mengwei, his voice a bit hoarse at this point.

"Deputy Commissioner Fang, it's nothing personal to check the accounts at the Central Bank's Peking branch and it is not directed at any individual. To prove this, Mr Fan Dasheng's tea set gifted by Comrade Jianfeng to Governor Fang last time speaks volumes for his good faith. I'm calling you now because I heard that Captain Fang drove with Miss He to the southwestern military line, and the Communist line is just beyond that, which is too dangerous. We all know his character and no one can stop him. I should have gone myself but out of respect for him, for Governor Fang and for you, I'd like to ask you to drive over there along the Jingshi Highway. Find Captain Fang and bring him back. I wonder if Deputy Commissioner Fang understands what I mean."

It turned out that Zeng Keda's request and Xie Peidong's purpose for bringing him back were identical! Fang Mengwei's eyes turned to Xie Peidong. Xie Peidong actually completely understood the purpose of the call and it was certainly better for Zeng Keda to ask Fang Mengwei to find Fang Meng'ao than to ask him to do it himself. But he could not very well reveal his true intention yet. All he could do was to look expectantly at Fang Mengwei.

"Excuse me, which direction did you say my big brother went?" Poor Fang Mengwei, in order to make Xie Peidong understand his intention, he had to ask again.

When the caller at the other end repeated what he had said, Fang Mengwei saw that Xie Peidong was still looking at him, as if he didn't understand. He couldn't ask for his permission, so he could only reply: "Thanks for letting me know. It's my job to bring my brother back."

"Why did my brother suddenly drive out of the city with Xiaoyu and out of the southwestern defence line in the direction of Zhuozhou?" After putting down the phone, he realised why Xie Peidong had been so anxious to contact him.

"Indeed. This is too dangerous! Can the inspection team split up by riding in several jeeps and find your captain separately? Anyway, he's the one who has to do the auditing." Xie Peidong had no time to explain the dire situation to Fang Mengwei. But in the presence of Shao Yuangang and Guo Jinyang, he had to say something.

"I don't need them to do it." Fang Mengwei took over and turned to Shao Yuangang and Guo Jinyang. "What's the point of checking the accounts when your captain isn't here? Go back to your barracks and tell them not to come here to check the accounts unless your captain is here. Move!"

Shao Yuangang and Guo Jinyang turned to leave but not forgetting to salute Fang Mengwei and Xie Peidong.

"Did Zeng Keda ask you to find your brother?" Xie Peidong had to find out the details of Zeng Keda's call.

"Yes. I really don't want to listen to his instructions." Fang Mengwei appeared quite agitated. "What's going on with my brother? Does it have to do with Uncle Cui's case again?"

"No more guesswork." Xie Peidong could not explain and was afraid of Fang Mengwei delving into the details. "Hurry up! Get your brother and Miss He back. What else did Zeng Keda say to you?"

"The Garrison Headquarters of Peking has been informed that the road will be cleared, which is a clear attempt to make it easy for my brother to go to the Communist side, framing him as a Communist. He told me to get him back in the name of the Investigation Department of the Garrison Headquarters."

"Then go quickly! When you find your brother, don't ask any questions. Tell him to send Miss He back first. Then come over because I'll wait for him here. First, tell him I will need his cooperation to bring in tomorrow's rations from Tianjin. After that, I will work with him to check the accounts."

"Got it."

Fang Mengwei sighed gently and strode out of the office door.

Xie Peidong picked up the phone on his desk and dialled. "It's me, Sister-in-Law. No need, just tell the governor that Mengwei has personally gone to look for Meng'ao and Xiaoyu. Please make sure the governor and Chancellor He don't worry about them."

"OK, I'll go and tell them," replied Cheng Xiaoyun.

"Also, tell the governor that I have to push Tianjin a bit so that they can ship the grain to Peking as soon as possible. I'll be back in an hour or two." As he was about to hang up the phone, another worrisome issue suddenly came to mind.

"By the way, is Mulan with you?"

"She just left, I think she went to see Professor Liang." There was silence on the phone for a little while before Cheng Xiaoyun replied.

Xie Peidong's heart almost missed a beat again!

He was startled as he looked over towards the chair near the balcony where Cui Zhongshi used to sit. How he wished he could have seen the smiling Cui sitting there.

"Uncle, Uncle!" Cheng Xiaoyun was calling out at the other end of the line.

"I'm listening." The call made the image of Cui Zhongshi disappear. A bird swept by outside the French window. Suddenly, Xie Peidong realised that the sky was so clear and blue today.

"Uncle, do you want me to talk to Chancellor He and ask him to contact Professor Liang so that Mulan can come back?" Cheng Xiaoyun felt Xie's concern on the other end of the line.

"That's not necessary. Hurry up and tell the governor not to be mad any more and to contact Mengwei at any time. I also have to hurry to get the grain shipped," said Xie Peidong urgently, coming to his senses.

At this point he pressed the phone button to hang up.

He had to dial another number. Xie Peidong felt his fingers tremble slightly and could not dial the right number any more. He paused, took a pencil out of the pencil case and wrote the number down one digit at a time on a piece of paper.

The call went through.

"Is that Mr Zhang from the Bank of China's branch office?"

"Speaking." The voice of Zhang Yueyin came across crystal clear.

CHAPTER 15

In a small room on the first floor of a trading firm, Zhang Yueyin saw Xie Peidong, who was waiting for him anxiously.

"How could this happen?" Zhang Yueyin looked at Xie Peidong, more anxious than ever. "Mr Xie, you personally met with Fang Meng'ao but why did he suddenly leave and drive Comrade He Xiaoyu out to the southwest defence line?"

"It was my fault." Xie Peidong was in a very heavy mood and no objective explanation could replace self-criticism at this time. "I overlooked the fact that he suddenly realised I was Comrade Cui Zhongshi's superior and he felt so strongly about it. After all, I am responsible for Comrade Cui Zhongshi's death."

"The organisation didn't instruct us to discuss the responsibility for Comrade Cui Zhongshi's sacrifice, Mr Xie!" Old Liu, who had been pacing back and forth restlessly, stopped. "The Central Committee has given a strict order to the North China Urban Works Department and Peking Urban Works Department to give a detailed report of the Kuomintang's action plan known as 'The Peacock Flies Southeast' by six o'clock. At this time, only Fang Meng'ao knows the details about this plan but he chose to run away! He even dragged He Xiaoyu along with him. What the hell does he think he's doing?"

Xie Peidong sighed. "The problem may be that I told him about Liang Jinglun's Iron and Blood Congress but I neglected the fact that he was worried about He Xiaoyu's safety. That's probably the reason why he suddenly ran off with He Xiaoyu."

"The situation is even worse than we thought!" Zhang Yueyin stood up. "If Fang Meng'ao tells He Xiaoyu about Liang Jinglun's true identity, we'll be completely passive in our next move. If Fang Meng'ao has really taken He Xiaoyu to the liberated area, the consequences will be even worse.".

"We'll have to wait for Fang Mengwei to bring them back," said Xie Peidong. "I'll see if I can make up for it."

"Will Fang Mengwei be able to catch up with them?" Old Liu had lost all his deep respect for Xie Peidong. "What if we can't catch up with them? What if Chen Jicheng and Xu Tieying's men seize them at the Zhuozhou junction?"

"The Iron and Blood Congress will use Fang Meng'ao to carry out their 'Peacock Flies Southeast' plan. Zeng Keda should also be calling the Central Army through Chiang Ching-kuo by now to intercept Fang Meng'ao."

"Really, he makes no distinction between friend or foe!" Old Liu was becoming very agitated. "Is Fang Meng'ao a member of our party or is he a member of the Iron and Blood Congress recruited by Chiang Ching-kuo?"

"Comrade Liu!" said Zhang Yueyin. "This is the grand strategy of the Central Committee. At the Peking Urban Works Department, we shouldn't jump to conclusions! Send a telegram to Comrade Liu Yun immediately and report it to the Central Committee. I will go to Mao'er Hutong and send the telegram immediately. I'll go first. Old Liu, you're supposed to leave in five minutes. Mr Xie, please don't go in your car. Tell your Peking branch driver to head back first. Grab a rickshaw instead."

Neither the Kuomintang nor the Communists expected Fang Meng'ao's jeep to suddenly turn off the Jingshi Highway en route to Zhuozhou, turning off a small road onto the Yongding River, a rarely travelled section of the riverbank.

July and August was the flood season for the Yongding River. Along the embankment were willow trees with willow silk growing profusely. The jeep was in the shade, as were the people; as a result, the summer heat was drastically reduced.

"It's nice and cool, isn't it!" said Fang Meng'ao.

He Xiaoyu did not answer as she stared into the distance.

Looking to the northeast, there was no Peking; looking to the southwest, in the distance was the vast grey expanse of the Taihang Mountains.

"Can you swim?" Fang Meng'ao asked.

"You brought me here just to swim?" answered He Xiaoyu, finally.

"You can or you can't?"

"I can, but I won't now."

"What if I force you into the water?"

"No, you won't."

"I will." Fang Meng'ao sat down facing the river."The last time I saw Uncle Cui was in Houhai. He told me he couldn't swim but I forced him into the water. It wasn't until he was submerged and didn't surface for a long while that I jumped in and saved him."

He Xiaoyu's heart almost missed a beat. She held her breath.

"Do you know why I forced him into the water?"

He Xiaoyu looked at his back, not daring to answer.

"On the tenth of September 1946, the fifteenth day of the eighth month in the lunar calendar, the Mid-Autumn Festival, Cui Zhongshi recruited Fang Meng'ao to join the CPC at Jianqiao Aviation Academy in Hangzhou. On the first of August 1948, in Houhai, Peking, Cui Zhongshi told Fang Meng'ao that he had never been a member of the CPC, and neither was Fang Meng'ao. Now, do you know why I forced him into the water?" At this point, Fang Meng'ao stood up and looked intensely back at He Xiaoyu.

He Xiaoyu could only look at him.

"Do you have a watch?"

"No. I gave my watch to Uncle Cui the other night," confided Fang Meng'ao. "Give me your wrist and I'll check your pulse."

He Xiaoyu subconsciously tried to hide her hands behind her back but she only moved them a little.

Fang Meng'ao smiled. "Then you can count it yourself. My pulse rate is sixty beats per minute, compared with seventy for a normal person."

"What on earth are you doing?"

Fang Meng'ao started to take off his shirt, boots and trousers. "In Kunming, I competed with members of the US Flying Tigers to hold my breath under water. The best of them could hold it for two minutes and ten seconds but I could hold it for up to two and a half minutes. Count up to a hundred and seventy-five! If I haven't come up yet, it means I'm going to join Uncle Cui."

He Xiaoyu was startled when suddenly she saw a figure dart forward!

Fang Meng'ao had disappeared from the river bank and there was a big circle of ripples in the Yongding River! Staring at the ripples, He Xiaoyu suddenly remembered to count her pulse. She put her finger on her wrist but couldn't find the pulse. She then quickly put her hand on her chest to count her heartbeat. She scrambled for a while, not remembering any of the numbers. She stopped counting, opened her eyes and searched the river. Upstream and downstream, all she could see was the river flowing.

"Fang Meng'ao!" He Xiaoyu shouted towards the river.

There was no response from the Yongding River, which continued flowing quietly.

"Fang Meng'ao! You're a bad person." With a terrible howl, she lept forward and threw herself into the water.

Indeed, she could swim. When she reached the centre of the river, she dived down to look for Fang Meng'ao. Unfortunately, the river was not too clear and the visibility under water was only two metres.

He Xiaoyu resurfaced, took a quick breath and shook the water off her wet hair, only to find herself downstream about ten metres away from the jeep.

There was no trace of Fang Meng'ao on the embankment, nor any sign of him in the river. He Xiaoyu was being carried further and further away from where she had plunged into the water. She felt her energy gradually flagging but still she did all she could to swim upstream and cried out loud: "Fang Meng'ao!"

While she was calling his name, He Xiaoyu suddenly felt that the power of the Yongding River was stronger than before while her own strength was diminishing. As she alternately sank and floated to the surface, she knew she was not able to swim to the shore, nor did she want to swim there. She began to let herself sink. Her last thought was that she might be able to see Fang Meng'ao under water. As her body began to sink, her school skirt floated up, resembling a round lotus leaf near the water's surface. The round skirt could no longer support He Xiaoyu and prevent her from sinking. The sunlight on the surface of the water became brighter and brighter as seen from under the water.

There was a pair of eyes that were able to see the sky through the water and through the sun's rays on it. Fang Meng'ao, who had actually been swimming under water following He Xiaoyu's shadow, could clearly see the round skirt sinking at an angle.

Like a fish, he sprang towards the shadow, grasped the feet underneath the skirt with both hands, and pushed them upward. He Xiaoyu's body rose out of the water and the underwater thrust was so great that her body rose a metre above the water's surface.

He Xiaoyu spat out a mouthful of water, her eyes dazzled by the daylight. She saw clouds in the blue sky. All of a sudden, a thought occurred to her that she wanted to stop between the water and the sky.

But soon the hand holding her up underwater loosened again. As her body fell back onto the surface of the water, a hand stretched out and took her arm in a strong grip. When she saw Fang Meng'ao, He Xiaoyu twisted her arm and tried to get away from him but she was so weak that she just couldn't manage to. Fang Meng'ao swam towards the shore with her on his arm, just like a large boat pulling a small one.

In the north room of the courtyard house at No. 2 Mao'er Hutong, Zhang Yueyin received the telegram from the radio operator. He was startled at the first glance.

"Did you get told off?" asked Old Liu.

"Told off for what?" Zhang Yueyin was in an even worse mood. He didn't look at him, only handing over the telegram. "Comrade Liu Yun is attending a meeting at the East China Field Army headquarters."

Old Liu became even more frustrated when he read the message. "Can we communicate directly with the East China Field Army headquarters?"

"No way," said Zhang Yueyin. "The Peking Urban Works

Department can only communicate directly with the North China Urban Works Department."

"Then we can't wait." Old Liu looked at Zhang Yueyin. "The Central Committee definitely needs our information before six o'clock. I propose that Comrade Xie Peidong takes a car from the Peking branch and goes along the Jingshi Highway to look for him. When you see Fang Meng'ao, convey the instructions from the superiors and tell him to meet with Zeng Keda to find out the details of Operation 'The Peacock Flies Southeast', and who that Liu Lanzhi is."

Xie Peidong pondered for a moment, then replied: "I can go and look for him. I don't know whether I can find him but even if I do, I'll definitely not tell Fang Meng'ao to ask Zeng Keda about details of the operation or to find out who Liu Lanzhi is."

"Then we'll not carry out the Central Committee's instructions?" asked Old Liu, staring at Zhang Yueyin.

Zhang Yueyin could only look at Xie Peidong.

"The Enemy Works Department has principles. May I explain this to the Central Committee?"

"Explain what? That the party members we've recruited don't obey the party's command?"

Xie Peidong also pushed back strongly. "Before the integration of the Enemy Works Department into the Urban Works Department, there was a draconian discipline which stipulated that no special member assigned special tasks could be sent on any other missions until ordered to do so by the Central Committee. Fang Meng'ao is a special member of the party that Vice-Chairman Zhou instructed to be recruited, and the Iron and Blood Congress was also using him by any means possible. Therefore any move he makes has implications for the central government. If we send him to get information from Zeng Keda now, we'll immediately arouse Zeng Keda's suspicion and there'll be dire consequences. If pressed to do this, I must have approval from Vice-Chairman Zhou."

"No need to seek instructions!" said Old Liu, looking very firm. "It was an instruction from Vice-Chairman Zhou to report to the Central Committee on details of the operation known as 'The Peacock Flies Southeast' before six o'clock. In fact, Chairman Mao personally asked about it. This is the big picture right now. Mr Xie, your Enemy Works Department can make an excuse about the special status of your special members but we at the Peking Urban Works Department can't disobey Chairman Mao's instructions!"

"Then send a telegram to tell the Central Committee that I, Xie Peidong, am not carrying out Chairman Mao's instructions!" replied Xie Peidong.

"What did you say?!" Old Liu was shocked. Zhang Yueyin was also startled.

"I'm willing to accept the harshest punishment from the organisation!" said Xie Peidong, closing his eyes.

The air froze.

The two CPC special members by the Yongding River had no idea that the debate among their higher-ups was locked in a dilemma. In the back seat of the jeep, He Xiaoyu, with her blouse and skirt wet, reached for a large US Air Force tawny-print suitcase.

As the latch popped open, she found a neatly folded American Air Force uniform. Under the uniform was a clean white shirt, also neatly folded. Holding up the shirt, He Xiaoyu's eyes were fixed on the two exquisite frames that were placed side by side. In the left frame, two men in American-style Air Force short-sleeved shirts were smiling brightly at her: one was Claire Chennault who was smiling like a Chinese, the other was Fang Meng'ao who was smiling like an American.

In the frame on the right side, one man was in a Western suit and wearing a pair of gold-rimmed glasses, the other was in an American Air Force uniform and wearing a wide-brimmed hat. Both of them were smiling warmly at her: Cui Zhongshi in the suit smiling like a big brother and Fang Meng'ao in the uniform smiling like a younger brother!

He Xiaoyu was a bit surprised and smiled, then felt her heart wrenched. She held up the two frames and saw a fine oak wine box with 'Chateau Lafitte 1919' printed on it. A bottle of wine, a suitcase of clothes and two photographs were all packed together and carried around with him. Obviously they were precious not only because of the '1919' vintage.

She carefully put down the frames and picked up the wine box. It turned out that the answer was written in two lines on the back. The line on the left was in English: "To my bravest Chinese friend, Claire Chennault, Kunming. 1942." The line on the right was in Chinese: "To my beloved Brother Zhongshi, Fang Meng'ao, Hangzhou, 1946."

Claire Chennault gave it to Fang Meng'ao who in turn gave it to Cui Zhongshi but the bottle was still lying quietly in the suitcase!

He Xiaoyu cast a glance out of the window. There was no more Claire Chennault, no more Cui Zhongshi, only Fang Meng'ao who was sitting alone by the river like an enigma.

In the north house in the courtyard at No. 2, Mao'er Hutong, silence still enveloped Zhang Yueyin, Old Liu and Xie Peidong. None of them spoke.

"Xie Peidong proposed to send a telegram to the Central Committee saying that he was unable to carry out the chairman's instructions. If the task was not completed, then the Urban Works Department would be collectively held responsible. This message, however, could have ended the political careers of an old Communist Party member and of Fang Meng'ao, a special member of the party." A voice was quietly lingering around Zhang Yueyin.

"Old Liu." Zhang Yueyin could no longer remain silent. "What did Mr Xie just say? I didn't hear him clearly, did you?"

Old Liu, of course, understood that Zhang Yueyin was trying to protect Xie Peidong. He looked down and replied: "This involves party principles. I am a member of the party and I heard it clearly, I can't say I didn't."

Zhang Yueyin was really taken aback by Old Liu this time.

"Send a telegram to the Central Committee, I take responsibility for what I've said," assured Xie Peidong.

"Mr Xie!" Old Liu was torn by conflicting emotions. He was both distressed and anxious. "As a veteran party member with decades of experience, you have also studied the documents of the Seventh National Party Congress which stipulate that the whole party, the whole army and those on all fronts must implement the chairman's decisions. What you've just said is no longer the responsibility of one person."

"You mean, my personal words and deeds have implicated the Peking Urban Works Department?"

"Is it just the Peking Urban Works Department? If that were the case, the Urban Works Department of North China would be held responsible and so would Comrade Liu Yun!" retorted Old Liu.

"Then who else would it be?" Xie Peidong suddenly became intense. "The Central Committee's Urban Works Department? Vice-Chairman Zhou?"

Zhang Yueyin broke out in a cold sweat and looked at Old Liu. "I don't think that's what Comrade Liu meant."

Old Liu did mean what he had just said but he just couldn't bear to say it explicitly. Now that Xie Peidong had hit the mark with his response, he had no option but to reply stubbornly: "I did."

"You can't possibly mean it. If you do, we should reflect on it and correct ourselves." Zhang Yueyin was extremely frustrated.

"Correct what? What's wrong if I meant it?" It was Old Liu's turn to get emotional. A moment ago, he was inhibited from speaking his mind but now he was simply showing his hand.

"Who masterminded 'The Peacock Flies Southeast'? Chiang Kai-shek and Chiang Ching-kuo! The fact that Chairman Mao personally asked about it means that this operation will affect his decision to deploy our troops! Mr Xie, since you've worked for Vice-Chairman Zhou, you should understand that Vice-Chairman Zhou will be the first one to make a self-criticism if the intelligence gathered behind enemy lines is inaccurate because it will mislead Chairman Mao who is commanding a decisive battle at the front. For the sake of Vice-Chairman Zhou, you should seek out Fang Meng'ao to find out more details. How can you say something like you won't carry out Chairman Mao's instructions?"

"Comrade Liu Chuwu!" Xie Peidong slammed the table with the flat of his hand. "Have you ever seen Vice-Chairman Zhou and Chairman Mao working together! Have you seen how Vice-Chairman Zhou helps Chairman Mao use the troops!"

Old Liu and Zhang Yueyin were shocked!

"Indeed, the Seventh National Congress of the CPC established the leadership position of the chairman but it also confirmed the collective leadership of the Central Secretariat," replied Xie Peidong emotionally. "Now, which major decision of the chairman was not discussed collectively with the Central Secretariat? Vice-Chairman Zhou has always been on Chairman Mao's side. When did the inaccurate intelligence sent from behind enemy lines affect Chairman Mao's deployment of troops at the front? Comrade Liu Chuwu's thinking today reflects the erroneous trend of thinking within the party, which is that whatever Chairman Mao's instructions are which are communicated to organisations at all levels, some people tend to be so terrified that they don't even dare to report them even if they can't implement them. I strongly suggest that my ideas and those of Mr Liu Chuwu be immediately reported to the North China Urban Works Department, to the Central Committee!"

At this point, Xie Peidong became so agitated that he was trembling slightly.

Old Liu was still in a daze and then became emotional again.

"Mr Xie!" Zhang Yueyin called out to Xie Peidong with the intention of stopping Liu with his look.

"I agree to report your opinions but could you be more specific about the causes so that the Central Committee can make a fair assessment of the causes and difficulties?"

"Thank you, Comrade Yueyin." Xie Peidong stood up and walked over to the window.

By the Yongding River, He Xiaoyu had changed into Fang Meng'ao's white shirt and was standing silently behind him.

'Did you see everything in the suitcase?" asked Fang Meng'ao, remaining seated.

"I did," replied He Xiaoyu. "Why didn't you give the bottle of wine to Comrade Cui Zhongshi?"

"He told me to save it for later, to open it on the day when the New China is founded, and to drink it together."

The answer to this riddle was so simple and so heart-wrenching!

"Keep it and, when the day comes, we'll take the wine together to Uncle Cui's grave to honour him."

"Who are we?" Fang Meng'ao stood up abruptly and turned to He Xiaoyu. "Who else is there besides you and me?"

"I can only tell you that it's you and me now," said He Xiaoyu, giving him a profound look.

"What about Comrade Xie Peidong?" asked Fang Meng'ao. "Do we have to count him in?"

"Did Uncle Xie himself meet with you?" He Xiaoyu was quite taken aback.

In the north room at No. 2, Mao'er Hutong, Xie Peidong looked out of the window and finally replied: "I don't want to emphasise the difficulties. Comrade Yueyin, please explain to the Central Committee in your telegram that Fang Meng'ao is a special member of the party whom Comrade Cui Zhongshi and I were instructed to recruit, and the Central Committee has clearly instructed that he is not to be allowed to participate in organisational life, that he is not to be allowed to read party documents and that he is not to be given any assignments. Please understand his actions today and maintain his status as a special member of the party."

At this point, he finally turned around and looked at Zhang Yueyin and Old Liu who were both looking straight at him.

"The reason is simple. In the front line, we are bombed by Kuomintang planes all day long. Not long ago Kuomintang planes bombed Fuping, their bombs even fell on the chairman's doorstep. We need special party members like Comrade Fang Meng'ao more than ever, we need an air force."

"Mr Xie." Old Liu finally became emotional too.

"Don't say anything," Zhang Yueyin interrupted him. "I'm going to personally send a message to the North China Urban Works Department and ask them to relay it to Comrade Liu Yun urgently, and then ask him to report the situation to the Central Committee."

"Lovers' relationship?" He Xiaoyu looked into Fang Meng'ao's eyes. "Was it the organisation's decision?"

"It was my own request," said Fang Meng'ao with a wry smile.

"How can you make such a request to the organisation?" He Xiaoyu also did not know why her heart fluttered.

"In the past, Uncle Cui contacted me on behalf of my family. In what capacity are you contacting me now?"

"I told you last time, I represent the Students' Union."

"The Students' Union cannot contact me." Fang Meng'ao stopped laughing. "There's something wrong with Professor Liang."

He Xiaoyu was shocked.

As the sun stopped in the sky, the Yongding River seemed to cease to flow.

"What's wrong with him?" asked He Xiaoyu, startled.

"Petty bourgeois fervour."

Cui Zhongshi's efforts at conversation with Fang Meng'ao over the past few years had worked. Fang Meng'ao managed to make up the smartest way to lie. He Xiaoyu slowly recovered and when she looked at Fang Meng'ao again, her heart was still fluttering.

"I'm sorry, this is what your Uncle Xie said. His real identity is a member of the Student Committee affiliated with our party organisation. But he often takes advantage of his membership of the Students' Union to take drastic actions, including sending you to recruit me. The Urban Works Department did not assign anyone from the Student Committee with the task, nor did the Student Committee tell him to do so."

"Was this the reason why you were reluctant to meet me last time?"

"I'm not from the Urban Works Department, so how do I know the reason?" said Fang Meng'ao with a cockeyed grin.

"Then, what is the reason?"

"Personal reasons, do you want to hear them?"

He Xiaoyu was beginning to understand him but didn't know whether she wanted to hear it or not. "Go ahead," she replied.

"I like you."

These three words seemed to echo in He Xiaoyu's ears as if in a hollow valley.

The Urban Works Department sent her to contact Fang

Meng'ao individually and the Students' Union also sent her to recruit Fang Meng'ao's auditing team, all because of the irreplaceable childhood friendship and the special relationship between the two families. Now, faced with Fang Meng'ao, the man who arrived on a commonly shared past, He Xiaoyu had not yet seen the planes flying over the New China but had already tasted the 'sweetness' of the childhood friendship.

She wanted to cry but didn't want him to see her, so she turned and walked away.

The sun, the river and the open fields were all laid out before her. She could see the Kuomintang-controlled Peking City where the people were deprived of their means of survival; while behind her was the liberated area they yearned for on the other side of the rolling Taihang Mountains.

Surprisingly, the two men to whom she was still emotionally attached were the ones she had fought alongside for the New China. What lingered on was Liang Jinglun's Chinese-style robe. What was unforgettable was Fang Meng'ao's life-saving lift in the water!

"Don't rush to tell me now," said Fang Meng'ao as he came up behind her. "It's our business to like you, which has nothing to do with our task. Let me talk to Professor Liang."

"Don't!" said He Xiaoyu, turning around with tears in her eyes.

"From today on, we will be together frequently. I will not only talk to Professor Liang but also to Uncle He."

"I didn't even promise you anything, so why should you talk to them!"

"You will," said Fang Meng'ao. "You saw the bottle of wine, didn't you? I will write another line on it. 'My wish is for Meng'ao and Xiaoyu to live happily ever after, signed by Cui Zhongshi, when the day comes according to Uncle Cui.'"

Finally He Xiaoyu began to weep.

Fang Meng'ao gently pressed his body against her back and whispered in her ear. "Don't cry, we've got company."

Slowly, He Xiaoyu stopped crying and wiped her tears. "Can't you be more serious when you speak from now on?"

"Well, see for yourself." Fang Meng'ao stepped away from her. "To the northwest, there's a jeep."

He Xiaoyu hesitantly and slowly turned back, looking in a northwesterly direction. In the distance, there was indeed a jeep the size of a bug slowly moving towards them.

"It's Mengwei's car." Fang Meng'ao's powers of observation were always surprising. "Don't let him see you wearing my shirt, go and change."

The door to the North Room at No. 2, Mao'er Hutong was pushed open. Although it sounded very light, it seemed loud to the ears of Old Liu and Xie Peidong. The two men stood up as Zhang Yueyin walked in.

"Have you got any instructions?" Old Liu said to Zhang Yueyin.

Zhang Yueyin nodded and walked over to the table.

"From the Central Committee or from the North China Urban Works Department?" asked Old Liu again urgently.

"Just listen to the message." Zhang Yueyin did not answer his question. He sat down and gestured for Xie Peidong and Old Liu to sit down as well.

"Where is the telegram?" asked Old Liu yet again, as he took a seat.

"Burned. I'll communicate it verbally."

Old Liu and Xie Peidong immediately understood that this was a special encrypted instruction with no transcripts. The next step was to hear the communicator dictate from memory.

"In the wake of the latest development in the War of Liberation, we merged the Department of Social Intelligence with the Urban Works Counter-Espionage Department and consolidated it into the Urban Works Department. Recent developments indicate that the Urban Works Department is still very much unprepared for this development. One of the most prominent and serious issues is the neglect of the principle that intelligence work and united front work cannot be intertwined."

"Is this the Central Committee's instruction?" remarked Old Liu, interrupting Zhang Yueyin.

"It is quite wrong for the Peking Urban Works Department to suggest today that special party members with special assignments be allowed to conduct intelligence-gathering activities in a certain core department of the Kuomintang." Zhang Yueyin stared at him, and then continued: "In this regard, we severely criticise this way of doing things, and take this as a case in point to inform the Urban Works Departments in all localities. It is our hope that we will never allow similar mistakes to occur again."

Old Liu stood up abruptly and asked: "Who's to be criticised?"

"The Peking Urban Works Department and the North China Urban Works Department. While forwarding the message to us, Comrade Liu Yun was already reviewing the situation with the Central Committee."

Old Liu was truly confused, then came to his senses and asked excitedly: "Which department of the Central Committee drafted this message?"

Zhang Yueyin was already uncomfortable, but Old Liu's question made him even more so. He frowned and asked: "Is this important?"

"Of course it's important!" said Old Liu, even more excited now.

"It was a direct order from Chairman Mao that the detailed action plan for 'The Peacock Flies Southeast' be submitted by six o'clock today and that the true identity of Liu Lanzhi be found out. History has proven that the truth is always on the side of the chairman. We may not defend ourselves regarding the criticism today. But what should we do if there is a conflict between the implementation of the chairman's instructions and the general principle in the future? Did the Central Committee explain this issue in its telegram?"

"Yes." Zhang Yueyin's demeanour became very grim. "I will now communicate the personal instructions of Vice-Chairman Zhou and Chairman Mao."

Old Liu opened his eyes wide and asked: "Did Chairman Mao personally give his opinions?"

"Mr Xie," said Zhang Yueyin, turning to Xie Peidong, who had been sitting reticently. "The instructions of Vice-Chairman Zhou and the first paragraph of Chairman Mao's instructions concern you. Please listen carefully."

"Yes," said Xie Peidong almost instantaneously.

"Vice-Chairman Zhou fully affirmed Comrade Xie Peidong's

insistence that intelligence work and united front work should not be intertwined, and his opposition to allowing Comrade Fang Meng'ao to gather intelligence. At the same time, he severely criticsed Xie for his remarks about not carrying out Chairman Mao's instructions. 'This is an unhealthy practice, and we must firmly put an end to it.'"

"I accept Vice-Chairman Zhou's criticism."

At that time, Zhang Yueyin fell silent and clearly looked emotional. After calming himself down, he continued: "At the end of Vice-Chairman Zhou's instruction, the Chairman also wrote a commentary on..."

That's where the most important instructions came in!

Zhang Yueyin tried his best to calm down and said: "The first sentence is: 'It is a righteous trend that should be advocated'; the second sentence is: 'The king's orders are not to be obeyed when the general is fighting in faraway places!'"

Xie Peidong felt unexpected sorrow in his heart and his eyes became wet. He conjured up the image of Vice-Chairman Zhou working beside the chairman with great loyalty and dedication.

Old Liu, however, did not expect this and was taken aback.

"Comrade Liu, the chairman's next comment is related to Vice-Chairman Zhou's criticism of our Urban Works Department. It's up to you whether you want to ask for disciplinary action after hearing this."

"OK." Old Liu was already confused.

"The chairman's comment was: 'A strong sense of the organisation, poor sense of principle. Criticism this time, punishment with discipline next time.'"

"I still ask for disciplinary action." It was Old Liu's turn to get teary-eyed and excited.

"Don't bother with disciplinary issues!" said Zhang Yueyin.

"Now, time for the specific instructions."

"Yes."

"The intelligence that we were originally required to submit by six o'clock has been obtained by the Central Committee from our sources in Nanking."

Xie Peidong and Old Liu both held their breath.

Zhang Yueyin continued: "'The Peacock Flies Southeast' was the code name of the Kuomintang's currency reform operation in Peking. 'Jiao Zhongqing' is Comrade Fang Meng'ao and 'Liu Lanzhi' is Liang Jinglun!"

"Really, it's him!" Xie Peidong cried out involuntarily.

"The situation is still out of control. Comrade Liu Yun has informed us that Fang Mengwei has found Fang Meng'ao and He Xiaoyu, and that they are now on their way to Yenching University."

"They'll go for Liang Jinglun, won't they?" retorted Xie Peidong, surprised.

"It's quite possible."

On the road to the east gate of Yenching University, Fang Meng'ao's jeep with the plate of the Inspection Brigade of the Ministry of Defence actually showed up. Following closely behind was Fang Mengwei's jeep with the licence plate 'Peking Police No. 002'. The road was bumpy but the two jeeps were still rattling along at a fast pace.

The setting sun shone in the west as they approached the east gate of Yenching University. Several students were hanging around the school gate.

Fang Meng'ao's jeep screeched to a halt while Fang Mengwei slammed on the brakes. He Xiaoyu looked at Fang Meng'ao in the driver's seat but the latter was looking over to the east gate of the university where a small two-storey building was located.

"Is that the building?"

"Which building?"

"The place where Professor Liang reads and sleeps."

"What do you want?"

Fang Meng'ao didn't answer but just stared at the small building.

"Big Brother," said Fang Mengwei, knocking on the door of the jeep. "Drive Miss He home. Why did you stop here again?"

"Do you see that building?"

"Which building?" Fang Mengwei's heart pounded with a fierce beat.

"The Foreign Languages Bookstore."

"Brother! You've messed with everyone in the world and now you want to mess with me! Do you get some sort of sick pleasure out of it?" Fang Mengwei's face changed abruptly.

"What do you mean... messing around? I'm helping you." Fang Meng'ao stared at him. "If you're a man, go and bring Mulan out of that building."

"Then it should be you that brings her out!" Fang Mengwei's voice was trembling. "That Liang Jinglun loves Xiaoyu, not Mulan!" he said, striding towards his jeep. Fang Meng'ao looked in the rearview mirror, watching Fang Mengwei get into the jeep and continued to watch as he turned the jeep around precipitously and drove off like a man possessed. It was rare to hear Fang Meng'ao let out such a long sigh. He pushed the door open.

"What the hell are you doing?" said He Xiaoyu, trying to pull him back.

"Mengwei is right. I should go."

It was impossible for He Xiaoyu to stop him. As she watched, Fang Meng'ao got out of the jeep.

While he was still in a daze, she saw Fang Meng'ao's back ten metres away from her. Then, before she realised what was going on, he had run a hundred metres and charged into the bookstore. Surprisingly, none of the students hanging around the main entrance of the university were sharp enough to notice him. He Xiaoyu knew that she had to follow him into that small building. She even surprised herself with the speed with which she was able to run. It turned out that was the second time He Xiaoyu had to put her life on the line to rescue him today.

———

"I'll go to the Foreign Languages Bookstore now," said Xie Peidong in the north room at No. 2, Mao'er Hutong. As he said that, he had already picked up his bag. "We must stop Fang Meng'ao and Liang Jinglun from meeting each other!"

"No way," said Zhang Yueyin, vetoing the idea. "Mr Xie, what Comrade Fang Meng'ao did today was the result of your meeting in the morning. According to Comrade Liu Yun, it's highly probable that the Iron and Blood Congress would suspect you."

"I must go. Please trust me, I have good reason to talk to Fang Meng'ao. And I've got a way to deal with that Liang Jinglun."

"I won't allow you to talk to Liang Jinglun face to face!" Zhang Yueyin interrupted him. "Comrade Liu Yun has ordered us to wait and see what happens next, and to wait for new instructions from the North China Urban Works Department and the Central Committee."

Xie Peidong knew that he couldn't go. He looked out into the dusk outside the window.

"I don't know what Meng'ao will say and what will happen when he meets with Liang Jinglun."

"Mr Xie, let's believe that Comrade Cui Zhongshi's work on him over these past years was effective."

The light inside the bookstore was fading as the sun was setting. He Xiaoyu stood at the stairs on the ground floor, holding the banister. She felt weak after gasping for air and looked at Fang Meng'ao who was already standing outside the room on the first floor.

With the door open, revealing the dusk through the door frame, Fang Meng'ao, like a big boy with a gentleman's education, stood by the door without looking inside while He Xiaoyu watched with a sense of helplessness and admiration. She could not bear to blame Fang Meng'ao, only hoping that he could be more reasonable and a little more restrained.

With a "Don't worry" type of look, Fang Meng'ao asked somebody inside the house: "Excuse me, may I come in?"

"Big Brother!"

Downstairs, He Xiaoyu heard Xie Mulan calling out in panic because she hadn't heard the sound of Fang Meng'ao going upstairs from the room on the first floor. As she realised she was blocking the stairway, He Xiaoyu turned around and walked towards the bookshelf nearby.

Inside the room on the first floor, Xie Mulan, like a frightened deer, tried to avoid eye contact with her big brother and looked towards Liang Jinglun.

"Please meet my big brother."

What kind of talk was that? Xie Mulan was even more flustered.

"By the way, Professor Liang knows that he is my elder brother."

"Miss Mulan's here to borrow a book from me," said Liang Jinglun, actually very calm and composed. "Captain Fang, please come in."

"Mr Liang is a learned professor." Fang Meng'ao walked into the room, hiding his disgust for this man. He looked at Xie Mulan. "You and Xiaoyu should both learn from him."

"Yes, big brother." Xie Mulan's voice was so soft, she could no longer avoid eye contact with her big brother. Yet her eyes were full of hope to obtain his love and empathy.

"'She is Mr Xie's most beloved daughter!'" Fang Meng'ao blurted out the poem as his heart was saddened. Then he grinned, remembering the poem that his father used to recite to Mengwei and him whenever he showed favour towards his sister and Xie Mulan at their home in Shanghai before 13 August. Today, at this moment, he found it all right and proper to share this poem. He looked at Liang Jinglun.

"Professor Liang may not know that my father, who is the governor of the bank, has always favoured my two sisters since their childhood. When my younger sister was killed in Shanghai on the thirteenth of August, my father came to love Mulan even more. But, Professor Liang, do please feel free to restrain them if she behaves capriciously."

"All professors favour good students. Among my students, I also favour her a little bit." Liang Jinglun was very sweet-tongued.

Fang Meng'ao stared into Liang Jinglun's eyes with a smile.

Liang Jinglun was not as calm and composed as before, as he could not understand the real meaning behind the smile. He had no choice but to smile back in response. Xie Mulan dared not move nor speak. She stood there as if nailed to the spot.

"Mulan may not be Professor Liang's only favourite student, right?" said Fang Meng'ao with a broad grin. "I've also brought He Xiaoyu with me."

"Oh?" Liang Jinglun's eyes could no longer afford to be unresponsive. "Why didn't you come up together?"

"She's reading downstairs."

Fang Meng'ao was ready to start fighting this guy. He turned to Xie Mulan and said: "I've got something to talk about with Mr Liang. Please go downstairs, Xiaoyu is waiting for you."

"Well," muttered Xie Mulan hesitantly, looking over at Liang Jinglun moving.

"Go ahead," urged Liang Jinglun. "Just in time to talk to her about how the Students' Union will organise food pickups tomorrow."

"Mmm." Xie Mulan's legs began to move but only when she reached the door did she suddenly remember that she should have said goodbye to her big brother. She hastily turned back.

"Big Brother, I must be going."

Fang Meng'ao felt utterly dismayed to see her trying to cover up her panic, so he didn't look at her. Xie Mulan tripped as she stepped over the threshold, throwing the book and pen out of her hands. Although she tried to hold onto the stairs, she fell outside the door.

This time Liang Jinglun was embarrassed! He wanted to help her up but her big brother was there. He quickly looked at Fang Meng'ao.

Fang Meng'ao had turned his head but he stood there without moving. He smiled at Xie Mulan who was still lying on the floor outside the door. "Look, you fell again, did you? What did I tell you when you fell as a small child?"

Actually, she was so amazed to hear her big brother utter these words that Xie Mulan stood up immediately, no longer feeling scared when she first saw him, nor embarrassed when she accidentally tripped. Yet the smile on her face as she turned back melted the hearts of the two men!

"Remembered yet?" Fang Meng'ao's laughing had firmly supported his little cousin who was already standing there.

"I did." Xie Mulan looked at her big brother without hiding her tears and replied by reciting the famous lines: "'On the expedition of thousands of miles to the war, she dashed across mountains and passes as if flying.'" With that, she smiled in response to her big brother's smile but didn't bother to look at Liang Jinglun.

Fang Meng'ao laughed and looked at Liang Jinglun.

"There're still quite a lot of things that Mr Liang doesn't know. In fact, our family has been comparing Mulan to Hua Mulan since childhood. She took it seriously and at a very young age, she made a promise to join me in the Air Force and fight alongside me when she grew up. During the war years, when I was fighting the Japanese Air Force, I imagined her as my wingman several times but unfortunately that was not to be."

He smiled and waited for Liang Jinglun's reaction but he felt obliged to look pensive.

Within a day, Liang Jinglun had already had two interesting encounters, one with his father Fang Buting early in the morning and the other with his legendary son at this moment. Each of them had given him a hard time which he hadn't anticipated. He suddenly realised that what he feared most was not the Communist Party-controlled Student Committee, nor the Communist Party's Urban Works Department, nor those within the Kuomintang who couldn't stand him, but Fang Meng'ao with whom he would have to work closely. "No matter how hard it is, we must carry out Comrade Jianfeng's instructions. Let's play it by ear."

"Mulan was also renowned for her sporting prowess at school. She fell down and refused to let go of the ball when she was playing basketball," replied Liang Jinglun, finally finding the smile he was looking for and leaving his thoughts behind.

Xie Mulan was able to look at Liang Jinglun and the kind of dependence that was reserved for her cousin appeared in her eyes again. It was Fang Meng'ao's turn to laugh bitterly. For his little sister, he could not tell whether he was heartbroken or angry; as for the man beside him, he could not tell whether he hated or pitied him.

"Xiaoyu is still waiting for you," said Fang Meng'ao with his pitiful eyes still on Xie Mulan.

"Mmm," muttered Xie Mulan diffidently, glancing at Liang Jinglun. When she went downstairs, she was no longer the original Mulan at all.

Fang Meng'ao turned and pulled out a book from the bookshelf beside the wall and opened it while Liang Jinglun walked to the door and tried to close it.

"Don't close the door," said Fang Meng'ao who seemed to have eyes in the back of his head.

"In that case, do you want me to turn on the light?" asked Liang Jinglun, stunned.

"Nope," replied Fang Meng'ao, still with his back to him. "I've got good eyesight."

Liang Jinglun could not speak any more and slowly turned his body. Fang Meng'ao kept reading there, so Liang Jinglun had to look at his back.

Inside his room, Zeng Keda started with alarm when speaking into the phone and sternly rebuked the person on the other end of the line in a loud voice.

"Shut up! I told you to stop talking, didn't you hear me?"

Fang Meng'ao's sudden return from the southwestern defence line and his visit to Liang Jinglun without prior notice turned out to be equally surprising to Zeng Keda. When the caller at the other end stopped talking, he asked urgently: "Where are you calling from? The Foreign Languages Bookstore?"

"No. Absolutely not, Comrade Keda." The caller spoke with less urgency than before, therefore his voice was crystal clear.

"He Xiaoyu and Xie Mulan are on the ground floor of the bookstore, we'd be found out if we went in. So we're now calling from a safe place, which is why there's a delay of ten minutes."

The expression on Zeng Keda's face eased a little and then he frowned. "What do you mean by saying He Xiaoyu and Xie Mulan are on the ground floor? How did Fang Meng'ao get into the bookstore? Wasn't Fang Mengwei with him?"

"Yes," answered the voice on the other end of the line. "At first, both Fang Meng'ao and Fang Mengwei arrived in separate jeeps. They stopped two hundred metres outside the east gate of Yenching University. Fang Mengwei seems to have had an argument with Fang Meng'ao and then left in a fit of anger. Then Fang Meng'ao suddenly ran into the Foreign Languages Bookstore, followed by He Xiaoyu. Now Fang Meng'ao and Liang Jinglun are upstairs and He Xiaoyu and Xie Mulan are downstairs. We can't go in either, therefore we don't know what's being said upstairs and we can't hear what's being said downstairs. End of report, Comrade Keda."

What a mess!

Zeng Keda's eyes glanced at the book on the table, *The Peacock Flies Southeast.*

With the phone still near his ear, Zeng Keda had already lost his concentration: "'*Southeast the love-lorn peacock flies. At every mile she falters and looks back!...*' Why pick these two people?"

Of course, the caller on the other end did not understand so he asked urgently: "Comrade Keda, Comrade Keda. Please repeat the instructions you just gave, I didn't hear you clearly."

"It's good you didn't hear it," said Zeng Keda, snapping out of his contemplation. "Let me reiterate to you, I don't have any instructions. Stand guard outside the door, keep me posted on the latest. No one is allowed to enter the Foreign Languages Bookstore without my further instruction! Do you hear me clearly this time?"

"Yes, we did, Comrade Keda!"

Zeng Keda put the phone down and turned his attention to the direct line to Nanking. He reached for the phone but then changed his mind, walked impatiently to the door and opened it.

"Adjutant Wang!"

"Yes sir!" In the twilight, Adjutant Wang's reply came from across the corridor.

"Set up the radio right away and connect me with the number two special line."

It was already dark on the ground floor of the Foreign Languages Bookstore. After Xie Mulan came downstairs, He Xiaoyu refused to speak to her for quite a while. The two sat quietly in front of the reading table, listening attentively to what was happening on the first floor. Finally, Xie Mulan couldn't resist saying to He Xiaoyu under her breath: "How come there's no sound at all?"

He Xiaoyu stood up and turned on the light.

The electricity used by the Foreign Languages Bookstore was also supplied by Yenching University, with diesel fuel supplied exclusively by the US, so there was no need to economise on electricity consumption. A hundred-watt lamp illuminated the room so brightly that it diffused up the stairs and towards the door of the room on the first floor.

He Xiaoyu returned to the table with two books she had taken. She gently handed one to Xie Mulan, sat down and began to read the other. Some of the light on the ground floor spread in, making Fang Meng'ao's back more visible as he stood in front of the bookshelf in the room flipping through books.

Liang Jinglun, who was sitting across the long table in the middle of the room, felt the urge to speak. "Captain Fang, you must have something for me, can you tell me frankly?"

Fang Meng'ao was waiting for him to speak. Holding the book, he turned his head back towards Liang Jinglun and asked, half-smilingly and half-scornfully: "Where can we start with *The Twenty-Four Histories?*"

Liang Jinglun didn't know how to answer him. He just looked at him with a trace of confusion in his eyes.

"I'm sorry, I don't usually talk like this, I learned this phrase from my father."

"I understand." Liang Jinglun could no longer be "bewildered" by "history no one can afford to forget".

"Yes, 'forgetting history means betrayal'."

Liang Jinglun looked Fang Meng'ao straight in the eye. "Captain Fang also knows this famous saying?"

In the faint light coming from downstairs, Fang Meng'ao's eyes were so bright. "I know, Lenin said so."

"Do you read Lenin?" asked Liang Jinglun with a curious look.

"Is it strange to have read Lenin's books?"

Liang Jinglun waited for him to say more. When Fang Meng'ao realised that he would not answer, he shifted the book towards the light coming from the door and looked through it, then asked: "Have you got similar books here?"

"It's through," confirmed Adjutant Wang in front of the radio in his room. He was sweating profusely with his headset on, looking towards Zeng Keda who stood in front of the radio nodding his head. Adjutant Wang then went to get the file folder and pencil on the table.

"Don't take notes."

"Yes sir." Adjutant Wang immediately withdrew his hand and held the transmitter key.

"Expedited and Top Secret." Zeng Keda began to dictate.

The ticking sound of Adjutant Wang hitting the transmitter keys rang out at the same time while Zeng Keda dictated his message.

"Comrade Jianfeng, Jiao Zhongqing returned to Peking at six pm and had an unscheduled meeting with Liu Lanzhi in private, motive unknown, details unknown..."

Zeng Keda suddenly stopped dictating and Adjutant Wang stopped transmitting as he waited. Zeng Keda apparently was weighing his advice and, after thinking quickly, he came to his senses. Perhaps any advice would prove negative at this point. He then dictated: "Look forward to your instructions. Sent from Peking. Urgent submission by Zeng Keda."

As Adjutant Wang hit the key for the last time, Zeng Keda ordered: "Report to me immediately you get a response." With that, he opened the door and disappeared into the twilight.

In the room on the first floor of the Foreign Languages Bookstore, Fang Meng'ao took the book and walked across to Liang Jinglun.

"No need to go to the library to find it."

He put the book on the table and sat down. "Now you tell me you've read it, I'll tell you that at the Flying Tigers' headquarters, Claire Chennault had all these books, including those by Lenin, Marx and Mao. We were curious and asked him: 'Why do you need to read these books to fly combat missions?' He answered very honestly that these books have not only influenced the history of the world but are also influencing the history of China, so they're all worth reading."

"Did you read them all?"

"No. The Aviation Committee issued a strict order that these books could be read by Claire Chennault and American pilots but that we, the pilots of the Nationalist Army Air Force, were not allowed to read them. Regarding Lenin's adage, I heard it from Claire Chennault. Professor Liang should have read all these books, right?"

Liang Jinglun had a deep feeling that this person's behaviour was sloppy but his mind was extremely meticulous, more complex and powerful than he had anticipated. He could only answer frankly: "At home and in the US, I studied economics. Marx's *Das Kapital* was an elective course and the planned economy of the Soviet Union was also a requirement of the selected readings in comparative study course."

"I don't understand this." Fang Meng'ao knew it was time to drop the topic and cut to the chase. "Professor Liang, you should know what I'm here for."

"Why?"

"He Xiaoyu."

"I told her to ask you to help with the Students Union?"

"That's not our business."

Liang Jinglun had to look at him again.

"I proposed to her today."

This was indeed something Liang Jinglun had not expected. His heart was tumbling but he had to remain calm on the surface. However, Fang Meng'ao would not allow him to settle. "You're Xiaoyu's teacher and Professor He's student. I came today because I specifically want to hear your advice."

"That's a bit hard for me. Let me think about it, OK?" It was Liang Jinglun's turn to go to the bookshelf to look through the books.

Night fell and swallowed up the twilight, leaving only the dim yellow of the street lamps to shine on Zeng Keda, standing on a stone path in front of a small building. Gu Weijun, who had long been based in Europe and the US on diplomatic missions and who had extensive knowledge of Western countries, was said to have hired Western botanists to transplant several plants in this garden that had never existed in Peking. Zeng Keda didn't know them either, so he just checked them out one by one, looking over at the tallest tree and at the thickest branch on that tree. A branch of the tall tree, which was strong enough to keep a person's feet off the ground and allow them to hang by the neck, was slanting away. There was a pool of water below it.

Zeng Keda was a bit dazzled. He seemed to see two people pass by the water under the tree! One looked like Fang Meng'ao, the other resembled Liang Jinglun. He found himself in something of a trance as he walked towards the big tree by the pool. There was not a soul over there, only his own blurred reflection in the pond.

He suddenly remembered two other verses from *The Peacock Flies Southeast*:

> Barefoot, she threw herself into the pond's dark waters.
> Beneath the courtyard trees,
> He hanged himself on the branch facing southeast.

An ominous feeling overcame him and he was startled as he turned abruptly.

"Inspector." Adjutant Wang stood quietly about a metre behind him. "Number Two's sent a telegram back!"

"Can't you even say 'Report'?" asked Zeng Keda, taking his anger out on Adjutant Wang whom he quickly walked past. He went up the stone steps of the corridor and walked towards Wang's room.

"Inspector!" Adjutant Wang called from behind Zeng Keda.

Zeng Keda stopped, having now calmed down, and looked back at Adjutant Wang who reported under his breath: "Number Two called back and said he will speak to you on the phone immediately."

This meant that there would be detailed instructions. Zeng Keda patted Adjutant Wang's shoulder comfortingly and walked back towards his own room. At this very moment, the phone from the Nanking special line in his room began to ring. Zeng Keda darted into his own room.

Obviously, Liang Jinglun declined to answer Fang Meng'ao's question. Instead, he continued to stand in front of the bookshelf with the book in his hand. However, the light that cascaded from the ground floor was not strong enough to allow him to read the words in the book.

"If Professor Liang really wants to read a book, let's turn on the light." Fang Meng'ao walked over and pulled the switch by the door.

The twenty-five-watt lamp, however, dazzled Liang Jinglun. He felt as though he was being stripped naked and exposed under the lamp. Apparently, it was impossible not to answer Fang Meng'ao's question. Liang Jinglun put down his book, returned to his desk and sat down. "I honestly don't know why Captain Fang wants to ask me this question."

"Then let me ask you in a different way, answer me if you will." Fang Meng'ao returned to sit opposite Liang Jinglun. "But let's lower our voices, it'd be better not to let them hear us."

"Go ahead," said Liang Jinglun, keeping his voice low.

"Professor Liang, in addition to your teacher-student relationship with Xiaoyu and your teacher-student relationship with her father, are you romantically involved?"

Liang Jinglun pondered for a moment and said: "Captain Fang has already proposed to He Xiaoyu, so is it still necessary to ask me this question?"

"Of course it's necessary. If you are, it would be immoral for me to propose, especially since it concerns Vice-Chancellor He."

Liang Jinglun had been warning himself to be calm and now he just couldn't bear it. "Captain Fang, do you think we're romantically involved?"

"I don't think so." This was exactly what Fang Meng'ao wanted, namely, a spontaneous exchange and debate.

"Please go on."

"If you had had a romantic relationship, you wouldn't have asked her to enlist me to help the Students' Union. First off, it's dangerous for her. Second, it's bad for you because she's likely to fall in love with me or I with her."

"I really hadn't anticipated this kind of analysis by Captain Fang. Anyway, please go on."

"Do you want me to continue? If I do, can you answer what I ask?"

"There's no question that'd be difficult for me to answer."

"Unless you are a Communist!"

The silence was broken by the sound of insects chirping and warbling in the grass outside the window. Fang Meng'ao stared straight at him.

"You can either answer me or choose not to."

Lights could be seen on the first floor and the sound of two people talking could also be heard vaguely. Then silence. Sitting at the table on the ground floor, He Xiaoyu and Xie Mulan looked at each other.

"No, something must be wrong." He Xiaoyu stood up.

Xie Mulan also got to her feet.

"Let's go up," said He Xiaoyu.

Xie Mulan, however, did not move.

He Xiaoyu was anxious. "What are you afraid of?"

Xie Mulan was embarrassed and then also became anxious. "What am I afraid of?"

"I asked you what they've just said, you didn't want to say a word. Now, you don't want to see them. What is it that's making you so evasive?"

"What is there to be evasive about?" She followed He Xiaoyu who was already walking alone toward the stairs.

He Xiaoyu's footsteps were so loud that she could soon be heard to have reached the end of the stairs on the first floor.

CHAPTER 16

By the time He Xiaoyu had walked to the door of the room on the first floor, Fang Meng'ao had moved with unusual agility and was already blocking the doorway.

"Can we come in?"

He Xiaoyu's eyes were full of reproach which Fang Meng'ao could see plainly.

"No, you can't." He remained in their way.

He Xiaoyu ignored him and gazed over his shoulder at Liang Jinglun inside the room. Xie Mulan had also come up by this time, standing behind He Xiaoyu, checking out Liang Jinglun who sat quietly at his desk, surprisingly motionless.

"Professor Liang," He Xiaoyu did not know how their talk had been going but didn't feel she could ask. So instead she said: "Can we come in?"

"Please ask Captain Fang."

"Why? If you have something important to discuss, don't make us wait downstairs. If you tell us to wait and don't tell us why, we'll be very upset!"

"We'll be done quite soon. You guys can read for another half an hour."

"Let's go down and read," suggested Xie Mulan, tugging at He Xiaoyu from behind her back.

He Xiaoyu had never behaved like this before. She broke away from Xie Mulan's grip behind her, and her eyes turned to Fang Meng'ao again.

"Do as you're told, ah!" urged Fang Meng'ao, blinking.

"Told us what? Why are we supposed to be told?"

"Of course, listen to me and to Professor Liang."

He Xiaoyu abruptly turned round, walked past Xie Mulan and rushed downstairs. Xie Mulan still wanted to pry something out of her big brother's gaze but Fang Meng'ao had already closed the door.

Again, Fang Meng'ao sat opposite Liang Jinglun.

"Captain Fang, perhaps we shouldn't involve them."

"I never got anyone else involved," said Fang Meng'ao. "Perhaps Mr Liang should answer my question."

Liang Jinglun pondered before responding: "If Captain Fang really wants to know if I'm a Communist, I can't say yes or no. But if you insist, there is someone you can ask."

He Xiaoyu, who was now standing in the doorway, flashed past Fang Meng'ao's eyes. "Do I know this person or not?"

"Yes, you do."

"Who is it?"

"Wang Puchen."

"Is he the station chief of the Peking station of the Military Council's Bureau of Investigation and Statistics?" Fang Meng'ao had not expected him to name this person.

"Yes. As for whether I'm a Communist or not, he interrogated me in his prison located in the Western Hills."

"Do you mind if I smoke, Mr Liang?" Fang Meng'ao stood up and took a cigar out of his pocket.

"Go ahead."

———

The shrill ringing of the telephone in the radio communication room of the secret prison of the Bureau of Investigation and Statistics in the Western Hills drew the gaze of Wang Puchen who was on a phone call and was somewhat nervous.

Looking at the phone ringing on the other end of the table, he said into the phone: "It's Chen Jicheng calling. Comrade Jianfeng... Yes, OK. I'll take his call first and then report to you."

In the room on the first floor of the Foreign Languages Bookstore, Fang Meng'ao did not flick his American lighter this time but took out his special box of extra-long matches, struck one and slowly lit the cigar. "But I remember that I'd already rescued you before Wang Puchen interrogated you."

"Captain Fang, can I ask you a question?" said Liang Jinglun, seizing the moment. "Why did you bother to save me when you didn't even know if I was a Communist?"

Fang Meng'ao sat down again and extinguished the cigar he had just lit.

"Quite simple, it was Vice-Chancellor He who wanted me to save you. Besides, Vice-President Li was also asking about you at that time."

"Oh..." responded Liang Jinglun casually.

In the radio communication room of the secret prison in the Western Hills, Chen Jicheng could be heard speaking in rapid-fire Chinese, his voice so loud that it made the phone buzz. Wang Puchen put the lower end of the phone between his neck and his shoulder so that the upper end of the phone was away from his ear. He then picked up a cigarette from the table, lit it and took a puff, followed by a series of violent coughs. The coughing proved to be a really effective antidote against the yelling. When the person at the other end stopped shouting, Wang Puchen also gradually stopped coughing.

"Are you done with your damn coughing yet!" The commanding voice from the other end was very clear.

"Sorry, Deputy Commander-in-Chief Chen. I was answering another important call just now. If you've finished criticising me, please give me your direct instructions."

The caller's voice was less raucous, so Wang Puchen returned with an intermittent cough and briefly replied with "hmm" and "yes". He listened patiently to Chen Jicheng's babbling in his ears.

"Then I can go and talk to Chancellor He." Fang Meng'ao paused. "But I can't go now, my father is still there. Do you mind if I continue to do some reading here, Mr Liang?"

"Captain Fang should be aware that the Peking Municipal Government and the Citizens' Food Distribution Committee have issued a circular to distribute food rations to teachers and students of major institutions here tomorrow, including the students from the Northeast. The students of the Students' Union are waiting for me at the Yenching University library. Captain Fang, shouldn't you go back and get ready too?"

Fang Meng'ao opened the book. "Do you trust what the Kuomintang said? That the grain you're expecting is still in Tianjin."

"Oh?" replied Liang Jinglun again carelessly.

"Don't worry, I'll make sure you're informed in time when Tianjin starts shipping the grain to Peking. Don't you want me to support you? Don't you want to get the true information from me?"

"OK." Liang Jinglun had no other option but to keep him company.

The yelling on the other end had finished and the caller was waiting for Wang Puchen to answer. Wang, who had the phone gripped between his neck and shoulder, picked up another cigarette with his long fingers and used the butt of the previous one to light it. He coughed a few times before replying.

"The last time Fang Meng'ao took Liang Jinglun away, we submitted a detailed report afterwards. Deputy Commander-in-Chief Chen should have known about it. We also notified the Ministry of Defence's Secrecy Bureau of his release. As it might be of concern to He Qicang and Ambassador Stuart Leighton, we can't arrest the man without evidence. I know that there will be a large distribution of food rations tomorrow so, evidently, if Liang Jinglun is inciting students against the government, we'll surely nab him. If Deputy Commander-in-Chief Chen wants us to arrest him now, I'll need instructions from Nanking because Captain Fang is also there."

All of a sudden, the look on Wang Puchen's face changed and his coughing stopped, yet no one knew what Chen Jicheng had said.

"What do you mean by the Ministry's Bureau of Reserve Cadres? Deputy Commander-in-Chief Chen, how can you associate my bureau at the Peking station with Mr Chiang Ching-kuo? If it is speculation, then I would ask you to refrain from speculation in the future. We are under the supervision of the Ministry of Defence's Secrecy Bureau and such speculation is not conducive to our work. OK, yes. I will instruct you whether to arrest or monitor him after consulting the Secrecy Bureau." He hung up the phone with a snap. Wang Puchen coughed loudly and looked at the direct line to Nanking Line Two.

Putting out his cigarette, he picked up the phone for the special line of Nanking Line Two and stopped coughing. "Please, put me through to Comrade Jianfeng."

The person who answered the phone was Jianfeng himself who turned out to have been waiting.

Wang Puchen stood up straight.

"Comrade Jianfeng, sorry to have kept you waiting for so long. As you predicted, Chen Jicheng told us to go and make the arrest now. ... Yes, to arrest Liang Jinglun. Also, he asked me out of the blue if I had received direct orders from the Bureau of Reserve Cadres of the Ministry of Defence. ... Yes, I also think it's the Central Bureau of Investigation and Statistics. Xu Tieying told him. ... Yes, they are already in cahoots with each other. I'm now ready for Comrade Jianfeng's instructions."

The instruction was very concise.

But Wang Puchen was a little surprised at it. He calmed down for a moment and replied: "No, I won't ask why. I don't need to reply to Chen Jicheng again. Next, I'll repeat the operation instructions: 'Send someone to monitor the Foreign Languages Bookstore immediately. Tell those with the Chiang Kai-shek Student Society to get He Xiaoyu and Xie Mulan out. Cover Comrade Zeng Keda when he enters the bookstore.'... No, I promise I won't let anyone see him."

Wang Puchen gently put down the phone, a sombre expression

on his face. Although not allowed to ask the reason, he understood fully that it was a dangerous move for Comrade Jianfeng to send Zeng Keda to meet with Fang Meng'ao and Liang Jinglun. It could be have been a last resort, otherwise Comrade Jianfeng would not have shown his hand like this. Thinking of this, his eyes again stopped short on the special Nanking Line Two. "One revolution, fighting on two fronts," Comrade Jianfeng had said on the day of the founding of the Iron and Blood Congress. Today he had personally experienced it!

Time to implement the plan.

Wang Puchen picked up another phone. "Operation Group One? Are you now at the east gate of Yenching University? OK, listen up. Execute the mission."

Wang Puchen's slender figure was getting farther and farther away, but it was clear that he was giving orders.

The lights of Xu Tieying's office at the Police Bureau of Peking Municipality were on. Standing in front of his desk, Xu Tieying pressed a phone to his ear. He said uncharacteristically: "Wang Puchen is stonewalling you, Deputy Commander-in-Chief Chen. The information from the Communications Bureau of the Kuomintang Central Committee Members is absolutely accurate, Wang Puchen is a card-carrying member of the Iron and Blood Congress... You are too kind, State Secrecy Bureau Director Mao Renfeng is the president's stooge, involving Mr Chiang Ching-kuo. If it concerns Mr Chiang Ching-kuo, he has long played deaf and dumb. We are not working against Mr Chiang Ching-kuo but against the Communist Party. Deputy Commander-in-Chief Chen, last time Fang Meng'ao had Liang Jinglun released from the Western Hills prison without authorisation. This time, he took He Xiaoyu out to the southwestern defence line and then went to see Liang Jinglun on his return. It is your responsibility to report to the president and Mr Chiang Ching-kuo immediately that the Defence Ministry's Inspection Brigade is so closely associated with someone who is suspected of being a Communist... How can we expect Zeng Keda to do it? Deputy Commander-in-Chief Chen, in order to please He Qicang, and let him talk to Stuart Leighton and get the US to support their currency reform, they won't arrest Liang Jinglun even if he is a Communist. As long as the president agrees, we can go and make the arrest if Wang Puchen fails to seize him!"

Chen Jicheng was silent for two or three seconds before replying in a loud voice: "I'm calling the number one line now but I can't make a case alone, what else can you do to help?"

"Fang Buting needs a kick up the backside! What does it mean 'anti-corruption on the one hand'? Fang Buting and the two big families behind him cannot always watch from behind the screen. I will call Fang Buting now so he understands that to save his son, he'll also have to find a way to get the Song and Kong families to speak to the president on our behalf. Well, um, I'll call him right away."

Hearing the other party hang up the receiver, Xu Tieying put down the phone, picked up another one and started dialling.

A hundred metres away, the lights were on at the east gate of Yenching University but it was already very weak when it reached the door of the Foreign Languages Bookstore. A crowd suddenly appeared, all student-like. Seemingly not knowing one another, they approached the road outside the door in twos and threes, scattering to stand in their respective positions. All of them were from Wang Puchen's Peking station of the Military Bureau of Investigation and Statistics. Upon receiving instructions from Wang Puchen, they took up their positions and set up separate controls.

The two students standing guard in the doorway were immediately alerted. One, who pretended to be lolling around, was walking towards them. The man was the head of the First Operation Group of the Peking station of the Military Bureau of Investigation and Statistics.

The students standing in the doorway were identified as the same group of the Youth Army who had reported the situation to Zeng Keda. They had double identities. In their public capacities, they were progressive youths of the Peking Students' Union but in reality they were under the direct leadership of the Chiang Kai-shek Student Society. Although they belonged to the core organisation of the Youth Army, they did not wear military uniforms. Usually, they would follow Liang Jinglun as infiltrators in the Peking Students' Union but at critical moments they could bypass Liang Jinglun and report directly to Zeng Keda for assignments.

Examining the man who walked up to them, the two men from the Chiang Kai-shek Student Society did not even bother to hide the hostility in their eyes.

"May I borrow your lighter?" asked the head of the operation group, pulling out a cigarette.

"We're students, we don't smoke."

The head of the operation group then took a lighter out of his pocket, lit it, took a drag and whispered: "Inspector-General Zeng will be arriving soon."

The two men from the Chiang Kai-shek Student Society were taken aback, then one of them looked at the Military Bureau of Investigation guy. "May I know who you are?"

"The coordinated operation of the Ministry of Defence Cadre Reserve Bureau, don't ask," the head of the Military Bureau of Intelligence group demanded. "Our task is to monitor from outside while yours is to get He Xiaoyu and Xie Mulan out of the bookstore in the name of the Students' Union. When Inspector-General Zeng arrives, no one is supposed to see him." After saying that, he turned and walked across the road.

Looking again at the people standing far and near, in the light and in the dark, the two members of the Chiang Kai-shek Student Society had no more doubts. One looked around vigilantly while the other turned to knock on the door of the bookstore.

———

The door opened. He Xiaoyu was on full alert while Xie Mulan was taken completely by surprise. They looked at their fellow student from the Students' Union, listening to him finish what he had to say in a raucous yet low voice.

"Why don't you go up and consult Professor Liang first?" replied He Xiaoyu.

"Professor Liang and Captain Fang are together," said the man from the Chiang Kai-shek Student Society. "The people outside are all from the Military Bureau of Investigation. If Captain Fang finds out about this, there will be a conflict, and you two will be involved. That's why the union has instructed you to leave first."

"We're here to talk about the distribution of food among teachers and students in all schools tomorrow. What's not clear about that?" Xie Mulan's voice was so loud that she obviously intended Fang Meng'ao and Liang Jinglun upstairs to hear.

The look on the man's face changed. He looked up towards the first floor then whispered to He Xiaoyu: "Ms Xiaoyu, please follow the instruction of the Students' Union and take Xie Mulan away immediately."

"Mr Liang is upstairs. Which Students' Union are you telling us to listen to?" said Xie Mulan in an even louder voice.

"You'll bring in the Military Bureau of Investigation and Statistics! Miss He Xiaoyu, please stop Xie Mulan immediately and leave!" said the man, becoming angry.

"Then why not let the Military Bureau of Investigation people come in so that we can fight them while my big brother is here?" What made Xie Mulan angry was his attitude of excluding them from the Students' Union, so she now spoke in an even louder voice.

"Mulan!" He Xiaoyu interrupted her. "You've been working hard to join the Students' Union, haven't you?"

"I'm already in!" shouted Xie Mulan. "Professor Liang approved it today!"

This news astonished not only He Xiaoyu but also the man with the Chiang Kai-shek Student Society.

Xie Mulan's voice was so loud that she could be heard from the room on the first floor. Liang Jinglun looked across at Fang Meng'ao, only to find him still immersed in reading. His heart was quite saddened. Thanks to his double identity, Liang Jinglun had to face the test of the Communist Party's Urban Works Department and that of the Peking Student Committee of the CPC, as well as being subject to suspicion from within the Iron and Blood

Congress from time to time, even though he managed to survive each time.

But at the moment, he felt quite at a loss as to how to deal with Fang Meng'ao. When he heard the students of the Chiang Kai-shek Student Society downstairs telling He Xiaoyu and Xie Mulan to leave, he could not tell whether it was an operation of the Peking Student Committee of the Urban Works Department or of the Iron and Blood Congress.

"Then, let me go up!" From the ground floor came Xie Mulan's voice again. "I'll ask my big brother to come down and deal with them!"

Liang Jinglun looked at Fang Meng'ao again but Fang did not respond. He couldn't afford to be more passive. He walked straight to the door of his room, opened it and stood at the entrance to the stairs.

"Ms Xiaoyu, please take Mulan home first."

Downstairs, He Xiaoyu didn't even reply.

"Ouyang!" Liang Jinglun's tone became stern.

The student from the Chiang Kai-shek Student Society downstairs turned out to have a compound surname.

"Get a few students from the union to take them home by bicycle. If anything happens on the way, come back and report to me immediately. Captain Fang is also here."

"Yes sir!" came Ouyang's voice from downstairs, followed by the sound of the door opening.

"Go and get some students with bicycles," instructed Ouyang.

On the roadside near Yenching University, four students were sitting quietly by their bicycles. The four stood up at the same time when they heard a jeep speeding in their direction; surprisingly it had no headlights on. At first, all they could vaguely hear was the sound of its engine, then the jeep gradually became visible in the moonlight. Seeing the approaching jeep, the students affiliated with the Chiang Kai-shek Student Society picked up their bicycles and pushed them to the side of the road.

Two of them set up their bikes, then went on to the ramp and pushed the other two bikes over. Four men with six bikes were waiting at the side of the road. The jeep screeched to a halt in front of them. The first one to jump off the jeep was Adjutant Wang, who had changed into civilian clothes. He immediately went to open the door to the back seat. But the back-seat door was pushed open from the inside and Zeng Keda, who had also changed into plain clothes, stepped out of the jeep.

Without saying a word, the two young soldiers had already pushed the bicycles in front of Zeng Keda and Adjutant Wang. Zeng Keda got on one of the bikes and rode off in the direction of Yenching University.

"Follow the general!" ordered Adjutant Wang, hurriedly getting on his bike.

The four young soldiers ran over and jumped on their bikes, pedalling hard to catch up with Zeng Keda's bike. Soon two Youth Army students' bikes were in front and two at the back, protecting Zeng Keda who was in the middle. Adjutant Wang was also pedalling his bike hard in the rear. The moon was bright and hazy, the shadows of trees were swirling and the bikes were running as smooth as silk.

Zeng Keda was a southerner. As he was cruising along the road in the northern part of the country at night, he found no wheat stubble on either side of the road. The chaos caused by war had led to the abandonment of farmland. Successful political governance would have resulted in thriving agriculture and industry. By that standard, the Kuomintang government at all levels was a huge failure because it had failed to sustain the livelihood of the people and people had failed to work in peace and contentment. The most immediate result was that he would have to collect food for the two million people struggling to survive in Peking. Now he understood why Comrade Jianfeng had recited sentimentally the poem *Wang Feng* from *The Book of Songs* to him after giving him the new assignment on the phone.

The strong Fenghua accent immediately rang in his ears again:

The millet looks green and lush,
And the sorghum is growing.
But slowly I plod along,
With my heart falling apart.
Anyone who understands me would say
I feel sad at heart;

Anyone who doesn't would ask
What I'm really looking for.

"With the king's order in mind", his heart began pounding with excitement. Zeng Keda abruptly straightened his body, raising his bottom off the seat of the bike. He started to pedal so hard that he soon overtook the two students of the Youth Army, with the night wind streaming across his face.

The youths who were left behind all scrambled. With their bums off the saddles, they pedalled hard to catch up with him. Poor Adjutant Wang had a hard time catching up. Even though he tried so hard, he got left behind. After all, he was a civilian and not fit enough.

———

In the room on the first floor of the merchant's house, no one knew when the kerosene lamp with the lotus-leaf lampshade was turned on. It was flickering above the table. Zhang Yueyin's seat was empty, only Xie Peidong and Old Liu sat under the lamp. While the two were waiting for Zhang Yueyin, silence fell and was frozen in the little light overhead.

Suddenly, the sound of someone's footsteps on the stairs came from downstairs. Both of them stood up. Zhang Yueyin walked in hastily, this time without asking the two to sit down. He himself also stood. "An urgent telegram from Comrade Liu Yun, new instructions from the CPC Central Committee."

Xie Peidong and Old Liu both looked at him.

"'The Peacock Flies Southeast' is just another Kuomintang operation in Peking and Tianjin to implement the whole currency system reform. The focus of the reform is Shanghai while the operation of Peking-Tianjin is the key point of cooperation. In order to secure American aid, they will initiate currency reform in five major cities in the Kuomintang-controlled areas and issue gold-dollar notes. And to firm up the newly issued gold-dollar notes, they will ship large amounts of food and supplies to the five major cities to keep prices down. These foodstuffs and supplies will not be attacked or intercepted by our troops or by the underground organisations of the party during the shipment. We'll cooperate fully."

"I'd like to ask why we have to cooperate with them?" Old Liu couldn't help but ask.

"For the sake of the people in the five cities."

Zhang Yueyin's reply was very concise. He went on to say: "In Peking and Tianjin, those of our comrades lurking in the various departments of the Kuomintang government, and those who are involved in the currency reform and the transfer of materials, must not resist and must actively cooperate. It is hoped that you will immediately carry out the instruction in that spirit and pass it on to every person concerned."

The instructions of the CPC Central Committee outlined the most essential points. Next, it was time for the Urban Works Department of Peking to discuss and put them into practice.

Zhang Yueyin looked at Xie Peidong and said: "Comrade Liu Yun pointed out that in the Peking-Tianjin area, Comrade Xie Peidong has the most arduous task and the most difficult situation. The train from Tianjin has already left, you will receive the grain in three hours on behalf of the Peking branch and personally escort it to the barracks of the Inspection Brigade. When you meet with Comrade Fang Meng'ao, find out about the details of his meeting with Liang Jinglun. The challenge is how to make it clear to him that he's supposed to act according to the party's instructions in the future, without making the Iron and Blood Congress suspect that he is already connected with us. Therefore, Mr Xie is fully authorised by the Central Committee and the Urban Works Department in North China to establish absolutely single-line contact."

"Please rest assured that I know what to do," assured Xie Peidong, lifting his bag off the chair as if to leave.

"Please, just a second," said Zhang Yueyin in an attempt to keep him from leaving. Then he turned to Old Liu and said: "It's futile for the Kuomintang to win the hearts and minds of the people by announcing the policy at the moment. On the contrary, it'll definitely intensify their internal strife. Based on the analysis of the higher authorities, the intraparty strife will soon affect our comrades who work underground, including the progressive students on the periphery. As a matter of urgency, we need to secretly transfer some of our people to the CPC-controlled base areas. Specifically, it is Comrade Liu's responsibility to instruct Comrade Yan Chunming to leave tonight after you leave here. As for others who are to be transferred, we'll arrange their departure in batches in the next few days. Comrade Liu Yun also gave special instructions to the Student Committee to find a way of telling Liang Jinglun to propose the transfer of Xie Mulan!"

"Understood," answered Old Liu thoughtfully.

"Much appreciated." Xie Peidong felt quite moved at this moment even though he was quite a veteran underground agent.

"This is what we should do." Zhang Yueyin looked at Xie Peidong with deep feelings. "Mr Xie, the train from Tianjin will arrive in three hours, please go back to the Peking branch first. Fang Buting should also be expecting you. He must be anxiously waiting for you to discuss how to control Comrade Meng'ao's next move."

Xie Peidong slowly extended his hand to him across the table and the two of them shook hands. Xie Peidong shook hands with Old Liu again. He found that Old Liu's hand was strong but the grip was not very firm. He just clenched it and prolonged their handshake. Obviously, he was doing this to express his apology, to reiterate his respect and to convey a more important message, which was "please rest assured that Xie Mulan will be safe". Xie Peidong's eyes showed his gratitude and he turned to walk out, followed by both Zhang Yueyin and Old Liu who accompanied him out of the room.

Zhang Yueyin's judgment was accurate. Fang Buting had already returned to the governor's office and was waiting for Xie Peidong. Contrary to his normal practice, Fang Buting did not turn on the lights when he returned to his office. Instead, he made several phone calls under the moonlight spilling in from the south-facing French window, all alone and with a hoarse voice.

"Well, keep looking. Call Mr Xu at the Mirror Spring Garden and ask if Mr Xie is with him and where he is now."

After all those calls, Fang Buting moved close to the balcony by the French window and sat down, overlooking the courtyard illuminated only by moonlight. It turned out that not only was the office unlit but also the whole building and the courtyard outside.

A thin, bright sliver of moon was high in the sky as Fang Buting surveyed the desolate courtyard in a daze. The abnormal move of his eldest son in taking He Xiaoyu out to the southwest defence line today had dismayed Fang Buting. The fact that his youngest son had found his elder brother and He Xiaoyu without telling him depressed him even more. Surprisingly, it was Xu Tieying who called to inform him that Fang Meng'ao had paid a visit to Liang Jinglun on his way back and that Fang Buting should return home. Also, Fang Mengwei was allowed to head back home as Xu himself had to continue to work himself. Beset with troubles both at home and outside under the current circumstances, Fang Buting relied on Xie Peidong who happened to disappear on him. He had no choice but to wait. Meanwhile, he ordered all the servants back to their rooms and had all their lights turned off while waiting.

Who would come back first?

Suddenly, he was shocked to realise that someone had returned. The sound of a jeep came from outside the compound. Needless to say, it was the sound of the jeep with 002 on the number plate of the Police Bureau of the Peking Municipality that he was so familiar with.

Fang Mengwei was back.

The gate of the Fangs' compound, which was left unlocked, was pushed open from outside. Fang Mengwei stepped inside and stopped where he was. In the past, he had been impressed by his father's depth of character but now he was disgusted by his superficiality.

Although blackouts were frequent in Peking, the compound had never had a power failure as it was equipped with special cables. Yet there was no light on in the courtyard at the moment, nor a single light on in the building that awaited him. He knew that his father had switched them all off on purpose. Although he had been absent for a few days, Fang Mengwei found that the mansion, which belonged solely to his father, was sinking like the dark night. He understood in his heart that his father's eyes must be hidden somewhere in the darkness, staring at him.

Why do you have to take such pains to deal with your son who has been obedient since childhood? He really didn't want to take another step forward but still walked towards the house where his father's eyes were hidden. Pushing open the living-room door, Fang Mengwei stood in the darkness for several seconds before finally reaching out and pressing the switch on the wall.

The chandelier in the lobby lit up, lighting up the whole house, but Fang Mengwei was stunned. Inside the large living room, Cheng Xiaoyun was sitting alone on the sofa. When she saw Fang Mengwei, she slowly rose to her feet. He was not the only one who felt alone among the members of the family. Suddenly he came to realise that his stepmother, who was not much older than him, was closer than usual today.

The two looked at each other. Fang Mengwei's mouth moved but didn't utter a sound, yet it was clear that he was struggling to call Cheng Xiaoyun "Mum". Cheng Xiaoyun walked over, stood in front of him, and said under her breath: "If it's not easy, don't call..."

After all, it felt unnatural to Fang Mengwei to be so close to her. He cast a glance at his father's office up on the first floor but still had no intention of walking up the stairs.

"Let me ask you one question. Answer me if you will." Fang Mengwei had to look at her again and nodded his head. "Are your elder brother, Xiaoyu and Mulan at Professor Liang's place?"

Looking gloomy, Fang Mengwei did not want to answer, but he nodded almost imperceptibly.

"These are trying times, everyone is in a bad mood. Your father is waiting for you upstairs. As you can see, he doesn't allow us to turn on the lights."

Instead of nodding his head this time, Fang Mengwei showed a hint of disapproval and walked towards the straight staircase.

Cheng Xiaoyun walked him to the stairs apprehensively.

"I'd like to ask you one question, answer me if you want," asked Fang Mengwei, spinning round to pose the question.

Cheng Xiaoyun nodded.

"How did you fall in love with my father?"

"I'll tell you later, OK?" Cheng Xiaoyun could only reply after a brief moment of silence.

"Good." Fang Mengwei stopped making things difficult for her and turned to go upstairs.

"If it's not easy, don't call..." Fang Buting uttered these ghostly words from the balcony in his office on the first floor, which was an exact copy of what Cheng Xiaoyun had said downstairs.

The chandelier in the drawing room on the ground floor was very bright, shining into the first floor office through the door. As expected, his father's eyes were hidden on the balcony looking down on the entire front garden. By standing in the doorway he was clearly visible to his father sitting on the balcony, while his father's figure appeared to him confusing or disgusting. In addition to disgust, he could not help but feel a sense of bitterness in his heart.

He remembered that every time he walked through the door, he had to call out: "Father". For many years, he had been doing it as a sign of respect to his father but not to his stepmother but today he wanted to call Cheng Xiaoyun "Stepmother", refusing to call him "Father". Fang Buting had no idea why this obedient son to whom he felt closest, had suddenly become so estranged, rebellious even.

"I know you don't want to see me again, so don't turn on the light. I've got something to ask you but you can't keep standing in the doorway."

Fang Mengwei was unwilling to move yet still walked over to his father. Besides being silent, he was also meant to maintain a distance, standing about two metres from his father.

"Where did you find your big brother?" Fang Buting continued to look out of the window.

"West of the Lugou Bridge, by the Yongding River," answered Fang Mengwei.

"Did he tell you what he and Xiaoyu talked about?"

Fang Mengwei didn't reply. Fang Buting turned his head to look at his youngest son. But Fang Mengwei was looking outside the window, as if he was speaking to the moon. "He said he wanted to marry Miss He."

"Then why didn't he go directly to Uncle He, rather than go to see Liang Jinglun?" Fang Buting stood up.

"You can ask him yourself," said Fang Mengwei, still looking out of the window.

Fang Buting was dumbfounded by what he had heard from his youngest son. He stood for a while, slowly sat down and said with a sigh: "I admit I am not a good husband, nor a good father. But I'm still your father. The Kuomintang has long suspected that your big brother was a Communist but they are still using him for their own ends. Besides, is Liang Jinglun a Communist or not? I have a feeling that sooner or later he will put your big brother in harm's way. Mengwei, you saw Cui Zhongshi's death with your own eyes, so you can't watch your brother end up the same way."

Fang Mengwei's heart was tormented but he still didn't respond to his father's words.

"Wait for Uncle Xie to come back, I know now you only listen to him."

There were two measured knocks on the door of the room on the first floor of the Foreign Languages Bookstore. Obviously, it was not students knocking because they had been assigned to take He Xiaoyu and Xie Mulan back home.

Liang Jinglun was horrified to realise that the one who should have been coming was actually coming! He looked across at Fang Meng'ao. But Fang Meng'ao did not react, he was still flipping through one of the books there.

"It should be their classmates." Liang Jinglun stood up and spun round towards the door of the room. "Is it Ouyang?"

There was no answer.

"May I ask who it is?" He looked at Fang Meng'ao again.

There were two more unhurried knocks.

Only then did Fang Meng'ao speak: "No host is afraid of their guest, open the door."

Liang Jinglun stepped towards the door. The hem of his long gown fluttered again and his steps showed hesitation. But he frowned as there were many questions running through his mind. Were they people from the Secrecy Bureau of the Peking Station?

With Fang Meng'ao being here, no. Were they with Chen Jicheng or Xu Tieying?

With Fang Meng'ao being here, it wouldn't be them either. Could it be members of the CPC Peking Student Committee? It could be Yan Chunming! Liang Jinglun was already standing in front of the door, yet he found that his hand reaching for the latch was as hesitant as his footsteps just now. With the latch being slowly opened, the door was pulled open slowly.

Liang Jinglun was left confused. Surprisingly, the person standing in the doorway turned out to be Zeng Keda! No, never before had Liang Jinglun been so surprised. But before he realised, Zeng Keda had quickly reached out his hand for his. Liang Jinglun felt the glaring gaze of Fang Meng'ao behind him but had to stretch out his hand too.

"This is Comrade Liang Jinglun." Zeng Keda made the introductory remark while holding Liang Jinglun's hand. Meanwhile, Zeng Keda gazed at Fang Meng'ao over Liang Jinglun's shoulder.

Liang Jinglun stood there in a daze, unable to imagine how Fang Meng'ao behind him would react. Fang Meng'ao's gaze seemed to be full of amazement but the contrary also seemed true. Although he had obtained Liang Jinglun's identity as a member of the Iron and Blood Congress from Xie Peidong, Fang Meng'ao was astonished by the sudden appearance of Zeng Keda which directly blew the true identity of Liang Jinglun, something indeed beyond his expectation. Therefore, the look on his face at that moment seemed perfectly reasonable and true to Zeng Keda.

"Let's go in and talk." Zeng Keda stroked Liang Jinglun's shoulder as the latter turned sideways to enable Zeng Keda to enter through the doorway first. Walking straight to the table across from the doorway, Zeng Keda stopped and found that Liang Jinglun was still standing at the door. While Fang Meng'ao was gazing at Liang Jinglun with a sharp, penetrating stare, Liang Jinglun could not avoid the gaze, so he could only stare back at Fang Meng'ao as well.

"Come in, come in and talk." Zeng Keda gestured to Liang Jinglun so as not to confront Fang Meng'ao. "I will tell you all about it soon."

Liang Jinglun walked over to his seat. All the concealment was meaningless. The hem of his long gown fluttered. Yet, without the pretentious hesitation when he had opened the door just now, he did it in a completely natural way. Fang Meng'ao turned to stare at his long gown that surprisingly still flowed so elegantly. He didn't stop until Liang's gown was hidden under the table opposite him.

"Please sit down, both of you," said Zeng Keda, looking at Liang Jinglun.

Liang Jinglun sat down silently.

Zeng Keda turned to look at Fang Meng'ao who sat down with one leg perched on the other. His face flashed with instant irritation, as he remembered that Fang Meng'ao had been sitting in the same position at the military court more than a month ago!

Unhappiness had to be forgotten and patience exercised today.

"The military, the civil service and the teaching profession." Zeng Keda sat down steadily and opened with these words in a tone that was neither haughty nor subdued. He had put a lot of thought into today's meeting. Both men looked over at him with great anticipation, indicating that his opening remarks had achieved the desired effect.

"Captain Fang is an enlisted member of the National Revolutionary Army and Professor Liang is a member of a university faculty. According to the Constitution of the Republic of China, you are both public servants of the Nationalist government. Let's agree to accept these identities of yours first."

Liang Jinglun did not answer, only looking at Fang Meng'ao.

Zeng Keda was actually also looking at Fang Meng'ao whose attitude was crucial.

"Of course, I agree," Fang Meng'ao quickly replied, without accepting Zeng Keda's word "accept". He continued: "Originally I served in the Air Force but now hold the title of colonel in the Bureau of Reserve Cadres of the Ministry of Defence. You'll have to accept that, Professor Liang."

Liang Jinglun held his breath while Zeng Keda was also expecting to hear what Fang Meng'ao would say next.

"Yenching University is a private university run by Americans and you are now on the payroll of the Americans. Perhaps you are not yet considered a public servant of the Nationalist government."

Liang Jinglun could not very well answer that, so he chose not to.

"Let's count him in." Zeng Keda replied on his behalf. "The professors and faculty of Yenching University are registered with the Ministry of Education of the Nationalist government and are considered public servants."

"Then be my guest."

Both Zeng Keda and Liang Jinglun looked at him, waiting for him to continue.

Fang Meng'ao, however, didn't say anything, picked up a cigar that had been lit but subsequently extinguished that lay on the table, then took out of his pocket, not a box of long matches, but an American lighter. He flicked open the lighter and lit his cigar. Only then did he spin round to look at Zeng Keda, totally ignoring the fact that the other two were waiting. Moreover, he pretended to be surprised. "Why don't you continue? We're all ears."

Liang Jinglun looked at Zeng Keda to see how he would respond.

Zeng Keda understood very well that having such a lively conversation with Fang Meng'ao was tantamount to having a dogfight with this ace pilot. Fortunately, Comrade Jianfeng had given specific instructions before he came to this meeting which was, frankly, to prepare for a showdown!

With Comrade Jianfeng's instruction in mind, Zeng Keda cut to the chase. "Before I arrived, I was thinking that you two must have been discussing the question of whether the other was Communist or not."

He glanced at Fang Meng'ao and then at Liang Jinglun to see how the two might respond. Neither of them offered to answer him.

"In fact, it doesn't matter who is Communist or not. Captain Fang knows I insisted you were a Communist more than a month ago but the Ministry of Defence's Bureau of Reserve Cadres, Comrade Jianfeng, is still using you. The reason is simple: there is only one truth, which is the Communists are fighting with us for *Tianxia*. What is *Tianxia*? It refers to everything under heaven. What is this everything under heaven? Comrade Jianfeng defines it as the land and the people. The armies of the two parties are fighting for territory at the front, but victory is no longer defined militarily but politically. What we, including you and I, are doing now is fighting corruption in the Kuomintang-controlled areas so that the people can have food to eat. Putting aside the disputes between the two parties, you wouldn't object to what we're doing even if you were a Communist, would you?"

"Then, do you think I'm a Communist or not?" Fang Meng'ao knew that the moment he was waiting for had finally arrived and he had to ask the question firmly.

This was precisely the issue that Zeng Keda could not dwell on. "I've already said that it doesn't matter whether you're Communist or not."

"Am I or aren't I?"

"The Party Communications Bureau and the State Secrecy Bureau conducted an investigation more than a month ago and did not suspect you of being a Communist. Up to now, I've not found any connection between you and the Communist Party either."

"What about Professor Liang?" Fang Meng'ao suddenly changed the subject. "Is he a Communist?"

Following the showdown was confrontation. Zeng Keda looked at Liang Jinglun and gave him a "no need to worry" look. With that, Liang Jinglun slowly stood up. He had not been able to answer Fang Meng'ao's question, but now he could.

"I am."

"It's good to tell the truth." Fang Meng'ao stared at him and suddenly asked again: "What about He Xiaoyu? Is she a Communist?"

Liang Jinglun suddenly realised that this was the main purpose of Fang Meng'ao's trip to the bookstore today: Fang Meng'ao wanted to protect He Xiaoyu! Instead of answering him immediately, he sat down. After all, having harboured strong feelings for He Xiaoyu for so many years, he felt quite sad at heart.

Zeng Keda also felt the same way. Whether He Xiaoyu was a Communist or not was directly related to whether the Iron and Blood Congress could make good use of Fang Meng'ao. He looked at Liang Jinglun. "Please tell the truth."

"She's not," said Liang Jinglun softly, feeling that he had Zeng Keda's tacit approval.

"Then why did you send her to recruit me several times?"

"I didn't ask her to recruit you to join the Communist Party. She's only a progressive youth of the union, she's in no position to recruit you. She contacted you to support the union and to assist you in cracking down on corruption."

Fang Meng'ao learned from Xie Peidong of Liang Jinglun's true identity as a member of the Iron and Blood Congress, so he was most concerned if Liang Jinglun would know about He Xiaoyu's secret identity as a CPC member. The death of Cui Zhongshi had already inflicted pain on him and made him feel as if he was unable to redeem himself. It was even more painful to see that He Xiaoyu was following in Cui Zhongshi's footsteps to meet with him. For eight years, he had fought numerous battles in the air, witnessing life and death, but things had never been as heart-wrenching as he had experienced recently, for which he refused to be recruited that day. Today he had taken her out to propose to her, then had driven her back to see Liang Jinglun. It all looked like he was taking her on a combat mission rolling in the air and dodging gunfire. Now, Zeng Keda had actually come to disclose the true identity of Liang Jinglun who had categorically denied that He Xiaoyu was a CPC member. In Fang Meng'ao's eyes, neither of these two look liked enemy aircraft any more.

"That's good." When he looked at Liang Jinglun again, Fang Meng'ao finally captured an accurate image – the Hump during the war years! Now he was about to fly over the first summit but there was still an invisible peak ahead. For sure, the next one to fly across was Zeng Keda. While watching Liang Jinglun, he asked again: "I want to ask you one more question. Was it Inspector-General Zeng who arranged to send He Xiaoyu to recruit me?"

Liang Jinglun did not answer.

Fang Meng'ao didn't need an answer from him. He spun round to Zeng Keda and said: "Inspector-General Zeng, you've been using me for more than a month but you've spent that time holding me under suspicion. Now, with your permission, can I hold you under suspicion?"

"Of course."

"Professor Liang is a Communist, are you a Communist?"

"Of course not, I couldn't possibly be."

Fang Meng'ao looked at Liang Jinglun again.

"How could he be?"

"I'll answer you both here. Please stand up." Zeng Keda stood up first, straightening the hem of his plain clothes. He stood upright in a military posture, waiting for Fang Meng'ao and Liang Jinglun to stand up.

Liang Jinglun stood up first, followed by Fang Meng'ao.

"Half an hour ago, Comrade Jianfeng gave the latest instructions: 'Comrade Zeng Keda, please inform Comrade Fang Meng'ao of Comrade Liang Jinglun's true identity and assign tasks to both comrades."

"In the thirty-first year of the Republic of China, Liang Jinglun, formerly a top student in the Department of Economics at Yenching University, was recommended by Mr He Qicang and guaranteed by Mr Chiang Ching-kuo to be sent to the Department of Economics at Harvard University in the US for further study. In the thirty-fifth year of the Republic of China, he returned to China after victory in the War of Resistance Against Japanese Aggression and served in the post-war reconstruction of the country. In April of this year, he joined the Iron and Blood Congress and was a progressive youth and loyal comrade of the Kuomintang. For the upcoming operation 'The Peacock Flies Southeast', Comrade Fang Meng'ao is codenamed 'Jiao Zhongqing' and Comrade Liang Jinglun is codenamed 'Liu Lanzhi'. I hope that you two will cooperate sincerely to carry out the currency system reform in Peking and Tianjin municipalities, save the economy from the verge of collapse, combat rampant corruption and save our suffering compatriots! Chiang Ching-kuo.'"

At this point, Zeng Keda also found himself touched, slowly closed his eyes and calmed himself. Without looking at the other two, he said to Liang and Fang under his breath: "As for Comrade Liang Jinglun's membership of the Communist Party, Comrade Jinglun himself will briefly explain to Comrade Fang Meng'ao. Please sit down."

The lights were on, and the governor's office on the first floor was brightly lit. It turned out that Xie Peidong had returned.

"It was you who drove Mulan out to school that day!" Xie Peidong had never been so angry with Fang Mengwei. "You can take it out on heaven, you can take it out on the earth but I've only one daughter. Where exactly is she now? Is there any danger involved? Tell me, will you?"

"They should all be in the Foreign Languages Bookstore," muttered Fang Mengwei in a muffled voice with his head bowed.

"Who the hell is in the Foreign Languages Bookstore? Who is she hanging out with now?"

"My big brother, Xiaoyu and Mulan."

"All with Liang Jinglun? Are they still together?"

"I didn't go in. I got a call from Xu Tieying saying that there was an emergency at home, so I rushed back."

Fang Mengwei had developed a strong sense of guilt by this time.

"We can't let them stay there any longer." Xie Peidong turned to Fang Buting. "Governor, please call Vice-Chancellor He and ask him to tell Liang Jinglun to leave the bookstore immediately and go back to help him sort out his feasibility report."

Fang Mengwei looked at his uncle and his eyes lit up.

The idea was so simple and practical that he hadn't thought about it because he was angry. But could it be that his father, who had always been wise and resourceful, was also angry and running out of ideas?

Fang Buting sighed.

"If Vice-Chancellor He was in charge of such a matter, he wouldn't be vice-chancellor. He is the only one who dares to lecture me in this world. Before I left his house, I had the chance to have an overdose of his pedantic opinions. Do I need you to remind me when I myself can make this call?"

"Then ask my sister-in-law to call him." Xie Peidong looked closely at Fang Buting.

Fang Mengwei's anger towards his father suddenly subsided. Fang Buting saw the emotion in his eyes and sighed softly again.

"Then tell her to make the phone call. The professor likes her, perhaps he'll do her a favour."

Xie Peidong immediately turned around and called out: "Sister-in-law!"

In the living room on the ground floor, Cheng Xiaoyun dialled the phone number and the operator put her through.

"Xiaoyu, ah!" Cheng Xiaoyun immediately covered the phone speaker and whispered to Xie Peidong who was standing beside her: "It's Xiaoyu, she's home."

"Is she home alone or are both of them home already?" asked Xie Peidong anxiously.

"When did you return? Is Mulan with you? Where is her big brother?"

Xie Peidong looked closely at the phone.

Cheng Xiaoyun listened until Xiaoyu finished what she was saying. "Got it. Now, both you and Mulan, stay put. I'll tell Uncle Fang, of course, and Uncle Xie, tell them to rest assured. By the way, talk to your dad and see what he thinks… OK, we'll talk on the phone if something comes up."

Putting down the phone, Cheng Xiaoyun found that Fang Buting was already standing outside the door of the office up on the first floor.

"Xiaoyu and Mulan just returned home. Members of the Students' Union escorted them home by bicycle. Meng'ao is still at the Foreign Languages Bookstore with Professor Liang."

Xie Peidong from downstairs and Fang Buting from upstairs exchanged glances from a distance.

"Peidong, come upstairs." Fang Buting turned around and entered the office.

"Stop analysing, Liang Jinglun isn't a Communist." Fang Buting stood up from his balcony seat. "He's a stooge of the princeling!"

Xie Peidong's eyes widened. Fang Mengwei was also stupefied.

Fang Buting was again acting like the governor of the first-class branch, as well as the sophisticated and resourceful father. "Cui Zhongshi was a Communist and is dead. But they sent a fake Communist to test Meng'ao, and involved Xiaoyu in their cabaret, and now together with Mulan. He has put three members of our family in harm's way."

Xie Peidong's forehead seeped beads of sweat. Decades of clandestine work had long failed to perturb him but at this instant he was overcome with a horrified bewilderment at Fang Buting's analysis. If this brother-in-law did not work in economics, he would be a secret agent, and a rare talent within the Kuomintang intelligence community. How did he manage to conceal himself for the past ten years? He did not dare to think about it.

Fang Mengwei had also become like the beloved son, his father in front of him had become the man of power and influence again, from whom he and his big brother would need protection. In addition, how to prevent Mulan from falling into the clutches of Liang Jinglun? It all looked as if they would rely on his resourceful father again.

All eyes were on Fang Buting.

"A man with a Ph.D in economics who has returned to China from Harvard University could not possibly believe in the Communist Party. On the one hand, he's organising young students to take to the streets in protest, while on the other, he's helping the economic adviser of the Nationalist government draft a feasibility report on the current currency reform. I read the report, I don't think it would represent the perspectives of the Communist Party. The Communist Party simply wouldn't be capable of developing such a perspective."

"The Communist Party may also use this very strength of his to access the core economic secrets of the Nanking government." Fang Mengwei finally spoke to his father directly.

"What secrets does the Nanking government have? It is well known that officials, big or small, are equally greedy. Your uncle manages their accounts at the Peking branch of the Central Bank. It is not the Communist Party that wants to audit the accounts but the party's princelings. Peidong!"

"Yes, Governor," responded Xie Peidong immediately.

"Will the rations for the teachers and students in Peking arrive tonight?"

"I think so."

"What do you mean by that?"

"I'm coordinating with Shanghai and Tianjin through Mr Xu. If they don't ship the grain tonight, I'm afraid it'd be the Americans who will check them out on that."

"Has the three million been wired to the American firm in Shanghai?"

"These families are pooling their money and will remit it tomorrow."

Fang Buting let out a long sigh. "For the sake of my eldest son, we at the Peking branch must try to cooperate with the Ministry of Defence's investigation group. Tomorrow is crucial. If the food is properly allocated, I promised Zeng Keda that I would cooperate with him in carrying out his currency reform. Just on one condition: let Meng'ao leave the country, don't use him as a gunner. Mengwei."

Fang Mengwei finally replied softly with the word "Father" again.

"Do you think I'm a bit too partial to him?"

"By no means, Father."

"Then I'll tell you my real intentions today. No currency reform can save the Republic of China, nor can President Chiang's millions of troops. They may not be able to defeat the Communist Party, that's for sure. Therefore, I'll try my best to send your brother, Xiaoyu and Mulan overseas. As for you, I'll send you abroad eventually."

"Send us overseas? How about you, my stepmother and my uncle?"

"After the 'Thirteenth of August' incident, I irresponsibly left all of you behind and went to Chongqing by myself. It's time for me to pay my debt. You younger ones should be leaving and the older ones like us should stay. Peidong, what do you think?"

"The governor's intentions, we all know." Xie Peidong could not bear to look Fang Buting in the eye. He turned to look at Fang Mengwei.

"The key is how to prevent Meng'ao, Xiaoyu and Mulan from being used by him right now, since you've seen through Liang Jinglun who has such a complex background."

"Now that Meng'ao has proposed to marry Xiaoyu, it's easy for us to do it. I'll ask Xiaoyun to go to Vice-Chancellor He's to ask for the hand of his daughter tonight. The hard part is Mulan. She's infatuated with Liang Jinglun, she won't come home even if we tell her to. Don't worry, I know what I'm talking about. Suppose there's a direct flight to the US someday, I'll send her away first even if I have to drag her on board."

Xie Peidong could not say anything but close his eyes while Fang Mengwei had a lot to say but didn't know where to start.

Fang Buting looked at his son.

"Go back to the bureau and tell Xu Tieying that tomorrow the rations will be distributed and you will lead the team."

"He has always put me in charge of internal affairs, he may not necessarily agree."

"Tell him, it's my idea that you must go. When you arrive at the venue tomorrow, you must control the Peking Police Bureau forces and make sure that they don't clash with the students again. Remember, forget what I just said in my analysis of Liang Jinglun and the Iron and Blood Congress he belongs to. I'll deal with them. Don't mess with them again."

Fang Mengwei's initial revulsion gave way to a sudden resurgence of pain. He wanted to look at his father but instead closed his eyes.

"Remember what your father just said. Hurry up! Move!" said Xie Peidong.

Fang Mengwei couldn't bear to look at them again when he opened his eyes. He turned and left.

"Tell your stepmother to come up," Fang Buting called out behind his son's back. It was the voice of a loving father.

"Got it," said Fang Mengwei without turning around.

Sitting on the sofa in the living room of He Qicang's house, He was talking on the phone. A rare glimpse of a smile flickered between his eyebrows and the corners of his mouth. He spoke with an uncharacteristic flirtatiousness. "Just look what time it is. Yes, it's past nine now. Only you, the famous *qingyi* role player Cheng, would dare to have me called out of bed to answer the phone. What do you want me to do? I'm at your disposal."

He Xiaoyu and Xie Mulan were standing a few metres away from him because they were not supposed to eavesdrop on the conversation which was a house rule. But both of them were very interested to know what the person on the other end was saying.

They could only guess at what was being said from He Qicang's reply and the look on his face. The smile on He Qicang's face diminished. "You'd come here now? Alone?"

Both He Xiaoyu and Xie Mulan held their breath.

The answer on the other end was clearly affirmative.

The smile on He Qicang's face quickly disappeared. He was silent for a few seconds. Obviously, he had to be mindful of the feelings of the caller on the other end and the two girls who were not far away from him. He reluctantly revealed a smile in the corner of his mouth.

"Xiaoyun, I enjoy your company because I enjoy not only your singing style but also value the fact that you never get involved in Fang Buting's business matters. Tell him that it is not appropriate to ask his wife to visit an old man like me at this late hour! For no other reason, I won't meet you tonight, it's just improper."

He Xiaoyu and Xie Mulan were both quite bewildered.

He Qicang was really kind to Cheng Xiaoyun. Although the smile was not very natural, it was a resigned smile: "OK. Thanks for calling."

When he put down the phone, He Qicang looked mildly irritated. He slowly stood up by supporting himself on the arm of the sofa. Even He Xiaoyu dared not go over to help him at this moment.

"Come to my room," said He Qicang to He Xiaoyu, glancing at them both. He went upstairs alone with his stick.

He Xiaoyu didn't follow him immediately. Instead, she looked at Xie Mulan and said in a low voice: "Wait for me in my room if you want to, if not, go to the Foreign Languages Bookstore."

"Can I go to the bookstore now?" Xie Mulan retorted, not just angrily but also in a challenging manner.

"Then what do you want?" Xie Mulan appeared such a stranger in front of He Xiaoyu.

"If you can, give me the key to Mr Liang's room. I'll go and wait for him there."

"How could I have the key to Mr Liang's room!" Biting her lower lip, He Xiaoyu found her face swiftly turning white. It took a lot of effort for her to swallow the airlock blocking her chest.

"Xie Mulan, you just heard my dad talking to your Aunt Cheng. That's my father! I'm his daughter, Mr Liang is his student, we have family rules in the He family!"

"What about freedom? What about progress? What about revolution?" asked Xie Mulan, throwing in several rhetorical questions in a row.

He Xiaoyu spun round and walked quickly towards the stairs, leaving Xie Mulan there alone.

The He family's living room was smaller than the Fangs'. Usually it felt more cosy but today it looked like a desert.

Xie Mulan resolutely walked toward the door.

The moonlight in the courtyard was brighter than the streetlights in the distance, shining on the two wings of Liang Jinglun's house in the western part of the courtyard. Guided by the moonlight, Xie Mulan walked to the door of the house and sat down on the stone steps from where she could see the light in Uncle He's room. But Xie Mulan just glanced at it and turned to the courtyard door.

Suddenly she found herself developing a dislike for the little Western-style house that used to give her so much comfort and warmth. And she resented the He family rules.

Mr Liang might not come back tonight, but she was determined to wait for him until dawn.

"Long live freedom!" she cried out from her heart.

"Long live the New China!" She looked up at the moon in the night sky.

ABOUT THE AUTHOR

Liu Heping was born in Hunan Province, southern China in 1953. He spent his childhood in the theatre and went on to become an acclaimed screenwriter, novelist and historian known for his deep insights into the events of Chinese history. His pioneering historical drama about the Ming Dynasty, *Da Ming Wang Chao 1566*, was first published as a novel in 2006 and sold nearly a million copies. The following year, it was broadcast as a 46-episode TV series that garnered popular and critical acclaim in China. His Chinese Civil War TV drama, *All Quiet in Peking*, gained a cumulative 400 million online views in the month following its first broadcast in October 2014. The series made waves among China's intellectual circles and was picked up for international distribution by Netflix. Liu's realist approach to the historical and contemporary transformation of China has been hugely influential and well received in the Chinese-speaking world.

ABOUT THE TRANSLATOR

Teng Jimeng lives in Beijing, China. He teaches interpreting, translation, and film studies. He also translates from Chinese into English and vice versa. Teng has translated over 10 award-winning independent Chinese films and documentaries, dozens of scripts, song lyrics, and essays by authors such as Wang Meng and filmmakers such as Chen Kaige of *Farewell My Concubine* (Palm D'Or winner, 1993), Li Yang of *Blind Shaft* (Silver Bear, Berlinale, 2003), Wang Chao of *Luxury Car* (Un Certain Regard, Cannes winner, Cannes International Film Festival, 2005), Geng Jun of *Free And Easy* (Grand Jury Award, Sundance International Film Institute, 2017), and Bob Dylan of *No Direction Home: The Life and Music of Bob Dylan* (by Robert Shelton, U.S.A.).

ABOUT THE SERIES

The *All Quiet in Peking* series follows Fang Meng'ao, a Communist Party member working undercover in the Chinese Nationalist Air Force. It is 1948, and civil war is raging between the Communists and the Kuomintang, ravaging the economy of Peking. Fang is ordered to investigate a corruption case involving the Peking Citizens' Committee and the Peking branch of the Central Bank, the president of which is none other than his own father. Fang's desire for the peaceful liberation of Peking is a race against the clock. The nation doesn't know it yet, but the happiness and peace of the people depends on him. *Behind Closed Doors* is the second of three books in the *All Quiet in Peking* series, translated into English for the first time by Teng Jimeng.

About **Sino**ist Books

We hope you enjoyed this exciting story of Feng Meng'ao's quest for peace.

SINOIST BOOKS brings the best of Chinese fiction to English-speaking readers. We aim to create a greater understanding of Chinese culture and society, and provide an outlet for the ideas and creativity of the country's most talented authors.

To let us know what you thought of this book, or to learn more about the diverse range of exciting Chinese fiction in translation we publish, find us online. If you're as passionate about Chinese literature as we are, then we'd love to hear your thoughts!

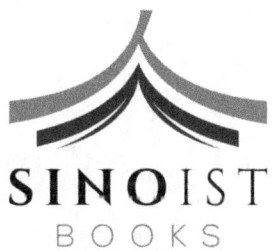

sinoistbooks.com
@sinoistbooks